James Birrel

was born in Glasgow in 1968 and now lives in Leeds. Since leaving university he has worked predominantly in HR and management consulting. He has also taken time out to go travelling and began writing *The Mañana Man* while he was in Belize managing a charity project.

JAMES BIRRELL

The Mañana Man

HarperCollins*Publishers*

Thanks to Judith at Greene & Heaton,
the burley wheelers and all at HC.

HarperCollins*Publishers*
77–85 Fulham Palace Road,
Hammersmith, London W6 8JB

www.fireandwater.com

This paperback edition 2003
1 3 5 7 9 8 6 4 2

First published in Great Britain by
HarperCollins*Publishers* 2002

ISBN 0 00 712236 5

'How Deep Is Your Love' (extract) reproduced by permission
of Gibb Brothers Music/BMG Music Publishing Ltd

Set in Postscript Linotype Sabon by
Rowland Photosetting Ltd, Bury St Edmunds, Suffolk

Printed and bound in Great Britain by
Clays Limited, St Ives plc

To those who had to go
before the music ended

The Mañana Man

crash and burn

She had this thing that she could do with her nipples. It was like a concentration thing that allowed her to erect one and leave the other sleeping. Left or right, she could do it with either or both.

That's when we hit the car. Not too hard, but solid enough for me to drop my bacon banjo, the can I'd been drinking from, and to get bruised by the seat belt. The back end of the Fiesta crumpled a little to allow Stan's Golf to mould and bend into it.

It was an accident. We were on our way to the Leeds City Crematorium and had been talking about Ting's failed romances when it happened at the lights off Town Street. We'd started drinking to ease us into the burning and scattering of our friend, except Stan because he was driving. We'd done Judy White, Jillian Grove and Rebecca Turner and were talking about Sally Finnigan.

Amazing nipples if Ting's account was anything to go by. It was when Pine explained how Ting could tell which nipple was erect by its growing against his cheek that Stan turned round to see if he was being serious and missed the lights changing and the car in front stopping.

Rubbing at my shoulder, I was satisfied that I'd suffered no permanent damage and, disentangling myself from the seat belt and coats, I went to check on the driver of the Fiesta. As I opened the door Stan was brushing the joint he'd been smoking from his lap. Jumping up and twisting round, he began calling Pine as many names as possible without repeating himself or resorting to not being offensive. As I approached the car, I glanced through the passenger window and saw a cake half in its box and half on the carpet, window, cowhide seat covers and dashboard.

'Oh, shit,' I mumbled, straining to see the driver.

Looking at the mess in the front of the car, I couldn't help but smile. This unfortunately didn't amuse the two hundred pounds of enraged driver who poured from the car. The cake was bad enough but when she stood up I had to cough to stop from laughing. She was wiping icing and jam from the pleats in her burgundy dress, which was the same colour as her face and only slightly lighter than her hair.

'Are you all right?' I asked, trying to appear more concerned than amused. I was of course, but I didn't look it. 'Sorry about that,' I said, biting my lip. 'We didn't see the lights change.'

Ignoring me, she glared at Stan and went to check the damage to her burgundy car. Walking round and opening the passenger door, she bellowed a sigh that could have blown the shuttle off course.

'Fuck.' She scowled up at me and I could see the wetness of her eyes. 'What the fuck do I do now?' I winced as I realised that her fifty-odd years on the planet had lent her voice a rasping quality that sprayed as she spat at me. Looking beyond me, she scanned the heavens as if searching for divine roadside assistance. 'I'm supposed to be at a christening in half an hour' – she pulled at her dress – 'and I'm wearing the fucking cake.'

The cosmic call centre must have been engaged as no angelic response team appeared to be reacting. Even if she was on God's catering team.

'I don't fucking believe this.'

Maybe it was her piety. I glanced back at Stan and mouthed 'help'.

Christ, was she hyperventilating? Calm her down, calm her down. 'Are you all right?' I asked again as she drew me a look. 'I'm sorry about the car.' I put my hands up in supplication. 'It was an accident.'

She put her hands up in mocking resignation. 'Fuck the car. What do I do about the cake?' She was about screaming now and her face went a funnier colour.

I turned as Pine and Stan got out of the car not talking to each other and told them that I thought she was okay, if a little upset about the cake she was presently trying to push back together. Stan apologised and went to get his insurance documents out of the car.

Thankful that it hadn't been me driving, I left Stan to placate her while Pine and I tried to separate the cars. They wouldn't cooperate.

This was great.

We were late before the accident, what with fastidious Stan, and now we'd have to find a taxi. Leaving the cars locked in an embrace, Pine and I pushed them onto the lay-by and waited a few yards away to flag down a taxi.

Once the initial shock had worn off, Stan was able to calm Mrs Doubtfire down, and, seeing us looking for a taxi, she asked for a lift. Pine, grinning impishly, told her, 'Sure,' and began singing, 'Always look on the bright side of life'. Stan glared him down and, kind-hearted if flawlessly stupid, agreed to take her to St Pete's in an effort to lessen his guilt. Stan had repeatedly apologised and told her he could get her a cake and she eventually became quite talkative as we waited, accepting a can of Stella and some spliff.

'Just to calm my nerves, you understand.'

She visibly relaxed and glanced at each of us as if seeing us for the first time. Her eyes narrowed. 'So what's your hurry?' She looked us up and down. 'Off somewhere nice?'

Pine accepted the proffered spliff and told her. 'To release our friend's spirit through the ritual of burning and lead him to eternal freedom.' He's always had a way with words that could put people at ease.

As she wiped up the spray of beer, she spluttered, 'You look a bit . . . eh . . . overdressed for a funeral.'

I suppose she did have a point even if she was being more than a bit of a cheeky cow for saying it out loud like that. Admittedly the skull-tight Peruvian hats, resplendent in primary colour and pom-poms, were enough to give the unaware the impression of frivolity not normally associated

with such occasions, but we were also dressed more appropri-
ately for a night on the tiles. She focused on the hats and
waited.

Stan shrugged. 'Ting liked them, he's wearing one and it
would be rude of us not to.' He glanced at me and I could see
what he really wanted to say, but he's usually too polite to say
things like that, even to his friends. She slumped and gave up
on us, too far out of her comfort zone to continue, so we waited
in silence until we hailed a taxi. She never spoke on the way
or even thanked us when we didn't ask for her share of the
fare. At St Pete's, Stan took her inside, told Josh to give her
the biggest cake and order her a taxi, and left her sat at the
bar shaking her head. Some people are just rude.

Back in the taxi Stan gave Pine a dead leg for making him
break his car, and Pine gave him a horse bite for calling him a
'Greasypastafuckinspangle' before we continued on Ting and
Sally. The irony of arriving at the crem in a taxi didn't escape
me as only two days earlier we had turned down Ray's offer
of a lift in the official cars. We could have gone in one of those
posh big black cars that the mayor uses but we were under
instructions laid out years before that had become as important
to us as string and shivering dogs to the homeless. So we took
Stan's Golf and ended up in a not so posh dumpy black car that
was driven by a strange man with an even stranger personality
dysfunction. He wouldn't even let us drink.

▭ * ▭

The cortege was already there when we arrived via a quick
stop in the gardens. At the doors, Ting's father and gran accompanied the coffin. His mother had left years ago. We joined the
thirty or so behind the coffin and followed them in.

I'd been in crems before ... well, once, when my uncle's
wife died in a syrup accident. I didn't like it then and I didn't
like it now. The place had no soul, which was ironic really. It
smelt of disinfectant and was adorned with plastic flowers
which set the tune for the whole place. Too much in salmon

and MDF, with pews straight from Rustic Pine on Swinegate. It tasted of milk gone sour.

Ting would have hated this place, but even in death we have to obey the conventions of our culture so Ray had booked today to burn his son in a crematorium rather than on the bonfire in Mull which he wanted. Ting, that is.

Ray waved us to his side. Nodding and smiling at each of us, he turned back to his mother and clasped her hand. If he was struggling to keep it together he was hiding it well, I thought. Then I noticed the white knuckles as he held the hymnal. Looking behind me, I winked to Molly as she sat with her arm around Sally Finnigan. The lights dimmed as The Doors began playing 'Break on Through' and I turned to the front, my gaze resting on Ting's coffin.

I closed my eyes when the music stopped and lost the next forty minutes in a haze of images. Even as a retired Catholic, I couldn't imagine that Ting was going to his reward in a Bible-defined afterlife. Mourn and rejoice. One of the many fundamentals that confused me as a catechism-reading child and one that I still couldn't come to terms with now, years later.

He was gone. Rolling behind a heavy curtain to the fires, leaving us to hope and actively pray for his redemption. Only I don't believe any more. And I don't pray, so there was little chance that I'd be doing any rejoicing right now. Instead I traced our friendship and fought my despair.

The curtain closed as the Fifth Element flew 'Up, Up and Away' in their beautiful balloon and I stood and shuffled out with everyone else. Outside, I kissed and hugged and mingled with the others. Some I just nodded greetings to, unwilling to enter into post-funeral chitchat. After a bit we moved off by ourselves and lit a joint, watching the smoke rise to join the trail that escaped from the chimney beside us. I wondered if they used smokeless fuel.

'Right, well, I'm happy to be out of that place.' Pine dragged clumsily on the joint, his eyes a bit wild. 'It's too fucking sad, and I don't mean the cheap carpets.' His hand trembled as he passed me the smoke and I knew and felt the same. He shook his head as though brushing off a shiver. 'Sad bastards.' He smiled thinly. 'Ting would be having a nightmare if he could see us now.'

We looked at each other, knowing that he was right but knowing that it didn't make a difference. We stood in silence as Sally and Molly, who had been talking with Ray, now walked towards us.

Sad eyes.

We all hugged and smiled the crooked sneer of resignation. Her arm around Pine's back, Molly held his face and gently kissed away an errant tear as we stood, speaking little and taking solace in our proximity to each other.

Safety in numbers.

Stan passed round the Stella and Sally produced another smoke from her bag.

Remote from the others, I watched as those fortunate enough to have been Ting's friends paid their own version of respect to Ray, who stood and reassured each of them in a perverse reversal of support.

'C'mon and we'll see Ray before he's off,' I suggested, stepping back into my happy place the way you do after a knock. It was the easy thing to do, it meant that I didn't have to examine myself too closely in the light of Pine's tears. If I had, I was afraid that I would have seen the cracks in the walls of my own dam and thoughts of never seeing Ting again would burst through. Walking over, I toyed with the distraction of finding Ting a different place in my psyche, a new place for him to occupy in my head. I was conscious of the attempt. I wouldn't miss him, I'd say, I'd still talk to him. He'd still be there, only vibrating to a different beat, so how could I be sad? Guilt-ridden, yes, but sad? That's what I was trying to convince myself anyway. Sally and Molly kissed their goodbyes and we left them walking to Sally's car.

'Ah, boys.' Ray looked up as we wandered over. 'I was wondering what had happened to you three reprobates. How you doing?' A smile and a warm handshake.

'Fine, Ray, just a bit fazed by this whole thing same as yourself. How are you doing?' I looked at him as his mother ambled over, wishing I hadn't asked what must have been both the most inane and popular question that he was being asked all morning.

'Aye, well, just as you'd suppose.' He drew back his lips and snorted. 'Thank fuck his gran's senile. God forgive me for saying it but this would kill her.' He turned towards her. 'You all right, Ma?'

All four foot of her was covered in a shawl; only her shoes and nose were visible. Pushing up her woollen hat, she smiled at him. 'Lovely concert, son.'

Ray looked at us knowingly.

'Pass us a toot on that spliff, Pennance.' He nodded to me and I handed it to him whilst Stan proffered a can of Stella. 'Cheers, boys,' he said, inhaling deeply.

'No problem, Ray.'

Mrs Sweetson raised her arms and we each leant down to receive our kisses. Her breath smelt of whisky and peppermint and the stubble above her lips didn't so much tickle as exfoliate.

'Hello, boys.' She peered up at us. 'Where's Charlie?'

Ting's gran had laughed when he suggested she call him Ting, then she agreed and forgot all about it.

Ray smiled at her. 'He's coming along later, Mam. Say cheerio to the boys and I'll see you in the car in a minute.'

She looked over to where he was pointing and started walking to the car, mumbling away to herself as she fended off wasps that only she could see. Ray watched her go and shouted, 'The other one,' as she opened the door of the hearse.

Calm as you like, Ting's dad, we all thought so. He'd brought Ting up single-handed almost since he was born. His wife, Ting's mother, had gone out one day and just never came back. Ting never mentioned her, but Ray was still fairly balanced when he talked about it. He'd told us about it once whilst Ting sat and watched television, pretending not to listen. They'd come back from a week in a caravan; it was their first holiday since Ting was born and they'd even bought a bottle of Asti to help them keep celebrating when they got back. 'We weren't that poor,' Ting had shouted, forgetting that he was supposed to be watching the telly and not listening, but Ray just smiled and continued.

'Gayle loved to walk, so we pushed the buggy round for days, picnicking by the cliffs and kicking sand at each other. We had a great time.'

We'd sat and listened how the day they got back she went out for a paper whilst Ray put Ting to bed and settled in front of the TV, waiting for her to come back with the telly page and a couple of Crunchies.

She never came back.

Ray found the note she'd left next to the kettle as the adverts started at the end of the news.

'What did you do then?' one of us had asked, absolutely gobsmacked that Ting had never told us about such a gigantic thing.

He shrugged. 'Well, I just kept flicking until I found something worth watching.'

He was like that forever. He did have a hard time dealing with not having Gayle there; he would always say that, but he managed. People do; the Rays out there always do. He moved from Mull and threw himself into being a single parent with all the energy and strength of someone who owned a piece of Wembley that he'd clawed up with his own fingers. Immaculately turned out in his three-piece and mirror shoes, he cut a dash that put us to shame in our nouveau GQ naivety.

Handing back the spliff, he straightened his already plumb-lined self and said, 'Right, Pennance, I'll see you tomorrow, what, at about three?'

'Sound as a pound, Ray,' I replied. 'You take it easy today.'

I hesitated, uncertain what I meant by that. Ray smiled tightly at my discomfort and patted my arm as he turned to follow his mother.

'I know what you mean, Pennance, don't worry.' He looked to Stan and Pine who were nodding vacuously almost in synchrony and shook their hands. 'Pine, how are you doing?'

Pine managed a half-smile.

'Any news about your house?'

'Not a lot, Ray.' He shuffled his feet, embarrassed by Ray's obvious concern. 'The fire brigade are still looking into it. Mostly there's smoke damage but I can't go back until they've finished investigating. I'm staying with Molly in the meantime.'

Ray nodded. 'Good, well, watch yourselves, boys.' He winked at them and strode off to the car.

We watched them drive off in silence until they disappeared through the huge iron gates. Feeling the insidious melancholy of the place seeping into my hair, I was thankful when Pine broke through the mists and suggested we follow suit and fuck off to St Pete's for some breakfast.

As we blagged a lift from the undertaker, I hoped that Ray was strong enough to deal with this. On reflection I was wondering if I was, and wished away the journey as I was gagging for a drink. That bastard Stan had finished the last of the Stella.

Chapter 2

heaven's above

In between mouthfuls of Egg Florentine and shots of brandy we sat in comfortable silence, each of us lost in our own thoughts as we stoked up on fuel to see us through the next few days.

I knew we'd need it.

Four years earlier, almost to the day, we had sat in the same booth deciding what we would do in the event that one of us died. A fairly surreal but not unusual conversation for us.

Back then we'd met regularly every week at the café. Even while we were students we tried to get back as often as we could. Ting, Stan, Pine and I shared pretty much everything and one of the most special things we shared was St Pete's.

The café belonged to Stan, or more accurately to Stan and the NatWest Bank. An uneven partnership where Stan got all the hard work and the bank took lots of interest. Financial as opposed to friendly. We'd all helped him to buy it and convert it from a butcher's shop into a tapas-selling no-jazz-allowed café bar, stripping decades of God only knows what off the piebald walls and ceiling, sanding floors and chiselling toilet tiles. Pine designed the layout and built the booths with Ting whilst Stan and I chipped and moulded the dirty great-big butcher's block into a bar that even vegans could fall in lust with. After three months, twenty-three bottles of Glenfiddich, eighteen bottles of tequila, six ounces of Moroccan hash, count-less limes, forty-seven pizzas, thirty-nine Chinese takeaways, seventy-two curries and far too much beer, we had an establish-ment fit for those keen to spend.

Leeds was on the up with lots of scooters and loft apartments and Stan had done his research well. Within days of opening, droves of suits, trousered and skirted, happily put the world to rights over sandwiches and wine that cost only slightly less than their parents spent to put them through university. Right from the start we reserved the booths at the back for ourselves and people we liked.

Whenever we were there, Stan rarely worked. He'd come and chill with us until it became a habit. Every Friday we'd meet, listen to our CDs and get stoned. We had a tab so cash was never a concern, Stan only occasionally accepting money if the bank was being particularly frumpy with him. Back then we were in our early twenties and hung around the café like extras from *Cheers* every weekend, too lazy and content to do much else.

I remember clearly how the conversation started

It was just another Friday when I arrived. Stan and Ting were sat at the booth under the kitchen window in the back corner of the café arguing.

'No, no way. It's got to be red wine,' Stan was telling Ting. 'It'd be hard but I'd have to take the wine.'

Ting looked at him and shook his head in disagreement. Seeing me, he motioned for me to sit next to him. 'Have you heard that fucking idiot?' Jerking his head to where Stan sat scowling at him, he asked me for reinforcement. 'Pennance, swimming or red wine?'

After a moment's hesitation I chose the wine, only to be told that I'd made the same mistake as Stan. Ting was for swimming. He knew someone who had drowned and he loved to feel like an astronaut when he was underwater. I thought that was fair comment but stuck to my gut, figuring that I drank wine more often than I swam.

'That's fine,' Ting had said with a sigh, 'but think about the implications of your rash choice: you'll never really need red wine but you may need to swim one day. You know, to save a drowning dog or to see hot chicks in swimsuits.'

He laughed as he revealed his driving influence. Stan shook his head again and told him to fuck off before joining him in laughing at the absurdity of his thinking. The night progressed as hundreds had before: food, drink and music, all enveloped in the safety net of our friendship. Pine, when he arrived, regaling us with a new instalment of the soap that was his life at Brian's Coiffure, Ting challenging us about our musical bad taste and me loving every second of it. The comfort of it, four people with hearts beating to the same rhythm.

Our booth had a drawer under the table and we each had a key for it. Inside was a collection of junk that we had amassed over the years. A picture of us at Blackpool, ticket stubs from concerts, a porno with a photo shoot of one of Pine's exes, assorted condoms of no fixed use, and all our pipes, bongs and smoking paraphernalia. Sometimes we'd play poker, so there were cards, chips, and a pot of money that we used if we wanted tickets for concerts or new CDs for the café.

This was our place, the leather of the bench had been worn by our continual use, and the varnish reflected years of memories. The rest of the café had been redecorated as cutting-edge style demanded, but we'd never altered our booth. That's how set we were in our ritual.

'This is "Fuzzy", Grant Lee Buffalo,' Ting told us as he passed the bong and reached for the garlic bread. We each nodded, he was rarely wrong about it. Ever since I could remember he always wore a Walkman. First a tape, then a CD and then a minidisc. Music was his great love affair, he could play too and had attempted to teach me the rudiments of guitar, admittedly with minimal success. I was, and remain, one of life's true musical challenges and would be hard pressed to keep a beat in a safe. Nevertheless he persevered, believing that music could free my soul even at a time when I was scarcely aware that it had been incarcerated. Music was food to Ting and he'd consume dishes from around the world with the gusto of a connoisseur, each plate appropriate for a particular time or mood. To him, and later to me, something like Nirvana's 'Teen Spirit' before 6 PM was as normal as chopped liver and mash for breakfast. But it was still part of the menu that Ting thought of as soul food. A soundtrack, if you like, that plays itself out, only waiting to be acknowledged, and that night, as Ting had said, was Grant Lee Buffalo. At least at that point it was, later it changed.

It was an easy night of bullshit and silence broken by the occasional guffaw as we scored the talent in the café at the top of each hour.

As the evening became night, Pine was in full flow. Born Mario Pinaldi, a second-generation Lothario, at twenty-five he was a well-respected hairdresser in a trendy salon in town. His mother had recommended either hairdressing or nursing as a good way of meeting girls and so at seventeen he had enrolled in nursing college to pursue his dream. Two months later he'd slept with nine student nurses, four qualified and a doctor who had him thrown off the course when naked pictures of her in surgical stirrups inexplicably appeared on notice boards around the halls of residence. Declaring a love for all things follicular, he became a hairdresser the next day.

'So because Jill was in Ibiza I said I'd do it,' he told us, mimicking himself pushing his dick into her shoulder as he always did when cutting hair and taking chances with his flirting sharper than his scissors. 'Talking away at her, I didn't notice the look on her face until I lifted a comb full of hair and realised I'd been cutting a wig. None of those bastards in the salon could look at me for pissing themselves, I'd never cut a wig in my life.' He stopped and looked at me. 'How was I supposed to know that it was meant to be wet before you cut it?' I could only shrug, how was I supposed to know? A smile of crooked teeth appeared. 'She now looks like an extra from a Flock of Seagulls video and I'm on my final warning again.'

Pine was, to be fair, a bit of a drama queen. I was never sure if it was part of his hairdressing persona or the real him and he'd never admit it either way. He was, to be sure though, very successful with the ladies and I, of course, was as jealous as hell.

'You bad bastard, what did you say to the poor girl?' I asked. 'And why was she wearing a wig anyway?'

'It wasn't my fault.' He camped it up. 'They all knew it was a syrup and not one of them told me.' The girl in question had been a regular client of Jill's for years and had lost her hair through stress. She was a redundancy counsellor and, far from being angry and demanding Pine's rubbing testicles on a plate, she paid for the restyling, left a tip, and accepted his phone number, agreeing to go on a date the following Saturday. We sat in mock disbelief as he concluded, knowing that this unusual turn of events was all too fucking common for Pine. He, along with Ting, was the archetypal babe magnet. Ting suggested that he would find it freaky dating a bald girl and a debate ensued as to which physical abnormalities Pine would actually keep his dick in his pants for. It turned out that there was only one and the chances of him propositioning a bearded hermaphrodite were slim. As the night grew late we moved from dating to marriage as Stan's sister was getting married. Her husband to be, Graham, had opted not to have a stag night and we were onto the relative pros and cons of this. It was academic in any case. Graham hadn't spoken to Stan since he stayed with them and pissed in a box of photos instead of the sink that he had been aiming for. We weren't on his A-list.

Through a haze of blue smoke I confided that I wanted a stag weekend at the very least with no fewer than twenty-four hours that I couldn't remember. Away in Barcelona along Las Ramblas or in Amsterdam taking in at least one top-level football match, a visit to a tattooist and a final ogle at beautiful naked women dancing. Ting's involved a remote beach, matches and being naked, and Pine's was too graphic so we didn't let him tell us about it. Sitting quietly as we spoke, Stan asked, 'Stag weekend or sex on your honeymoon?'

That was a good one. Over the years we'd had plenty, but that was a beaut. Toast or chips, oral sex or deodorant, bath or shower, coffee or Lara Croft. We'd had some choices to make, some easy and some that brought you out in a sweat. If for the rest of your life you could only have one or the other, which would you keep? (I'd opted for toast, oral sex, bath and Lara. Ting: chips, deodorant, shower and Lara. Pine: toast, oral sex, shower and coffee. Stan: chips, oral sex, bath and Lara.)

I played different scenarios in my mind, images flicking like Victorian penny arcade boxes, but in the end, having been talking and thinking about stag nights, I seriously wanted one. Never mind that I wasn't in a relationship, hadn't been for eleven months and had none in the pending file. It was a moot point, but I wanted one anyway. Then I checked myself. Thoughts of sex took over and I realised that a sexless honeymoon would probably be a bad precedent to set that early on in a marriage so I opted for the sex instead, feeling slightly put out that I wouldn't be having a stag do. Stan and Pine were with me on this one but Ting said he would hold out for the stag do. Moving along, we did hair or pinkie fingers, tits or a testicle, *The Fast Show* or *Blackadder* – series four, cremation or burial. It was over coffee and Jack that we pondered the serious choice that we could one day in reality have to make. Both shows could be scheduled for the same time and we might not have access to a VCR that we could fathom.

Talk of death, far from depressing us, gave rise to more and more sophisticated conversations of how we would like to go and, more often than not, how we would like our funerals. Details for all of us changed over time. Pine no longer wanted to be buried with a lock of hair taken from every woman he had slept with, Stan now wanted an Elizabethan theme as opposed to the Gladiatorial Extravaganza he first chose, Ting introduced Mull and I gave up on cryogenic freezing.

What didn't change was our insistence that it should be an event. A final booking. A notion from that first conversation about stag nights gave birth to an idea that grew to be an oath. A promise that no matter when it happened we would get together and have a stag wake. A final send-off. With the plans for our long walk back to the dressing room mapped out, we visited it less often, believing that we'd all be too long in the false teeth to even remember when one of us actually died.

But that was then.

▭ ＊ ▭

Lately we hadn't seen as much of each other. Life seemed to get in the way now. Or at least for some of us.

Pine was some kind of high-flying touring stylist hairdressing guru these days, rarely in Leeds. When he was at home he was usually catching up on his sleep. Ting had moved twenty miles and a cultural chasm away to head up a team of troubleshooting teachers in a clutch of Bradford's lower-division schools. He was so frequently snowed under with homework that it had become all but impossible to arrange for us all to get together as we once had. Only I was readily available when Stan suggested that we should have an Elvis party.

It was five days ago, after the party, that it happened. Ting was returning the 'Vegas Years' costumes to the hire shop. He'd taken his headphones off and, wearing them around his neck, he had listened to Boccherini (Minuet from String Quintet in E, predictably) being piped through the shopping arcade speakers when it happened. They said he'd been looking up. That was so like him; he'd walk past a tenner, never seeing it, if he could find an excuse to look up instead of down. He could always find an excuse. A patchwork sky, the roof of the Sistine Chapel, a sparrow sailing through the trees. Not only that, but he thought it made him look taller. His shoulders back and his chin up, he would pontificate. 'We don't appreciate the simple beauty of life that goes on around us because we spend all our time watching our feet.' He didn't believe that it was necessary. 'We know how to walk, we've all been doing it for long enough. Our brain knows what muscles to manipulate without our conscious thought. Contract and expand in the rhythm we call walking, running, hopping and jumping. It's as mechanical as blinking, why pay attention to it?' He believed it enough to be willing to accept the bruises and contusions that arose when he walked into benches, bins and beggars. He had convinced himself that years of dedicated dope smoking had heightened his senses and that he was attuned beyond the majority of the hoi polloi, thus allowing him to avoid serious injury to himself and others whilst following his heavenly focus. He'd go everywhere as if straining to hear distant music or deep in contemplation of a speck of a bird. I did ask him once if he had discovered his love of all things skyward as a result of trying to look taller or the other way round. He'd smiled magnanimously and told me to fuck off and get some. He didn't mean music or fish.

It was the Art Deco roof that got him.

With the light spilling through the multi-hued glass tiles, tiny prisms split the spectrum and beamed as colour took aspect and danced in challenge to the dark that rose to meet it. Ting's words, not mine. It held him in rapture as he walked through the arcade. That's what he told me one night as we lay on the cold marble floor looking at the stars distorted by glass and tequila. I think if the security guard hadn't gotten all anal on us he would have lain there to watch the sun come up and go back down again.

He got stabbed as he walked past Ted Baker.

Just once, but often that's enough.

If he'd been looking down or into the gaudily displayed shop fronts or even watching where he was going he might have seen it coming.

But probably not.

A man, any man, stepped out of a swell of passers-by and drove a four-inch carving knife into his heart.

Just like that. No preamble. No reason. No chance.

Security held the man, who never tried to leave, until the police arrived. They appeared almost immediately, and too late to do anything. The ubiquitous *they* said he was a known offender. A released patient. A nut.

God bless the Mental Health Act.

▭ ✳ ▭

We were in St Pete's.

St Peter's Rendezvous.

Stan, Pine, and I had been there all day, our new friend Lurch having dropped us off at about noon. The others had been arriving in dribs and cabs for the last several hours and we had pretty much taken over the back of the café where the orange booths were. Across the debris of our indulgence, Sally sat with Molly, both of them drinking doubles at full steam and showing signs of catching up with our drunken train. The remaining three tables were filled with other friends, those on the periphery of the inner circle, who felt a sense of loss no less keen than our own despite never having known Ting as we did.

We ordered tacos and tequila, sat in woollen hats and got stoned 'Immaculate' as Jim whispered from the speakers. It was the top of the hour again and we were toasting Ting, as we had been all day.

'Ting.' Pine raised his glass.

'Ting,' we chanted and clinked our glasses, shot, grimaced and refilled.

'Wake.' He started again.

'Wake,' we repeated.

'Wake?' Sally hesitated and emptied her glass slowly. 'Wake who?'

'Ting,' Pine answered her and raised his glass again, smiling.

Sally followed suit but her furrowed brow said that she wasn't following him.

'Tomorrow,' Stan told her. 'We're having a wake for Ting.' We clinked. 'His stag wake.'

'I thought that's what this was?' she said, gesturing round the café.

We shook our heads and made fun of her naivety until Molly began passing round her look.

'Sorry, Sal.' Pine grinned. 'This is more in the way of a warm-up. The main event doesn't kick off until we get Ting back. Tomorrow. I know it sounds a bit . . .' He looked at Stan.

'Bizarre,' Stan suggested.

'Fucked up,' I offered.

'. . . Unusual, but we planned it ages ago. The four of us.'

And so he went on to explain about Ting's perfect weekend. It was nothing particularly unusual. He wanted us to remem-

ber him well and to give him one last party before he got on
his way. He wanted us to have a night out, go clubbing, like
we used to. Hitting a few bars early and going on to a club,
maybe a game of pool and a kebab, dancing girls and a memorable hangover.

And he wanted to come.

Sunday, it being God's day and Ting wanting to hedge
his bets, we were to have a day of rest. Since this was also
the night that traditionally we would spend dissecting our
previous night's performance we were to combine them both
and have a major chill time in the café before taking him to
Mull. Ting had said that he thought there could be no more
appropriate place for him to begin his journey than at the gates
of heaven, St Peter's Rendezvous. We would take the train to
Mull; he stipulated that we weren't allowed to drive, as no
excuse for sobriety would be humoured, we were to speak
fondly and flatteringly of him and let the sea have his ashes.
He'd accepted the fact that it was unlikely that the Sanitation
Department would allow us to consign his mortal remains
to a bonfire on the beach and had given us a certain amount
of leeway in interpreting this final wish. Once back from Mull
we were to reconvene in the café, raise a final glass and smile
on with our lives. I knew that was going to be the hard bit.

◻ * ◻

As the candles burnt down I wandered from booth to booth,
talking the talk. The day slipped out and then the night drifted
into a false dawn. Stan locked the door and pulled the blinds.
We were having a fry-up, Josh was in the kitchen, and I could
smell the bacon. I was pissed. I couldn't think straight. I could
smell bacon. It reminded me of nipples. That threw me for a
bit until I got the connection. I was thinking of the bacon banjo
that I'd been eating in the car this morning.

Christ, was that only this morning?

Bacon and nipples, now I couldn't separate the two. Natural
as the focus was, I felt guilty that thoughts of pleasure maybe

were slightly out of sync with the moment. Unfortunately when I tried to find other trains of thought or catch tangents to go on, I always ended up with a return ticket.

Nipples, and it was such a funny word too.

In an effort to move on I went back to the table to wait for the bacon. Molly and Pine were sharing an omelette and Sally was skinning up. I determined to avoid looking at her cleavage and definitely did not think, even in passing, about the cause of the crash again. I budged up next to her and tried to play not being pissed while I waited for the bacon. Pine giggled at me and I took that to be an indication that I wasn't going to get that call-up for *Friends* after all.

'How fucked are you?' Molly asked, although I think she already knew. Sally had joined Pine in giggling and I was wobbling away all unawares. Her giggles subsiding, Sally continued to smile as she looked past me.

'Pennance Ward, this is Halifax,' she told me.

I felt as confused as I must have looked. It couldn't be, not unless Stan had moved the café when I'd briefly passed out after the misunderstanding with the tequila. I looked at her, then followed her gaze.

'Ali Fox, this is Pennance Ward,' I heard her say over the rushing of my blood.

My heart grabbed onto my ribs and held on for dear life as a torrent of testosterone raced round my veins. The sun actually did come up when she smiled, tripped, and dropped the bacon butties she had been carrying onto my lap. I leapt up and smacked my knees against the table as she shuffled in next to me, placing the empty plate and the bottle of Oban she had been drinking from on the table.

'Shit, I'm sorry,' she said, helping to retrieve the bacon. 'I'm really sorry.'

The smile came back and I went gaga.

It may have been the brush of her fingers as she picked up the butties from my thighs. It could have been the smile that eclipsed the sun. It was probably the copious amounts of drugs smoked and alcohol imbibed over the last week or so. Whatever the reason, I found myself unable to speak. Ali mistook my inability for an unwillingness and threw me a rubber ear.

'Well, I'm sorry anyhow,' she said, turning away from me and drinking her whisky.

She was for me at that time the most beautiful girl I'd ever clapped eyes on. I was knackered, I was sad and now I was in the presence of a Drop Dead Honey. Or at least that's what I think caused my paralysis. Suddenly I opened my eyes and, looking around, I knew I'd fallen asleep. I needed to go home. Ali had moved to the other side of Sally, and time being the great healer, she smiled in forgiveness as she noticed my staring.

'Alicumomewivmipleez?'

I felt my lips move but it took a fraction of a second longer before my brain caught up with them. I was obviously pleased that I had recovered the power of speech, but I was mortified because she heard me. With only a slight quiver around her mouth she said 'no' and continued talking to Sally, who had resumed giggling.

Another great outing for the Silver-tongued Cavalier.

Miserable, I slid off the seat and went to look for my coat. I found Stan using it as a pillow and woke him up. As he uncurled himself from the bar top I caught him before he hit the floor and pointed him in the direction of the door.

Sally shouted good night and waved us off. When we reached the door I turned one final time and saw Ali kneeling back on her seat looking at me. Sally was giggling again. Even emotionally dulled as I was, I could feel my face flush and made to turn away. Then Ali smiled and I definitely saw her wink. New testosterone elated me as I returned her wink and casually pushed the door open for my now to be swirling exit. Stan stood outside holding the door as I pushed at nothing and tipped onto the pavement.

I jumped up with an enthusiasm I didn't feel and pretended nothing had gone awry. I thought I'd gotten away with it too until I heard the rich peals of laughter from behind me. Refusing to look back in the café, I took Stan's arm and we walked up the road. He patted my arm 'there, there, there', but I missed what he said. All I could hear was Ali laughing at me. I am sooo fucking suave, Pierce Brosnan must be shitting himself.

Chapter 3
flat busted

I got the key in the door at the fourth attempt. The first and second were the wrong door, the third the wrong key. Helen, my neighbour – the second door I tried – found the correct key for me and helped me negotiate the escalator that had replaced the hallway some time after I'd left this morning. Helen must have been practising because she appeared to be having little difficulty with its mechanical devilry. In such accomplished company I was soon safely beyond its teeth and pushing through my junk mail. With the sensitivity of a tornado, Helen put me to bed, fed my cat, and tidied my kitchen. Thankfully the Hoover was broken.

I woke up with a heavy heart and panicked until I realised the cat was on my chest. Pushing her away, I pulled the clock to my left eye, moving it away from me until I was able to focus on the hands. Good, I'd managed four hours' sleep. Relieved that I had ages yet before I had to meet Ray, I skinned up and got undressed.

With Van the Man pushing clear the air in front of me, I searched for the Nurofen. I'd only been in the flat nine months and still lived out of boxes; finding things was a challenge, although I was determined that I would get around to unpacking some time soon. After moving out of student halls, living with Kirsty, and renting damp rooms from basement entrepreneurs, I had bought this flat in defiance of my instinct not to. In a masterstroke of gamesmanship I fooled myself into believing that I was ready to handle a mortgage. I was taking things slowly, assimilating at a careful pace. Once I'd become adjusted to the let-down of being a homeowner, I started to transform my soon-to-belong-to-me-and-not-the-bank-if-I-faithfully-paid-my-mortgage-for-twenty-five-years flat into the tack that was my taste. I was in no hurry to finish and that's why I was still finding stale bread Frisbees in piles of boxes. The bathroom, that most essential of sanctuaries, was finished. Racing Green paint and the original Deco tiles. No shower. The kitchen I started stripping in May and was almost halfway through finishing. I had yet to make a start on either bedroom but was quite satisfied with the living room. The couch used to be my parents' and even though the leather's cracked I was loath to part with it. Remembering the scoldings I got for actually sitting on it as a child, I revelled in my ability to do on it what I liked. Of course mostly I just sat, but it did look good. The best thing about my home was that there was no magnolia. Orange, yellow, puce and red, but no magnolia. No wood chip and no Anaglypta either. I threw that out with the Artex. Finding the Nurofen in the sink, I washed three down with stale Irn-Bru. I needed to wake up, properly, and my flat with its badly fitting windows and bowed walls was well placed for clearing the head with a belt of fresh air exercise. One of the main reasons I bought it was its proximity to trees and grass. Jumping on my bike, I headed down the avenue of oak that drew me in to Narnia.

▭ * ▭

Once I was pumping, I headed to the lake and chained my bike to the railings dedicated to the new age cyclist. Originally the railings came complete with bikes that were intended for the use of the park-going public. There were four points where bikes could be picked up and left, all free of charge, for a day's riding in the park or a short commute from end to end. A good idea, very philanthropic. Very myopic. The bikes disappeared before lunch on the first day of the project. Like bowling shoes, they were purposely garish to deter theft and make for easy identification if they left the park. Like bowling shoes, they disappeared anyway. Like No Ball Games signs placed precisely where they make an excellent goalpost, the bikes were a good idea – if slightly out of kilter with those who use the park. Maybe the next generation of local councillors would invest in something less transient. Like flowers.

Despite a few bike thieves and local authority ineptness, the park was a popular retreat relatively free of junkies and drunks. Climbing to a bench above the tree line, I lit a smoke and watched the swans and geese below in the lake. Cackling at each other, they fought for the attention of their host, a boy of about seven who was throwing bread – probably fresh by the look of his off-road-driving parents – more at them than to them. I imagined him a Tristan or Rupert. The birds, however, had other ideas and launched a blistering attack on the Marks & Sparks bag, forcing Tristan to jump away yelping as Mr Land and Mrs Rover dived over him as if fearing a Hitchcock moment.

I heard Wagner send his Valkyries in to play.

Warm though it was, the wind was pulling at my shirt, cooling my sweat, and making me shiver. Someone walking over my grave. Down in the bowl before the lake I could see families and couples ambling past each other in aimless fashion. A pondering advance to the ice-cream van that seemed to draw them like a lodestone without conscious thought. For most that was the attraction. A day of misdirection and shoe scuffing. In lives mapped by timetables, routes and convention, the park was rebellion. No 'queuing in an orderly fashion' or 'keeping to the left', it was smoking at your desk and leaving lights on when you left. Their alternative was cartoon ties and chunky jewellery, but that was thankfully only during the week.

Looking again, this time less casually, it struck me that in the whole park, if you discounted the two guys with dogs flirting outside the toilets, I was the only person on my own. This was not normally something I worried about. Relaxed and confident, I muddled through life and did okay for myself. It's been adequate. Stumbling from job to job, I didn't see myself as needing this park time. The people below me came here to get what I had. They strived to be able to sit in front of the telly and do nothing. It's what everyone wants. That's why holidays are so popular.

With my eyes closed, I imagined talking to all those people in the park, a manic street preacher extolling the virtues of Pennance, a latter-day Nietzsche promising salvation in sloth. But as I scanned the crowd for agreement I saw consternation in the eyes of the hugging couples, disapproval in the stance of the fathers as mothers led the impressionable away with a sad shake of the head. Freedom from responsibility scares the masses and I am reviled as all good prophets should be.

Ting had always been more pragmatic than me and had sat on this bench and argued that it was with freedom that responsibility came.

I wished he was here with me now. He could help me to understand his death, what to do next. Work out how to move on. The park wasn't a haven any more where I watched and remembered why I was happy. Now it was full of people with life, even the Land-Rovers, and my memory would always be of a different day.

▭　＊　▭

Last week I'd been running through the park, past the lake and on to the incline, panting up the hill with the sun almost drying the sweat as it soaked my shirt. And Ting dying as I fought for breath on the rise. Ironically, at the time when his life stopped, I remember that I was thinking that soon I'd be too old to qualify to go on an 18–30 holiday. Not that I wanted to go, I just didn't like the idea of not being able to. The two girls who had breezed past me barely out of breath had reminded me that I was getting older, and I was thinking it a drag.

There was already a generation out there who only knew of Spangles and Choppers, *Runaround* and *Tucker's Luck* because they were hip to retro, thanks to cheap TV programming. The DJs who had brought me up had been canned, or, worse, moved to Radio 2, and I couldn't believe that I was having conversations that I knew my parents had had before me. Bad as that was, the worst came when strangers, even those I would put at only a few years younger than me, started to refer to me as mister or sir, as in 'do you need help with that?'

What, like getting my Zimmer up the stairs maybe?

Fighting for breath, I'd shaken my head as I'd looked round at the generation that came before me and saw what my future held and laughed, spluttered really, at the absurdity of it. Maybe I didn't want to grow up, grow old.

Then home and news that Ting was dead. At that point the lifeless existence of a middle age that I believed to be the future – the responsibility and inevitability of it all – disappeared in a flash of understanding.

Now I knew the alternative, getting old didn't seem such a big deal.

My problem, as I sat at the top of the hill again, was how to do it without becoming what I despised. How to avoid the cardigans, slippers and living for weekends.

My life, for what it'd been, wasn't exactly a success story. Closing in on thirty, I was still in temporary employment, still waiting for the proper job that a university education owed me but which no one had seen fit to approach me with. I was sat alone in a park. Alone because I didn't have anyone to share it with. I had friends, but no one to share the days with, especially now with Ting gone, and I felt an emptiness. Like the career that had eluded me, the One had still to come forward and make herself known, my very own Eris. My goddess of trouble and strife. Where was she?

I closed my eyes and forced a smile, remembering where I was. I was losing myself to the new middle youth devotees and was in danger of becoming a caricature from a cheesy coming-of-age movie.

Oh me oh my, I need a girlfriend. Oh me oh my, I'm turning thirty.

It was so twentieth century.

I wasn't worried about getting old; it was more about not getting the chance. Suddenly I could feel my grounding in the park turning mean. Fear of what I would and might not become hung behind my eyes and I struggled with it. Time to move on.

Reaching for my water bottle, I saw a pair of young lovers walking through the park, smiling as their toddler chased their dog through the trees. Sitting back, I took over the dad's role. Pennance the doting father. Pennance getting back from Ikea with his wife and opening a bottle of wine. Pennance making love regularly. Pennance being balanced, less neurotic and without the beer belly. Sitting up straight, I wobbled my stomach with both hands and listened to the water swooshing round. What can you do? Attractive, it is not. But try as I might, it's here like herpes.

In search of a better body image, and thus a better me, I joined the gym and even went at least once a week with Ting or Stan. Not that they needed to, they only went out of friendship and to flirt. I'm heavier now that I use the gym than I was before. It doesn't bear thinking about. My only solace is in imagining how big I'd be if I hadn't felt I was fat in the first place. My logic assured me that I could maintain a balance of low self/body image, gym, and beer without having to shop at High and Mighty.

I was hyper-aware of how I felt, here today with blotched flesh oozing through my fingers, the sun burning my nose, the sweat sticky and damp on my back, my obsession and its total fucking irrelevance exploding before my eyes. Insulated by time, distance, and hypotheticals, I wondered, what if it was me? Stopped, frozen, preserved in a jar. I knew what I would think as the red card appeared and he pointed over his shoulder with his thumb, and it wouldn't be fair do's, ref. Would I be content? Would I fuck.

Following the tree line, I found the Land-Rovers and saw them walking to the car park armed with a brace of double cones. A nest of young tripped around their feet as they held the ice creams out of reach until they had been distributed in orderly fashion, a throwback to non-weekend behaviour. Only Mrs Rover didn't have one. She took a bite of her husband's and handed it to him, shaking her head that she didn't want any more. Her denial made me conscious that my insecurity had traditionally been a single-sex issue.

Girls worried about weight, girls worried about stretch marks, cellulite, droopy tits, fat arses, thunder thighs, ankles – the mystery one. Double chins, flabby arms, chunky fingers and swollen eyes. Now, thanks to Lycra, I was only too aware that not only did *they* worry about it, but I should too. For myself. And as if to confirm what cycling shorts had suggested, the magazines that once determined what would make a girl shaggable now explained to me why I and most of the other sixty per cent would remain unshagged until our buns could crack the porcelain. For me the dream of a six-pack was just that.

I'm built to withstand the rigours of a winter on the Steppes, not to play beach volleyball. Where it was once enough to have clean fingernails and control over body odour, now I had to groom, preen and try to fit into trendy clothes or spend every unfucking night alone. To make matters worse, I could feel the sun burn my head where my hair used to be as I walked back to my bike. A few days ago this would all have meant nothing. A blip that would be carried away as I slipped back into life again, back in the traffic. Today it seemed to need to be part of me and I wasn't sure if it would want to go away.

Freewheeling down to the car park, I blinked the wind out of my eyes and breathed in the sky. This was what needed to be done. Twenty-six minutes of fat-fed self-pitying despair when Ting couldn't ride his bike any more.

Because he's dead.

Over the cattle grid that rattled like a Tommy gun and screaming past the swing park. So I'm fat. Into the car park for a skidding arc stop that had gravel punching through the air. I saw the Land-Rovers; two kids were being dragged into the back seat while their father threw a demented look to his wife, smug with her I-have-them-all-week expression. She glanced my way and I smiled before sucking in and shooting off. Leaving them to face their own screaming futures as I worked on mine.

◼ * ◼

I saw my obsession for what it was: a shaper, a limiter, an excuse. It gave me a reason to be me. Something to focus on so I could forget about the things I wasn't ready to face, like life. It had taken me a week to realise that mine wasn't necessarily in front of me, waiting patiently for me to like myself. I was right in the thick of it, possibly with more behind than up ahead, and the bits that had gone, well, they had gone. I couldn't die waiting not to be fat, alone and ignominiously, forever projecting my complex onto those not sufficiently disgusted to be put off dating me. That would be too fucking sad.

If I could go at any minute, and I could, as Elvis and Ting had shown, then I wanted to be either enjoying what I was doing or content with what I'd done, and since I had no idea of the when, all I could do was stop making excuses for the now. I grabbed my stomach and wobbled like before, this time finishing with an affectionate patting that made me feel sick. There were more important things to be thinking about than this. Like how my new confident self could fit into Ali Fox's knickers and just possibly her life before she noticed my ankles.

Back in the traffic I decided to accept my lot with new abandon, I'd be thin enough when I was dead, so fuck it. True as a fault line, as soon as I passed the mirror in the hall back at the flat I sucked in again. And there was no one around. Programming and its big brother, public opinion, came and kicked optimism out of the swing park with a swift boot to the balls.

▭ ＊ ▭

I ran a bath and phoned Helen to see if she wanted a coffee. She did, so I asked her to bring me one too.

Helen was good to me. She was a twenty-six-year-old nurse and already the girl who watered my plants, fed the cat, and brought me groceries any time she went shopping. When I'd moved in she had greeted me with a bottle of rum and a spliff. Helping me move in meant we became friends. During the week she would come over with soup or a bottle of Jack and every

Friday after she had driven the quarter-mile back from her parents' house we would have a toot to relax her whilst I would wait for a taxi to the café. Saturdays we would have bacon sandwiches while deconstructing her evening. Friday is Shabbat for Helen, and as testament to her upbringing she religiously goes home for dinner every week. The smoke afterwards is a symbolic as much as a physical high in that it signals the start of her own weekend which is about as religious as Bubbalicious. Parental and devotional duties ticked, she wants to party. Helen though, if not especially zealous in her religious duties, has that particular temperament found mostly only in Jewish women. She can talk straight without taking a breath for up to four days. Not only does she talk but she punctuates every word with a potentially fatal stabbing hand that scares dogs and small children.

Last night I'd missed our downtime; she understood that and held no malice, but just looking at her, I could see her filling almost to bursting. I knew by the state of my unusually tidy kitchen that she'd had too much nervous energy last night. She needed release and that was why she was walking through my door with a steaming mug of coffee for me rather than having told me to go do something rude to myself as she normally would at such a demand. Handing me my coffee, she took the joint and began talking. I missed the first part of her monologue as I was adding the cold water to the bath but that didn't deter her.

'. . . And he's a Gentile so of course they wouldn't even let him in the house which put me in a position . . . don't you think . . . I mean how could I ask for commitment from him when I had to hide his bike every time my parents visited even though they knew that he stayed but never never talked about it to my face when . . .'

She spoke on, oblivious of me being underwater.

'. . . So I asked Dad to pass the wine and ignored the question which was probably rhetorical anyway because she never listens to my opinion or credits me with any sense of my own on account of that I don't settle down and marry a good Jewish boy and where would I find one anyway . . . I mean it's not as though I haven't looked.'

Unexpectedly she stopped. Realising that I was in the bath, she had sat herself outside the door and, having paused in her recital, she pushed it open and looked at me in the mirror. I saw her eyes refocus as she decided that it was probably appropriate to be asking me about the funeral, even if she did still want to exorcise last night's demons.

'Pennance, I'm sorry for going on, you must think I'm terrible yapping it up when you're fresh back from the funeral and not even bothered about hairy Daphne and my night because you've probably got a hangover, judging by the state of you this morning . . .' Hearing my name, I consciously began listening to her and found myself staring at her over the edge of the bath, unsure how to deal with the onslaught of guilt that put even me to shame. '. . . When I put you to bed and fed the cat and, by the way, did you know that your Hoover isn't working . . .'

'Don't worry about it,' I said. 'I'm fine.'

'You want me to feed Kato this weekend?' she asked.

'That would be great, thanks.' She was a sweetheart. 'There's food in the cupboard and I'll be back on Tuesday, Wednesday at the latest.'

She smiled then and regained her momentum. I lay in the bath controlling the temperature with the hot water tap on trickle and some dextrous toe and plug work. This was a great skill to have and meant that I was able to spend hours reading in a bath that didn't go cold. Lying with only the tip of my nose out of the water, I practised being a crocodile waiting for an unsuspecting lunch to come within reach. When the cat jumped onto the rim in search of her meal ticket I sprang with the guile of an adolescent lion and made a grab for her. Unmoved by my floundering, she sat in mute testimony to my hunting skills and regarded me with curious eyes. Sinking below the surface again, I waited for less proficient prey and promised myself to pay more attention to wildlife programmes. From underwater, Helen's voice was distorted and too late I realised that she had finished her account.

My back arched and every nerve end screamed as I rose out of the water in a spectacular reverse belly flop. The shock of cold water created a tidal wave as I struggled to avoid it. Helen stood above me. Her hands were still dripping as she grinned malevolently.

'That's for not listening.'

As I continued to hyperventilate, she leant down and gave me a kiss which if I'd stopped to think about it should have been a bit strange. I didn't think about it and in a rare moment free of self-consciousness I forgot to breathe in and flex.

'And that's because it doesn't matter. Good night, Pennance,' she said, her body clock still on night duty. 'I'll see you later.'

⚊ * ⚊

Alone again, I made the mistake of revisiting last night and groaned at my embarrassment. Another dazzling display of my legendary pulling power. My lack of appeal as good boyfriend stock was incongruent in a life where I had so many female friends. I was unwilling to let Ali join my already over-subscribed 'oh well at least we can still be friends' category and would be sure to pay more attention if the opportunity arose. I ran through the rest of the day as it came back to me in barely swallowable chunks. Over and over again I thought of the funeral and my clumsy attempts to rationalise Ting's death. While I wasn't ready to face it yet because it was still too raw, I was drawn to it. Sunburn on my eyes. I sat up and shook off the chill brushing along my spine.

Life had changed inexplicably, becoming fragile as a broken wing. My friend was dead, his death a waste like they all are, but not one I could tune out of or turn the page on. I tried to imagine the world if I was dead, substituting myself for Ting and willing him back into this existence. I could only picture life going on. People going through their lives as normal, the momentary discomfort of loss, no matter how keen, smothered in the minutiae that was living. Death was about not being in people's lives any more, no more thought of than a relative who lost contact or that best friend whose number was lost years ago. When Ting went travelling after university he came back full of enthusiasm for the experience. It took about two days for him to slip back into the life he'd left. After catching up on what we'd been up to and as interest in his trip flagged, he realised that although we did want to know about his adventures we had our own stories, albeit rather more prosaic than his but as important to us. Life went on while he was away, work, parties, laughter and disappointments, and when he got back he became part of it again. That's how it works. Only this time he would not be coming back and the knowledge weighed me down like a bad trip.

I hauled myself out of the bath, pausing as I saw my reflection in the mirror. The paunch and what Pine gleefully informed me was second-stage male-pattern baldness, a widow's peak where my hair used to be. Still not thirty and I was starting to look like my dad. I saw the beginnings of wrinkles around my eyes and the lines when I smiled. Here I was worrying about getting old again. With Ting's death came the richness of tomorrow and an almost reverent belief that I had to take advantage of each one, its transience having been revealed.

Intellectually, I was aware of death as a concept, but in the invincibility of youth I'd never paid it much notice, secure in the knowledge that, like winning the lottery, it was something that happened to other people. That is until Ting's ticket came up. Now I was awash with the guilt of the wastrel and determined to make adjustments. I just needed to work out how to do that while dealing with the mood swings that were afflicting me like PMT week. Post Mortal Ting.

▭ * ▭

Looking for a towel, I noticed that the answer machine was flashing. I noticed because it was so unusual. I had for years avoided the curse that was the answer machine, thinking that like the cash dispenser it was simply another way to control, mechanise and ultimately do away with human interaction. Then I got such a hard time from everyone for not being contactable that it became a fait accompli when Stan gave me his old one. As it turned out, I wasn't missing many calls anyway and I had gotten used to the synthesised voice dispassionately rebuking me every time I asked for messages. 'You-have-no-friends,' I would hear it say.

But not today.

'Hi, Pennance, it's Kirsty. I thought I'd try and drop in today at about one if you're going to be in. Phone me if not or I'll see you then. Bye.'

Ignoring the presumption that I would be at home to phone her back, I was glad to hear her voice. I had left a message for her, explaining about Ting, but hadn't heard anything back. I was pleased that she was coming.

Chapter 4
one got away

Realising that Kirsty would be here soon, I dried in the vortex created by my frantic cleaning spree. When we had lived together she had constantly admonished me over what she lovingly called my 'durtihabits' until I became a domestic automaton. At least for a while. Kirsty loved a clean flat. Or she loved the idea of it, if not the actual practice, in what my mother would call a 'top tidy' manner. I'd found her once literally sweeping stuff under the carpet. That was no defence, as I had found out, against her own prejudices, which was why I knew that she would judge my life and me by the state of my living conditions. Even though we were no longer together, old habits die last, and I knew she'd take it as a personal affront if I didn't make the effort.

Assessing the task I had allotted myself, I had a rethink and banished all undesirables to the back room, threw a blanket over the lot and closed the door while concocting a decorating saga to do justice to the lunarscape I'd left behind. At least Helen had cleaned the kitchen to recognisable proportions. A dishcloth over the sink and a pot of fresh coffee would have to do for the rest.

Satisfied and exhausted, I lay back on the bed and in an effort to thwart Kirsty rewarded myself with a quick one off the wrist. I nearly hit the ceiling when the bell rang to announce her. Boxers and a T-shirt later I opened the door.

A mass of tresses upon which sat a pair of Blocs, all tiara-like, waved through the door, stopping only to give me a rather perfunctory kiss before seeming to rethink its action and delivering an all-embracing hug from the body below it. Kirsty

loved big hair. And rightly so, for the shock of hair that had
served her through adolescence as a hiccup cure had captured
the sun and now used it for its own dastardly means. Bright,
warm and responsible for rationality blindness in the Inca chief-
tains that worship it, it strode ahead of her, sending out ripples
of warnings that you, Mr Ordinary, were about to come eye
to vision with one of God's Own.

Luckily I was immune now. Below the hair and enveloping
me round the waist, two perfect arms slid out of sight into the
light summer dress that had been designed to delicately hover
out of touch from her body. Not quite perfect enough to compete with the honey skin it adorned, it nonetheless delivered
the goods and I could feel stirrings where moments before there
had been fast-earned sleep.

Immune system must be down.

On floating away from my rough embrace, she left the
tingling push of her nipples to confound me as she breezed into
the flat.

'Did you miss me?' she breathed.

'I never threw anything at you.'

She curled her lip before smiling and arching her brow.
'Pleased to see me then?'

Not too quick today, I said, of course, before following her
gaze and covering myself. With my best boyish grin, I giggled
past her, secretly delighted with the impression I had made
against the cotton.

'Sorry.'

I left her exploring and made the coffee before steering her
away from the leviathan in the back.

'How long did you have after my message?'

I made a deal of pouring the coffee as she lifted the dishcloth
from a pile of dirty plates and shook her head.

'About twenty minutes.'

'Not bad,' she gave me, having scanned the whole of the
flat and appreciated my efforts. 'I guess that means the back
room is out of bounds then.'

Busted.

'I don't know what you mean. You still take three sugars?'

'Got any saccharine?'

She had started walking from the kitchen and I was in danger of losing her to the black hole in the back room. Knowing that she would get all righteous on me when she found that I'd merely thrown everything behind the door, I thought to deflect her. She was thinner than Bruce Willis's hair and I knew how to get her attention.

'You're kidding, you on a diet?'

'Fuck off.'

'Very nice. Do you still kiss your grandmother with that mouth?' I was already shrivelling up for using such an expression outside a De Niro movie before she came back and added her death stare.

'You kidding or what?' she asked incredulously.

'Sorry.' I hid behind my embarrassment as her eyes flashed. 'It was the best I could do on short notice.' I knew I'd probably overstepped the mark, but at least she'd given up on the back room. 'But I don't have saccharine, so do you want sugar?'

Indecision etched her face and I knew that she still had her demons.

'Of course.'

She regained control and I guided her to the living room, handing her a steaming mug as she relaxed back into the folds of the couch.

'So' – her smile was back in place – 'the back room. Out of bounds?'

'I'm decorating it, it's still got paint everywhere, I'll show you it next time.'

This was our way of re-establishing ourselves as friends: she would show her concern for me through disapproval, and I would pretend not to care that I was a slob.

We sat together with our coffee, chain smoking, and talking small. We were comfortable doing this, strangely so considering that we had been intimate, even dirty with each other for such a long time. I knew what made her flush and she knew how to reduce me to jam. But we'd lost that relationship. It was apparently doomed from the start. Ting expressed it best of all.

◻ ★ ◻

'You should have married Kirsty.'

He had it all worked out, and went to great pains to make sure I appreciated his effort. 'But you drove her away.'

Standing up so that I would know to prepare for oratory genius, he had jumped straight into one as we sat in St Pete's one night.

'Pennance, you have low self-worth, a common enough phenomenon. You, however, are a natural master. Your behaviour could be mapped and used as a model in self-actualisation classes for Neil from *The Young Ones*. A hubris deficiency, if you will. Your relationships can't work. Your needs and those of a partner are diametrically opposed. A relationship needs to be a meeting of equals, each giving the other a part that they receive back in equal measure. Thus remaining a whole person. Your difficulty is, as I've said, self-worth.'

He went on.

'You choose a girl who does it for you. You dine, date, flirt and charm, all the time building her in your mind into the One. When you catch her, case in point Kirsty, she becomes a goddess, Eris returned to dazzle you with her goldenness, and you assume the role of chief disciple at the altar of her pubis. You taking from her in full measure but fearing you give nothing back. How can you have a goddess?'

And on.

'The doubt starts. How can she love you with all your faults, real and imaginary? She's a goddess after all, she can see your soul and the colour of your aura; she knows what you are. So when she holds you and declares her love, you back away, wondering how she can accept your flawed love. Maybe she's flawed after all.'

And on.

'Oh, my goddess, that's it, she's a fallen Eris. Enter resentment.

A step of minuscule proportions for one of your depreciating ability and one that she won't comprehend. Goddess or not. Now you're convinced she's a false idol, one of the ones Father McGonagall warned us about. So now she's flawed, no longer worthy of your devotion. How can you love someone who loves you and accepts your faults when you can't accept them yourself? You create this reality with no difficulty and yet remain unaware of ever having done so, an unconscious competency developed to protect your fragile self-worth. By loving you, she is lessened and no longer worthy of your devotion.'

I remember slowly clapping and telling him to fuck off.

Ting would analyse a dust mote in times of boredom, but he did display an unhealthy interest in pointing out my deficiencies whenever I was in a relationship, or going into one, or coming out of one or looking for one or eating a cheese pasty. I kind of understand what he meant although I do think he could have summed it up more succinctly.

GET OVER YOURSELF.

Not that it would have made any difference even if he could curb his verbosity. I was, and am, too far gone to reprogramme myself, there's just too much power in negative thinking for that.

And so as our relationship developed, it spiralled to accommodate my conditioning. After that it was just a matter of time. We went from the giddy heights of holidays together and setting up home to the uncomfortable certainty of TV meals and a quick cuddle before the lights go off, hiding two distinct bundles in bed where there used to be only one.

According to Ting, I was trapped, choking on the spastic orgasm of visceral conjugation. I had to ask him what that meant. The fantasy of being in a relationship so much more fun than the reality. Lazy Sundays in bed with the papers, brisk walks in snow-dusted parks and smouldering looks over the fruit counter at Sainsbury's become battles of wills about washing up, paying for petrol and never getting to pick the film you want at the video shop. At the peak, or bottom, of my relationship curve, I was adept at recognising the signs. I had to be to survive, because as everyone over the age of seventeen with a dick knows, girls and their mentors, women, have a mastery of playing at not playing games, and then only when it suits them. She may have said she loved me, but as John Cleese asked, what have the Romans ever done for us? At least that's how I perceived it at the time, and even Ting agreed that perception is reality even when based on a shaky pedestal set on a bed of wet sand on the back of a truck with a puncture on a cobbled street. Once I had convinced myself of her intentions, I recalibrated my sights.

From the day we first moved in together I started preparing for the war. Storing annoyances and idiosyncrasies like provisions, polishing the armoury of my take-downs, cutting remarks and mood swings in easily accessible army-surplus webbing belts that I could don at a moment's notice. I'd embark on training exercises in the video store, Ikea, at her parents' and when she was pre-menstrual. The war became my reality and I was trapped in the truth of it. I believed it would happen and prepared extensively for it.

All the time I was on exercise, Kirsty was involved in her own guerrilla war in the suburbs and country lanes of my head. Her tactics baffled me to begin with and in time I realised that she was fighting a dirty war with no respect for the rules of engagement unwritten every Friday night in St Pete's. She was being nice. She countered my sarcasm with benevolent understanding, my unreasonableness with humour, my moods and intractability with senseless nakedness and random blow jobs. I intensified my attacks and with deliberate disregard for the safety of my troops I finally won a pitched battle at Garlic Bread Hill, the cliché where I finally overcame her with superior firepower and willingness to sacrifice everything on a point of principle. Drunk of course.

'If you loved me you wouldn't eat that garlic bread.'

'Eating garlic bread doesn't mean I don't love you. You like garlic too, so does that mean you don't love me?'

'Don't turn it round, you know garlic gives me heartburn so you shouldn't eat it.'

'No. That means that you shouldn't eat it.'

'Or you.'

'Are you saying it's garlic or you?'

'No, that's what you're saying.'

'Eh?'

'Whatever.'

'Pennance, what the fuck are you talking about?'

'Look, just stop manipulating everything I say.'

'I'm not manipulating you.'

'You're manipulating me by saying you're not manipulating me, can't you see that?'

'There's nothing to see.'

'Yes, there is. You'd rather eat garlic than love me and you're trying to make it my fault.'

'Fine, I won't eat the stupid bread, just forget it.'

'How can I forget it? It's impossible to deliberately try and forget something. It's like telling me to be spontaneous.'

'I'm not telling you to be spontaneous.'

'Well, you can't.'

'I'm not.'

'Fine.'

'Fine.'

Those were the last civil words we spoke to each other for nine months. Kirsty ate the garlic bread, paid for the meal, and drove home. She packed up the iron, the contents of the bathroom (leaving only the inflatable breasts bath pillow) and went to live in an episode of *This Life*.

When I next saw her she caught me unawares as I left the gym. I was a beetroot with flat hair and a beer belly pushed into my shorts. She was a vision of unattainable beauty in clothes that were obviously new and with an air of knowing superiority that comes from turning every head, male or female, within a two-hundred-metre radius. Fuck, she was back to being the goddess, once more worthy of my unworthy love. We traded civilities for a few seconds before I made the excuse of rushing to catch an imaginary train to Manchester for an imaginary soirée, went home and got drunk on Stella.

Over a period of months we started to see more of each other, albeit on a strange ex-lovers level. We'd be at the same parties, the gym, the café and we'd get on fine. Kirsty was great company again. No pressure now, I could enjoy her company without trying to live up to the expectations generated by my hang-ups. Then she got a boyfriend. She'd complained about not having sex which made my loins ache, and then came to St Pete's one Friday with after-sex glow written all over her face. That left me with two choices.

Immaturity.

Maturity.

I was a grown-up able to hold sensible conversations, vote and take responsibility for small children when I had to. I took the only sensible option and ignored her. I'd had sex since we'd split up, occasionally with someone else there, but I wasn't ready for Kirsty to have it with someone other than me. After all, it had only been a lifetime ago and we'd developed this special bond where we were great sexless friends. Visions of her sweating a new disciple confused me, and that led to long conversations, hand holding and sleepovers. All very platonic apart from the occasional faux pas, and then it began to spiral again.

It was time for me to find a new goddess, and, pleasure be damned, I stopped calling. Undeterred, she had continued to visit whenever she was in town and after a while we managed to control our carnal instincts again.

The phase that we'd gone through in our lives together meant we could sit as we did now, and where before there was electricity, there was energy of a different kind, a more delicate weave that soothed instead of pulsed, but that was just as powerful. We were no longer sexual together and so we got our dosage from being friends. And, better still, we were flirting friends. Flirting for flirting's sake as it should be, with no confusion when the means is the end.

▭ * ▭

Old care reaffirmed, Kirsty turned to face me.

'I'm so sorry about Ting.' There were tears welling in her eyes and her voice shook as she spoke. 'I came as soon as I got the message, I just can't believe it.'

'I know,' was all I could think to say as I reached for her and we fell into a hug.

Eventually I had to pull out as I had been tensing my stomach the whole time since we sat down and was, not surprisingly, in extreme pain. It was with Kirsty that I had first learnt to hold myself tensed and flexed for hours at a time so as not to appear unsightly, even in bed. One of my great fears of the time was that I would crush her in my relaxed state whilst attempting to rock her to orgasm. As though sensing my discomfort, Kato walked in and hissed, her hackles raised in warning.

'You've still got that evil cat.'

Kato hadn't taken well to Kirsty and she never saw fit to tell me why.

'She's not that bad,' I said, knowing that she could hear me.

'She never liked me.' Kirsty stood in front of the fire, putting the table between them. Carefully, we moved to the kitchen and with the relief of standing straight I let the fall of my T-shirt do the work for me. We spoke about Ting and of the fun we had all had together, reminiscing because we had no future to talk about, not together. She smiled when I explained about the wake. I could sense that she was building up to something as she rebuffed any attempt I made to find out about her own life. I plugged the iron in and went to the wardrobe to find a shirt. Zappa's 'Catholic Girls' followed us into the bedroom, distorted guitar warbling over our voices. She flopped on the bed and I held up a selection of shirts, shouting for her to choose one.

'Which one says sex god?'

She was either shaking her head at them all, or at me, or at Frank.

'What about this one then?'

'No.' She took a length of hair and started chewing it, a

sure sign that she was uncomfortable beyond my choice of dress.

I held up another.

'No.' She wrinkled her nose at one of Frank's less melodic chord changes in a way that I once had no defence against. 'Ben has asked me to marry him.'

'What did you say?'

'I said Ben has asked me to marry him.'

'No, I mean about the shirt?'

'No.'

'What did you say?'

'Yes.'

'You like it?'

'No.'

'What about Ben?'

'No, he wouldn't like it.'

'Really?'

'Yes.'

'What about Ben and getting married, what did you say?'

She knelt up, as though in devotion before the Blessed Virgin.

'I said yes.'

I watched her lips form the words. Before the sound reached my ear I had covered the full spectrum of reaction, looking to find the one that would be me while I played out the shirt pantomime. I heard 'Welcome to the Cruel World' through to 'Starting Over from Scratch' before the lump in my throat unplugged the speakers and time became linear again.

My smile grew as I moved next to her and held my arms out.

'Congratulations.'

She sighed into my arms and we held each other tightly while my brain caught up with my emotions and nodded in agreement at my reaction. I knew she'd been distracted since she'd arrived – initially I'd thought it was because of Ting but now I realised it was because of me. I think she was genuinely relieved at my response, my opinion and blessing being important to her, and I felt good that I was sincere. I really wanted her to be happy. It had taken me a long time to realise that I didn't have what she needed, or maybe I just didn't want to have to try that hard; if she had found somebody who was able to, or didn't need to work at it, then I wanted to buy that man a drink and say well done, and thanks.

Even though I'd never met him I knew who he was. He was a career man, square-jawed and secure. All the things she'd wanted me to be until she realised that was someone else.

Kato shot from under the bed and ran out the door as though her tail was on fire and I felt Kirsty's fragile body heave with those sobbing belts of laughing syllables, a bout of hiccups while you're sniffing, that men can't carry off with anywhere near the same effect.

'Thank . . . you . . . hic . . . I . . . don't . . . hic . . . know . . . why . . . hic . . . I'm . . . car . . . hic . . . eyeing . . . hic . . .'

Our bodies heaved together as my giggling matched her sobbing. Now I just wanted to wrap her in cotton wool and cute her all day.

'. . . Hastop . . . hic . . . hal . . . hic . . . haffing . . . hat . . . hic . . . me.'

She stopped hugging once we had assured each other of our mutual respect and I had promised to dance at her daughter's wedding. Not that she was pregnant, it was more a declaration of long-term friendship than anything else.

'So what's he like then?' I asked as she blew her nose and took a deep breath.

'He's just what I need.' She let out a strange mix of hiccup and giggle as she determined to stop crying. 'Travels light.'

'What?'

'No emotional baggage.' She made big eyes at me as she smiled and too late reached to stifle the sneeze that sent jets down both nostrils.

'Serves you right.' I pretended to push her away in disgust as she frantically grabbed for a tissue. 'And it's not just me you know. Everyone has history, yourself included.'

'I know.' She shrugged once she'd dried her face. 'But you know me, if I wanted to handle baggage I'd work in an airport.'

'Fine. But that's enough about you, how's about we get back to me and the sexy shirt search,' I said, getting up and moving back to the wardrobe. 'Sexy shirt search,' I repeated, trying not to sound like Sean Connery.

'What?' she asked, then screwed up her face as she stepped off the bed and onto a wad of scrunched-up tissue. 'Eeugh.'

'What?'

'Have you had a cold?' she asked, while she scuffed her foot clear.

I think I may have blushed as I said yes, but I cunningly faced away from her and reached for a shirt as far in as I could.

'So are you loved up yet?'

'Why do you think I need the sexy shirt?'

'You are going to need some help then.'

'What about this one?' I climbed out of the wardrobe and over the mound of Oxfam waiting to happen. 'Does it say va va voom?'

'Run out the room, maybe.' She pursed her lips and pushed me aside. 'Let me see.' She knelt in front of me and I had to concentrate on images of puppies in plasters.

'Clubbing tonight?' she asked, oblivious.

'Definitely.'

'Any ladies in your need-to-impress box?'

'That would be Ali, and before you ask I've only spoken to her once but she's a friend of Sally's and I'm thinking big things if I see her again.'

'Okay then,' she said, all business. 'I think we may have just what sir requires.'

She passed me a charcoal button-down that I hadn't seen in years.

'Didn't you buy me that?'

'I did.' She smiled. 'And it's still the best shot you've got.'

She declined my offer of the iron and led me to the kitchen.

'I'm fairly sure you know how it works,' she told me as she left to pull her boots on.

By the time I had placed the shirt on the ironing board, she had used whatever it is you can fit in a purse the size of a mobile phone to remove any trace of tear damage and walked into the kitchen, triggering involuntary gulping on my part. She saw the effect she was having on me and lowered her eyes.

'See what you gave up?'

You can only be unhappy about losing something if you want it in the first place, I thought, remembering why we were here like this. Her smile faded when I didn't reply and I put it down to hormones. Hers or mine.

'Ready to face the world.' I smiled as though I'd missed her jibe.

She shrugged a breath of cleansing dimension and settled her tiara in place.

'No problem.'

She took my hand as we walked to the door. 'Will you say hello to Stan and Pine for me? Tell them I'll catch up when you get back.'

'Of course I will.' I squeezed her hand and smiled expansively. 'We'll have a drink when we get back from Mull. Have a drink and celebrate and you can introduce us to the man who stole your heart, see if I approve.'

'I won't get married if you say not to,' I hope she joked through a straight face. 'Just say the word and we'll run away together.'

'It's a bit late to elope.' I played dumb as I opened the door. 'He's already asked you to marry him and he won't want to run off and jump a broom now.'

'I didn't mean him.' She stooded silently for a few seconds and tightened her grip on my hand. 'You're okay, aren't you? I mean about . . . everything?'

I thought about Ting going and now her getting married. I knew which one would take the most to deal with and wished it differently. I didn't love Kirsty any more. Sometimes I wasn't sure that I ever did. Well, probably I did, but I was genuinely pleased that she had gotten what she wanted. That part of everything was fine.

'I'm getting there.'

She reached up and gave me a kiss, her hair poking me in the eye and making me recoil.

'Easy,' she sang. 'It's just a kiss.'

'Sorry.'

I wasn't sure what was going on in her head but she reached up and cupped my face as I rubbed at my screwed-shut eye, her eyes reflecting my tears but for reasons I couldn't fathom.

'Like they say, one day at a time, eh?'

'More like the Doobie Brothers, "Minute by Minute".'

At that I pulled her into a hug.

'Bastard.'

She unhooked my arms, her eyes hardening as she stepped away.

'What?' I held up my hands and shrugged pathetically.

'You've undone my bra again.'

'Oops.'

I couldn't help myself, I'd always found it hard not to automatically search and snap when I'm in a hug. The first had been Carolyn Murray when I was twelve, the last was Pine's mother when I was drunk at the Elvis party.

Finding my frivolity out of place or mistimed, she shook her head and punched me. 'What time are you out?' she asked, stepping through the door and adjusting herself with a wiggle.

'About ten minutes.'

She reached up and, tilting her head, her hair safely out of harm's way, she kissed me with what could only be described as a mischievous look in her eye. 'Probably got time for another cold then.'

And then she giggled her way down the stairs, leaving me with a smirk.

'Bye, Pennance.'

◻ ＊ ◻

I could hear the Fun Lovin' Criminals, so I found the CD and got dressed after a treasure hunt for underwear and socks. I only owned seven socks in the whole world and no two came from the same pair. But that was okay because I knew socks needed to be matched by thickness and not colour. Today was going to be a black ankle sock and blue football sock day. I could trace this blasé attitude towards the appropriateness of foot underwear to my early youth rebellion. My mother would only ever hang washing to dry in size order and with each pair of socks matched, hung, and dried together. In my role as fifth columnist I sabotaged her washing line with unsolicited aid and hung washing out with no regard for her conventions. This and a learned inability to hoover properly or put plates away correctly gave rise to a studiously observed idleness. My mother's reply was to mismatch my socks for the remainder of my tenure. I attempted to continue in that vein when I lived with Kirsty, but she was too reactionary to play along even if she did understand about thickness over colour. Content with my efforts, I fed the cat again and walked out ready to face the day.

In contrast to my mood, the air was light and the wind brushed soft as down. In the height of summer the street was celebrating life. The flowers straining to reach the sun, offering their perfume in reply to the day, were well tended. I saw Mrs Baker, my neighbour from downstairs, soothing her roses. All spring long she had coaxed the earth with her mysterious ministrations. Pottering, potting and pruning, she was the perennial gardener and her roses were her reward. No matter if I met her queuing in the post office or at the bookie's, she always smelt of mulch.

'Hello, Mrs B.' I smiled, reaching over her wall and picking up a crushed cigarette packet. 'Growing B & H now, are you? It'll be marijuana next,' I said as she peered over her half-moons, squinted, and pushed them up to focus on me. Recognition lighting her eyes, she knelt back on her knees and smiled as she pulled off her gloves.

'Hello, Pennance. Was that you trying to get into my flat this morning? I heard Helen shout at you.' I gave her my sheepish but cute smile and she tutted in mock disapproval. 'What do you think to my roses then, can you smell the beauty?' She cupped a yellow rose and drank deeply, oblivious of the bee that she had disturbed. 'That you off out again then?' she asked, coming to sit on the wall.

Pushing the fag packet into her rubbish bag, I made a show of breathing deeply. 'They smell great,' I assured her and took a seat next to her. 'I'm off to the dancing tonight, I'm going to get my pals now. How's the hip?' When I'd first moved in, the removal van had blocked the ambulance that eventually rushed her to hospital. She tapped at her side.

'Good as new,' she laughed. 'I wish they'd replace the rest of me and I'd come dancing with you.'

For a moment there was a flame in her eye as I watched her remember her faded youth. She'd told me before how she had loved to dance and that she and Mr Baker had once represented Yorkshire in the regional finals of *Come Dancing*.

'I bet I could still cut a rug better than those youngsters that I see on the telly,' she said seriously.

'I bet you could, Mrs B,' I started to say but she cut me off and told me not to get sarky with her, emphasising her point with a trowel that she lifted from her apron.

'I remember saying the same thing to my gran and that was fifty years ago. You're not the only one who's ever been young, you know.'

'Away with you, Mrs B, you're still young,' I told her.

'Pennance, my false teeth are older than you,' she replied, standing up and flashing them at me. 'But that's okay, I'm happy enough.' She looked up to my open window. 'Now go and turn your music off or at least put something on the wireless that I like.' She dismissed me with her Queen Mother wave and I went back to the flat to change the music I had forgotten was playing outside my head. I set the timer, 'Scooby Snacks' became Puccini and I headed out again. As I passed her garden Mrs B was softly humming away to herself, worrying at a weed climbing her wall. Without looking up, she said, 'It takes too much moisture out of the soil, the roses don't like it near them.' I stopped and asked her what she was talking about.

'Marijuana, it leaves the other plants dry.' She still didn't look up and I left her there as I laughed out loud for the first time in days and walked down the street.

Chapter 5

the king and i

As the gate closed behind me, my mood nose-dived again. I looked up at the closed curtains and wondered if Ray was home. I rapped on the door and waited. Turning away, I gazed out over the street. A mother with a pram walked past and smiled as two kids dribbled a can across the road.

Suburbia.

Distracted by the arrival of an ice-cream van, I didn't hear Ray open the door behind me.

'Want a cone, Pennance?' he asked as he followed my gaze.

Startled, I mumbled my apologies and said, 'Sorry, Ray, I was miles away.' He held his hand out and I followed him into the house, closing out the rest of the world as the door shut behind me. Walking behind him as he led me through to the living room, I watched his back as he took off his jacket. 'All suited up, Ray, and it's a Saturday.'

He tugged at the hem of his waistcoat, pushed back his hair and forced a grin. 'Need to maintain the sensibilities, old boy,' he said with aplomb.

We sat opposite each other at the small table under the window. With the curtains closed the room was dimly lit by a standard lamp in the corner. Ray topped up his glass and poured me a malt. I sat in silence playing with my glass, unsure how to proceed, while Ray sifted through a pile of photographs on the table. Watching him squint in the half-light, I thought he would do better to open the curtains but somehow I knew that would be wrong. The sunshine didn't belong in here, it couldn't brighten this house, not today. Ray began passing me pictures of Ting and we spoke about him as if he were still with us. The photos became Top Trump cards as we tried to outdo each other. My Ting climbing a rock face beats your Ting on a moped, in a pram beats graduation, sat in a puddle beats playing the guitar. Then I found one from school. A team photo from when Stan and I used to play. Ting was kneeling at the front holding the only cup we ever won in four years of playing, the lid was on his head. Pushing the photo over to Ray, I noticed the writing on the back.

'District Cup Champions, courtesy of Charlie Sweetson's three-goal bonanza.' I recognised the handwriting.

He scored the winning goals that got us the cup and was christened Ting when he refused to give up the lid, wearing it in the shower to cover his 'ting' from all the poofters who wanted to hug and kiss him that day. It sits on the bookshelf in his flat, a reminder, along with the name, of his day of schoolyard glory. Game, set, and trump.

Drawing strength from the whisky, I watched as Ray quietly stacked the photos and slotted them back into the Nike box at his feet. Seeming to shake off the spell of forgotten times, he was watching me oddly when the photos were returned to their out-of-sight out-of-mind home.

'Are you all right, Pennance?'

Good question, I thought. Here we were sitting drinking over pictures of his dead son and Ray was concerned for me. I was a pillar of rock, a support that would help him through this. A selfish prick with guilt too complex to see beyond my own discomfort. It was a good question, but one that I should have been posing. 'How are you coping, Ray?' I should be asking. 'Oh, by the way, did I tell you that it's my fault that Ting's dead.' I felt nauseous. 'Here,' I should be saying, 'let me pour you a drink in apology, that'll make me feel better.' Instead I sat mutely and caught the tears as they fell, driven out by the burning in my veins.

'Easy, son,' he said, putting a reassuring hand on my shoulder, using the other to fill my somehow empty glass and then his own. 'It'll get easier.'

He didn't say it but I could see the 'I hope' in his eyes.

Sighing deeply to catch myself, I emptied the two fingers and felt the fire compete with the acid to settle my nerves. I made no move to stop the free flow of tears that exposed my guilt.

'It was my fault, Ray,' I whispered. 'Ting's dead because of me.'

I said it before I lost the nerve and, true to my belief, it didn't make me feel any better for saying it. The weight of my confession added impetus to the nausea I felt, and, far from thoughts of absolution and contrition, I shook with renewed fervour. After a moment that encompassed the birth and death of suns, I raised my face to Ray, thinking that maybe he hadn't heard. He sat frozen in the moment, the raised glass immobile inches from his thin lips. This is how the anthropologists would find us, excavated from the ash of our own Pompeii, confused and unprepared to guess at the import of why we were caught off guard. Submerged in the pain of my guilt, I needed confession, a throw-back to school assemblies and the force-feeding of dogma too embedded to ignore. But Ray wasn't a priest, he was a bereaved father in need of consolation. Not confession. Too late I saw my need for forgiveness for what it was, a selfish act of indulgence that rode roughshod over everything else in a gesture of exotic narcissism. Guilt on two counts.

Ray put his glass down, his eyes unreadable in the soft light. I crushed out a cigarette I didn't remember lighting and brushed at the pool of tears collecting on the table.

'It wasn't your fault, Pennance, it was . . .'

'It should have been me,' I interrupted. 'It should have been me that was there.' My voice croaked as I leant forward with my head in my hands.

'Where?' Ray indulged me. 'Where should you have been?'

I looked through my hands at him, his face confused. 'I said I'd take the suits back, but Ting, he offered to do it and I . . .' I shook my head. 'It should have been me, I said I'd do it and I didn't.'

'Pennance, it doesn't matter.' Ray was speaking slowly, quietly, the way you do to a recalcitrant child. 'Don't you see? He was there, it happened. You can't plan for these things, a

million-to-one chance that can't be predicted or avoided. It's
fucked, but it's not your fault.'

I placed my hands on the table to disguise their shaking and
looked up. 'It was, Ray. I should have taken the costumes back
the day before, I said I would and I didn't.' Pregnant tears were
hurtling from my chin to the back of my hand, exploding in
silent rebuke at my continued expurgation. 'If I'd done what I
said I would, none of this would have happened. Ting would
still be here.'

Ray glanced quickly at the fireplace and, following his gaze,
I saw Ting's brown travel bag. He's in there, I realised, over-
come once more and forcing my eyes closed to hide from the
reality. Like a child who believes he becomes invisible when he
closes his eyes, I regressed and looked for sanctuary in the
darkness. I gripped the edge of the table tightly, using the pain
to ground myself. 'I am so sorry, Ray.' My overworked glands
fought to swallow the bile rising in my throat. 'So sorry.'

I heard him move but didn't open my eyes until I felt his
hand on my shoulder in silent benediction. There were tears in
his eyes as he looked at Ting's bag and stood over me. Without
a word he walked off behind me and I let out a shuddering
sigh, the kind that collapses you and pinches at your belt. Ray
came back into the room, his leather shoes muffled by the deep
carpet. He handed me a handkerchief and gave me the moment
to compose myself.

'It's not your fault,' he reassured me quietly as he poured
another drink. 'It's nobody's fault. Not even the poor bastard
that did it.'

'But, Ray, if I'd taken them back when I said I would . . .'

'But you didn't, Pennance.' He stopped me, his voice firm
and without compromise. 'You're not responsible.'

'I am,' I said petulantly, unable to accept his understanding.

Ray was shaking his head at me in disagreement or in pity,
I wasn't sure which, being too caught up in my own wallowing
to know.

'Okay, Pennance,' he agreed, 'it's your fault.'

I looked at him then.

'You should have taken the suits back. No one would have died then.' He held up his hand. 'No, someone would have died but it wouldn't have been Ting.' He shrugged his shoulders and exaggerated his hypothesis. 'Thinking about it, maybe you shouldn't have had a fancy dress party, or maybe you should have gotten the costumes from a different shop.' His voice was becoming more animated as he continued. 'As a matter of fact, maybe you shouldn't have had a party in the first place.' He cocked his head as though thinking something for the first time. 'Whose idea was the party, Pennance?'

I looked at him dumbly, unwilling to follow him, but he beckoned with his hand. 'Whose?'

'Stan's,' I told him quietly, aware that he already knew.

'So it was Stan's fault then.' He held his hand up, stopping me from protesting. 'Stan's party killed Ting.' He pursed his lips and nodded sagely. 'Hmm, why did Stan have a party?' He prompted me and I felt compelled to play along.

'It was the anniversary of Elvis's death.'

'Ahh,' he exclaimed in surprise, 'so maybe it's Elvis's fault.' He stood up dramatically, his chair falling silently to the floor behind him as he leant forward on the table. 'Local headlines, Pennance.' He threw his hands in the air and stood like an evangelical preacher.

'ELVIS KILLED MY SON!'

I let it sink in. What he'd said. Ray was absolving me even if I couldn't forgive myself. Ting's death a link in an unconnected chain that I could not predict, much less influence.

'Forget it, son. If it's anyone's fault it's mine.' He righted his chair and pointed behind me. 'I introduced Ting to the magic that is the King.'

Looking over my shoulder, I saw the Elvis mirror above the cabinet, a discordant note in the otherwise classical decor in the room.

'Thanks, Ray.' I walked over and we hugged. 'I know it's stupid, but I can't help it.' Sitting back down, I tried to look better. 'It's eating me up.'

'Pennance, are you even listening to me? I'm his father and

I don't blame you. This is not about you, stop letting your imagination run riot. You've got to deal with this same as the rest of us and this is not helping you.' He looked down and picked up the box of photos and I almost missed the 'or me'.

With that statement I finally stopped projecting my guilt. It wasn't about me. Ray said it and I knew he was right. Stop crying over your son, Ray, and make me feel better. Me, me, me. Look at me and make me feel better. This was shite. I'm a shite. There was nothing else to do that wouldn't compound my stupidity, so I apologised again, this time for the right reasons, and raised my glass to his.

'So have you got everything sorted out?' he asked, as much to change the subject as to find out.

'Pretty much.' I nodded. 'I haven't got the train booked, but there's plenty of time yet.'

His eyebrows raised, he let that one pass. 'When are you going up?'

'Monday.'

'And until then?'

'Well, we're starting with a pub crawl tonight. All our old haunts, before a club. There'll be a kebab involved.'

'Of course.'

'Tomorrow night we're in the café then the early train to Mull on Monday.'

'Have you booked anywhere to stay yet?'

I shook my head and then he did the same.

'What am I going to do with you, Pennance?' He took a piece of paper out of his waistcoat pocket and handed it to me. 'Phone this number and give them my name, they'll sort you out.'

'Thanks, Ray.' I half smiled as I took the number. 'I was going to . . .'

'I know.' He held his hand up and grinned tightly. 'You were getting round to it.'

Embarrassed, I finished outlining the rest of Ting's wake.

I was aware of how difficult it must be for Ray. We'd asked him if he wanted to come to Mull, but he'd said no, he'd said his goodbye, made his peace. He knew what Ting wanted and was happy that we were honouring it. But I needed to check in one final time.

'Are you cool with this, Ray? I mean the whole idea of partying with Ting?' I heard the uncertainty in my voice. It had taken a couple of days for me to actually accept that we were going through with it, and I knew that it wasn't the most normal of send-offs.

'I'm fine, Pennance. I've been listening to you all talk about it for years. I suppose, like you, I thought it was just something to talk about.' He looked at me and pursed his lips. 'But Ting would make damn sure that he did it for any of you, so I guess you don't really have any choice but to go ahead with it.'

'We won't if you say not to, Ray, you know that.'

'I've no problem with it at all, Pennance. But you're going to have to turn yourself round if it's going to count for anything, otherwise you're just going through the motions.'

I thought about that and blew my cheeks out in agreement. 'I know. This has helped, even if it's the last thing that you need right now.'

Ray sniffed in response. 'It's no loss what a friend gets, son.'

'Even if it's getting dumped on by a stupid prick like me?'

'Even so.' He laughed. 'Especially so.'

━ * ━

I sat and listened to him then, as he spoke of his life before he left Scotland, his own eulogy. The same stories he'd told Ting through the years. About Mull.

'God's own country right enough,' he said. 'Where heaven meets the earth and you can't see the join.'

His eyes misted but I didn't have the words to clear them so I sat in useless silence as he remembered.

'You only ever have one home,' he told me with quivering authority. 'Everywhere else you're just visiting.'

'Is that why Ting wanted to go there?'

Ray nodded slowly.

'He wants to go home.'

He pushed away the now full ashtray in front of him and took a moment to collect himself.

'What time are you meeting Stan and Pine?'

I glanced at my watch. 'About five.'

'You'd better make a move then,' he told me, walking to the fireplace. 'I thought it would be better to use his bag, make it easier than the box he came in.' The corners of his mouth twitched. 'It seemed appropriate since you're going away for the weekend.'

A smile.

I nodded without looking away from the bag.

When Ray handed it to me, I was surprised by how light it was, but then again I didn't really know how heavy it should have been. My hand shook slightly when I took him, as though realising for the first time that 'oh my God, my friend's in a bag'.

I started crying again. I couldn't help it. I knew, no matter what Ray thought, that this was my doing.

'Take care of him for me,' he told me as we walked to the door.

'I will. We will. I mean, well, you know what I mean. We won't do anything daft.' He laughed as I grinned through the tears. 'Honest.'

'Yeah, right.'

We stopped at the door and I took his hand. 'Thanks, Ray, I'm sorry about before.'

'No more sorrys, eh?'

I nodded and turned to leave but he kept hold of my hand. 'I mean it, Pennance, let it go.'

'I will,' I told him without much conviction.

Ray smiled and stared at me. 'We all feel guilt about something,' he said seriously. 'I feel it every day. Today it's for being alive, about outliving my son, about . . .' He hesitated and I could do nothing but wait for him to go on. '. . . About pretty much anything I can be bothered to think about.' The smile drained from his face. 'It's the Catholic curse, Pennance: life is pain, the more the merrier and the greater the reward.'

'But you've done nothing to feel guilty about,' I protested. 'You've done nothing wrong.'

'And neither have you, but you feel it just the same.' He looked across the street, nodding hello to a neighbour. 'You've just got to get on with it and do the best you can. Right now you owe it to Ting to go out and enjoy yourself.' This time the smile turned into a lopsided grin that made him look ten years younger. 'Otherwise you'll give yourself something else to feel guilty about, so fuck off and show him a good time.'

'Thanks, Ray, I'll try.'

'I know you'll try, Pennance, but I'm telling you to actually do it. Go have a good time.' He passed me a tenner. 'And get those other eejits a beer on me.'

'Thanks.'

He reached behind the door for his jacket.

'What are you doing tonight?' I asked as he pulled the door closed behind him.

'I'm going down to my mum's now to see how she's doing.'

'Have you told her then?'

'Not yet.' He shook his head. 'She was here this morning making sandwiches for Ting so I decided against it just yet.'

'Making sandwiches?'

'She saw his bag when she came round and I told her that he was finally getting to go back to Mull. She decided to make him some pieces for the journey.'

'Bless her.' I smiled. 'Any plans for later?'

'I'm meeting Harry and Jojo at the club for a game of doms. They came round earlier and talked me into going out. I didn't want to at first.' He looked at me sheepishly as he buttoned his coat. 'I felt guilty about it but they convinced me that it's no good sitting at that table on my own all night. And trust me,' he said, placing his palm against my chest as he stopped walking, 'they were a lot less subtle about it than I've been with you. Think yourself lucky.'

And I did. Lucky to have talked to Ray. Lucky that he was such a sound bloke.

I watched him walk off towards his mother's.

His shoulders straight and his head high. I knew he was hurting and I took strength from his resolve. I smiled as I watched him disappear round the corner. The tears dried in my eyes as I tried to feel better about myself. No, not tried but actually did. Tightening my grip on the leather straps of the bag, I lifted it in front of my face and said, 'Right then, Ting my boy, let's see if we can't have ourselves that good time,' and set off down the street listening to Loudon Wainwright III telling me about his 'Bad Day on the Planet'.

Chapter 6
the good old daze

Molly gave us a lift from St Pete's and dropped us at the cash point on the Headrow. She was going to Sally's and said she might meet up with us later.

'Where to first, then?' Stan asked, rubbing his hands together. 'Fancy a quick one in Whitelock's to get started?'

'That'll do.' I nodded.

Our first round was on Ray and we toasted him with a whisky chaser to run the demons off. Stan suggested a game plan and looked to us for confirmation.

'That'll do for me,' I said to Pine.

'With cocktails,' Pine agreed and, after another pint, we headed to Mojo's.

Too early to be trendy, it was relatively empty and we stood working our way through the cocktail menu, sharing the bar with the only others there, a group of student types grunged up in designer wear. Stan was beginning to get a bit antsy over their practice of leaving big tips on the bar to ensure that their choice of minidisc was played, over and over again. The bar staff were getting demented too, but they were big tips. Understanding their dilemma, Stan insisted that we would have to leave soon before he died of 'bubble-gum pop' exposure. As it was, they were removed not long after for throwing their shot glasses at a poster of a flame-effect fire in the manner of Russian Cossacks. One of them was thrown out in the same style by the army of bouncers who appeared from nowhere.

'Thank you,' Stan told the Mongolian cavalry as they returned and he smiled for the first time all night. 'Fucking retards,' he said, raising his glass and looking out the window. 'Cheers.'

We watched as they picked themselves up and retreated down the street. Having heard them cry out as they left, I knew they were Welsh, but I didn't say anything to Stan because he would never accept that as an excuse. He hummed merrily as a barman invited him to work through the MD playlist, happy that it did contain more than Steps and S Club 7.

Tom Waits saw us off as we headed downtown and upmarket where the cattle go to be seen. We went up through the arcade. Past the café seats and the bread booths we walked without talking. Past Reiss we slowed until, without thinking about it, we stopped outside Ted Baker. This is where it happened. We stood and gazed about us at the ordinariness of it. This was why we were standing here with our friend in a bag. Looking round, I could see no evidence of what had happened. A life gone in a flash of steel, blood pooling on the tiles and running to the gutter, washing away dreams. For how long? An hour? 'Clear up that finished life, we've got a business to run.' I looked up at the roof. This was Ting's last sight as he felt the life drain from him.

The glass reflected red that wasn't on the floor and I shivered. Pine tapped my shoulder and whispered, 'Come on,' as if talking normally would have been out of place. Only for us though, as the rest of the Saturday revellers filled the air with their coarseness. A group of marauding girls on a hen party screeched by, breaking my reverie anyway, so, with a deep breath and my arm around Pine, we continued through the arcade to the bar. This was more like the Saturday night Ting needed. Music too loud to hear and a queue to the bar three deep. Sharking country.

▭ * ▭

We used to be what people would call big clubbers, heavy weekenders, party people. But as with all things in life it was a phase that came to a natural end. And one that carried few regrets. But I was determined to forget all the reasons we didn't do it any more. I think that was Ting's point in wanting us to do it, to remember it from when. Back like it was before, when they played music with words.

We used to go clubbing virtually every Saturday, unless we were loved up. Single Saturday was clubs. Couple Saturday was movies, meals, visiting other couples and generally doing things together. It was understood. Only by prior agreement and under mitigating circumstances were Saturdays freed up for the boys, or the girls. That's the way it works.

So we slipped into character. A double round at the bar and then we secured an observation post to survey the playing field. Possibles at three o'clock, negative, bogeys moving in. Contact. Start again. With Pine and Stan vigilant in their role as spotters, only I was active tonight and was honour-bound to give it large. Plenty of opportunity. Summer. Students. Saturday. Bingobango.

'I'm off for a wander,' I told them as I finished my drink and pushed myself afloat. 'I'll get the drinks in.'

I pushed through the crowd to the bar upstairs, smiling and pouting my way to the back of the queue and accidentally stumbling into a Honey in a feather bra and hot pants that I'd spotted from the table.

'Sorry.' I beamed at her. 'I'm not used to these high heels.'

I got a forced 'ha ha' and a toss of dark teenage hair, no eye contact and a rubber ear. That'll be a no then, I thought, and squeezed ever onward. We know we are too clumsy to be attractive to some of those we worship from afar and that's why most of the time it's easier to look than to risk the danger of rejection, but as Ting was often heard to say, a faint heart and all that shite.

The open doors and windows did nothing to thin the air at the bar, which was thick with tobacco and tasted of perfumed sweat. Leaning on the bar, I felt my arm nudged as someone was crushed forward by the throng. I looked at her cursorily in the practised manner of the auctioneer and decided that it was far too early for me to be thinking that she was attractive, so I concentrated on getting served, remembering Ting's oft-voiced belief that the difference between a fox and a hound was only a matter of hours and about ten pints. When she caught the barman's eye, I shouted over her and ordered three pints in a tone that left no doubt that I was to be served first. She tutted and drew me her best Paddington but I was still too sober to be affected by it. Chivalry is fine but shouldn't be overdone in a busy bar, unless a play is being made of course. So I ignored her and smiled at the girl who suddenly appeared on my other side. That didn't get me anywhere though, as she was intent on getting served and was too busy throwing her smile behind the bar to notice me.

I took the long way back to our table. A glance here, a stare there, all the time checking for eye contact. I was relying on peripheral vision for this, while surreptitiously focusing at chest height. I know it's rude but I have difficulty not looking at tits. Their impact is quite profound regardless of size or cover. It's not an easy thing to admit either, even when you're in the company of over half the population, and rational explanations of reproductive drives and triggers notwithstanding, I had acknowledged that it made me a bit sad. Sad but happy. Strolling through the groups of party makers, looking distant as though searching for someone, I smiled like a kid at Willy Wonka's. The abandon shown by the girls grinding and swaying round the bar left me feeling light-headed, and once again I imagined there was a God and that She probably spent all day laughing at our dicks and playing with her breasts. Even in a healthy sexual relationship, when I'm happy and keen to be with my partner, I gaze longingly at the girls passing me in the street. Sometimes the guilt of adultery is stronger when it's all cerebral, the need to cheat is less because you're already doing it with every girl you see. Or can imagine. Maybe if I'd been breast-fed it would have been different, but I doubt it. I don't know a straight guy who can see lightning and hear thunder who doesn't think the same. They might not say it out loud too often or get caught out by their partners, but it's there. Like farting every time your girlfriend leaves the room, it's natural obsessive-compulsive behaviour. We are programmed by our genes and influenced by our environment and my only excuse is in the genetic memory of the need to be physically attracted to a female to reproduce – and not just one at that. I know that in a partner I need more than mamillae to stimulate me, but that only counts once the initial feeling of 'hubbahubba' kicks in. And it's not just me. There is a double standard employed by our sisters in professing disdain at this admission, as it is irrefutable that they are just as guilty as we. Yes, they claim attraction to more emotive stimulation, but in the main they are dependent on these feel-good attributes being tightly packaged in Calvins and washboards. Walking back to the table, being no Diet Coke ad myself, I couldn't see one sense of humour or hear anyone click with me, so I continued my titillating search, knowing that, offensive as girls might say they find it, how else do you judge potential? And anyway why wear the bingo dresses and Wonderbras and tit tops if you don't want to be looked at? I think the relationship is more symbiotic than is admitted.

◻ * ◻

Ali was leaning against the railings talking to Stan. She hadn't seen me and I stood on the stairs watching her. She had dimples when she smiled at something Stan said, and I studied the movement of her body as she sipped her drink. The shirt she wore was fitted, and the hipster jeans were faded from wear. Looking at her, I saw the reason for cold showers, and, hoping that I hadn't made too much of a prat of myself last night, I donned my best Bruce Willis smile, à la *Moonlighting*, and walked over, quickly swallowing to force my heart back out of my mouth. Sally smiled and gave me a kiss. 'Hi, Pennance.'

'Hey, how you doing?' I didn't turn to Ali. 'When did you get here?'

'We just nipped in to use the toilets, we've been up at the Regent with Molly, she's meeting us again later.' She reached behind me and grabbed Ali. 'I'm here with Ali.'

'Hi.' She looked at me, bored, and brushed a non-existent hair from her face. No smile.

'Hi.' Look sheepish and wipe the grin off. 'I'm sorry about last night.' Look cheeky. 'I was a wee bit drunk, I hope I wasn't too much of an arsehole.'

Bruce. Result. A smile.

'Don't worry about it.' Another smile and then she went back to talking to Stan. I looked at Sally and she winked at me before turning away. Cool, I get a second chance.

Listening to them talk about the funeral, I tuned out and scoped the bar again while waiting for my opportunity to speak to Ali. Fire exit to the bar to the stairs to the toilet to the door to the . . . Ali? And look away quickly and take a drink. Was she looking at me? Risk another look, same drill, and . . . yes. There she is again, out of the corner of her eye. Just caught it . . . and . . . yes again. That's a smile. Contact. When Stan went to the bar I moved closer and signalled to Pine that the game was on. He brought me into the conversation and I looked as though I was listening to him. 'Uh-huh. Uh-huh. Yip, I agree.' Listened enough, now time to engage with Ali. She obliged by reaching for her cigarettes and offering me one.

'Have you got a light?'

Yes, and it's green to go. By the time Stan's back, I'm deep with Ali and haven't had to use a line once. What's more, she's giving me her full attention; with Pine and Sally on autopilot, she's turned to face me. Desperate to make up for last night, I try not to look at her tits and only do once when she reaches for her drink and it would have been rude not to. Risky but worth it. Always a dilemma in a bar, it's important how you manage the whole thing. When you're sharking and spot a Honey it's easy to check her out from a distance. When you make your move and start talking to her it's deemed rude to pay attention to those bits which helped attract you in the first place. The stuff headaches are made of.

With Stan back from the bar, she moved back to share herself with us both before turning to Sally and saying it was time to leave. 'Where are you going?' I said, too quickly to sound casual, and felt my neck flush as she turned to answer. Damn.

'We're meeting Molly and then going on to the Fruit Cupboard.' She slugged down her glass and picked up her bag while Stan smiled at my gaffe.

'We'll maybe see you later.' She waved over her shoulder as Sally took her arm and they minced off.

'Bastard.'

'She is lovely.' Stan winked at Pine and then looked at me. 'But way out of your league.' His face smiled but I didn't believe it.

'Cheers, mate.'

Bastard. I thought I was in there. This bar is a fucking jinx, I never get a break in this place. The first and last time I pulled here, George Michael could still use public toilets. Georgina Banks was her name. I left with her and Ting took her friend home. We spent four minutes kissing on the couch and that was it. When I flicked her bra loose she pushed me away and got all holier than thou on me. She was a Godsquadding happy clapper and, I very much suspect, a virgin to boot. Christ, she wore an anklet with WWJD braided in it. She wanted to court, she told me. She wanted dates and a relationship. I wanted sex. She came home with me from a bar for Christ's sake, what did she expect? So I went in a huff.

'What Would Jesus Do?' she asked righteously as she fastened her bra.

I was walking round the room in frustration, cursing the toss of the coin that had left me with her and Ting with her drunk friend. I shook my head at the question and picked up the phone. Get you a taxi and have a fucking wank, I thought I whispered.

She didn't wait for the taxi.

Now Ali blows without a by-your-leave and I'm back to square one. And Stan was being a prick.

'I'm only saying it how it is, Pennance.' He held his hands out, one above the other. 'Portvale and Man U.'

'Stan, shut the fuck up,' I told him as Pine laughed. 'Yes, she's gorgeous but you're not qualified to judge, so just shut the fuck up, okay.'

'Easy, tiger.'

'Leave him alone.' Pine came in on my side. 'He's having a bad day, can't you see the poor boy just bombed out?'

Well, thanks, Pine, I thought, working on my 'no, I didn't take a drink of your pint, perish the thought' look.

'No, I did not.'

They exchanged glances as I tripped over my petted lip and took a sulk. What was it about this place? 'You'll see when we get to the Fruit Cupboard.'

'Who said we're going to the Fruit Cupboard?'

'I did.' I challenged them to disagree, but they shrugged and asked for handbags at dawn. 'Come on and we'll go to the Cuban Heel, this place is shite.'

In the Heel, Pine decided it must have been a school disco night, so he said it was time for Bristol's. Stan skinned up while Pine and I held Ting's bag up so he could take a look. Stan wanted to listen to the end of a Glenn Miller track so we ordered nachos and slammers before forcing him to leave on the 'Chattanooga Choo Choo'. Crossing the road to the canal, I mistimed the traffic and my cool saunter was forced into a nerdy dance/run that I tried to cover by continuing long after the bike had passed. I fooled no one. Behind the car park a cycle path raced along beside the canal, lamps topped the railings and you could see the skin of diesel on the water fan out as ducks silently sailed past. This was the shortcut to the dark arches on the city limits where Bristol's was to be found. We smoked and giggled our way along behind the ducks, and Pine was adamant.

'It's a stag do.'

'It is,' I said cagily. It's not that I was against lap dancing but it was Ting's do and we were supposed to be doing what he wanted. Getting pissed and chasing girls, not paying for them. Also, I thought that if a future girlfriend ever held it against me, I could always say I was the one who questioned going. We reached a set of stairs that led down to the water's edge; the frayed end of a mooring rope dragged lazily against the current, its journey halted by a shopping trolley.

'Well, he said he wanted a stripper at his stag. Bristol's is where we'll find one.'

I pursed my lips like I wasn't sure. 'This is Ting we're talking about. I mean a stripper? Ting? Come on.' I shook my head in disappointment. 'I don't even remember him ever mentioning a stripper.' We stood three abreast at the top of the stairs, unzipping and waiting for Stan to give the word.

'Yeah, but you can barely remember which end of a toothbrush to use at the best of times and, anyway, this is different. Stan?'

Stan nodded his head. 'Definitely different.' His voice hardened. 'Right, lock and load.'

'Toothbrush?' I looked at Pine sideways and pinched the end of my dick. 'What the fuck are you talking about?'

'You and Ting, when you went climbing and he told you to take a spare toothbrush to clean the rock.'

'No, he never.'

'Stan?'

'He did.'

'Well, I don't remember.'

'That's kind of my point.'

'What is?'

'When you forgot to take it and Ting had to use his to scratch off the lichen, he told you and you forgot about that as well. That's why you ended up sand-blasting your teeth that night when you were being clever and used his toothbrush without telling him. He used the other end.'

'Five seconds,' Stan reminded us.

'Pine,' I said, exasperated, 'I've no idea what you're talking about. Why would I use Ting's toothbrush, and what the fuck has it got to do with a stripper?'

'Nothing.' He shrugged in confusion. 'All I'm saying is that you don't remember everything.'

'Fine, we'll go see the fucking stripper, stop making such a big fucking deal of it.' I shook my head and concentrated on the target, surreptitiously running my tongue over my teeth. I could still feel the grit in my gums.

'Would you feel better about it if we called them dancing girls?'

I ignored him like a good twelve-year-old. I told him I wasn't speaking to him if he was going to insist on being clever.

'Two, one, and go.' With the precision of those bombers during the Gulf thing, I let go a golden tracer. This was a competition not only of accuracy but of duration. In the absence of a tree to climb or swings, pissing competitions helped keep us young, and this version took me right back to my discovery of the foreskin balloon. Using it to good effect, I outstayed Stan but lost on points to Pine who had the greater accuracy.

'That's that then.' Pine clapped us on the shoulder and started singing 'Patricia the Stripper' as we chased the ducks. We waited by the bridge whilst I finished smoking. I was having a moment. Maybe it was the spliff, but I felt tranquil looking at my reflection in the canal. I held tightly to Ting's bag and felt good. Almost a full seven seconds later I tasted tepid malt on my tongue. Dropping Ting to the pavement, I held the railings in both hands to brace myself and started racking. Behind me, Stan had turned and, unaware of my condition, proceeded to slap me on the back by way of telling me to move. The tortilla chips flew, undamaged from their sojourn in my gut, with the grace of shurikin, and rained down on the confused ducks. What could only be cheese followed, along with the peanuts and chips I'd eaten earlier. I wiped my mouth and looked at the globular mass floating towards the bridge and nearly gagged again as the ducks began eating it. Picking up Ting, Stan took my arm and led me away.

'That boy never could do tequila,' he said from behind Ting's bag in case I breathed on him.

'Those nachos were off.'

'Of course they were.'

'Pine, will you tell him?'

'Don't worry about him.' Pine shot Stan a glance. 'If you're really good, I might pay a nice young dancing girl to sit on your knee. Who knows,' he said, moving upwind from me, 'she might even kiss you.'

'With the way his mouth reeks, I don't think we've enough money between us to get him a Glesga Kiss, never mind anything else.'

'Pine,' I whined, but Stan was already giggling away to himself anyway so Pine just shrugged. Swallowing again, I contemplated licking my arse to get the bad taste out of my mouth.

▭ * ▭

Bristol's was at the top of the stairs and along the alley behind the railway arches. It hadn't rained for weeks and it still smelt damp, as if the weather wanted to add ambience to the place. We squeezed between two bouncers who were just slightly smaller than Microsoft and paid to get in. I thought they were going to refuse when I asked for a ticket for Ting rather than check him in to the cloakroom, but revenue beats refusal. It cost a tenner each, and for that we got a small table away from the podium, a ten-minute limit, and a tumbler of whisky and water. We didn't ask for the water. It wasn't as seedy as I had imagined. Low lighting, a fair DJ, and dancers light years from the Friday afternoon strippers I remembered from my father's local. Funky chicks dancing naked are great for making you feel human again. Our tenner spent, we left before being asked for more, and I enjoyed the fresh air on the way to the Elbow Room. I felt naughty. A lap-dancing club, and me a good Catholic boy. Lapsed, but Catholic nonetheless.

The Elbow Room was busy and we had to wait at the bar for a table. Eventually we paid a couple of students for theirs and played doubles at a shot a ball. I had Ting as my partner and naturally we won, seeing as how Stan and Pine couldn't sink a rowboat with an axe. We only got a couple of games as the table was booked so we decided to pub crawl to the Townhouse to see us through to a club.

▭ * ▭

I'd lost track of where I was and hadn't seen Pine or Stan for ages. When we got to the bar I did a quick sweep of the room and went upstairs for a look. I hooked onto a promising student but got cut free when her friends asked if it was 'grab-a-granddad night'. After that I went for the wet puppy look at the bar before adopting the more common sad-drunk-drooling-in-his-drink approach. It took me a while to get downstairs and after searching and not finding them I resigned myself to loneliness and went to the toilet for a seat. All I wanted to do was sit down. Five minutes' peace and quiet and I would be fine. I took a seat on a bench outside the toilet, or rather outside the communal wash area between the toilets. In front of me was the water fountain where both sexes washed their hands in a non-bashful grown-up manner. The area was surrounded by glass bricks with kaleidoscopes behind them and the hand dryers had perspex covers. The unisex facility probably helped increase the incidence of boy hand washing in the place but did nothing for retaining dignity when you had to dry the front of your pants when you forgot to shake. I closed my eyes and thought ska to clear my head.

'Peter?'

It was a girl's voice and it was inches from my ear.

'Peter.'

Same voice only accompanied by a prod in the ribs this time. I turned my head as she sat down next to me and tried to work out who these two girls, twins no less, were and why I was getting prodded.

'Are you on leave?'

My eyes wouldn't concentrate and I was confused.

'Uh.'

'Are you back for good?'

'Uhh.'

They paused for a moment when I stared and one of them disappeared for an instant, causing me to jerk away in fright.

'Are you going to be sick?'

'Uh-huh.'

'Urrggh.' They stood up sharpish and peered down at me through identical glasses.

'Pennance, you look fucked.'

Their voice sounded deeper when they stood up and it took a moment for me to realise that it was Stan who was speaking to me as he walked down the stairs. Or at least it was one of the two Stans that I could see, I wasn't sure which one. Feeling decidedly odd, I closed one eye to rest it without appearing rude and had déjà vu as the Stans became one.

'Uhh, think I'm going to be . . . Urrggh.'

'Urrggh,' said the Stans.

'Urrggh,' said the prodders.

'Urrggh,' said everyone who had to jump away from the fountain when I threw up in it.

'Ohhhh . . . that feels better.' I sank to my knees and rested my head against the cold steel of the fountain. I could feel my cheek go numb and it felt great. Stan's twin turned out to be evil and manhandled me roughly back to the bench.

'Did you say Pennance?' prodding twin asked Stan, peering at me like a visitor from Saturn.

Stan answered without looking away from me. 'Yeah, Pennance.'

'Not Peter?'

Stan shook his head and she looked even harder at me and was rewarded with a dry heave and fetid breath. Her puzzlement became disgust as she righted herself and gurned. 'Sorry, I thought you were someone else.' She turned to Stan and said, 'I hope your friend feels better.' And walked up the stairs without a backward glance.

'You were nearly in there, son.' Stan nudged me as he watched her go. 'Wait here and I'll get you some water.'

Of course I'd wait, I could barely stand up.

Now I remembered why I didn't do this so much any more.

Head in hands, elbows on knees, I cursed Newton and his accursed gravity for rendering me helpless. I needed a new place to live that could do for me what this place did for Superman. I wanted X-ray, not double vision. Stan had said I was nearly in there. He was wrong though, because I'd already been there. Sue – I had recognised her almost immediately but my memory was as blurred as my vision and I was pissed off because I couldn't remember who I'd been when I was with her. Now I remembered and it was too late because she knew who I was. Otherwise the play could have been on. Again. Too late I remembered Captains Peter Barton and Durham Scott, those two rakes who had been on their first night's leave since returning from the jungle. Their regiment was being rotated and they had a weekend pass. After meeting Sue and Fiona at a club, they spent the remainder of the weekend acting like bounders and shamelessly seducing them. Dishonourable as it was to make such a play, Ting and I had adapted it from what we thought were a couple of air hostesses who fleeced us when we first started hitting the clubbing scene. I hadn't seen Sue since my regiment had returned to Bosnia the following Monday and she waved me off, all tearful Vera Lynn. I should have known we'd meet again.

'You fucking cunt.'

I opened my eyes and looked in front of me at a pair of polished black Docs that disappeared into a pair of khaki Gap combats. The thing that held my attention beyond the need to find out who the fucking cunt was, in case it was me, was the perfectly formed soggy tortilla chip sitting in a patch of cheese just below the trousered knee. Oh shit.

'Look what you've fucking done.' A meaty hand grabbed my shoulder and pushed me back against the wall. The sudden movement threw floaters before my eyes and I experienced the strange sensation of being underwater; all my actions were in slow motion. As my back hit the wall my head flicked up and I was face to bollocks with a pinch-faced terrier wearing my nacho. This couldn't be good, and here I was on double-gravity world, and underwater. Blows started raining down on my head as he began working himself into a berserker and I knew that I had to begin examining my options fairly swiftly. With a bump and a bruise, my glands began producing more than rancid sweat and my veins coursed with the survival instinct. The entirety of my fighting prowess was based on the repli-cation of Jackie Chan choreography and I feared that my drooling dance partner would be ignorant of celluloid fight etiquette. But what could I do? I slowly stood up.

Hoping that he could not see me shake like wattle, I squared up to him and pushed him away. He didn't move and I realised that he must have had Kryptonite stitched in his shirt.

'Come on then, you cunt,' he snarled a skelf of a second before Stan's punch hit him like a meteorite. His eyes were closed before he hit the floor.

'Fucking Welsh,' Stan spat as he stepped over the recumbent form and led me up the stairs. 'Are you all right?'

I sipped at my water as I nodded, the adrenaline rush making me feel better than I did ten minutes ago. 'I had it covered, but thanks anyway.' He had the grace not to answer. Behind us people started talking again, while at the head of the stairs there was a commotion as two swarthy bouncers shouldered their way through.

'There's a drunk guy down there,' Stan said helpfully as they approached. 'He's been sick and passed out.' They ignored him and imperially shoved me to one side as they bounded down the steps, leaving Stan smiling in their wake. He patted me on the back. 'Let's find Pine and get a drink.' He glanced back at the bouncers as they grabbed the fallen Cossack. 'Come on, we'd better move.'

I followed Stan, letting him carve out a trail through the crowd as he headed to the bar. Pine waved when he saw us and made space for us beside him. 'What you drinking, Pennance?' he asked, handing Stan a bottle of Dog.

'Vodka and Red Bull,' I told him, thinking that I needed the boost.

'Wouldn't you rather have a pint?' a voice asked from behind me. I knew it was Sue and for a moment I thought it was back on. With a quick wink to Stan, I turned, ready to charm, and caught my breath as she poured a full pint over my head. I became the epicentre of a silent tremor as conversations stopped and people moved away like ripples in a pond to avoid the splashing. I stood frozen, the grin still on my face, as Sue handed me the empty glass and walked off without another word.

There can be few moments in life when you feel more of a prick than this. The grin slipped off and was replaced with the head of the pint as it worked its way down my face. I licked at it and was unsurprised to discover that I still didn't like Guinness. Maybe Sue didn't know that. Scrunching my shirt, I wrung it out into a puddle on the floor and shook like a dog in from the rain. I wasn't making any new friends, judging by the response this got.

'What was that about?' Pine asked, watching Sue melt into the crowd and disappear.

Stan shook his head and I could see his eyes shine with suppressed mirth. 'A case of mistaken identity, I think.' He raised his eyebrows and covered his mouth. 'Peter?'

'Pennance?' Pine waited. I stared at the dark pool at my feet and felt foolish. Stan was openly sniggering as Pine looked between us, confused. 'Well?' he demanded, beginning to laugh.

'Evil twin.' I added to his confusion by joining Stan in sniggering and we stood like that until the storm troopers ran back up the stairs and escorted me out.

saturday night fervour

Late as it was, it was still mild outside and what wind there was helped dry me off as we walked to the kebab shop. Never a great fan of congealed offal, I nevertheless enjoyed a good doner when I was drunk. Toasted pitta and a pound of spitted roast, a slice of tomato and chilli pepper sauce lined the stomach like no other foodstuff at this time in the morning, except for maybe a curry. The only difference between them was that you could stand in a queue for a club with a kebab and you can eat curries when you're sober. Keen to be on good form when I saw Ali, I was picking the onions from my kebab when a group of girls pushed a shopping trolley with a sleeping L-plated moose bundled in it behind us as we weaved down the street. They were joined moments later by bucket-wielding boyfriends as they collected money in exchange for kisses from the moose. Never one to miss an opportunity I threw all my coppers into a bucket and gave the comatose bride-to-be a smacker. A buzzer sounded and I came up for breath as Pine took my place with a rather more chaste peck on the lips.

'Shit. What did I do with that kidney?'

The buzzer I heard turned out to be a mobile phone and one of the bucket carriers seemed to be having a panic. He searched through his pockets until he found a notebook and then walked off for some privacy to talk on the phone. Pine dug in his pocket for change to throw in the bucket but stopped mid toss as the new bucket carrier turned to him and said hello. He smiled in return, genuinely pleased if surprised to see her.

'Hello, Donna. I haven't seen you in ages. How you doing?'

At mention of this name I peered over Stan's shoulder to

check who Pine was talking to and nearly dropped my kebab
when I saw her. The last time I'd seen her had been at a wedding
in Edinburgh. We'd been going out for about two months and
were still in the throes of passion that's normal when you only
see each other every other weekend. We didn't have a great
deal in common other than a mutual friend – Pine – and a
loathing of jazz. Up until then we'd spent most of our time in
bed, on the couch, in the shower, in the car or back in bed. It
was fair to say that sex played a major part in our relationship
and that was just dandy with me. Prior to meeting Donna I'd
been a practising celibate, more through necessity than choice.

With no steady girlfriend I had embarked on a course of
nightclub slapper sex, and after a few outings the doctor had
advised three months' abstinence to allow my pubic hair to
grow back. Well, she actually said I could have sex again after
the six-week treatment but I started to enjoy taking myself in
hand again after a long period of neglect and to be honest I
was slightly uncomfortable about exposing my prepubescent-
looking genitalia to people I didn't know. By the time I met
Donna, I had been one hundred and twenty-seven days without
assisted orgasm. We met at a party in Pine's flat, she was drunk
and I was the only single guy in the room. She was three days
out of a long-term relationship, vulnerable, rebounding and
gorgeous. Ever the romantic, I immediately took advantage.

The day in Edinburgh was typical of our relationship outside
the bedroom in as much as we barely spoke to each other, the
exception being the twenty-three minutes we spent in the toilet,
which according to the ticket inspector was loud if muffled. The
thing was, Donna had a predilection for phone sex. Nothing as
prosaic as sex lines, but a more proactive approach where she
would call her friends, her mother, her ex, and engage in matter-
of-fact conversation whilst holding my head between her legs
or sitting astride me. Initially I found this to be highly disconcerting until I realised that it was an ideal method to maintain
wood and avoid the curse of the undersexed, early delivery.
Not for me the need to count Premiership hat-trick scorers or
to pierce my fingers with my thumbnail. After a couple of weeks

I even started enjoying it and it became a game where I would try to make her squeal or moan by biting a nipple or taking her to orgasm on the phone. It may not have been romantic or the basis for a long-term relationship, but it was by far the most erotic sex that I'd ever had. Not even Ting was having sex like this.

Our day in Edinburgh started well enough as we went straight to the church. An old school friend that she'd kept in touch with was getting married to her childhood sweetheart and it became obvious almost immediately that Donna wasn't handling it too well. She had planned to get married to David, her ex, but they had split up over trivia and now she was feeling sorry for herself as her friend walked up the aisle looking like a princess. When she started to cry I took her to the back of the church, through the glass doors and up the four steps to the porch, where all the prams and buggies had been parked. Now while I still harbour doubts as to who actually knocked the brake off, I suppose I need to take some responsibility for it. I'd sat on a wheelchair with Donna on my knee in an effort to console her, and I'd manoeuvred it so that she could still watch the service through the doors at the bottom of the stairs. With her head on my shoulder I had to fight against the tightening in my pants when I felt her breasts push against me as I rubbed her back in consolation. Try as I might to combat it, I have no defence against a pert nipple and as it brushed my chest I was forced to react by drawing her down and kissing her. I could taste the tears as I dug deeper into her mouth with my tongue and she gave an involuntary moan as she ground on my thighs. Always a sucker for a damsel in tight dress, I could only oblige by lifting my knee to let her rub on it while our kisses became more passionate than sorrowful. After a minute or so of trying to erase the material of my trousers, she satisfied herself that no one could see us, unzipped me and guided me under her skirt. Donna didn't wear underwear. It was at this point, naturally, that we began rolling forward towards the stairs.

With twenty-twenty hindsight I realise that I too should have leapt off the chair at that point and no damage would have been done. As Donna jumped she landed solidly on her bum while trying to hold her dress down. I frantically attempted to grab the wheels before I reached the first stair and almost made it. Almost – one of the sorriest words I know. The chair and I bounced down the stairs and crashed with a dull thud against the doors at the bottom. At that point the priest looked up from his hymnal. As he looked up the conjugal couple looked round to follow his gaze. The front row of guests turned to see why the service had faltered and in order to get a better view they stood up. What followed was the first recorded incidence of a Mexican wave in St Thomas's Roman Catholic Church as the whole congregation turned and stood by rows until they were all staring at me. I looked behind me and saw Donna scurry out the door and with as much dignity as I could muster I turned back to see ninety slack jaws and one hundred and eighty eyes focused on my now flaccid penis as it curled against the cloth of my trousers in shame.

Now here she was, almost six months later, and by the look of it another friend was getting married. 'I'm good,' she said, smiling, as her friend finished on the phone and took the bucket from her hand, replacing it with his own.

I leant past Pine and grinned at her in that inane way that can only be achieved when you know that it will cause the most discomfort. 'Hey, Donna,' I gushed. 'How you doing?'

Her eyes took on a wild aspect and she looked ready to flee into the night. Her friend winced as she tightened her grip on his hand. 'Hi, Pennance,' she said quickly, the smile running for cover. 'This is David.' She confirmed his boyfriend status by wrapping her arm round him as he shook the circulation back into his hand. When she said my name I could feel the hairs stand up on the back of my neck as some preternatural instinct kicked in like a Leeds fan at a scum match. David went rigid, his hands frozen like he'd just sung how he loved his dear old 'Mammy' and I knew I was his audience. I would have played sticky sticky statues with him but I was struggling to maintain equilibrium.

'I want to fucking talk to you, pal,' he snarled as my legs shook in protest at yet more glandular activity. His tone of voice and the inflection on 'pal' confirmed what my brain had already told my body: he didn't and I wasn't. Pine took over the small talk at that point as Donna did her level best to calm David down. That suited me fine as David her boyfriend turned out to be David her ex and I was not prepared to have any kind of conversation with him, given that the only time I'd ever heard his voice was when I was hanging from his girlfriend's nipple. His remonstrations apparently arose through a discrepancy over what seemed to be a grey area about whether Donna was single when I met her or still officially his girlfriend. Too much reality to deal with right now. I needed to move on. Turning to Stan, who was watching impassively, I walked away, careful to put him between Slabberboy and myself as I passed.

▭ ＊ ▭

As it happened, one of the bouncers at the Fruit Cupboard recognised Stan and we had to throw away most of the kebabs as we were let through the emergency exit. This suited me fine as queuing and kebabs are okay initially, but the longer they go on the less of a good idea they become. Inside the club was the seventh level of Dante's Inferno, only hotter and with less air. I put Donna and David from my mind as Stan and I took up positions at the bar while Pine went in search of Molly.

'They're on the dance floor,' he shouted when he came back. 'They've got a table over here,' he mouthed with a nod of his head and we followed him to the back of the dance floor.

Sitting with Ting on my knee, I was in charge of coats and bags as everyone danced. Ali had been playing it cool with me since I'd arrived, asking Stan to dance and only talking to me between records; she was making it clear where she stood. Or at least that's how I interpreted it. She was oblivious to my plays, and the groundwork that I had invested in earlier appeared to be forgotten as she gyrated with anyone who took her fancy and wasn't me. Molly took the piss out of me when

I refused to dance and then Sally and Ali disappeared and I thought they'd pulled and left. I had almost convinced myself that I was in with a chance with Ali until I remembered that she was a DDH, and I had missed the opportunity to make a play. She met me before I had the wherewithal to build a persona to hide behind, and by the time I could, it was too late. Now with the spectre of my conversation with Ray rattling my conscience, I regressed to the unworthiness that Catholicism had assured me I should feel. You can take the boy out of the church, but you can't unlearn its dogma.

Feeling sorry for myself, I clutched at Ting and bemoaned the lack of decent unattached girls in my life. Ting didn't say a word, which I took as confirmation that he agreed, and I spent the next ninety minutes sat mostly on my own.

Molly kept Pine dancing long after he would rather have been sitting, and Stan needed no such encouragement as he enjoyed it with the fervour that only comes from knowing you have real rhythm. Except for the occasional dodgy song or the need for a drink, they spent the remainder of the night on the dance floor.

Pine had bought some whizz from a guy in the toilets and they were all up for it. I declined, amid cries of poof and lightweight, but remained firm in my refusal. It wasn't from some moral high ground where I was above a bit of stimulant that I refrained, it was just that I couldn't handle the gnashing of teeth that came with it, not with bits of kebab still stuck between them. Also I was a bit wary about toilet dealers since the last time I bought a tab of acid from one, I had to sit at home all night whilst a pissed-off plum tree from my garden walked through the kitchen, packed a bag and left me for a Victorian terrace with walled garden. I still get flashbacks to the trail of mud I found on the doorstep and carpet the next day.

With little attention from my friends I sat alone, pulling in my stomach, and pondered at the inequality inherent in being a man, a subject that had kept Ting busy in his role as my therapist. I was, as he told me, the victim for the new millennium.

Tarred by the festering brush of a culture that I didn't buy into, I was condemned to Laddism and ridiculed for the stereotypical behaviour that it believed I wanted to exhibit. I honestly didn't want to moon lollipop ladies or drink pints and eat curry till I dropped; I read papers that weren't tabloids and could talk about more than football and sex sometimes.

I was a post-Laddism deconstructionalist and that was just not cool. Far from the confidence-oozing brash lad that the magazines demanded I be, I wanted nothing more than to be a happy boyfriend secure with the love of my life and to buy bonsai trees without fear of banishment from the pub. Ting agreed. The inequitable part was obvious in the lack of female interest in me as I sat all alone in a nightclub. If I'd been female I could be guaranteed that I would be sat by myself for all of a millisecond before I had company. I might not have wanted the company but at least I would have had options. Ting and I had experimented with this with Kirsty and Sally last year and the findings of our straw poll proved a landslide in opinion for our hypothesis.

The four of us went to a club and split up between the dance floors. The object of the experiment was firstly to see who could get the most telephone numbers from members of the opposite sex in half an hour and secondly to ask ten different people for sex. Ting got three telephone numbers, which was only two more than me and sixteen less than Sally. Kirsty won with twenty-two numbers in less time than it took me to get my coat off.

For the second part of the experiment we laid ground rules that we could only approach people we didn't know and that they had to be people that we would actually sleep with in real life. Of the ten I approached, one slurred yes but fell asleep as I spoke to her, one slapped me, three laughed and the other five told me no in a number of different ways, only one of which was polite. Ting fared no better, and both Sally and Kirsty got the go-ahead from all twenty, seven of whom were in the club with their partners but were on for it anyway. I knew girls were empowering themselves and that gave me a buzz, power and strength of character proving to be the best aphrodisiac.

The reason I thought of myself as a victim was less to do with them and more to do with what they were empowering against. The Lad Club. By default I joined the club simply through the mischance of birth, that and finding women attractive. Defined by *Loaded* and confirmed by lager, I was portrayed as an uncouth moron with no redeeming qualities and to be avoided at all costs by any member of the opposite sex with even a modicum of taste. When Donna ran out on me at the church, leaving me alone to face the organ music, she was only doing what she had been told by her own anti-Lad mags that I would do to her if my opportunity had been greater. Spurred by this knowledge, she made like lilac, secure in the belief that she had dealt a swift blow to a minion of Lad.

My problem was that, short of liking to sneak a peek at a Honey, which was about as sinister as chocolate, I didn't want to be branded a buffoon because of what they read. I'd rather meet on equal terms and at least have a go at standing upright before I was labelled. I didn't mind the labelling as long as it was all on my own merit and I don't need any help from misrepresenting media to act like a fool.

And so I sat alone in the knowledge that no one in their right mind would talk to me, clutching at Ting and watching Stan pick Pine up from the floor.

▭ ＊ ▭

'Wanna dance?'

'Sorry?'

'I said do you want to dance?'

'Sorry?' I leant forward on my seat to hear better and he backed off slightly as though startled, or scared.

'Oh, I'm sorry,' he said, clutching his hands to his chest just so. 'I thought you were . . .' Pause. 'Oh, never mind, I'm sorry, okay.'

'Relax,' I said easily, and then I got it. 'You think I'm gay?' My eyebrows went north to counter my chin's southward sprint.

'No offence, mate.'

'Oh, none taken,' I assured him. 'But you really thought I was gay?' I was watching Stan and Pine pogo to the Clash.

'Well, yeah, I do. Did. I mean did.'

'Well, I'm not.'

Then he dropped his hands to his side and pulled a comedy teapot look of puzzlement. I was hoping for a 'well, what a waste', or at least a 'the good ones never are', but he said: 'Are you sure?'

I heard the machine gun that was both my laughter and my voice saturate him with a definitive answer.

'Of course I'm fucking sure.'

'Oh, well, shame really.' He smiled and minced off.

'*Am I fucking sure!*' I was still laughing when Pine sat down with Stan while Molly went to the toilet.

'What are you laughing at?'

'A guy just asked me if I wanted to dance,' I told them.

'Which one was it?' Stan asked, standing to survey the room.

'The ugly one probably,' Pine answered for me, pulling him down. 'And you're coming for a curry, so forget about it.'

'All I want is a couple of hours alone with him in a dark room. Go get a curry with Molly.' Stan stood and demanded that I tell him what my gentleman caller looked like until Molly came back and told him he didn't have time because he'd promised her a curry for getting him new curtains and she wanted it tonight. Or rather this morning because it was way past normal closing and only Stan's 'café contacts' could secure her a chicken rogan josh at this hour.

And that, as she finished telling him, was, 'The only thing that can stop me from spontaneously combusting over your nice new shirt. So abandon this selfish quest.' She went all Shakespearean. 'And seek thee absolution amidst the bountiful trestles of ye olde Curry Shoppe with these, thy fine companions.' A hand brushing her brow, she continued, 'Oh, how

dost foul famish fatigue me.' And with a flourish she feigned
fainting into his arms.

Stan then felt so guilty for not paying attention that he forgot
about everything else to help Pine pick Molly up and staunch
the blood. I got a beer mat in the eye from Molly for laughing
but that was much better than Stan – he got the look.

'Are you coming, Pennance?' Stan was all meek now.

'No, I've had fuck-all luck with food tonight. You go and
I'll see you in the morning. I'll just finish this and get a taxi.
I'll be fine.' We did that whole kiss and hug thing even though
we knew that we'd be seeing each other in a matter of hours.
It seemed more necessary sat there with Ting on my lap. Stan
was the last to go.

'If that shirt-lifter comes back, you make sure you give the
fucker my address, okay.'

'Absofuckinlutely, mate.'

'Seeya.' He left with a wink.

With them gone I returned to feeling sorry for myself and
generally miserable. I looked around at all the Feargal Sharkey
haircuts and had the same thought as the last time I was in a
club. I tightened my grip on Ting's bag. So many freaks, not
enough circuses.

◻ * ◻

'Wanna dance?'

It was Donna, and before I could answer she landed on my
knee clutching at her drink as she grabbed me to stop from
falling. She giggled her way comfortable and turned to face me,
her dilated pupils inches from mine. A salacious grin revealed
her teeth. 'Sorry about earlier.'

'Earlier when?' I said blandly, remaining unruffled by the
quickening in my chest. 'Here or Edinburgh?' Part of me was
seriously annoyed with her but I was too deep in the cups to
be clever about it, and truth be told, I was sat in a nightclub,
alone on a Saturday night bemoaning my lot, and here was
Donna sitting on my lap. Rethinking my approach, I was about

to apologise for being such an uncouth clod when she started giggling.

'Well, I meant here, but . . . Edinburgh too.'

'Don't do me any favours,' I told her sulkily, again just a tad put out.

'Aw diddums,' she purred, caressing my face. 'Let me make it up to you.'

'Donna, I'm serious.' I pushed her hand away.

'Don't be such a baby. You didn't know anyone there and, anyway, you were sat in full view of the church and I was out of sight. What would you have done?'

'I wouldn't have left you.'

Her eyes said 'yeah, right!' but she just tutted and took a sip of her drink.

'Donna, at the very least you could have waited outside the church.' Although I was trying really hard, my drink-addled resolve was failing me and I was finding myself wanting to forget talking about Edinburgh and concentrate on the girl sat on my knee, even if only for tonight.

'I panicked, okay.' She shrugged in resignation. 'I didn't think it would be such a big deal.'

Was she kidding or what? Not a big deal! As big deals go, this one topped the Manhattan Island for shiny beads affair. She was slumped on the couch next to me, having slid off my knee, and was explaining her way out of it. The unfortunate thing was I was sober enough to recognise a play on her part, but too drunk to defend against it.

'. . . And then I got back with David so I didn't think it would be right to phone you.' She shuffled upright and jabbed at me with a finger. 'You could have phoned me.' This I understood. She abandoned me, ignored me and now was making it out to be my fault. An honours graduate from the Transferable Guilt School, or a good convent girl, Donna was not taking no for an answer. She leant in closer and I could taste the rum on her breath. Using the last of my reserves, I pushed her away again.

'C'mon to grips, Donna. You left me with my dick out in a

church for God's sake.' I wanted to sound hurt but came in somewhere between whiny and petulant. She grinned maliciously and beckoned me with her finger conspiratorially. As I leant towards her, she put her arm round my neck and pulled me to her. She held me so that her lips brushed my ear and her chest pushed against my hastily flexed bicep.

'We could always finish what we started,' she breathed.

I'd been through any number of different scenarios about how I would react when I met up with Donna again after Edinburgh, but this hadn't figured in any. Looking at her glazed eyes, I knew she was serious.

'Where's Demonic Dave?' I asked. She relaxed, knowing that with those words she had me.

'On his way to Manchester General Infirmary to deliver a kidney. He won't be back until tomorrow now.' Playing the coquette, she raised her eyebrows and placed a finger to her lips. 'Well?'

What else could I do?

I heard Sally cough and giggle as she sat down next to us. I ignored the thumbs up she gave me behind Donna's back and felt thankful that Ali wasn't around to see what a catch she had missed in ignoring my advances. Donna whispered that she was going for her bag and I was to meet her at the door in thirty seconds. Swaying slightly as I stood, I smiled rakishly at Sally and left her with a nonchalant wave that said, 'I'm off for sex.' I caught her returning my smile as I made my way to the exit. At this point if I'd had a hat I would have cocked it to a suitably jaunty angle and skipped out the door. I didn't have a hat and, rather than skip to the door, I tripped as I reached it and fell into the arms of Ali as she walked through it.

'I can't stand up for falling down,' she sang at me, before letting me fall flat onto the sticky floor. Looking down at me, she shook her head, her mouth open in a cute question. 'Is it a love of Morecambe and Wise that drives your exits or don't the callipers work properly?'

All I managed was a confused and slurred apology before

Donna scooped me up and levered me into a taxi and hopefully to a galaxy far, far away. Unaware of my inner turmoil, both Donna and my libido fumbled around in the back of the taxi, much to the delight of the driver who was straining to see what we were doing. Pathetic as it made me, I was aware that the tingling in my pants was as much to do with the brush against Ali as Donna's hand cupping me. After a short journey we got to the flat she shared with her sister Claire. Our clothes were ripped off and led a trail to her bedroom where we collapsed on the bed, tangled in the mystery that was her bra.

'We need protection.' Since my days with the surgical umbrella and razor, even pissed I am now the captain of careful, the arch-nemesis of non-prophylactic sex. That I didn't have any condoms wasn't an arrogance on my part nor in this case a deferral of responsibility, but a sad indictment of my own self-confidence. I hadn't thought it would be necessary.

'In my bag.' She pointed as she jiggled off the bed and into the bathroom to do those things girls always seem to want to do behind a closed door before sex. I took the opportunity to sniff at my own armpits, and satisfied that the deodorant was still working I had a quick fluff and air of my pubes before reaching for her bag. Filofax, chewing gum, phone, two pen lids, a lighter, the mandatory lippy, a beer mat with a scrawled phone number for someone called Jed, a water pistol and . . . condoms. Game on. Happy, I lay back, waiting until she returned before sucking my gut in.

'Now where were we?' She pouted and sashayed clumsily to the bed in her drunken interpretation of eroticism. The next two hours passed in a blur of uninhibited hedonism that I realised was more a release of my own frustration over Ting's death than any real desire for Donna's company. And it was payback. She rode me like a seesaw as we fucked, sucked, blew, chewed, licked, laughed and screamed until, exhausted, she fell asleep in my arms, snoring like a walrus with chapped lips. After a while I gathered my clothes and let myself out into the new day.

Endings are strange things. Since Edinburgh I'd thought all

kinds of things about Donna without ever thinking that I would get the opportunity to realise them. Now I had achieved closure. I would not need to see her again. Humming to Cast's 'Walk-away' as I left, I did have a momentary twinge of angst about David, but he had, after all, revealed himself to be a bit of a cunt earlier. So that was that. And, anyway, just because he answered the phone whilst Donna was in the bathroom didn't mean that he would have listened the whole time, did it?

Chapter 8
make like frankie

I could hear the cat gurgling at the magpies through the bedroom window. The flat was cold and I remained under the quilt as the sun climbed through the gap in the curtains. I shook my head slowly and then more vigorously as I tested out the intensity of my hangover. I felt okay, I had a hangover but thankfully it was more Gabrielle than Xena. The chill in the flat, not yet found the morning's breath, left me tingling with goosebumps as I opened my eyes and unglued my tongue from the roof of my mouth. Shrugging out from below the quilt, I stepped gingerly from the bed and shivered at the touch of the wooden floor. Stripped floorboards looked great, but I knew I'd have a fitted carpet by winter. I reached under the bed for the pair of semi-solid balled socks I knew would be there. The crispy material buffered against the cold as I walked to the kitchen. I poured a glass of water, swallowed Nurofen and looked for my cigarettes to soothe the cough that rose in my throat. Wrapping the quilt around me, I dismissed the thought of coffee in favour of turning up the thermostat and lying in bed until the heating woke up.

Crushing my cigarette in the ashtray, I pressed the play button on the answer machine as it sat flashing in mute testimony to the depth of my sleeping – the phone was beside my bed and I hadn't heard it ring.

'You-have-three-messages.'

Message 1: 'Pennance, I'll see you and Ting at the café at about seven.'

That was Stan.

Message 2: 'Hi, Carol, it's me. I'm in the bath reading this amazing book that you will love and I just thought I'd phone and say hello. So what have you been up to? Have you seen Mel?'

I turned round to face the machine as though doing so would help me to recognise the voice. Feeling ridiculous, I shook my head and frowned, concentrating on listening.

'. . . I'm going out with Joe tonight, I fancy a shag and, well, you know Joe, he's always up for it.'

Listening to her giggle, I forgot the absurdity of it and leant in close to the machine, looking at it expectantly.

'Work is just stressing me out, I can't believe I slept with that dickhead Brian again, and I can't believe Suzy is now, even though she knows that I was. She's a fucking slag.'

I smiled, thinking of poor Joe, as she continued in the halting fragmented manner of magnetic conversation.

'Anyway, I'm giving it all up and fucking off round the world, that's why I was phoning, want to come? We can talk about it when you come over. What do you think to a tattoo? Only, Emma got one and it looks so cool that I just thought fuck it, why not? I'm only going to get a henna one first though, to see if I like it. Maybe a tasteful sunburst round my belly button ring. I got that green dress but I haven't worn it yet coz I'm on and feel too ugly and I don't know if it was a mistake or not coz I think my tits are starting to sag. Maybe I just need a new . . .'

The message ended abruptly, cutting her off and leaving me agog at the intimacy she had shared with a complete stranger. Me.

Message 3: '. . . mascara. I hate it when I get cut off like that. Anyway I need to phone my mum and go buy something sluttish for tonight. I'll speak to you tomorrow from work. See you, bye.'

'You-have-no-more-messages.'

I stared at the now quiet machine for a moment before collapsing back on the bed and smirking. I pictured her, who-ever she was, lying in her bath, bubbles up to her ears, and couldn't imagine for one second that her tits were saggy. With that thought and the promise of a clear head after a quick sleep, I closed my eyes and slipped into the bath with her. I was distracted by a nagging pull at my eyelids but quickly learnt to ignore it as we pencil-tested her tits.

I sat bolt upright and threw off the quilt, the warmth forced from my body with the subtlety of a sucker punch. I slapped at the machine and it leapt to the floor with an ominous crash.

'You-have-three-messages.'

Message 1: 'Pennance, I'll see you and Ting at the café at about seven.'

I scrunched my eyes as I realised what was bothering me about Stan's message.

I didn't have Ting.

'Fuck. Fuck. Fuck.'

I sat hunched over the machine, staring at it without seeing it. Knowing it was pointless, I jumped up anyway, ignoring the giggling and splashing as the tape played on, and skidded from room to room like a demented flasher under house arrest. Back in front of the machine I waited expectantly for it to give me an answer. Where was Ting? I was cold-sweating alcohol as I frantically tried to remember what had happened.

Unable to do much damage on her own, Gabrielle whistled and like a good sidekick moved aside as the Warrior Princess stepped up and cleaved her bastard sword though my brain. Now that's a hangover, she said. I clenched my eyes shut in time to stop them from shooting across the room as my defence-less mind ran from her blade, desperate to find a way out. Instead I moaned and frantically searched through my dissected brain for the memory. He was on my lap, I was sitting . . . sitting where? I flopped onto the bed and stared at the constellations on my ceiling. He was on my lap, no, Donna was on my lap.

So where was Ting?

'Oh fuck.'

I'd left him in the club.

Pulling on last night's trousers, I held them up with one hand and pushed down on my skull with the other as I hopped round the room looking for my door keys. Then I froze and fell. Donna had a bag in the taxi. Was it hers or Ting's? I couldn't remember. Flopping like a merman, I grabbed my phone book and found Donna's number.

After about a million rings someone said hello. It was her sister.

'Hello, Claire.' I coughed lightly to steady my voice. 'It's Pennance. Is Donna there?'

Where the fuck are my keys? I roamed within the radius of the phone cord.

'Erm, yes,' she said quietly. 'But she's a bit busy right now. Can you call back later?'

Stopping looking for my keys, I gripped my head harder, trying to crush the life from my swinging hangover, and strained to hear. Voices in the background, raised but muffled by distance or bricks and mortar.

'Is David there with her?' I was surprised by the lump in my throat.

'Yes.' She paused. 'How did you know?'

I ignored her question and cursed silently; timing was fucking everything. But I had to know if Ting was there. 'Claire.' I spoke with the same confidence I had fifteen years ago asking old Grumpy Bastard Harrison for my ball as he picked it from amongst the broken glass of his greenhouse. 'I don't suppose you'd go get her for me?'

'Look, Pennance.' I could tell from her tone that she suspected that the shouting match in the bedroom and my call must somehow be related. 'I don't know what's going on but you'd better leave it just now.' Whatever her suspicions, just like old GBH, she'd obviously decided that my mere presence was an admission of guilt and my unspoken assurance that it wasn't my fault, a big boy did it and ran away, wouldn't change her mind any more than it had stopped him taking his garden fork to my ball with inevitable results. 'I'll tell her you rang.'

'Okay but just . . .'

The insensitive bitch put the phone down on me and burst my bubble.

Masking the pain from my temple by forcing my thumbs against the upper rim of my eye sockets, I focused on when I'd last had Ting. It must have been before Donna sat on my knee. Which means I must have put him down, probably at my feet and left him there, assuming, that is, that the bag in the taxi was Donna's. As this was all I had to work with, and the fact that I hadn't just lost an umbrella or a hat, but my best friend, I started having palpitations. I dressed and ransacked the flat looking for the keys, able for the moment to ignore my hangover, distracted as I was by the throbbing above my eyes.

Not on the table, not in the kitchen drawers, not in the bathroom. Still not on the table, not in the bedroom, not in my pockets and still not on the table. I stared at the table seven times before I eventually found them under a towel in the back room.

Jumping on my bike, I burnt rubber all the way to the Fruit Cupboard. When I finally banged my way in, the cleaners were having a break. Well, maybe they were, it was hard to tell. They weren't working, didn't look as though they had been and were sitting surrounded by a barely penetrable fog of smoke; maybe that was the job. The air was fetid and I coughed as the reek of stale beer and tobacco cloyed in my throat. The carpet I walked on valiantly attempted to escape as it clung to my shoes with every step. Without the flashing lights and bumping of the system, the room looked pasty in the stark brightness of the house lights.

'Excuse me.' I smiled with forced politeness. 'You haven't seen a brown leather bag lying around? I think I left mine here last night.'

The cleaner I addressed, resplendent in stained pinny, with dirty fingernails and dishwater blonde hair, didn't bother to look up from the scab she was picking from her knee.

'You're not allowed in here.'

'I know, but I've lost my bag,' I said reasonably, fighting back the urge to throttle the sloth-like lump of Jabba.

She deigned to look at me from below a frown and sighed

as her head fell back under its own weight and she looked over her shoulder at a dark mass in the corner.

'Sadie, have you seen a bag?' she asked lazily, bored. The nicotine gruffness in her voice was flattened by her obvious disinterest, my predicament being an unwelcome distraction from the excitement of peeling herself without bleeding.

'A bag,' she repeated louder and looked heavenward as the hoovering black hole launched a packet of Lambert & Butler. The responding grunt seemed to satisfy her sense of Christian charity and she wrinkled her face back to me and shrugged. Audience over.

□ * □

I cycled home in a daze, a sense of dread moving me with the speed of a shooting bullet through wet cement. This was not good. Fucking karmic payback for Donna and David. But so soon, and so huge. This was definitely not fucking good.

'I cannot fucking believe this!'

I began yelling while banging and pulling the handlebars, jerking my front wheel and causing me to swerve to avoid an oncoming car.

'What the fuck are you going to do now?' I asked my reflection in the mirrored glass of the bus shelter that I stopped and leant against because I was hyperventilating. Not twenty-four hours after promising Ray that I would take care of his son, his son whose death was on my hands, what do I do?

'YOU GO AND FUCKING LOSE HIM!'

The mirror screamed at me without embarrassment as the church groaners shuffled past the bus stop. Now I was in the throes of a well-formed panic attack and sat gripping my bike and shaking it as though possessed, while my stomach had its own white-knuckle ride.

Breath-two-three, breath-two-three . . .

'Okay,' I told the mirror. 'Calm down. Go home and try Donna again. Find out if Ting was in the taxi.'

I grimaced.

'Apologise? Say it was an accident? Deny it? Oh, fuck, just phone her and see how it goes, they may have been arguing about something else.'

The mirror smirked in response.

Yeah right.

Even with the wind in my ears, I couldn't get Beck's 'Loser' out of my head. The best I could do was to ignore him as I pedalled furiously home, rehearsing what I would be like with Donna and imagining how good I would feel when she gave me Ting. Problem solved, two grown-ups acting maturely. 'Oh,' she'd say, 'you left Ting here when you took my relationship this morning? Don't be silly, 'course we're still friends, come on round and get him.' She'd laugh. 'I'll just put the kettle on.'

I shouted hello to Mrs B as I leapt off my bike and into the flat, determined to speak to Donna before I bottled it. Flying through the door, I dived on the bed and grabbed the phone and dialled. No answer.

Dial, no answer.

Another panic attack, a spliff and I tried again.

No answer.

Repeat ad nauseam.

'Hello?'

I stopped breathing as I recognised Donna's voice then took a deep breath.

'Hi, Donna.' I did my best to sound upbeat. Scared that if I stopped talking I'd never be able to start again, I raced on. 'It's Pennance, I'm just phoning to say thanks for last night and to see if I left anything there, like a bag maybe?'

She left me hanging.

'Hello? Donna? Are you there?'

Silence, and with it the knowledge that hope had fled and taken any chance of cooperation with it.

'Donna?'

'Fuck off, Pennance.'

Click.

'Nooooo.'

I wailed at the phone, unwilling to go quiet into the dying

of the line, and threw it against the wall in a display of mature stress control.

And breath-two-three.

I dialled. Engaged.

'Bitch.'

Again. Engaged.

'Bitch.'

Breath-two-three.

Bitch-two-three.

Think-two-three.

I wasn't even convinced that Donna had Ting in the first place; maybe all this ranting was for nothing. If she did have him she would certainly give him back, if not to me then surely to Pine, although I'd rather avoid having to involve anyone else as I'd just end up looking like a fool. The problem really started if she didn't have him. I picked up the phone and tried again.

'Hello?'

I scrambled to catch the phone as I jumped.

'Donna, it's Pennance.' I sat on the bed and took a deep breath, concentrating. I sounded hurt. Confused and hurt. 'What was that all about?'

'Pennance,' she spat. 'Fuck off.'

'Donna, what . . . ?'

'Fuck off.'

I shivered as the phone iced over in my hand and threatened to make like the Blob. To misquote Tom Waits, she was colder than a welldigger's ass.

'Look, what is this?' I tried.

'Pennance, you are a cunt. Now fuck off.'

Hearing the venom in her voice and reading the subtle undercurrent between the lines, I realised that I was going nowhere and not likely to get there soon so I gave up on her and decided to returned the pleasantries. Fuck her, what's she going to do, keep him? I'd get Pine to phone her. There was no need to be rude.

'No, Donna, you fu—'

Click.

I held the phone out and stared at it in disbelief, I couldn't believe she'd gone, just like the last time. Now I was angry, how dare she be like that with me. She started it in Edinburgh, and it wasn't me that came on to her all moist last night. Childish and highly inappropriate as I knew it was under the circumstances, I demanded the last word. Then I'd have to phone Pine and ask him to go get Ting – assuming she had him. If she didn't, it was all fucked anyway so it wouldn't matter who knew about it. I phoned her back.

Engaged.

'Bitch.'

This time before I slammed the receiver down a very nice cyberlady told me how to use automatic ringback. I sat waiting, seething.

Kato, who had been asleep on the bed throughout my whole tirade, woke and lazily cat-crawled to my shoulder, curling round my neck like a centrally heated muff. As I had come to expect, the phone rang just as she got herself comfortable and she showed her displeasure at her imminent removal by digging all her claws into me for added security. I leapt for the phone and she scratched down my back on her way to the bed, leaving me with Bruce Lee, Enter-the-Dragon scars. Ignoring the pain, I grabbed the phone and hissed in a voice coated with malice.

'No. You fuck off.'

I waited for her to respond so that I could put the phone down, mission accomplished.

After a brief pause I heard 'Hello', but didn't hang up because it wasn't Donna. Whoever it was, they sounded a bit perturbed by their reception. I didn't recognise the voice and thought back to the message earlier. Maybe it was the same girl. Confusion washing away my anger, I lay down carefully, the scratches on my back stinging as adrenaline was swept away in the flood of emotions coursing through my body with dizzying effect.

'Hello?' I ventured gingerly.

'Pennance?'

Not the bath girl then.

'Yes.' I closed my eyes in embarrassment as recognition bobbed in front of me. Unwilling to trust my own misfortune, I asked anyway. 'Who's that?'

'It's Ali,' she confirmed. 'Sally's friend. We were talking last night?'

My God, did she think that I wouldn't remember?

'Yes, sure, of course.' I cringed. 'How are you?'

'I'm . . . eh . . . fine, yes, fine, thanks.' She answered quickly, as if not actually sure of herself. 'What about you, you sounded a bit . . . stressed.'

'I'm fine, thanks, you know.' I stopped, realising what I was saying. 'Oh, you mean that "fuck off" bit. Sorry about that, I thought you were someone else.' I sank into the bed.

'Having a bad day?' she asked.

'Something like that.' I sighed. I felt emotionally drained. Ting, Donna and now I'd told Ali to fuck off. The cat approached me and I sideswiped her but missed and predictably got bitten on the back of the hand.

'Maybe I can cheer you up a bit,' she said, teasing a smile from me with her dulcet tones.

All I could think was: sure, you could invite me round, open the door wearing nothing but jam and be carrying Ting's bag, but settled on, 'That would be good.'

'I got your number from Sally and thought I'd better phone you.' She paused slightly before continuing. 'You were pretty drunk again last night.'

'I know.' I said it as though I was only just realising that that wasn't a good thing. 'But there are mitigating circumstances.'

'Anyway,' she said, dismissing my self-pity, 'when you left with that girl . . .'

'Donna,' I prompted.

'Yes, Donna.' She paused again. 'She was really pretty.'

'I know.' I nodded impatiently, my hand all but crushing the life out of the phone as I remembered how I felt about Donna. Let's not talk about her right now. 'What about it?'

'I'm just saying she looked nice, I didn't mean anything by it.'

'No, I mean what about when I left?'

'Oh, right.' I could hear her get back on the track. 'You left your bag.'

Relief flooded me and I began to breathe again, unaware till then that I had stopped. I couldn't hear if Ali was saying anything else for the blood pounding through my body, tattooing my salvation with every beat.

Breath-two-three, yes-two-three.

I strained to listen.

'Sally said it would be too weird for her to take it, so she asked me. I hope you don't mind, but we weren't sure if you were coming back for it.'

'No, that's okay, I did go back for it, but a bouncer told me that a girl had taken it, so I kind of assumed that Sally had him. I was just about to phone her to go collect it.'

I'm sure my voice was choked as I glibly lied for no apparent reason. Habit taking over until my brain got control and started working again. I stopped punching the air as Xena started to wake and unsheathe her sword.

'That's why I was phoning, I didn't want you to worry about it. I've been trying for ages, but you've been engaged constantly. I ended up using that auto ringback.'

Man, what a head rush.

'Ali, you have so cheered me up.'

'I wanted to catch you before you started going demented and racing round looking for Ting.' She laughed. 'If it was me, I'd have freaked.'

'Me too.' I nodded sagely, joining her laughter.

'Okay, so I'll bring it, I mean him, round to the café tonight. I hope you don't mind but Sally invited me.'

Mind? This day was just getting better and better. I bit my lip as a whisper started in my head, suggesting that such a serendipitous phone call could only mean that things were looking up. Ting in a bag aside, life could be getting interesting. The casualness of the thought and the subsequent lack of lightning strikes convinced me to take a chance.

'Of course it's okay.' I drained the last of the laughter from my voice, replacing it with easily recognisable longing and hope. 'But do you think it would be all right if I came round and got him now?'

'Well, my parents are coming for lunch in a couple of hours and I still need to have a bath and get ready and stuff . . .' Her voice tapered off and I waited, once more holding my breath.

Please, I kept whispering to myself, cocky again now that I had recovered Ting.

'Oh, what the hell, if you come over now it will be okay. Have you got a pen and paper?'

Chapter 9

smelly cat

In premeditated payback for my lacerations, I left Kato cat food from my punishment stock in the freezer and wondered again why I didn't have a dog. I was chaining my bike to the railings outside Ali's flat thirty minutes later. Old terraces converted into des-res apartments for the affluent youth, not an area that I was familiar with. Wiping toothpaste from my lips, I took a couple of deep breaths before walking to her door. I'd spent last night chasing and not catching her and she knew it. The two times I'd met her I'd been drunk, and to compound my embarrassment I'd left my friend's remains in a nightclub in a bag. The guilt I was amassing. Finding her name, I pressed the right buzzer, thinking to myself that I owed it to her and to myself to appear slightly less pathetic than when we met before.

'Hi, Ali, it's Pennance,' I answered cheerfully as she said hello.

'Come on up.'

Framing myself, I checked my zip and ran my tongue along my teeth. Dishevelling my hair, I pushed at the door. It wouldn't open.

'Hi, Ali, it's me again,' I said sheepishly when she answered again. 'I missed it.'

She still had her finger on the buzzer when I topped the stairs of her landing. Her door was open so I gave it a quick knock.

'I'll just be a second,' she shouted as I stepped in. 'Go sit down.'

Her voice came from behind a door at the bottom of the hall and as I walked I could smell cooking to my right. That'll be the kitchen then. Which meant that on my left – I opened the door – yes, the living room.

It was spartanly furnished in expensive tat. I searched the room for clues as I made my way to the open bay window overlooking the road. Past the steel-framed suite, I circumnavigated the cream shag pile and checked out her shelves either side of the fireplace. Ali and her friends, Ali and probably her parents. No Ali and boyfriend in any of her photos. No man stuff in the room. Looking out onto the street, I allowed myself a quick smile. This would be a good place to wake up, sun streaming through the window and the smell of cooking from the kitchen floating by. Cooking and something else. Something feminine? Something homely? But no, my brain stumbled through records to identify the source. I took a deep breath and closed my eyes. My face screwed up in recognition, it was . . .

'Shit!'

I turned at the sound of Ali giving voice to my summation.

'I know, do you want me to close the window?' I asked helpfully. If her parents were coming soon, she wouldn't want them to catch a whiff, it was rancid.

'Just don't move.' And then she was gone

She wore a pair of faded jeans and a white T-shirt that had to have been painted on. Barefoot and with a towel turban, she was an advert. I could hear her mumble distractedly as I wondered where she had gone and took a few tentative steps back towards the door, away from the window.

'I said, don't move.' Ali was back, and while I swayed slightly against the sudden force field that held me in stasis, I almost toppled over when it registered that she was wearing Marigolds and had fallen to her knees.

Kinky.

'Take your shoes off, please.'

At that point I bent down and picked up the penny.

'Oh, shit.' My hand rose to my forehead and then reached out to her. 'I'm really sorry. Here, let me do that.'

Before I could say any more she held her hands up and shook her head.

'It's okay, I've got it. Just take your shoes off.' I was relieved when she spoke, there was no trace of anger or annoyance there. 'You can leave them outside, no one will touch them.'

I felt a bit abashed, edging past her with my shoes as high above my head as I could carry them. I left them outside the door, secure in the knowledge that she was right: the gelatinous covering on the sole would deter any would-be miscreants from offing with them. On my way back, I could see dollops of damp where she had sprayed bleach after kitchen-rolling away the evidence of my passing. Whispering a long-thought-forgotten prayer in thanks for not walking across the carpet, I stood behind Ali and ranted apology after excuse after expletive as she crouched along the floor clearing and bleaching.

'Don't worry about it, I'll only be a minute.'

She dismissed my grovelling with a nonchalant wave of her hand. Even feeling hand-on-heart guilty, I couldn't help simply watching her. Suddenly I was awash with desire. Every move of her hand travelled the length of her body, and when she shuffled forward she was almost feline in her grace. Now I wished I had walked on the carpet as all too soon she stood and gave the floor the once-over. Satisfied with her work, she let out a sigh and smiled.

'Hi.'

'Hi,' I replied, still watching her last breath's momentum work out of her T-shirt.

She rolled a glove off and used her naked hand to adjust her hair under the towel, with the other she picked up her cleaning bucket and pointed at the hi-fi as she walked past me.

'Why don't you turn that tape over and I'll stick the kettle on. Okay?'

Rousing myself from Marigold fantasy, I turned the tape, noting and questioning her choice of Fatboy Slim as good Sunday music and followed my nose to the kitchen.

▭ ✱ ▭

'Coffee or tea?'

'Coffee, please,' I replied nonchalantly, sitting at the huge farmhouse table. Making a display of it, I slowly surveyed the room. In contrast to the living room nothing else could have fitted in. 'I take it you like to cook.' I motioned to the well-appointed work surfaces and burgeoning shelves.

'Yes, I suppose I do.' She didn't turn round and I watched her fill the kettle. Fox by name . . .

She placed two mugs on the table and sat down. Shaking her hair from the towel, she tilted her head to one side and smiled.

'You really were fucked last night,' she stated matter-of-factly.

'I know.' My head hung in shame, not only from last night. 'I've barely met you twice and both times I've been out of my tree, then I walk dog shit around your flat.' I looked at her and smiled sadly. 'You must think I'm a right wanker.'

She had a golden laugh.

'Don't worry about it. I know the mitigating circumstances, remember?' As an after-thought she added, 'Sally says you're not usually that bad, so I'll let you off.'

So you've been asking Sally about me, have you? I thought to myself. Pleased with the way it made me feel, I fought to keep the smug grin from showing through.

'How do you know Sally?' I asked, thinking it a good idea to change the subject and also because I was sitting in her kitchen and I knew nothing about her; we hadn't even had sex as a point of morning reference.

'We used to live together at college,' she explained. 'I moved back to Leeds a couple of months ago and we've kind of picked up where we left off.'

I found it strange that Sally had never mentioned her before and even stranger that Ting hadn't. A Honey of Ali's obvious standing would have been too much for him to keep to himself, and, anyway, I felt sure that if he'd known about her he would have introduced me.

'Did you know Ting?'

'Only what Sally told me of him.' She shook her head. 'I never met him.'

I knew it.

It would have been Sally thinking that I wasn't good enough for her, not for one of her friends. She knew that Pine was with Molly, Stan . . . well, Stan had nothing in common with Ali so was no risk anyway, but I was single, she knew that and that was the only reason that she could have had for keeping Ali under wraps. That pissed me off, even if she had introduced us the other night.

'How come we've never met before?'

'We must travel in different circles, different pubs and stuff.'

That had to be true. If I'd been within scoping distance of Ali before, I would have remembered where, when, and who I would have wanted to be.

'Sally's never even mentioned you.'

'She's spoken about you.'

I fucking knew it.

'Nothing good, I hope.'

'Nothing specific.' She laughed.

Before I could delve any deeper, her cauliflower bubbled over and she went to the stove to sort it out. I felt nervous now, wondering what press Sally had written for me and why she had chosen this time to bring Ali into my life. Maybe with Ting's death she had seen it as a way of keeping close with us, his friends. If I was going out with Ali, Sally would still be our friend by association and not drift off as ex-lovers so often do. It was possible that she liked me that much, right up there with my scoring the clincher on Cup Final day. Whatever the reason, I was going to make up for lost time and make sure Ali was here to stay. It was time to be charming.

'Can I help you with anything?'

'Pour the coffee,' she replied distractedly. 'Milk's in the fridge.'

'It's okay, I take it black.'

'I don't.'

'Sorry,' I said, standing up. 'I wasn't thinking.'

'Relax,' she told me, echoing my own thoughts. 'Do you want a biscuit or anything?'

'Have you got any jam?' I muttered under my breath.

'What?'

'Nothing, I was thinking out loud.'

I was putting the milk on the table as she wrapped her hair back up and walked towards the door.

'Do you want to roll a joint?'

She got me her stash tin from a drawer and left me to skin up while she dried her hair.

□ * □

I was feeling better now, more human. I relaxed and let the spliff massage my mind, refocusing my energies into happiness. I was still put out with Donna, but now I knew she didn't have Ting it wasn't worth thinking about. Things had worked out reasonably well. I had sex last night, and here I was in Ali's flat the next morning. I went for the kettle and cast a look over the food. I looked for signs of burning and checked out how much food was being cooked – maybe if I was a really good boy Ali would invite me to stay for lunch. It smelt delicious, a roast sizzling in the oven, potato and two veg. I imagined that the Yorkshire puddings would be making an appearance any time soon. I was convinced that Ali was a great cook, and on opening the oven I was rewarded with a blast of mouth-watering heat as the aroma of roasting beef filled the room. After a moment the mouth-watering became eye-watering the further from the oven I was. Not dog shit this time, but something infinitely less attractive competed with lunch. A cloying smell that tasted warm on the throat a nano-second before it made you gag. A bit like ammonia but with none of its redeeming features. When I sat down I noticed it was also stronger the closer to the floor I was. Then, once more, I bent down to retrieve another penny and had to squeeze my eyes closed as they came into direct view of my socks. My crusty socks that grazed when I pulled them on from under my bed this morning. They had defrosted in my shoes and were now all but squelching every step I took. Instinctively I stood up and held my breath until I was comforted by the continued drone of Ali's Ferrari-powered hairdryer.

I needed to make toast, and quickly.

When Ali came back, I passed her the joint as she walked through the door, stalling her for precious seconds.

'What's burning?' she asked worriedly and made her way round me to the cooker.

'I'm sorry about that.' I walked behind her. 'Lunch is fine, don't worry. It's just that I thought I'd have a slice of toast instead of a biscuit. I hope you don't mind.' I stood against the sink and opened the window. 'I shouted to you but the hair-dryer must have drowned me out.'

'The toast's no problem,' she told me, pulling it out from under the grill. 'But you've let it burn, it'll stink the flat out.'

'I just realised it was burning as you came in, I was pouring the coffee. Nice cafiter by the way,' I said, sitting back down at the table.

'Cafetière.' She laughed, thinking I'd joked.

'That's what I meant.'

Stan was going to get such a kicking for that one.

'Do you want me to make you some more toast?'

I looked up in time to see her walking to the bin. 'No,' I said, probably a bit too loud. 'I like it like that.'

'You sure?'

'Absolutely. Any toast is good toast and you should never not eat it lest it be your last.'

'You're a bit weird, aren't you?' She didn't so much ask.

I shrugged like Shylock, not really having a suitable answer to that.

'At least the smell of the toast will cover the bleach.' She stretched up to a cupboard. 'Do you want Marmite?'

'That would be an emphatic no thank you.'

I gagged at the thought of yet another olfactory assault and had a momentary worry about our long-term future.

'See, definitely weird.'

Satisfied that her kitchen had suffered no long-term damage, she stirred and tasted some more and joined me at the table while I devoured the carcinogenic remains of the toast that I had smothered in butter. I watched her run her finger round the rim of her cup while her eyes wrinkled slightly as she appeared distracted.

'You don't mind me coming to the café tonight, do you?'

'Mind?' I spat crumbs and she moved out of range while I covered my mouth and hastily swallowed. 'Why would I mind?'

'Sally told me about your wake for Ting, I just didn't want to think I'd be intruding or anything.'

'Trust me.' I smiled. 'You're more than welcome.'

'Thanks.' She seemed to relax again. 'I was glad when Sally asked me but I felt a bit awkward, you know, with it being a wake and me not knowing Ting or anyone. But she wants me to go.'

'Me too,' I whispered. And then louder. 'You'll be fine. I'm here so you must know me, right? And Ting? Ting was just your common-or-garden, all-round one in a million.'

'I can imagine.' She grinned. 'A guy has to be something special to catch Sally's eye.'

'Well, he was that.'

'You miss him, don't you?'

I nodded.

The day after he died was the worst. I'd sat in the flat, alone, staring at nothing and not hearing the phone ring. Sighing, I'd stood up, walked listlessly back and forth and sat back down, about a million times. No histrionics, no melodramatics. Only numbness. Only denial.

Ali smiled tightly and shook her hair, perhaps purposefully shifting my focus.

'And what about you?' she asked, pouring more coffee, not so subtly dropping a piece of kitchen roll on the table in front of me. 'Are you one of the good guys?'

'I'd like to think so.' I smiled. And I'd like you to think so too, I thought, as she beamed back.

'So what do you do? I mean you're here' – she gestured

vaguely round the kitchen –'but I don't really know you. Are you a teacher as well?'

'A teacher?' Thoughts of Ting vanished into the ether as I faced this new affront. 'God, no. Why would you think that?' I pulled at my clothes as though examining them and checked for bicycle clips. 'Do I look like a teacher?'

'Well, you've got black bits of toast between your teeth.' She pursed her lips and pointed. 'But it wasn't that. I know Ting was a teacher and I just thought that might be how you knew each other.'

Fair comment, I suppose, but the thought of being categorised as a teacher without due reference had shocked me almost as much as Ting becoming one. He'd said it was a necessary part of genius on his part as the only way to change the system was to work from the inside. I wasn't convinced but had no recourse other than to allow him to still be my friend but insist that he looked into aversion therapy.

'I'm a temp.' Much to her obvious delight, I'd tongued away the last vestiges of the toast before I dared answer.

'You're temping?'

'No. Well, yes. But I'm not temping, that's my actual job. I'm a career temp.'

'Eh?'

So I tried to explain. I'd left university with a Desmond in law. Not really up on the idea of real work, I began temping in the meantime. After a while I began to enjoy the variety of work that I was doing and started to think of temping as my job.

'So do you enjoy it?'

'At first I did.'

At first it was quite exciting. I remembered reading about POWs in Colditz pretending to escape but in fact hiding in the prison to be available to 'temp' for prisoners who really had escaped and buy them time to get away. They were the original temps and I'd convinced myself that what I was doing was similarly worthy. At least that's certainly what I told people when they asked. Like now.

'Moving from job to job, it wasn't just the different types

of work I'd be doing that kept me interested. I realised that I'd be working with lots of different people all the time and thought my social life would explode.'

'And did it?'

'Like a wet squib.' I shrugged. 'As a temp you're never anywhere long enough to become one of the in crowd. My closest friends now are the same as they were ten years ago.'

'So why don't you get a real job if you don't enjoy being a temp?'

'I suppose that's what has to happen next.'

'Should be easy enough.' She nodded. 'You've got a law degree.'

'Only a 2:2.'

'Me too and I've got one of those real job things you're talking about.'

With that revelation we spent the next twenty minutes comparing student horror stories and remembering past lectures and papers that we had in common. She took me back to stuffy libraries and stuffier shirts as she talked me through her articles and made fun of her chosen profession's pomposity. We talked about being students, we talked about not being students, and then we talked about how we got to here.

As the silences began to outgrow the talking I began to feel as though I was on a date, a first date where we looked for and found commonality through emotional depth, but then I feared we'd gone too far too soon. We risked becoming depressed about life being a complete bastard sometimes; case in point, how I got to be here now. It was, I had to remind myself, only sometimes. There's a time and a place for soul searching and emotional honesty and there's another for being the guy who makes you smile. I wailed like a siren as I became that guy again.

'Saddo alert, saddo alert. Please head to the nearest sexist.'

Entirely on my wavelength, Ali immediately smiled and brought the temp back up. I was happy that we'd been able to sit and talk so easily and hoped that I'd managed to redeem myself in her eyes after Friday's fiasco, but it was time to move on before I ended up in tears again.

'Did you have a good time last night then?'

She nodded. They'd stayed and danced until the club shut and then gone back to Sally's for a smoke. I laughed when she aped some of her less gifted dance partners of the evening until I became uncomfortable that I could recognise myself in her gesture. I was glad when she moved on to the fashion and fake-up disasters of the night, picking at them with the subtlety of a vulture with aspirations of a stand-up career and giving me ample opportunity to watch her body live each emotion as she spoke. After more deconstruction work I thought it might do me no harm to apologise again for my behaviour. With one eye on the roast beef, I went for it.

'Sorry again if I was a dick last night.'

Encouraged by her shrugged response, I pushed on.

'Or if I said anything stupid.'

'You mean when you were coming on to me?'

Butter wouldn't melt in this girl's oven if she didn't want it to.

'Mmmm . . . yes.' I squirmed.

'Maybe if you hadn't been so drunk . . .' and the buzzer went, announcing that her parents had arrived.

'Shit.' She jumped up. 'I forgot about the puddings.'

She buzzed them up and turned back to me, still sat in the kitchen, unable to believe my luck, good and bad.

'I think you're forgetting something too.' She raised her eyebrows but I must have looked confused. 'Your bag, Pennance, it's behind the door in the bedroom. I'll get it now.'

I had to remain sitting until the wash of guilt poured out the window. How could I have forgotten? Then a thought came to me. I realised that this was exactly the kind of thing that needed to happen. I was supposed to focus, the possibility in life taking precedence over consideration for the dead. Otherwise why bother keeping going. Somehow I knew Ting would agree.

'Get the door for me, please.'

I was forced into action as I realised I was being shepherded out. Ali strode towards me with Ting and I forced a smile.

'You slept with Ting in your bedroom last night?'

'The door please.'

Hearing footsteps as I opened the door, I guessed lunch was a no go.

'Here you are.' She handed me Ting. 'Try not to lose him this time.'

'Thanks,' I said drily, then repeated with a smile as I caught her questioning look.

Her eyes danced mischievously as she glanced past me and whispered, 'First man I've had in that bedroom.'

I stood to one side as her mother and father walked through the door and they hugged and kissed hello, and I nodded hello goodbye as Ali informed them that I was leaving.

'I'll see you tonight,' she called after me as she followed her parents into the flat.

I smiled in acknowledgement as I headed down the stairs before putting my shoes back on.

'Is that a new boyfriend?' I heard her mother ask before the door closed. I stopped breathing, trying to hear the answer before giving up and making like a Cheshire as I practically skipped out of the door.

Chapter 10

planned breakdown

Cotton wool lazed in the sky as I rode to the train station, my head pushed through the clouds. I'd gone straight home after leaving Ali's. I'd thought about taking Ting into town with me but *Rio Bravo* was on and he never missed a Duke film if he could help it. The evidence in the kitchen spoke of Kato's displeasure with me so I left her more food, not frozen this time, as a peace offering. Ting safely in front of the telly, I'd set off for the station. That the summer had decided to stay around as long as it had encouraged me to cycle instead of taking a taxi or getting the bus, and the film of grime that coated me was but a small discomfort compared to the joy of riding with the sun on my smile. Hiding behind my sunglasses, I meandered slowly, gravity and time having no reference in the dreamscape that led me past the tit tops and shorts of the students and the diaphanous blouses of the too-hot sunny-day shirkers on summertime lunches. I smiled past the university gardens that did for the traffic what Gossard and Eva started and then headed back to the station, shaking my head to clear it as I realised I'd been going in the wrong direction. I needed to pick up our train tickets and thoughts of Ali had led me astray. I'd left her flat with an air of demented satisfaction that things just felt right. Knowing that Ting would approve and be smiling with me kept my mood light as I saw her face in those I passed. All too soon I got into the city centre and felt out of place in my creased and sweaty clothes.

I hurried through the shoppers and into the cooling sanctuary of the station, clothes hugging my body as the sun and nipple count took hold. In the echo chamber of the ticket hall

I wanted to shout and tell everyone that I, Pennance Ward, waster with the waistline, had just been bonding with one Ali Fox, Drop Dead Honey, but judging by the looks I got as I passed through, the smile was loud enough for everyone to hear, and I felt happy, content even. My good mood lasted almost another full minute before it all went horribly Pete Tong as the clouds returned and Ali's spell broke.

'But there's got to be a train,' I said for the fourth and loudest time.

Mull, it appeared, was not part of the network and no matter how much I raised my voice or asked her to check she wouldn't change her mind.

'I can't help you,' she said in a way that made my eye twitch, all smiles and frankly I don't give a fuck if you curl up and cry. She looked me up and down before continuing, 'I sell tickets, I don't drive the trains or tell them where to go.' Her mind made up, she sneered, 'But if you want to take the bus, I'll happily tell you where to go.'

I took my sunglasses off and looked at her. I couldn't work out if she was naturally this charming or if she'd learnt it in a training course when they gave her the job. Either way I had to force a smile and ignore her obtuseness; politeness was my only weapon.

'If I wanted a bus,' I said pleasantly, swallowing the urge to throttle her, 'I wouldn't be in a fucking train station.'

'And if I thought you were funny I'd be laughing.' She raised her eyebrows and I knew that if she'd been standing her hands would be on her hips and she would be shaking her backside. She had watched too much Jerry Springer.

'Sorry,' I said, meaning it not at all. 'I didn't intend to swear.' This was my fault, not hers, and even if she did have the personality of a dead badger there was no excuse for me being rude. She couldn't help that there were no trains any more than she could uncross her eyes. I'd expected there to be trains. I hadn't checked, I'd assumed.

''S'okay.' She looked behind me at the queue that had formed. 'You want a ticket or not?'

'Fuck.' I shook my head, unsure what to do. 'I don't know where to go now.'

'Well, you need to move if you don't want a ticket.'

With a glance behind me I shrugged, her belligerence filling the void left when my good mood evaporated five minutes ago. 'I'm at the front of the queue, so you have to serve me. They can fucking wait until I decide where I'm going.'

'Whatever you say.' She folded her arms and spat, 'Sir.'

'Thank you.' She nodded in agreement as I worried about my choices, or lack of them. Yet again I had fucked up. I could taste the disappointment on my tongue as I lived through Stan and Pine's, and probably even Ray's, reaction to my mistake. Beyond their caustic remarks I felt the cold breath of Ting, sealed in a jar, expecting release that I was responsible for arranging. I almost jumped when a hand tapped my shoulder and the Transport Police led me outside as the now smiling clerk mouthed 'prick' through the glass.

'Bitch.'

Now I was in trouble, not from the wannabe cop standing at the door in his ill-fitting uniform and shiny badges, confident that he could stop me going back in by the power of his misanthropic smile, but from the inescapable fact that I was living down to the expectations of all who knew me. Sitting on the kerb outside the station, I held my head in my hands and shook with anger. Not at anyone else, only at myself. Ting was my best friend and I'd taken responsibility for getting him to Mull. More than that, I had insisted, vocally, that I wanted to do it, I needed to do it. Now at the eleventh hour, I knew I had taken on more than I was able. Not intellectually – even Stan would have admitted that I had the gumption to use a credit card – but emotionally. Planning and arranging took thought and action, neither of which, outside a carnally gratifying chase, I had been able to do. Maybe it was a form of denial. Sorting out the arrangements would make what we were doing real, but, in the less visited part of my brain called honest-to-Murgatroyd truth, I knew that was only me grasping for the branch as I sank in the

sand. I was lazy. Simple as that. And I had fucked up again.
Time for another panic attack.

◻ * ◻

'Spare me a cigarette?'

Caught up in self-flagellation, I hadn't even noticed him sit
down. Judging by the smell, he was homeless or bath-averse,
but I nodded and handed him a smoke, lighting one for myself
as well.

'Don't worry,' he said, sucking and wheezing simultaneously.
'I get thrown out all the time.' He glanced over his shoulder.
'You'll be able to go back in in a minute; they change the guard
on the hour and that wanker will be off to polish his helmet.' I
mumbled something in return, not wanting to get into a conversation that I knew would lead to me giving him my shoes. 'You
want a drink?' He held up a crushed can of Special Brew and
shrugged when I pushed it away. 'Suit yourself.'

It was an indication of how low I felt that I paid no attention
to the legs and midriffs that passed by. I couldn't even find
comfort in Ali. I was lost in my own despair, unable to lift
myself out, when I heard a pschssscht from next to me and
quickly swapped my packet of cigarettes for the freshly opened
can before it reached his crusty lips, using it to wash the taste
of disappointment from my mouth. I knew I looked scruffy,
the amorphous lump behind the ticket counter had made that
plain, and as I drank Special Brew sitting at the side of the
road, I knew that even if I had noticed the talent walking along,
they wouldn't have noticed me, only the grubby clothes and
the Special needs Brew that spilt down my shirt as my partner
in grime nudged me.

'Look depressed,' he whispered while I brushed at my shirt
in a futile attempt to stop it dissolving. 'Here come meals and
heals.'

'I am fucking depressed,' I said, shaking my head and swiping one of my own cigarettes.

'That's the spirit.' He smiled a tooth at me.

'God bless.'

'Same to you, Father,' I heard from beside me as my new friend pulled at his forelock. I nodded in greeting as his holy shadow blocked the sun and the sky threatened to fall on my head.

'You boys hungry.' He didn't ask.

'Oh, yes, Father.' My man nodded vigorously. 'I haven't eaten properly since twelve.' I turned my head slightly to look at him, thinking he was possibly talking himself out of a meal, but he winked at me and smiled. 'Since I was twelve.'

Ignoring him, the priest looked at me through eyebrows only slightly thicker than the sheaf of leaflets he was shuffling in his hand. 'If you come to prayers' – he held out a brochure for heaven – 'there's food afterwards in the hall.'

Without a backward glance, my cigarettes disappeared on their way to church and a plate of hot soup. I shook my head and wished my own problem could be so quickly turned round.

'No, thanks.'

With a fatherly sigh, he sat next to me and nodded. He took a moment to take a world-weary wipe at his brow and to look out over the car park to where the spire from his church rose like the antenna he believed it was.

'You're new to the street, aren't you?'

'I'm not –'

He held his hand up to silence me, choosing to doubt my word and believe his eyes as he'd been taught. Years of conditioning and good old-fashioned God-fearing preaching had him cast me as a soul in need. I was, but not in the way he had assumed from his temple learning. Another leaflet.

'Don't be too proud to accept the hand of God when it's offered to you; we all need a lift when we're down. Don't be blinded by your pride. Take this to the address on the back and they'll give you a room for the night.'

'After prayers?' I asked archly, too pissed off to be civil. First the debacle at the ticket counter and then my ignoble exit, now I was a fucking tramp, not to mention that his God had knocked my nose out of joint when he murdered Ting.

'Praying brings us closer to God,' he reminded me, choosing to ignore the sarcasm in my voice, 'and God is the only one who can save you, son.'

The hackles of history rose unchecked, now was not a good time for theological theorising and with a shiver I readied to prick at his altruism.

Although I was adamant that I didn't believe in his God, the ghost of Father McGonagall occasionally haunted me, reminding me that I didn't actually know for sure that He didn't exist and it took a belt of Danish to banish him back to the classroom. I'd had a fear of talking to priests since primary school and my first real encounter with the confounding conspiracy that was religion. Teachers, who looked a lot like normal people, were telling me about sensible things like a-r-i-p-h-m-a-t-i-c and the alphabets, encouraging me to make logical decisions in fun games with bright blocks and balls, and generally promoting thinking. Then one period each week I'd be told that if I didn't learn my catechism I'd go to hell and spend eternity with the Protestants. I didn't even know what one of those was. Father McGonagall made us sit, arms crossed, knees together, while we learnt by heart the Ten Commandments and our part in the confirmation ceremony where we would become Gold card members in one of the least exclusive clubs around.

It was at that point that I learnt to my utter disbelief that I wasn't joining, I was confirming my membership. I had been enrolled years ago, about the same time that some sicko in a frock tried to drown me and apparently once you were in you were in, the cancellation fee being a killer. Even into high school Father McGonagall would insist we believe everything he read to us from his Bumper Book of Fairy Tales (King James edition) and ban questions that began with words like: How can that ... That doesn't make ... You've got to be jo— He was as normal as the straining black dress he wore even in the heat of summer and the scowling crucifix he made us kiss as we left the room at the end of prayers. He couldn't comprehend how we weren't able to grasp the nuances of a book written by a bunch of people who believed that God lived in the sky and that the earth was flat.

I'd asked him once, before I knew any better, where do we go when we die? I wasn't even sure I knew what dying was; I knew it happened to very old people although that didn't help as I had no real concept of time anyway beyond knowing that it was frequently up or flying. I'd heard the words but I didn't know where they were, one was up and one was down, one was good and one involved Protestants. I got confused about which one was which. Mostly when he spoke I daydreamed, only catching occasional words or learning parrot fashion with the class; his blatantly made-up stories couldn't compete with *Warlord* or *Roy of the Rovers*, but sometimes his booming kept me awake and he'd say something else to confuse me, that's why I asked.

'Your soul flies to the Pearly Gates,' he'd said, glassy-eyed. 'St Peter checks his ledger and if you've been devout, if you've lived a life of sacrifice, poverty and chastity, you join the eternal chorus in eternal alleluia.'

'Is that heaven or hell?'

After that, the lessons were shouted in my ear, religiously. They weren't lessons as such, more anti-lessons, contradictory to what my expanding mind was realising about how things worked and why things happened. It didn't make sense but I'd heard it enough times for the edges of reason to be frayed. Today it was my anger at Ting's death that put the acid on my tongue as I abused the good Father's intentions.

'No, you're okay. I think I'll take my chances. Your God couldn't save His own son, or my very good friend Ting. What makes you think He'd have better luck with me?'

'Jesus died to –' He began his sermon, but it was my turn to hold my hand up.

'Forget it, Father, I'm no prodigal son and I don't need a fatted can of soup or a bed.'

He stood up and I could see him weighing up his vocation against the need to punch my lights out and exorcise my demons in traditional seminary practice. Surprisingly for a man of the cloth, duty won over pleasure and the benign smile reappeared.

'Here.' He grabbed my arm as I stood and thrust another card into my hand. 'Life's a journey, son. It's up to you how you travel.'

I surprised myself with a laugh. 'Not according to GNEfuck-ingR.' In spite of myself I felt my cheeks redden under his flaming gaze, any hotter and his eyebrows would spontaneously combust.

'Sorry.' I could taste the soap in my mouth, my mother pinching my tongue as she scrubbed. 'Thanks for trying, but you can't help me.'

'Are you sure?'

'Can you drive a train?'

He scowled for a moment and then shook his head, looking at my stained shirt and the empty can I had picked up to put in the bin.

'Give these people a call. You don't even have to pray unless you want to.' He nodded his head sharply and walked off. 'God bless.'

I knew I looked rough – unshaven, the look of the damned in my face – but I still had to laugh at the card he had left me. One side had a number for a drugs helpline, the other for Alcoholics Anonymous.

I shook my head. Ting always said I'd end up in the AA.

After a moment my laughter stopped and I looked at the card again, dumbstruck.

Ting was right, the AA would be my salvation, but not in the way he'd predicted. I looked back at the priest as he moved to another helpless soul, maybe his Lord did work in mysterious ways after all.

I walked back to my bike, thoughts of tickets and trains replaced with an unsettling feeling of gratitude coated in a thick covering of redemption.

We'd get to Mull in Stan's car. Courtesy of the AA.

Chapter 11

ali gaga

When I got to the café Stan and Pine were already there, lying prostrate in the booth. After last night both of them were subdued. I sat down and nudged them out of their stupor. Pine was nursing his pint and Stan screwed his left eye shut whenever he spoke. Cocktail hangovers are always the worst; Ting would be proud. I could only think that my adrenaline rushes and panic attacks from my day's activities had leeched my hangover as both Stan and Pine watched me from behind their grey pall.

'How are you feeling?' Pine asked in a voice two steps from pathetic. Stan squinted at me. I pursed my lips and drew my hand along my chin. Need a shave, I thought, nodding.

'I'm okay,' I said cheerfully. 'A bit delicate, but okay.'

'I feel like shite,' Pine said. 'Sick as necrophilia this morning and it's gotten progressively worse.'

'You should have stayed in bed,' I suggested, but he shook his head carefully.

'Not a chance, this is how the man wanted us. I'll feel better in a while.'

'What about you?' I asked Stan as Pine sat shivering.

This was why we were here, why Ting wanted his night in the café. To compare cringes over last night and work through our hangovers. I'd almost cracked mine.

'Not good. Not good at all. I think I've got a tumour where my eye used to be.' The left side of his face twitched as he held his eye shut.

'How come you're not hung over?' Pine interrupted him and shot me a look of shaky disgust. Beads of sweat popped through his jaundiced skin.

'I drank a shitload of water before going to sleep,' I told him glibly, 'and of course I must have sweated out all the alcohol when I went home with Donna.'

'You went for it then?' he asked with a forced casualness.

'I did.'

'Spare us the gloating.' Stan grimaced. 'I thought she was a bitch and you wanted her to die of bad teeth and piles.'

So I told them what I'd done, about phoning David, only stumbling a bit about why I called her this morning. They both winced and did a lot of sucking in of deep breaths but nodded in agreement at the justice of it.

This was another part of our café nights.

Reinforcement.

'What about Ali?' Stan asked, surprising me. 'I thought you were making a play for her. You were up to your elbows trying to pull her in.'

I thought about today and how I'd spent time with her. Not awkward morning-after-drunken-conquest time either, but real time. Of course I'd tried all night to get her but I'd failed miserably, until today. Stan was right about last night, I told myself. Ali was out of my league. But today wasn't a league match, it was the Cup and the only qualification needed was to turn up. We'd had the first leg and now, tonight, I was hoping to cause an upset. Pennance the giantkiller.

I shrugged. 'Donna was there.'

Pine grimaced and stood up. 'Back in a minute.'

I looked over to Stan and put my glass down, finishing rolling for Pine.

'Thanks for last night. I was in a state for a while.'

'Don't even mention it.' He tutted. 'You know I hate Welshmen.'

He made light of my thanks and avoided embarrassing either himself or me. In spite of our closeness, the need to keep face was still an important function of our relationship. Even with a friend dead we were careful how we worded our regard for each other. The banter, the jibes, the sarcasm, all of it amounted to a statement of love that had to be disguised as rapport. Looking at

Ting's bag, I realised that it was easier to say 'I loved that man' because he was dead. Never when he was alive. We'd hug and we'd even cry when it couldn't be helped but we didn't wear our hearts on the outside where they could be bruised and broken. I don't know why it should be like this. Maybe it's just me, and Stan, and Pine, and Ting, and . . . maybe it's not. We could well be from Mars. One day, I promised myself, I'm going to tell my friends exactly what they mean to me. Not in a drunken embrace or when stoned to the bone but sober and without provocation. And not when they're dead either.

'Cool,' was all I said, falling back on a smile until tomorrow. 'What's to eat?'

Stan looked to the kitchen and asked what I fancied, before disappearing through the door, leaving me to guard Ting against loss and misadventure. My hand sat reassuringly on his bag and I could feel the outline of the jar that came from the crematorium. I realised that I hadn't looked in the bag since Ray gave me it yesterday and wondered if I should. After my emotional roller-coaster of a day I decided that I wasn't up to it and settled on a reassuring pat on the soft leather, whispering, 'You know I love you, don't you?' while surreptitiously check-ing that no one could hear me. I laughed a throaty chuckle at the absurdity. Ting's dead. He could be hovering above me, his wings suspending him out of my reach as he lounged and listened to his music.

'I know' – he'd shake his finger silently at me – 'but don't tell anyone.'

I looked around and above. No Ting. Nothing.

'What are you laughing at?' Pine asked as he came back and followed my gaze skyward. Embarrassed, I shook my head and self-consciously took my hand from the bag.

'Nothing.'

Stan returned from the kitchen then, saving me from having to explain.

'You all right?' He nodded at Pine.

Pine took a long drink from his pint. 'I feel like a new man,' he declared heartily.

'Me too,' Stan mumbled, turning as Josh approached him from the bar.

'Some dirty bastard has just been sick in the toilets,' he told Stan with disgust. 'It's all blocked and it stinks to high heaven.' He shivered and went past us to the kitchen, returning seconds later with a pair of Marigolds and a plunger. 'I fucking hate doing this,' he spat as he pulled on the gloves and headed back to the stairs.

Stan watched him go and then turned to stare at Pine, one eye closed, the other arched questioningly. Pine couldn't return his gaze and fidgeted sheepishly with his glass.

'Well?' Stan drew out the question.

Pine looked at me but I looked to Stan, not trusting myself to keep a straight face.

'Yes, thanks,' Pine said meekly.

Stan shook his head and sat down, looking from Pine to me and back again.

'Couple of lightweights,' he sniggered. 'You two couldn't hold your breath.'

I exhaled slowly so that he wouldn't think I was purposely contradicting him. Sometimes Stan goes off on one, and anyone, and that includes us, who pisses him off can usually expect a hard time. Relieved that his hangover was obviously keeping him mellow, I relaxed and smiled, listening to Pine ingratiate himself by changing the subject and debriefing last night.

After leaving the club they had gone for a curry before heading home. I listened to how one of the waiters had flirted with Stan to such an extent that, along with the bill, which undercharged them, he left Stan his phone number.

'So you got lucky last night?' I asked excitedly while he squirmed on his seat.

'Did I fuck.' Stan took a swing at Pine, who was grinning outrageously. 'He was a sweaty, lime-sucking, ugly, gap-toothed, spotty student.'

Pine put his head down and made a neighing sound before convulsing with laughter and palsy. I looked from one to the other.

'Maybe lucky is the wrong word,' Pine suggested helpfully.

Stan looked at Pine again and sighed.

'Come on,' I urged them.

'He was a horse.' Pine nodded.

'He was a horse,' Stan agreed.

'And not a bad jockey apparently,' Pine added, giggling at his own cleverness.

Stan's silent blushing spoke volumes.

'You never did!'

He nodded and started sniggering with Pine.

'I thought you didn't get lucky.'

'I didn't,' he said simply. 'He only looked like a horse.'

Pine held his ribs for the next round of convulsions and dodged Stan's sideswipe.

'Are you going to see him again?' I asked.

'Am I, fuck!' Stan said, sounding surprised. 'It was just sex.'

Our friendship notwithstanding, I wondered at the fundamental difference in attitudes between Stan and me. Gay and straight. In a culture where sex was highly dependent on relationship potential most straight men were faced with courting, buying drink and food and even stretching to holidays and clothes in their pursuit of sex. Even casual sex after a pub or a club was usually the result of exchanging money for Bacardi or some such and then confounded by the unstated knowledge that at least one partner was looking for something that would outlast the night. Sex for the straight man, even if single, was seldom gratuitous. There are conventions and norms that specify behaviour and expectations, a process with only occasional shortcuts that we hope will lead to sex.

I flirt, she flirts.

I buy her a drink. She lets me.

I think sex. She thinks free drink.

I ask for her phone number. She gives me it.

I think sex. She thinks more free drink.

And so on through the game until something gives.

She gives out or I give in.

That's how it works when you're straight. It's almost

impossible to bypass any step. The civilities demand it. The gay man on the other hand, like the straight female for that matter, can choose when, with whom and how often they want to have sex simply for sex's sake.

Where for the straight man gratuitous sex is the exception, when you're gay it can be the rule. Same goes if you're a predatory female. The dichotomy arises out of what is available and what is wanted. Stan's statement about not being lucky arose not from having sex with the not horse but from wanting a relationship. He hated being single and I smiled at the irony.

I'd lost count of the number of nights we'd all go sharking with mixed success, the only constant being Stan's ability to go out at any time and pick someone up with the sole intention of having sex. A subculture of consenting adults happy to shag and move on.

Looking at Stan, I thought, there are similarities between us. I think that I want a relationship. I think I'm ready. The difference is that in my search for a lover, a significant other, the chances of random sexual encounters, Donna not included as we've got history, are fairly limited. Stan, however, is still able to meet, phone and fuck all in the same night. I shook my head and smiled. Sure, I was jealous, but mostly I was pleased; he'd waited long enough to be able to.

◻ * ◻

When we were greasy-skinned moonscapes, all hormones and newly sprouted hair, every Saturday night we would go stand at No. 7 with a bottle of Merrydown and wait for the girls to show up. Any girls. No. 7, as anyone in the know knew, was the number stencilled on the lamppost outside the chippy, and for generations had been a beacon witnessing teenage rites of courtship. For as long as I could remember it always wore a tyre, a rubber necklace sat on the hunched shoulder of the pavement, thrown there in games of testosterone-gorged Hoopla. We would lean against the wall, coughing on stolen cigarettes, hands thrust deep in trench-coat pockets in our interpretation of cool – cool with a threat of menace and sophistication. With the curse of hindsight, I know we looked what we were, sacs of spunk in Sta-Prest pants all but leaking from every orifice. Ting with his headphones and sunglasses, and me all Brylcreem and Brut with imitation spats. We were fucking insane. Stan had known he was gay even then and it became clear he was ready to tell us. He knew that we knew, but in the years of our friendship we'd never spoken about it, we had waited for him to broach the subject.

He chose when we were big enough to go to No. 7.

The last incumbents had begun looking old enough to get served in pubs and so just like school we moved up a form. As we drank snakebite in his bedroom in preparation for our inaugural visit, he was rooting around in his wardrobe for his parka and we were trying to convince him to buy a trench coat when he broke it to us gently.

'I don't care who's wearing them,' he'd said. 'I refuse to look like a cunt.'

That we were standing in front of him at the time modelling said garment, new from Oxfam, and looking as trendy as sixth-formers when he stepped out of the closet and smiled mattered not a jot, it was nothing personal.

'No offence.'

Embarrassed by his own candidness he blushed but didn't look as though he regretted saying it. His bold admission confirming his sexuality in words we could understand and accept.

In our hearts we knew that he was right, we looked fucking stupid – cunt was probably going a bit far, if not by much – but *Smash Hits* told us and *TOTP* showed us that trench coats were cool. Wearing one was in actual fact about as cool as Eddie the Eagle being your dad; the ones we could afford smelt of dead old men and bleach, they scratched through cotton, and didn't fit. The sleeves had to be rolled up, frayed lining showing. That we were bog-eyed crazy enough to don them wasn't our fault, we were going through 'the change'. From back when No. 7 first saw a pack of sharp-suited sharks, through loon pants and punks, Newmanoid clones and New

Romantics in legwarmers, they, we, have ignored sense and reason and gone along with what we were told was going to work, never mind that it made us look like we got dressed in the dark at a jumble sale.

'Look like this and the girls will think you're cool.'

So we did.

And they did too. With Buck's Fizz-like enthusiasm, they glittered and flicked, all eyeshadow and pixie boots, acting Bananaramas. Stan didn't want to play, but we had to. His refusal to compromise himself, not to mention run the risk of fleas or scabies, shouted loud the fact that he wanted different things; we would have tied pelts to our hides with cat gut if Steve Wright told us one afternoon that chicks found it groovy. Stan wasn't interested and so had decided to tell us.

Having been friends since forever, we treated his outing with sensitivity and immediately began using him as a babe magnet. Our stock with the girl set at No. 7 rose at once and the kudos we accrued from having the gay friend more than made up for the discomfort of being an eighties fashion victim. Ting used this time to learn and refine his art while Stan and I would walk home alone for entirely different reasons. On the strength of my association with Stan, the same girls that Ting was kissing and groping on the swings were flirting with me. Unfortunately, intuitive as I am, I laboured under the belief that if one was talking to me it was to kill time until Ting noticed her. My misery at that time, unlike Stan's, was of my own making until, after a night of being particularly dense, Coreen Manson, and for this I still can't say her name without grinning, took my hand and shoved it up her tank top. Game on.

Stan had to wait until much later. Being boy gay was one thing, doing something with it was a different thing altogether. We were still at school and it was the eighties. As the novelty of adolescence wore on and we handed down the key to No. 7, the girls became less inclined to encourage a casual fumble and we graduated to the bars and clubs in town. Initially Stan was terrified, and it was almost a year before he let us drag him to a gay bar. That's when things changed and Stan discovered a life of hedonistic abandon that left us dead in the water. After years of watching us master the breaststroke, Stan found a different pool, and dived straight in with the other beginners.

▭ ✶ ▭

'You are a jammy bastard,' I told him. 'I bet you didn't even have to promise to ring him, did you?'

'Did that last night, I bet.' Pine laughed disgustingly.

Stan dismissed us with a nonchalant wave of his hand. 'Phoned him at three, fucked him at four and was home by five.'

'But you want a relationship,' I reminded him. 'Are you not going to give him a go? He might be one of the good guys.'

Pine neighed again and Stan punched him quiet.

'I know what I want, Pennance,' he said, standing up. 'But as our over-clever young friend here has so elegantly reminded me, the man was a horse. Only not.'

Stan stepped into the kitchen, returning with our tapas, and Josh brought us a round from the bar as the early ravers came to St Pete's en route to the clubs. Sunday was becoming the new Thursday, the magazines were saying, but I didn't think too much about it as I got confused. What would happen to Thursday, I wondered, would it go the same way as Saturday, or Black when that young upstart Brown came along? Another one to ponder on in the bath.

We attacked the plates, lining our stomachs to begin drinking again.

The first part of Ting's wake had gone well, apart from the losing him this morning bit. But even that added an element of adventure that will make a great story when I admit to what happened, in about a thousand years.

We toasted our success and Ting's foresight. His weekend was something special.

Then Stan reminded me who I was.

'You have got the train tickets for tomorrow, haven't you?'

'Not on me.' I smiled tightly, not wanting to lie outright. I couldn't tell him that there were no trains as he would undoubtedly use that as an excuse to rip my head off. 'But I've sorted us out.'

'So you've got the tickets then?'

'Stan.' I sounded exasperated. 'I said I'd take care of it and I did, okay?'

'So we –'

'Yes, we're going to Mull first thing in the morning. Okay?'

'Sure.' He shrugged. 'If you say so.'

'What about somewhere to stay?'

Now it was Pine's turn.

'That's taken care of,' I said curtly, showing them my disappointment at their lack of faith in me. 'Do you want the phone number to double-check?'

They looked at each other and shook their heads, dropping the subject. I let out a quiet sigh. I knew I'd need to tell them that there were no trains, but I figured that if I left it until the morning then I wouldn't have to face a whole world of shit tonight. Tomorrow there would be no time for them to point their fingers and cry 'fuck-up'. We'd be on our way to Mull.

□ * □

They were getting my elbow to smoke when Molly arrived with Sally and Ali.

'Here come the Beverley Sisters,' Pine announced.

'What?' I asked, twisting my arm to see what he was talking about.

'Not you, you dumpling, them.' He nodded at the door. 'Molly, Sally and Ali. Their names all stop in Lee,' he explained.

'So why the Beverley Sisters?' I asked, seeing them come in.

He shrugged. 'Coz it rhymes.'

'Are you a good hairdresser?' Stan inquired, but Pine told him to fuck off.

'Show time.' He smiled as he stood up to meet them. 'And Ali is looking like one Drop Dead Honey. Time to be cool, lover boy, you up for the Cup?'

I'd told them of my intention to make a play for Ali. Even

though I'd made no mention of this morning or why I thought
I might have any luck with her, they were supportive in my
time of need. Stan had stopped laughing long enough to wish
me luck and Pine had offered a couple of lines that he knew
but hadn't used since he met Molly. Since I was neither Italian
nor hung that way, I decided to go it alone. Cornier than corn,
I would just be me and hope that I hadn't read things wrong
at her flat. I was fairly sure that she liked me and I was determined to make her want me just as much. I would carry on
where we left off before her parents arrived, witty and charming
without being a smarmy bastard, and stay sober enough to
chivalrously offer to see her home. Up for the Cup indeed.

I smiled warmly at Ali as she followed Molly and Sally and
kissed me hello.

'You smell nice,' she said playfully against my cheek and I
all but collapsed into her arms as her hot breath melted me.
Thankful that I'd had the foresight to tell Stan only to give me
single measures for the last hour while we'd been goofing
around, I was taking my play seriously. I almost fell to the
floor entirely as she stepped past me when I realised he had
forgotten. I moved carefully to let them sit, steadying myself
against the booth, and we all squeezed together round the table,
unwilling to put Ting's bag on the floor. I was tingling because
of the pressure of Ali's leg pushing against my thigh. Her slight-
est movement caused my muscles to spasm and I could feel her
hips move as I shifted my weight. Six people can sit comfortably
around this table. Thankfully, seven is a tight squeeze.

Josh brought over a round of drinks and I took a moment
to frame myself as they swapped stories about last night. I was
surprised and grateful that Sally didn't mention about Ting,
and felt myself blush as she winked at me when no one could
see. I smiled back my gratitude. Pine was bursting to tell them
about Stan's equestrian outing but lost the chance when Sally
asked if she could come to Mull with us and the mood round
the table turned away from his jocularity.

She was looking at Ting's bag. She had purposefully sat next
to him and now she sat with her hand resting on the leather.

Sally had had an off-and-on relationship with Ting since they'd met six years ago on a kibbutz. They were seldom together for longer than a few weeks at a time and went for months without seeing each other. They were comfortable getting what they needed from being together when they wanted to. Stan was sat next to her and he put his arms round her as her eyes welled up.

'No problem, Sal, you know you're welcome.'

She looked up gratefully at him and then at Molly, a question on her face. Molly pursed her lips and nodded.

'Why not?'

Pine squeezed her knee and winked at Sally, all Arthur Daley-like.

I was nodding in agreement, distracted by Ali's unconscious manoeuvrings against my leg.

I knew that I had to stop playing the role of drunken spectator if I wanted Ali to notice me but I wasn't sure that my tongue could get off the roof of my mouth. I took a drink and it squelched clear.

'Ali can come too if she wants,' I blurted suddenly, my tongue running away with itself as it fell. I blushed instantly as I heard myself sound like a twelve-year-old excitedly inviting someone to be their girlfriend. No one spoke and I had no recourse but to fumble on. 'I mean . . . if you want her to, Sally . . .' I was floundering. '. . . If you don't want to come on your own . . .' Molly just said she was going. '. . . You know what I mean . . .' No one helped me. '. . . Well, if we're all going it seemed unfair not to ask Ali . . .' That didn't sound right. '. . . I mean, she's here, we're all talking about going and . . .' Through my thigh I could feel Ali raise her eyebrows and I involuntarily clenched my backside. 'Forget it,' I said, shaking my head. 'It doesn't matter.'

Pine was staring, slack-lipped, as Stan said, 'Way to be cool, Pennance,' and began to giggle. One by one, they started to smile and then they were all laughing. Not with me, but at me. Pine held his hand up for quiet and their laughter became a mumbling snigger as he spoke.

'Are you asking her out on a date, to a wake?'

'It wasn't a date,' I answered too quickly.

Sally must have been storing some residual good feeling because she came to my rescue.

'Right, that's settled then.' She turned to Ali. 'Ali, want to come to Mull with me?'

Still sniggering, Ali nodded. 'Yeah, it'll be cool.'

'Cool,' I said under my breath, pleased with the outcome of my little tirade. Ali pushed against me as she sat back again and I pushed my leg in response, relieved when she didn't pull away. I sat back and relaxed, listening to Elvis being 'All Shook Up' while outside my head they arranged what we'd all do in Mull.

Throw Ting into the sea. That's what we'll do, I thought. But when I pictured standing on a cliff, the wind in my back pushing me at the abyss, Ali's there and we're throwing kisses, not to the sea but to each other and there's no cliff, there's only a bed, and she's no clothes on, and . . .

Calm down, boy, I said to myself, starting to breathe again.

'Thanks for saying yes,' I said quietly to Ali, checking that no one else looked like they were listening.

She turned her head and smiled. 'I've had stranger dates,' she said warmly and turned back to Sally, leaving me staring. Racing to come up with a stranger date, I was stopped and sidetracked by Molly when she noticed my elbow.

'Why do you have lipstick on your arm, Pennance?'

Ali twisted away from me to get a look at what she was pointing at. Sally leant forward and they peered closely at my elbow. 'It *is* lipstick as well,' she said in astonishment.

Holding my arm against me protectively, I scored a point for men everywhere.

'Don't smudge my lipstick! I've only just put it on.'

Molly threw a lighter at me to show her appreciation and Sally said 'ha ha'. Best of all, Ali smiled.

'We were making his elbow smoke,' Pine told her. 'Ours can't do it, but Pennance and Ting's can.' He brushed off his mistake with an apologetic glance at Ting. 'He can smoke and sometimes we'd do gangster films or they'd have false moustaches and monocles and be all evil and sometimes' – he glanced at Stan – 'we'd do gay theatre. I'd be the narrator since I'm too tight to be gay,' he said proudly.

The girls continued to look on in confusion and Stan took control, pushing round to where I sat and taking hold of my arm.

'Look,' he told them pointlessly, as they were each leant on the table staring at my elbow. I tensed my bicep instinctively.

'Relax,' Stan admonished me with a sharp slap on my arm.

'I am,' I hissed from behind my smile, promising myself to beat him to within an inch of his life. He pulled the slack skin of my elbow with two fingers, and, stretching it enough so that he could grab it in his other hand, he showed them 'Old Man's Willy'. They groaned at the realism of it. They were less impressed by 'Unfolding Flower', the various stages of female arousal, but became enthusiastic again when Stan manipulated my elbow lips to talk to them in a voice somewhere between James Bond and *Highlander*.

'Sean Connery.' Molly clapped in delight.

Warming to his audience, Stan gave them Jack Nicholson.

'YOU CAN'T HANDLE THE TRUTH.'

Julian Clary.

'I've just been in the back fisting Norman Lamont.'

A naked hurdler, twice, because they groaned and once he'd reapplied the lipstick and drawn a pair of glasses.

'You're only supposed to blow the bloody doors off.'

Ten minutes later Molly had a thick-lipped librarian for her elbow face, Sally a bow-kissing cherub, and Ali was able to have anyone she wanted as her elbow proved to be as elastic as mine. Stan, impresario extraordinaire, threw his voice around the table, carrying on elaborate conversations while we concentrated on lip-synching. Our impromptu show ended with Thelma, a wall-flower waitress emancipating herself and finding true love with Troy, a 1950s detective whom she rescued from femme fatale Gloria and her henchman Stelvessio.

'Cool game.' Ali smiled at me and turned to Stan as Sally helped Stelvessio smoke. 'I didn't know you were a ventriloquist.' Sally and Molly shook their heads in agreement.

'I'm not,' Stan protested modestly. 'I'm just arsing about.'

'You're really good.'

Ali turned back and asked if I could do it and so I immediately began forming the excuse that would support my affirmation. Needing to buy time until I was ready to prove myself, I looked to Pine.

'Yes,' I replied, setting him up with a nod. 'Not as well as Stan but better than him.'

Pine took on a mischievous look and smiled. 'I can't throw my voice but I'll put my hand up your skirt and make your lips move.'

Ali laughed at him while he rubbed at his arm where Molly casually thumped him.

As our elbow dramatics came to a natural close and faces were rubbed out, Ali picked up the lipstick and asked whose it was.

'It goes in the drawer,' I told her, explaining that it was kept there for elbow theatre.

She handed it to Pine and he slipped it back in the drawer under the table but not before Molly caught a glimpse of something and held his arm to stop him closing it.

'What else have you got in there?' she asked.

'Just stuff,' Pine assured her, removing her hand from his arm and shutting the drawer.

Molly looked at Sally, her interest piqued. She was not giving up. 'Do you know what's in there?'

Sally shook her head. 'Ting would get papers and stuff from it but I've never really seen it open.'

'How come you've never mentioned it before?' Molly threw Pine a look.

'I don't tell you everything,' he said lightly.

'We'll talk about that later,' she replied archly, too preoccupied to deal with his foolish answer. 'Come on.' She motioned to Stan and me. 'Show us what's in it.'

Stan's shrug told her he didn't mind and I nodded for Pine to open it.

'No secrets,' he said easily. 'It's just stuff.'

He put it on the table and they leant forward to peer at it. It was a fairly ordinary drawer with ordinary things that we had collected and used over the years. In the way an old story has mystery when heard for the first time, so it held the girls.

Sally held up a tatty porn mag and gave Stan a level gaze.

'Yeah, right,' he said, raising his eyes.

Molly was flicking through Polaroids and snapshots that spanned haircuts, showing everyone the ones that made her laugh the most. Ali was looking through the official Vodka Roulette Rule Book. Amongst the papers and filters and pipes and poker chips and loose cards and condoms they sifted and poked.

'And this is whose?' Molly asked, flicking through the magazine she'd swapped from Sally.

'That'd be mine,' Pine told her matter-of-factly.

On pages 39–45 'Sindee' undressed and showered in full soft-lensed glory. Long before Molly, when Pine was still collecting stuffing for his pillow, he had a fling with a dancer he met through a client. He did her hair when she put a portfolio together and after not seeing her for months she appeared at his salon on her way to a video shoot in Barbados and gave him a copy of the magazine.

Cindy Preston.

Pine told them about her with Stan and me lending verification to his disclosure amidst the dubious glances Molly and Sally exchanged.

Molly passed Sindee around and Ali smiled at Pine as she nodded in appreciation at the photo story. Sally gave a snort of derision when she looked and went back to the photos in her hands.

'And you feel it's necessary to keep it because . . . ?' Molly asked Pine.

I could see him make the adjustments needed to turn up the charm as he took a hit and passed her a pipe. 'I can't remember the last time any of us even glanced at it,' he said, looking for and getting our support. 'It's just there. It would be a strike against childhood dreams to throw it away.' He shrugged beautifully. 'But you can if you want.'

She searched his face for any sign of duplicity before appearing to settle on a decision. Pine remained magnanimous.

'Why would I want to throw it away?' she asked him, sounding puzzled. 'If it was me, I'd keep it.'

Pine flashed her an evil grin. 'If it was you, I'd remember when I last looked at the pictures.'

'Maybe you'd better get a camera,' she retorted with a straight face.

As they continued to ferret round the drawer, he laid his head on her shoulder and closed his eyes, either power napping or porn snapping.

Suddenly, Sally guffawed. She was staring at a Polaroid and covering her mouth as though in shock. She looked up and showed me the photo before passing it to Molly.

Ting's final attempt to break into the world of show business, captured by Kodak.

Molly took it and shrugged. 'Why a picture of Tarzan?'

'Look at his face.' I pointed. 'Then look at the guy dressed as a monkey.'

She held the photo closer to her as though trying to find the right distance to bring it into focus. Ali was straining to see as Molly yelped in pleasure when like a Magic Eye she worked out what she was looking at.

'What's the monkey holding?' Ali asked, still unable to work it out.

'Well, it could be a banana,' Stan suggested. 'But it looks a little too straight for that.'

Her eyes went wide like Sally's as she got it.

'What's he wearing?' Ali was pointing at Tarzan's head.

'That would be a porn perm.'

'Ting was in a porn film?' they screeched in unison.

'Not quite,' Stan told them. 'He ran a mile when he realised.'

Ting had enjoyed a short trek along the boards for an

amateur dramatics group under the patronage of an ageing queen from the theatre set that Stan had befriended in the café. After a walk-on in *An Inspector Calls*, Ting's ego was massaged enough for him to believe his greying friend when he suggested he could get him a part in a promotional video being shot locally and put him in reach of an Equity card. Locally had meant upstairs in his town house, and the production team was a bloke called Bubba in a monkey suit who was warming up by screwing a camcorder to a tripod at the bottom of the bed. Although drunk on ambition, by the time the first Polaroid had dried, Ting had snatched it and run from the house, leaving half his clothes and all his theatrical aspirations behind.

He combed his perm out the very next day.

Intrigued by what other golden moments lay captured in the drawer, they started to root through more photos just as I heard a wet cough behind me. We all looked round together to find the diminutive Jojo approaching the booth.

'C'mon,' he coughed at Stan. 'Yir car.'

□ * □

Harry and Jojo had brought Stan's car on the back of a borrowed truck and he'd gone to open the gates to the back yard while we put everything back in the drawer. Ray had told them about our accident and asked them to bring the car round to the lockup behind the café for safekeeping until Stan had time to get it to a garage. Ray's nice like that.

Pleased as Stan was that his car would now be safely locked up until we got back from Mull, it stuck me right in the glue. I needed his car, broken down and sitting by the side of the road waiting to be recovered. I needed the AA.

I needed a drink.

It was too late to rethink my plan, and due to the fact that I didn't have a plan B, I was stuck with it. What I needed to do was to believe that it would still work. At least that's what Ting always told me. 'What you expect to get, is what you get,' he'd said.

I tried to believe him and though the fear rose ugly in my stomach, I thought positively. It would still work. We would get to Mull.

Sally and Ali had gone to the toilet. In that way that I will never understand, they seemed able to orchestrate their toilet visits so that when one stood, the other knew where she was going and automatically followed. I knew that they'd lived together and that when girls share houses they get into the habit of doing some things together – shopping, menstruating. But even then there were some things that had to be done separately. I didn't suppose for a second that if they were in a house or a flat with friends they would need to go to the toilet in twos, even at a stranger's house, but in that case why did they, and most of the sisterhood, do it when they were out? Scared of the bogeyman maybe. Stan gimmicked this to the delight of his female customers: one cubicle, two toilets.

They were still not back when Stan returned with Harry and Jojo.

'We're no stayin',' Harry said as we made room for them. 'Ah'll huv this an then wir off.'

He filled two half-pint glasses from a bottle of whisky Stan handed him and passed one to Jojo; they clinked tumblers and we raised ours and toasted Ting with them. I'd known Harry through Ting. He was a graduate from the Carter school. Connected in some very low places, he was what they called a 'Known Man'. As a child Ting had called him Uncle Harry, and for his part, Harry was just that, a friendly giant of a man with a big heart who would chase us around the garden or park. It wasn't until later that we found out that other people had an entirely different perception of him. If he walked down the street the hard men would climb lampposts to avoid catching his eye. Occasionally, when we got older, he would give Ting and me cider tokens to help him at his warehouse, an Aladdin's cave of crates and boxes that had shown no obvious distress at having fallen off the back of various lorries. Ray found out about our extra pocket money and told Harry to stop it; he didn't want Ting involved. That was the last time we went to the warehouse to this day. I'd never worked out Ray and Harry's relationship and it wasn't the kind of thing you just come out and ask. 'Oh, by the way, Ray, how come you can make one phone call and a big man like Harry does as you tell him?' But it was as strong now as it was then.

I'd nearly fallen off the floor when I found out that Harry actually was Molly's uncle, and Ting had put her obvious refusal to be attracted to him when she first moved here down to the fact that they were practically related.

'How are you doing, Molly doll?'

Harry gave her a smile as he squeezed his considerable bulk into the space beside her. She lifted Pine's head from her shoulder, reached over and gave him a kiss.

'Good, thanks, Harry.' She smiled as Pine snuggled up again, caught between his dreams and knowing he should be awake. 'How are you? I haven't seen you for ages.'

He shuffled in his seat as though caught stealing the teacher's apple. Jojo coughed and he looked round at him for a second.

'Bin away workin' so we huv, me and the man here.' It was obvious that he didn't want to be drawn. 'How's yir da? You been away home?' he asked with his eyebrows raised.

Sometimes Harry's gruff manner and over-developed frame led people to believe he was not quite the full shilling. His bulk disguised a sharp mind that was more than able to deflate those who believed the misconception of their eyes. Now it was Molly's turn to squirm. She hadn't visited her parents in over six months and apparently Harry knew that.

'Whit aboot Pinaldi there?' He nodded at Pine, who had regressed again to his own Polaroid fantasy. 'He treating you okay?'

Molly stroked Pine's head as he snuggled against her shoulder and sighed. 'He's just dreamy, Uncle Harry.' She giggled, nudging him awake.

Miffed at being woken but unable to think of a suitable rejoinder in his dream-fuzzed state, Pine probed at her with his elbow and earned a questioning look from Harry and a cough of surprise from Jojo. I'd barely heard Jojo speak at all in the years that I'd known him; his vocal cords seemed to be worn out.

He had a cough bubble lodged in his throat that he'd been trying to shift for at least two decades and had decided long ago that the less he spoke the less he was irritated by it. Strangely enough, the less he spoke the more he was irritating; his word rationing reduced even the most straightforward of sentences to almost unintelligible and seemingly random exclamations.

Pine sat up straight under Harry's stare, unsure whether he was being reprimanded or the butt of a joke, though wisely he decided it wasn't worth making a mistake.

'Y' styin'?' Jojo coughed and Pine froze, his eyes darting from Molly to Harry to Jojo, confusion painted on his face.

'Wair yeh crashin' oot noo?' Harry tutted and repeated for Jojo who had disappeared into an off-white hankie as he held his hand over his mouth to catch a lung.

Pine looked on helplessly. When he first began dating Molly, he had turned up at my door one night with a bottle of tequila and a need to lock the door and close the curtains. Halfway down the bottle he was calm enough to explain that he'd just been for a drive with Harry. Nothing happened, he was spoken to for twenty minutes then dropped off back home. He knew Harry so he wasn't afraid at the time, not until he was dropped off and Harry thrust his head out the window as the car drew away.

'In yeh bet hirmember that,' he'd said.

'Pennance,' he told me, 'I don't know what he said, if I've been warned off, been welcomed to the family, or been propositioned, I couldn't understand a word he fucking said other than "Mamolly", "Ya wee spic cunt", and something about "greeting cards, Marx and doing something". What the fuck am I supposed to do now?'

'We phone Ting,' I'd told him. 'He'll sort you out.'

And we did, and he did. Greeting, he explained, was crying, a doing was what the wee spic cunt could expect if he ever made Molly greet, his card would be marked and it involved big sticks, bones and pain. Other than that he had the big man's blessing, which was nice.

'He's staying with me,' Molly answered for him. 'His flat's a mess. The fire burnt out in the front room, but there was smoke damage throughout the whole flat.'

'Aye, so ah hear.' Harry nodded.

'Fucks.'

Pine nodded; sometimes Jojo's conciseness hit the spot.

'Okeydokey.' Harry smiled to Pine's comical relief. 'You got the keys?' Pine looked on in surprise as Molly lifted his house keys from her bag and handed them to Harry. 'Right then, Jojo, let's shoot the crow.' Harry kissed Molly and slapped Pine affectionately as he stood. 'Watch yourselves, boys,' he said, shaking our hands and patting Ting's bag affectionately.

'And girls.' Molly told him that they were coming with us.

'And girls,' he amended. 'Take good care of this boy now, don't go losin' him neither.'

We mumbled our assurances that we'd be fine, and I told him we would take good care of him. He smiled again and shook his head. 'I doubt it severely,' he said as he turned and Jojo coughed his goodbyes. 'But I'm sure you'll try.'

Pine was staring at Molly while Stan walked them to the door, thanking them again for bringing his car round. 'What was that about?' he asked her as I scanned the café, looking to see where Ali had gotten to. I was working hard remembering not to think about the car and was in need of distraction.

'Nothing to worry about.' Molly patted his head and settled back into her seat.

'Why did you give him the keys to my flat?'

I'd given up searching for Ali, deciding that they must still be in the toilet, and turned to listen to Molly. I was wondering that myself.

'He's found out who did it and they've volunteered to re-decorate it as an apology.'

'Oh.' The casualness in her voice had left him speechless.

'Nothing to do with us,' she continued, squeezing his hand as he came to terms with the enormity of her understatement.

'Harry'll take care of it and let us know when it's done to his satisfaction.' She looked radiant as she finished. 'He said to think of it as an early wedding present.'

'Oh.'

I loved Molly like a sister, but I didn't envy Pine becoming part of that particular family. If nothing else it would certainly curb his natural tendency to play at being clever, at least with Molly and certainly with Harry, but more than that it would be an education. For once, he was to be the one with the cold corn-beef legs. Molly had sneaked into his comfortable wardrobe and thrown out all his suits from Miss Oginy for Men. The only trousers to be found in their relationship were the ones that Molly sat wearing. The gradual debagging which normally paces a couple's time together became an overnight certainty last week when Pine was forced to move in with her.

He lay his head back against her shoulder and I passed her a drink as she winked at me.

I smiled, thinking that Pine had just felt the first rush of cold air up his skirt.

▭ * ▭

Sally and Ali were still not back from the toilet by the time Pine was sufficiently composed to skin up and I was beginning to think they'd done a runner. Stan was helping Josh behind the bar and Molly and I were on paper, scissors and rock to see who would go to the bar. Best of three wins had progressed to best of one hundred and twenty-seven before they came giggling back. Molly asked them if they wanted a drink and sat smiling when they told me what they wanted. I mumbled my way to the bar and cleared my head by looking through the CD collection while Stan poured our drinks. Smiling as I found Luther Van Dross, I slipped him into the system and effectively brought the lights down.

'A bit obvious?' Stan was giggling as we walked back to the booth. 'Why don't you go the whole hog and get all Big Bad Barry on her, let the girl know what you really want?'

'That's my secret weapon,' I said, tapping my nose, 'but I'm only going to use him if all else fails, and at that point if big Baz doesn't work, I'll know it's not me she's not attracted to, it's men as a species.'

'Not that I could even imagine such a thing.' Stan shivered. 'Not being attracted to men, how could that happen?' He cleared his head of such disturbing thoughts and raised his eyebrows. 'But what then, what if she was a weirdo like you and liked women?'

'Then I'd have to rethink my strategy, maybe ask her if she knew I had breasts.' I stopped short of the table and watched Ali as she laughed at something Molly was saying, her arm round Sally's waist as they sat together. 'I'll tell you what though, Stan, I get the feeling that this is going to happen.' I looked at him and felt a lump rise in my throat as I spoke. 'It feels right, I don't know why but it's more than just getting her into bed, it's . . . it's . . .' It's what? I asked myself as I paused to swallow. Love? It was absurd. I didn't love Ali, I didn't know her. I couldn't love her when all I knew about her was that she smelt of easy mornings and that she left me gooey every time we touched; that couldn't be enough. I was drunk but I wasn't that drunk. But I must have been. 'I'm not sure what it is, but I think I've fallen for her and I don't even know who she is, I just know that I want to find out. And so what if it doesn't work out? I won't even think that because it will. I'm totally serious, Stan, I'm doolally for this girl.'

'Fuck sake, Pennance, I was only having a giggle.' He was looking at me funny and I felt I'd just confessed to wanting to shag his gran, then his eyes sparkled. 'Go for it, and I'll watch out for the right moment for Baz.' He smiled. 'Only if you need him of course.'

''Course I won't fucking need him,' I said with a self-deluded grin. 'Step back and let me get to work.'

Chapter 12

same world . . .

The café was shut and Big Bad Barry boomed from every speaker. Stan was arranging six shot glasses on a tray in front of him and explaining the basics of Vodka Roulette. Now that I was in love with Ali I'd hoped to get drunk enough not to tell her before she fell in love with me. I was flirting with the subtlety of Tyson in your ear and pulling it off as Ali thought that a performance this bad had to be staged. She laughed at my lines and looked straight at me when she spoke, the rest of the table minor players as I got her full attention. She nodded enthusiastically when I confessed that I didn't know where to look when I was talking to her, to anyone, whether to look at one eye or the mouth, or to flit between the eyes really quickly. She giggled when I showed her what I meant and got dizzy when she tried it and fell into my arms in delight. I might have been clumsy and trying to be charming but I seemed to be winning with funny, even if it was inadvertent. I think I may have made a sound deep in my throat as I felt her weight against my shoulder. It was at that point that I decided to slip my arm round her back. Naturally Stan chose the same moment to clap his hands to get our attention and she sat out of my reach as he explained the rules. Foiled, I leant forward and prepared the drinks and listened to Stan, not because I couldn't remember the rules, but to make sure he wasn't adding any of his own; he'd need committee approval for that but he wasn't above trying to sneak one in anyway. That's why the rules were in a constant state of flux for such a long time. It got so out of hand that we spent more time checking the rules than playing and had been forced to write them all down, leaving out some of the more outlandish. We still had a full set of secondary rules addressing issues such as time-keeping, dry-heaving, spillage and style with a whole subset dealing with forfeits and non-compliance but, having glanced through them, Ali announced that she found then too restrictive for an introduction to the game. I imagine that she found the attention to detail outlined in the official rule book to be a tad anal but was too polite to say so. We had, if truth be known, spent an inordinate amount of time constructing the game parameters. I felt proud of it, both in its simplicity and its sophistication, not to mention the creativity we had shown in writing and colouring in the rule book. Stan was giving them the beginner's version.

Those rules are simple enough. Six shot glasses on a tray. One with water, five with vodka. The tray gets spun and the glasses emptied one at a time until the water is reached. After each round the glasses are filled again so that each player has a full tray to begin with. The winner was usually the last person to be sick but tonight, being amateur night, it was to be last man standing. Waving Stan on, the girls were eager to play, so with a flourish he spun the tray.

'Ladies first!' he shouted, picking up the first glass and toasting Ting. He got water on his third glass, Molly on her second and Pine on his third. I was unlucky enough to get it on my first but was ignored when I asked for another go. Pine reminded me that we weren't using the proper rules. Ali hit it on her fifth making her gag and giggle in equal amounts, whilst Sally choked on her third but got water on her fourth. By the time Barry had played out we were groggily clapping as Molly took a careful bow, having beaten Stan in a final quickfire round that ended when he ran to the toilet. I stood and staggered after him.

▭ ★ ▭

Leaning with my forehead on the wall in front of me, I had a pee on Jimmy Hill. I soaked his beard and made a waterfall from the end of his chin, so that I had to step back to avoid it splashing on me. The toilets at St Pete's had always been popular. Stan had ripped out the original urinals and replaced them with a perspex trough behind which there were four television monitors playing videos from behind the bar. He encouraged his customers to bring their own videos in and was happy to play them. Opera, Michael Bolton, Australian cricket, ex-girlfriends, football teams and politicians all had a showing. Along with Maradona and Beadle, Jimmy Hill was a firm favourite.

I stood at the hand dryer until I got bored. Rubbing my hands dry on my trousers, I gurned in the metal plate mirror and practised smiling as Stan dialled the big white telephone. Pine came through the door with a pint of water for him and asked how I was getting on with Ali. I explained that my subliminal strategy was working better than I had hoped. She thought I was funny, and I was ready to go in for the thrill.

'Don't leave it too long,' he said over his shoulder. 'Sally's upstairs ordering a taxi.'

Armed with this new information, I headed back to the table with Pine one step behind me. I was determined to win her hand before Sally snatched it out of my grasp.

I settled in next to her and tried to catch her attention by looking serious. I think I must have climbed the stairs from the toilets too quickly because I was feeling light-headed. Nothing to do with the vodka.

'Have you had any Italian in you?' I slurred as she turned to face me.

Pine pushed in beside me and casually collapsed into a heap of giggles.

'What?' she said. She looked at Pine and then slowly smiled at me. 'Oh. Right, I get you. Em . . . no. Have you?'

'No,' I mumbled, unable to see where I'd gone wrong.

'What he meant to say' – Pine shook his head, wiped his eyes and helped me out – 'was do you have any thick useless bastard in you.'

I was trying to kick him under the table but drove my heel into my own ankle. I stifled a cry, hoping that Ali's giggling meant she thought this was all part of my dumbing up my flirting.

'And then he says . . .' He turned to me and drew his lips back in a grin.

'He says fuck off, Pine, and leave him alone.' I pushed him off the bench and he sat round with Molly and laughed.

I sat there, mortified.

'I'm just going to lie under the table for a little bit,' I told them. 'I won't make any noise.'

Pine was still laughing when Molly lifted him away from the booth. She gave me an encouraging smile as she passed. Alone at the table with Ali, I slowed my descent and peered up at her from just above the table's edge. She was still smiling.

'I'm crap at this, aren't I?'

She stopped laughing and looked at me for a few seconds as though seeing me for the first time. She grinned, but didn't shake her head.

'Yes.'

I collapsed onto my knees and gave her my best shot. Nothing to lose now, said the vodka. 'Don't go home with Sally.' I stuck my bottom lip out. 'Please.'

'I'm not.'

I pulled myself up straight and squinted at her as Stan started to turn off the lights and Sally shouted from the door that the taxis had arrived. 'So what are you doing?' I could feel myself slowly leaning forward but I was powerless to stop it. She put her hand on my chest to stop me falling and I could feel its sobering power as her touch worked its magic.

'I was hoping that you were going to offer to see me home, but if you're wanting to stay here . . .' Her voice trailed off as I became one big sparkling smile.

She took my hand as we walked to the door and in a moment of sensitivity I asked her if Sally was okay about it, us.

'Us what? You seeing me home? I think she can handle it. I spoke to her earlier when Molly's uncle was here and she's cool.'

'You mean you've known all night that you . . . that we . . .'

Stan was leaning on the bar tapping the Barry White CD box and whistling. I wasn't the only one who was out of tune. 'Why didn't you tell me? Why didn't you let me know?'

She shrugged and pulled me out to the taxi as we shouted good night to everyone. 'You were trying so hard and it was so much fun that we thought it would be a shame to stop you.'

'We?'

She nodded and laughed and I realised I didn't care that I'd been outplayed all night, it was the result that counted. I'd scored and was walking to the undressing room with the trophy.

▭ * ▭

We held hands in the taxi. I was unwilling to let go in case I woke up. I'd watched enough films to know that the dream scene always ended when you stopped holding hands and I wasn't ready to fall yet. I shut my eyes as I stepped from the taxi and sighed with relief when I heard Ali step out behind me, still real. As she ran her hand down my back I knew for certain I wasn't dreaming. Barefoot in the flat, Ali handed me a bottle of wine and a corkscrew and suggested I put some music on while she got herself together and found some glasses. Dana Gillespie whispered moodily in my ear as I walked to her bedroom and waited for her to finish in the bathroom.

In the bedroom I found the rocking chair that just had to be there and placed the open wine on the dressing table beside it. Almost in a trance, or a stupor maybe, I glided around the room lighting candles, softening images and creating expectations with the distorted balance so essential in seduction. Satisfied that the rocking chair was in sufficient shadow for me to relax, I sat back and waited for Ali, feeling myself grow in anticipation. Rocking gently, I smiled; this was turning out to be the best wake ever. Ting, you are a genius right enough.

▭ * ▭

I was so stiff it hurt. And I was cold. And I was alone.

It took me a moment to realise where I was and another to realise that it wasn't dark any more. And I was still sat, stiffly, on the rocking chair. Fully dressed. And waiting for Ali.

I rocked myself out of the chair, careful not to wake my headache just yet, and looked round me in confusion. Where was Ali? Where was her duvet? Carefully I walked from the bedroom and stood in the hallway listening. My head tilted and my ear cocked, I turned towards the living room where I could hear the sounds of morning traffic. Stepping gingerly towards the not quite closed door, I peeked inside and saw that the window was open, the TV was sizzling away quietly and Ali was asleep on the couch. The bottle of wine I'd opened lay empty on the table in front of her. Thinking that the noise from the street would wake her, I made my way over on tiptoe to the window to close it. It was an old sash window and, as I began to slowly slide it shut, it juddered and then slammed down noisily on my thumbs. I bit down on my lip to stop from screaming and jammed my hands under my arms. I'd have to leave the room before I allowed them to start throbbing and allowed myself to cry.

'Oh, you've decided to wake up?'

Ali had shuffled onto her side and squinted up at me. The duvet that covered her had slipped and I could see that the straps of the T-shirt she was wearing had fallen down. I forced a smile.

'Morning.' I sounded hoarse. 'I was closing the window to keep the noise out,' I said by way of explanation of her waking to me standing staring at her.

'So I heard.'

She leant up on one arm and stretched and I fell into the chair opposite.

'The sash is broken on that window.' She yawned. 'I hope you didn't catch your fingers when it fell?' She shook off a chill and pulled the duvet tightly around her.

'I'm not entirely stupid,' I lied, placing my hands casually in my lap. 'I can manage to close a window.'

'What time is it?'

I looked at my watch as she uncurled herself and slowly stretched her muscles.

'It's nearly eight,' I told her when I was able to speak again. 'I'm going to have to go. We're meeting at the café and I've got to get home first.'

She nodded but didn't say anything because she was yawning again.

'Ali.' I paused, unsure how to ask the right question. 'What happened last night?'

'Well, we all spent the night in the café.' She looked at me for confirmation.

'No. I mean after that.' I sat up in the chair and hugged a cushion to me so as to breathe out and keep my thumbs subdued. 'I know we got a taxi here, I opened a bottle of wine and waited for you in the bedroom.'

'Yes, I want to talk to you about that.'

'Then I woke up and you're in here. What happened?'

'What happened is that you fell asleep on my rocking chair leaving every candle in the room lit.'

'But where were you? I was waiting for you to finish in the bathroom and I must have dozed off. Why didn't you wake me?'

'I wasn't in the bathroom. You were putting some music on and I was in the kitchen. When I came back I thought you'd gone to the bathroom so I sat and waited for ages and then got worried that you were being sick or something.' She sat up and wrapped her duvet round her once more. 'When I came to see if you were all right I found you asleep on the chair.'

'Why didn't you wake me?' I asked, embarrassed.

'There didn't seem much point. You were obviously in no fit state to talk, so rather than wake you and send you home I thought I'd just nip into bed and leave you in peace. But now that you're awake . . .' She folded her arms meaningfully. 'Tell me, what did you think you were doing in my bedroom with all those candles?'

Eh? Had I misread every sign? I was invited back here, she

did tell me to get comfortable. I thought we were going to go to bed. She thought we were going to sit and bond some more. What planet was she from? I could feel my face burning as she fought a smile at my discomfort. She knew exactly what I'd had in mind. I shrugged.

'I was going for a bit of mood lighting.' I grinned sheepishly to distract her from my embarrassment. 'I was hoping you were going to ravish me.'

'Well, at least you're honest.' Now she did allow the smile to take hold. 'But no, sorry. I'm strictly a second-date girl.'

'And I'm sorry for falling asleep.'

'Don't worry about it,' she assured me. 'If you hadn't you wouldn't be here this morning and I would have had no one to make me a quick cup of coffee.'

Sharp as ever, I was on my way to the kitchen almost before she pointed.

I handed her a steaming cup of wake-me-up.

'I've got to go. But I'll see you in Mull.' I stepped away and gazed down at her as she blew on her coffee. 'You are still coming, aren't you?'

She nodded and took a scalding sip from the mug.

'Good.' I leant forward to give her a kiss and she turned her head so that I got her cheek.

'Egh.' She recoiled and laughed, careful not to spill her coffee on the duvet. 'Morning breath.'

I laughed and said goodbye walking to the door. Then I stopped, my hand on the handle as confusion grabbed me again. I turned back to Ali who was now leaning over the couch watching me go. She was still smiling.

'You said you left me to sleep and went to bed?'

She nodded.

'Then how come you're lying on the couch this morning.'

'Pennance.' She laughed delightedly and I instinctively knew that I was blushing again. 'You snore so loud you should carry a health warning.'

I mumbled some apology, shuffled out of the flat, curled into a ball and sobbed.

the road less travelled

'You've forgotten your bag.'

I turned around in panic as I was putting the key in the door. Not again. But no, this time I was sure, Stan took Ting home last night. I remembered making damn sure that it wasn't me. Molly was grinning at me from the passenger seat of Sally's car. They had drawn up alongside the door as the taxi I'd gotten from Ali's dropped me off. Realising that she thought I was leaving the house, I shouted that I'd only be a minute and ran into the flat to pack a bag, grab a quick wash and phone the AA.

Apologising for being late, I jumped in the back of Sally's car as she headed to the café to drop Pine and me off on her way to pick Ali up.

They'd decided to drive to Mull.

'What time's your train?'

I had my head resting against the window and was trying not to fall asleep as the engine purred against my ear. Pine elbowed me in the ribs and nodded at the mirror. Sally was talking to me.

'Change of plan,' I said with a confidence I didn't believe. 'Just drop us at St Pete's.' Pine and Molly exchanged glances as I turned back against the window. 'Trust me.'

'I hate it when he says that.' Pine shook his head and shut his eyes.

I was woken by a slap of cold air as Molly opened the car door. We stood outside the café saying goodbye. We arranged where to meet and stood watching them drive off.

'Well?'

'Let's get Stan and I'll explain.' I held the door open and ushered him into the café where Stan was busy with the breakfast crowd.

Stan stumbled between the tables, the convivial host in grey skin and sweat sheen, topping up cups and conversations with the ease of the consummate professional. He had an unerring ability to remember names and faces, who had what kids and dreams, where they worked and what they came to the café for. It's why he was successful. He was everyone's friend; even this morning when he was obviously not at his best he still managed to smile at his customers and carry a tray of drinks without spilling too much of them.

Pine went straight to the toilet and I waved to Stan before walking through the kitchen to the yard at the back. His car had been left in front of the steel security gates holding the street at bay. Now even more than before I was worried that I had really fucked up. Calming myself down, I walked back into the kitchen and found the keys for the gate.

I was sitting uncomfortably at our table by the time Stan brought Ting from behind the bar and sat across from me with the bag on the table in front of us. Our booth was the only one not full and Stan sat with his back to the café to get away from his demanding public.

Pine slipped in next to me and folding his arms on the table in front of him, he looked over Ting at Stan.

'So how are we getting to Mull?'

'What?' Stan glanced at me through hollow eyes and then frowned at Pine. 'What're you talking about? We're getting the train.'

'I thought you said there was a change of plan?' Pine sat back on his seat, looking at me, confusion clear on his face.

Now that they were both staring at me, I felt my brow dampen.

'What time is the train, Pennance?' Stan spoke slowly, precisely.

'There're no trains,' I said as they both closed their eyes without a word. 'But it's not a problem. I've got it under control, trust me.' I was proud of myself for keeping a level tone.

They sat in silence, nodding, and I was touched by the faith they had in me.

'So how are we getting to Mull?'

'Stan. I thought I asked you to trust me?' I looked at Pine. 'See, Pine trusts me.'

'Of course I do,' he said with a quick look to Stan. 'But how are we getting to Mull?'

'Thanks very much.'

I still wasn't sure how to tell them when I wasn't so sure myself. But I'd run out of time.

'We're driving.'

'Who's driving?' Pine asked, looking round quickly. 'I'm not driving, I can't drive, I'm still pissed, and I've just been sick.'

'Don't worry, you're not.'

'Don't look at me,' Stan said, folding his arms.

'Relax, none of us are driving.'

I knew I was infuriating them but in a way it was too good an opportunity to miss. Both of them were storytellers, spinners of yarns. Their sense of occasion always had an edge of drama about it, explanations always elaborate and confusing until they revealed all and produced the flowers from their sleeves. But they suffered the affliction of the extrovert. The need to be in control. To create the mystery, not be a victim of it. Although I was tense that I'd screwed up getting the train, I was enjoying my moment while there was still a chance that it would work out.

'So?'

'A little bit of faith is all I'm asking for here.'

'Sure. Who's driving?'

'Let me see if I've got this right, Pennance.' Stan spoke quietly as though too exhausted to be bothered, too used to it for it to require any effort. 'We're not getting the train, we're driving, but we're not driving.'

'That's about the size of it.'

'So who,' Pine asked while Stan calmed down, 'is driving?'

Pausing for maximum dramatic effect, I slowly pointed beyond Stan's shoulder.

'He is.'

'I most certainly am fucking not.'

'Not you,' I said, disgusted that my theatre was lost on him. 'Him.'

I stood up and walked to the door, leaving Pine and Stan to wonder at the sudden appearance of the fourth emergency service.

□ ★ □

Yesterday, outside the station, I did what all lapsed Catholics do in an emergency. I told God that this would be a good time to work one of those miracles that priests are so fond of if He wanted me to even think about relapsing. Then the priest turned up and dropped his leaflet in my lap. An hour later I was a fully paid up member of the AA with breakdown and recovery cover.

For an additional premium, which the helpful assistant thought she talked me into paying, we could be taken to our destination, and our vehicle repaired there or towed home again should we ever require such a thing. God forbid. The best thing about it was that even with the added premium, it was still cheaper than taking the train. When I had called from the flat this morning the operator commented on my foresight in taking out cover before embarking on such a long journey and assured me of a prompt response. Divine providence, she had laughed. Possibly, I thought at the time, but there was still a lot of work to do to repair the damage Father McGonagall had inflicted before such a small gesture would sway me. But it was a start, and I most definitely appreciated it.

I walked round to Stan's car with the patrolman and showed him the damage.

'Damnedest thing,' I said, shaking my head. 'We were sitting having a coffee and then we heard an almighty crash.'

I stood in front of the car, looking outraged.

'The fucking bin lorry had reversed into it.' I turned to face him but he had bent down to examine the damage. 'Can you believe it?'

'No,' he said, before disappearing under the bonnet.

'What?'

I bent down to look at him in shock. Did I just hear right? I knew it wasn't the best of stories, but considering the alternatives it was the best I had. I hadn't anticipated that the car would have been moved here. Stan's Golf had concertinaed, and since it was backed up an alley, the only way it could have happened, if it happened here, was for something to have rammed it. Otherwise it would have had to have been thrown off the roof. The alley behind it was closed off by bollards so there was no way it could have been travelling fast enough to hit something and sustain the damage it did. My first thought had been to roll the car out the gate and onto the road, but images of policemen and breathalysers rolled it back in. All in all, the bin lorry was my best option, and the cynical bastard was already scuppering it.

'I don't believe it.' He started scribbling on his pad. 'Do you know how fast that lorry would have had to be reversing to cause this damage?'

'No.' I didn't have to pretend to be confused.

'Where is the broken glass from the lights?'

He resumed walking round the car.

'I don't know. It was a bin lorry for fuck sake, maybe they cleared it up.'

He stopped walking and slammed the rain cover on his clipboard.

'That's it, smart arse.' He threw a slip of paper on the roof and turned to walk away. 'Sort yourself out.'

'Okay, I'm sorry.' I was beginning to panic. 'It wasn't a lorry, it was a car. I ran into it.'

'Go on,' he prompted me. Standing with his arms behind his back, he looked for all the world like a disinterested Bobby listening to yet another tale of circumstance and woe. 'I'm listening.'

I told him I had been too embarrassed to tell him the truth and he smiled and asked where the other car was.

'It drove away.' I shrugged.

'And took all the glass?' He made a deal of brushing down his uniform and I got the impression he was waiting.

Behind him, Stan and Pine appeared from round the corner and began walking towards us. My mind was racing, this was not turning out how it was supposed to. With nothing to lose I offered him money.

'Fifty quid.'

He snorted in derision and walked off.

'A hundred.'

'What's happening?' Stan asked as he came over.

In spite of the testimony of the medical profession, I think I sobered up enough in the next two heartbeats to drive us to Mull, as it now seemed likely I would be forced to do. If I could borrow a car. And learn to drive. The patrolman stopped in front of Stan and Pine and pointed back at the car.

'Sorry, boys, that car's not going anywhere.' He turned as though looking at the car and winked at me. 'I'll just bring round the truck and we'll be off. Back in a minute.'

'Pennance?'

It took a moment for me to swallow my heart before I could explain.

We piled into the cab of the truck while Stan's car was loaded on the back.

'And he believed you?' Pine was passing round the Stella and shaking his head.

'Yes.' I spoke in an offhand way. 'Why wouldn't he?' I shrugged and took a can. I needed a drink.

'Didn't he ask about the other car? Or where the bumper was?' Pine was amazed that it had worked. 'I can't believe he didn't suss you.' He raised his can in salute.

'I don't think he's that bright,' I said quietly and settled into my seat, Ting on my lap.

Pine was smiling and even Stan had a wry smile on his face. I felt relief wash over me. Things were turning out all right after all.

The door opened and the engine fired up with a throaty

growl. Colin, according to the name sewn in his shirt, shrugged out of his coat and picked up the two fifties I'd left on the seat. He smiled at me in the mirror and I winked.

'No drinking in the cab,' he said, pulling onto the road. 'Sorry, lads, I don't make the rules, I just follow them.'

The irony wasn't lost on me as I shut my eyes, my ears ringing from New Order's 'Blue Monday' competing with the sound of Pine and Stan snapping their heads round to stare me to death.

CHAPTER 14

re member

As we joined the traffic, curiosity got the better of him. I watched in the mirror and could see him shifting his eyes trying to work out whether he could talk to us. He knew we had reacted badly to his jobsworth attitude and could feel the tension it had caused, but it was going to be a long drive.

'So what you boys up to in Mull?' he asked lightly.

Always open to opportunity, and able to recognise it for what it was, Pine slipped into character and explained about Ting and the wake and how we were now on our way to send him on his. He called him Colin when he spoke, establishing an intimacy that brought him into our story. Somewhere in Pine's backwater cousin-loving ancestry, his family had lived through famine by selling curses and potions. In his mind it was true and not the Puzo fable we sceptically believed he was ripping off. Names gave power, everyone in his family knew that, that's why he gave up on nursing. Name badges. Allegedly.

His eyes a little wide, Colin went silent for a bit before licking his lips and asking, 'Is that him there?'

Pine patted the bag on my knee and went back to contemplating the road without a further word. Pissed off with the way things had turned out, I folded my arms and closed my eyes. I could feel the weight of Ting's bag on my legs and the heavier weight of Stan's disappointment. I leant against the window and tried not to think about how it had turned out, this last journey of ours, hoping sleep would come and take me.

It did.

The road cut an endless path of grey through the countryside, a scythe through the grass taking us along for the ride, oblivious of our reasons. I could feel my mood being drawn down into the bitumen.

An angry horn woke me to a traffic jam, and in true Monday morning style I opened my eyes to find that we were still within the city limits, bumper to bumper in every lane. Stan was sleeping and Pine was staring quietly out of the window that I was leaning against.

'Sorry about this,' I said quietly to his reflection. 'This hasn't worked out as well as I thought it would.'

He smiled in the window and I turned to face him as he laughed lightly.

'Don't worry about it.' He punched me softly on the arm. 'How could we give Ting a wake without having you fuck up at least once, if only for the sake of authenticity?'

'What?' I pushed him away, feigning injury.

'Well, you know what I mean. Ting even told us once' – he shook his head as though lost in thought – 'years ago, not long after we first came up with the idea . . . I don't remember where you were but he told us not to give you a hard time if he went first and you fucked up. He said it would make it more memorable. More real.' He looked at Stan and laughed again. 'Something for the man here to moan about.'

'Well,' I sniggered. 'I'd hate to disappoint anyone.'

'No fear.'

He reached down to his feet and then handed me an open carton of milk. Parched, I took a long drink before spluttering and blowing as though my mouth was on fire.

Vodka.

My milk moustache covered me from Colin's inquisitive gaze but my eyes were watering when I handed the carton back to a smiling Pine.

'That's my tree.'

Pine was pointing at the border of the park that we were crawling alongside.

And it was too.

'And there's yours.'

'There's Ting's.'

'That one with all the blossoms on is Stan's.' Pine glanced at Stan's recumbent form. 'Do you think we should wake him, he might want to see it in bloom.'

'Mmmm.' I screwed my face up in concentration. 'Maybe we'll just leave him, eh? Safer that way.'

He nodded and we sat back, drinking the milk and watching life in the park slowly slip by.

They were our trees. Or at least we planted them.

It was part of our community service.

◻ * ◻

For Ting's eighteenth birthday we'd organised a party.

A Lethal Weapon party.

We hired the church hall and fitted it out with film posters and strobe lights. We had a glitter ball, a DJ with his own kit, and had printed up the BYOB invites as flyers. Everyone agreed that it was the best party they'd been to in years.

We went as Martin Riggs, the Mel Gibson lead. Lots of people did. Each of us hoping to be the most realistic in character as well as costume. We prepared balloons filled with red food dye as bullets for our cap guns. Stan and Ting choreographed a four-way shoot-out for us to perform at some point in the night that would have us each claim to be the true Riggs and shoot an impostor. At the climax we wouldn't throw balloons at each other, we'd tape one to our chest beforehand and pierce it as we fell. Everyone would applaud. Taped almost flat under our T-shirts, the balloons would be undetectable until our well-timed demise.

We drove from Ting's house to an off-licence for our cider and our fifteen minutes of fame began ticking.

We left Stan outside in the car with the engine running and walked through the door with our cap guns in our waistbands. We wore tight worn Levi's and leather jackets, vests, and the biggest mullets we could handle. It was obvious we were in disguise even if the butts of our pistols weren't. We selected our cider – scrumpy and Merrydown; the first one gets you merry, the second one puts you ... and took our place in the queue. Bored of waiting, by the time Ting was getting served by the nervous-looking shopkeeper, Pine and I were deep in character, deciding how we were going to get to the church hall once Stan had dropped his car off. Our mundane conversation was enlivened by our liberal use of film speak and fantasy, more 'mo'fu'ers' getting whacked than there ought to be for such a harmless discussion.

'Shit.' Ting was rooting through his pockets. He looked up at the slack-jawed shopkeeper and smiled like Riggs. 'I don't have enough money.'

'Don't worry.' The shopkeeper shook his head and then pushed the bulging bag towards Ting. 'Take them. Please.'

'Eh? You're having a laugh?'

But he wasn't.

Ting shook his head and shouted for me to give him the money he needed. Still in character, with a terrible American drawl, I gave him it with a warning that I wanted it back with interest.

'Otherwise I'll pop a cap in your ass.' My hand formed into a gun, thumb up, two fingers pointing, and I held it angled down above his head. 'Blam! Blam! Blam!'

They took the piss out of my accent as we laughed at our menacing realism on the way back to the car.

Once we'd dropped Stan's car off we decided to walk through the estate and on through the graveyard to the church hall. It was the long way round but it gave us plenty of time to Scrumpy Jack up as we planned our assault on the party. Our entrance would be a spectacular and well-executed shutdown. We'd shoot our way in, dispatching impostors and bad guys pretending to be good guys.

As we came through the graveyard we saw a small group in costume mooching around the doors of the hall, possibly planning their own entrance. We each silently grabbed a handful of balloons. Giggling, we sneaked up to them as far as we could before they spotted us. Whooping loudly, we let fly with our cap cannons and missiles. We showered the cops with noise and balloons and gleefully chased them as they scarpered. We stopped at the door and gave each other high fives while we waited for them to reappear so that we could have a proper laugh at them. The doors beside us slammed open and three guys dressed in SWAT gear walked outside.

'Down!' I shouted, pushing Ting to the ground and throwing the last of my balloons.

I turned to Stan and Pine and thought it odd that they weren't firing at the doors. Instead they were standing shaking, with their hands above their heads.

'Argghh.' Ting looked up at me in disgust. 'You've gone and killed me.'

He stopped pulling at the dampness on his chest and stared behind me at the doors.

As soon as we'd left the off-licence the overly conscientious and scared shitless shopkeeper had phoned the police. The cops we splattered were real police who had been sent along with the armed response unit to the church hall. The armed response unit were the ones standing in front of me with food dye dripping off their flak jackets.

They bound us over for the rest of the weekend and we made the local rag.

The judge gave us community service because of the seriousness of our stupidity.

And those were the trees that we planted next to the swing park we helped to build in the park we helped to clean up. It was the best party ever.

◻ * ◻

The memories grown from the park were both fond and harsh, a smile at the days we'd had, tempered by the ones we'd never have. Ting's loss struck me afresh and I felt him heavy on my knee as Pine spoke, too obviously thinking the same.

'Happier days.'

Then he caught his breath and pointed towards the running track that weaved through the park. 'Did you see that?'

'What?' Refocusing, I couldn't see anything worth pointing out.

'Never mind.' He shook his head and filled the carton again. 'There was a rollerblader but she's disappeared round the corner.' He handed me a drink and sat back as I scanned the park searching for a sight to lessen my load. Ting would have been the first to point out the vulnerary powers of a girl on skates. Pine, however, had already dismissed her from his mind. 'So, how did you get on last night?'

I turned towards him but before I got a chance to answer he was lost again, pointing out the window.

'She's back.'

This time when I looked I had to agree.

'Hubba, hubba.'

'I know,' he said, shaking his head. 'She's a Honey.' He exhaled slowly and loudly. 'But what about last night, how'd you get on? What was Ali like?'

He still hadn't lost sight of the girl in denim shorts rollerblading towards us. I shielded my eyes from the sun and watched her as she approached the path that ran parallel to the road we were shuffling along.

'Strong legs,' I whispered as she swung round ninety degrees and began haring along the path. 'Firm tits and a stomach you could bowl on.' Soon she would be alongside us and then powering away. 'Good stamina and perfect rhythm.' Her arms were pumping as she swung past us in a blur. 'Hubba, hubba.'

Silently then, we both followed her until she disappeared over the hill. Waiting for a second to see if she'd reappear, we were rewarded by a jogger sweating past in the other direction. We followed her until we were back facing the park again. This was a fairly common pastime for all the people in all the cars that jammed the road. Skin watching. Sometimes it even caused the jams. With the intensity and passion of apathetic stalkers, we craned and swung our necks in concert, attracted by the flash of flesh in the warmth of the sun. We only had to sit; the park brought new opportunities as old ones escaped our lech as we lumbered along.

'Were you talking about Ali?'

Well, no, actually, but now I'm thinking about her. The rollerblading Honey gave me flashbacks to the stolen glimpses of her shoulder and the firmness of her body that I came so close to last night. The chemical reaction in my system was palpable as my thoughts took flight to fancy and I had to look to be sure that there was no physical evidence of its effect.

But I had another problem. I wasn't sure how to tell Pine that I fell asleep in Ali's bedroom without her, without him annihilating me all day. Then somewhere in my brain the pin-bright image of Ali pricked a carton and it spilt. It soaked me to the skin. Thinking about Ali and about last night reminded my body, my tired lazy body, that sometimes I did get it right. Well, up to a point. Even though illusionary, the buzz took me and I basked in its warmth, only one eye on the horizon for the pain cloud I knew could come back. This was one of the moments. A synapse that could occasionally contradict my negativity and let me remember how to smile. A warm memory. It wasn't Ali particularly that did it. It was a log fire when you're stood at a bus stop in the snow. Adam's ale after a run. It was a remembered joy. It was life.

'No.' I smiled easily. 'I was talking about the rollerblading Honey. But I could have been.'

'Oh.' He snuggled up close to me and we sneaked a smoke out of the now open window. 'Do tell.'

'What do you want to know?'

'I want to know how you got on, for fuck sake,' he said with his eyes wide. 'I want to know if you got lucky.'

'Lucky being got a shag, I presume?'

'Natch.'

'Then falling asleep in a chair would be the opposite of that?'

Our noses almost touched as we faced each other.

'Tell me you're joking.'

'I only wish.'

Pine then did a strange thing. He didn't laugh.

'Fuck sake, Pennance, what a 'mare.'

'Nightmare doesn't even come close.'

He sat back in the seat and I waited for him to say something funny, something that would have me laugh at myself, but he didn't. He surprised me.

'I want you to help me pick an engagement ring.'

It took me a moment to catch up with him, he'd changed track and my train of thought had only just pulled out of the station. Since we'd been talking, he'd only had eyes for legs; he'd been on the automatic pilot he used when cutting hair, and now he wanted to get married. Because I was as much a victim of the blades as he, my own attention had been compromised and I'd failed to notice the uncharacteristic seriousness in his voice as he'd been talking. He was distracted and it had taken me this long to work it out, and only then because he all but told me. That's not to say that I wasn't glad of the distraction myself now.

'An engagement ring?' I echoed, finding that I had his full and now undivided attention. 'Why do you want me to help you pick an engagement ring? Surely you might be wanting to do that with Molly. I'm presuming it is for Molly?'

'Of course it fucking is.' He screwed his face up and scowled. 'And I will pick one with her, but I need to buy one first.'

'Wait a minute.' I held my hand up and sat up. 'Let's start again. Have you asked Molly to marry you?'

'No.'

'But you're going to?'

'Obviously,' he stated petulantly.

'Okay, so far so good.' We risked another smoke. 'What's brought this on?'

That Pine was in love with Molly there was no doubt. He never lost that doe-eyed look whenever she was around. They were good together, they had none of the paranoia or choking that I was used to, they did their own thing, didn't fuck around and made a point of getting their quality time together, SNI they'd call it.

It didn't matter which night but at least once a week they'd have a special night in. The rest of the world locked out, they would be a couple. It didn't matter what they did or if they did nothing but watch TV as long as they were alone and together. Pine wanted them as much as Molly and even contrived to have them on a Saturday if United were on *MotD*. Dinner, wine, quilt in front of the fire, and thirty minutes before the football started he'd turn the central heating up, whack the fire to full pelt and cuddle in with her until she'd drift off to fuzzy warm cosy sleep. A few minutes before kick-off he'd yawn and pass his arm in front of her eyes, slowly to see if she was awake, and then snugly and smugly switch *MotD* on, lower the music and watch the game. Even once Molly had cottoned on to his game plan, which was roughly about after the first time, she confided that she didn't mind because it was sweet of him to go to all the trouble and she liked falling asleep like that anyway because he always ended up having to carry her to bed afterwards. She said it made her feel like a princess.

My somewhat blunt question was more to do with his oft-voiced assertion that marriage wouldn't suit his image. Exactly what image other than single hairdresser – probably gay – I had no idea, but that had always been a fundamental for him.

'Nothing.' He shrugged. 'I've been thinking about it for a while.'

He fidgeted and tutted, taking the cigarette from my hand. 'Who am I kidding?'

I didn't say anything, but watched the road as we slowly picked up speed and waited until he was ready to tell me.

'Last night in bed with Molly, she was asleep, her head was on my chest and I thought I could get used to this. No, it was more than that. I wanted to get used to it. I remember thinking, don't let this get away. Don't risk losing this. I was up all night thinking about it.' He looked up at me. 'You know me, Pennance, I never talk to myself so I knew I was serious. It shook me. Ting, the flat, the fucking timing. I'm going to ask her to marry me.'

Despite the gravel in his voice and the sincerity on his face, I found myself smiling. Not at Pine, although he was responsible for it. But because I was happy.

Another moment to tuck away for a rainy day. Pine marrying Molly made perfect sense. I knew that. Everyone knew that. I'd known both of them for years and couldn't think of one without the other.

'I'm serious.' He sulked, misreading me.

'I know you are and I'm happy for you, for you both. Congratulations.'

'She hasn't said yes yet,' he pointed out ruefully as I shook first the hair on his head and then, after pushing him away from me, his hand, opting for a complicated and frequently changing cool combination of grips, brushes, turns and flaps rather than the more traditional interlocking approach.

'She will, Pine. I wouldn't worry about it.'

'But what if she doesn't?'

'She will, trust me,' I assured him. 'But tell me, why do you want me to help you pick a ring?' I didn't quite understand that bit.

'Because, I'll need a ring to give her when I propose, but of course she'll want to take it back and exchange it for one that she'll want. You know what she likes, so you can share the blame for not buying one that she wanted. Seems simple enough to me.' He sounded exasperated, as though I was being unreasonably dense.

'I don't get you. Why not just wait until you've proposed, then shop for a ring together?'

'We will.'

Maybe he was right.

'So why buy one with me?'

'She'll need to have a ring when I propose. You know Molly, she'll expect it.'

'Okay,' I said, finding the perfect solution. 'Here's a novel thought, why not buy her a ring she will actually like and want to keep and give it to her when you propose?'

'How?' he asked simply and waited for me to answer.

And waited.

I understood now what he meant. How indeed? There are some things that we are just not genetically designed to get right, like recognising all but the most extreme changes in hair wearing, and this was undoubtedly another.

'A good point well made, sir.'

I accepted the proffered carton that marked the end of that conversation.

'So, back to the sex and sandman story.' He settled back in his seat as though preparing for an epic.

'Was Ali really like that rollerblader?'

I nodded, as sure as I could be.

'Not for me.' He shook his head. 'I like to see it in a bikini or skating through the park, but in bed I want to close my eyes and have to guess if I'm holding a boob or a tummy, nipples notwithstanding. Skinny women just don't spoon right, but if you're happy you're happy.' Then he grinned. 'Look at it this way, you've always wanted a stomach like that and now you're almost in reach of one. Go for it, if you can stay awake long enough. See if she's the One.'

Now that was a good thought to hold.

'How did you know that Molly was the one for you?'

'She told me.' He shrugged.

'Maybe I should ask Ali?'

'Easy, tiger,' he winked. 'One wedding at a time, eh?'

'Absolutely, mate.' I smiled.

'Don't say anything to Molly.'

'Don't worry.' I shook my head.

'I won't. And don't you worry about anyone finding out about you falling asleep on the job. I'll be the soul of discretion.'

So, assured, I let the rumbling of the truck rock me to unexpected but welcome sleep as thoughts of Ali inured me to the sounds of the spluttering traffic.

◻ ✱ ◻

The crunch of gravel woke me as we pulled in to a service station and I heard Colin tell Pine that he had to make a phone call. We left him at the doors of the services talking to a colleague at a promotion stand and walked through to the café for a coffee.

Stan groggily followed Pine to a table and sat down with his head in his hands while I got us a drink. Looking round, I could see that the services were busy. Queues at all the tills, video arcade filled to bursting with kids driving and drivers shooting as they expunged their road rage, and already the floor at my feet was squelching with spilt tea and coffee from the chrome pots that never quite pour properly. Pine was out of his seat and walking to the toilets when I got back, so I sat opposite Stan and thought to find out if he was still in a nark.

'If you don't stop looking like that,' I told him, glancing round the room, 'people will think I've just broken up with you.'

He squinted at me through heavy lids and pulled a flask from his jacket and made the coffee Irish. He almost managed a full smile before he grimaced and emptied the rest of the flask in one swallow.

Relieved that he seemed to be verging on humanity again, I sat back and sipped at my coffee, watching Colin talk agitatedly with his pal through the window.

'How'd you do last night?'

I had to lean forward to hear what Stan had said, his voice no more than a whisper. He was fighting his way back from his self-inflicted solitude and I was more interested in getting to the bottom of his mood than telling him about Ali. His attitude in the café and his subsequent silence were not natural and I wanted to clear the air before we went any further. We were in this together after all, we all felt like shit but were making the best of it for Ting.

I shook my head. 'In a minute. Tell me why you're in such a shitty mood first.'

'I am absolutely fucking knackered, that's why,' he said, surprising me. I thought that he was depressed because of Ting or annoyed because of me. 'I couldn't sleep last night. It was too weird, too fucking weird.' He shook his head and took a steadying drink. 'I couldn't handle it, Pennance, it was doing my head in. Knowing that he was in the flat, only not. I couldn't

handle it.' He looked at me. 'You must know what I mean,
you did it on Saturday.'

Well, actually . . . I squirmed.

'So what did you do?'

He stared out the window and drank his coffee.

'I phoned the Horse,' he whispered.

I heard him but pretended I didn't, forcing him to say it
again. Louder.

'I thought you said . . .'

'I know what I said.' He blushed. 'But I was sat there on
my own with a bottle of tequila, crying like a baby with Ting
in my arms. I was fucking low. Christ, I put the blues on to
bring the mood up but I was too far gone.' Now I felt terrible
for mocking him. 'After a while I needed a hug.' He shrugged.
'You know how I get when I'm maudlin.'

We said it together and I smiled while he struggled with it.

'One tequila, two tequila, three tequila, whore.'

'Did you take Ting with you?'

'No, I was in no state to go out, the Horse came to me and
I left Ting in his old room with the Duke.'

Stan chewed on his lip and I thought I knew why he was
feeling bad. When he and Ting had lived together they had
agreed not to have anyone back for sex unless one of them was
out. It was a rule they'd agreed on after a weekend when they
both pulled. Because their bedrooms shared a wall they could
each hear the other having sex. Whilst that was no problem
for Stan or Ting, their respective partners had shown more
interest in what was going on through the wall than in their
own bed. As they lay there, both their partners had shushed
them in order to pay attention to how the other half made
love. Stan and Ting lay in separate beds smoking while their
conquests sat motionless, separated by two layers of paint only,
commenting on how quietly gay people or straight people had
sex. That nobody had sex that night didn't emerge until the
morning when they compared notes and complained about the
draw of vicarious gratification. After that they stopped double-
dating even by accident.

'Which film?' I asked, trying to draw him away from his guilt as he had done on innumerable occasions for me.

'*The Quiet Man.*'

'I bet that pissed him off.' I shook my head and patted the bag, hoping he'd laugh. 'He watched that yesterday at mine.'

'I didn't know,' he said seriously, too seriously. 'It was one of his that he'd left.'

'Chill, dude.' I raised my hands to mollify him, realising too late that he was in the wrong mood. 'I'm only messing with you.'

'You sure?'

'Of course I am.'

'Well, what did he watch at yours?' He slowly forced a smile in response to my own and I sighed with quiet relief.

'So what's up then?'

'Nothing.' His smile became a snort of contempt. 'Me, that's the problem, I couldn't get it up. The Horse came over and I sent him home less than an hour later. I know I was pissed but that's never happened before. He left and I went back to sitting with Ting and the tequila until the sun came up, feeling sorry for myself.'

'Don't worry about it,' I said gently, not wanting to be dismissive of his confession. 'You've been strung out all week, it was bound to catch up with you. You were just knackered, that's all, and you said it yourself, it's not as though he was a looker.'

'That's bollocks and you know it, Pennance. You were drunker than me and you got on all right, didn't you?' I shrugged. 'And you've seen some of my past conquests. It's not as though they all fell off the catwalk, so why was last night any different?'

'I don't know, maybe you just needed to be alone –'

'But I wasn't alone, was I? That's the point. Ting was there and it drove me crazy. I sat with him on my knee watching the end of his film, guilty about trying to have a good time while he was in a bag.' He shook his head. 'I don't think I'm handling this as well as I thought I would. I didn't even look in the bag

because I didn't want to see Ting squashed into a fucking jar.'
He pushed the bag towards me and looked out through one
bloodshot eye. 'I'm telling you, Pennance, I'm not cut out for
this losing friends lark. If you or Pine get yourselves killed any
time in the next sixty years, I'll fucking murder you.' I smiled
as he pulled himself back from the brink. I knew to keep quiet,
he was working through it himself and nothing I could say
would get him there any faster. 'Fuck this for a game of soldiers,
I've got to get out of this mind-set, it's giving me the right
hump.' He grinned tightly. 'Come on then, depress me even
more, tell me how you got on last night so I can get more upset
and take it out on you.'

'You know.' I smiled, glad that he was moving on. 'Just
your average night in the café, then a taxi and eventually sleep
in Ali's bedroom.'

'I'm amazed, Pennance,' he said honestly. 'I never thought
she was interested.'

'Thanks for the vote of confidence, big man.' I tutted and
kicked him beneath the table. Not too hard because there was
still a shadow of his mood sitting above him and I didn't want
to push too much. 'But you saw for yourself, she was the one
that dragged me out last night.'

'Yes, and don't forget who helped you to get her to that
stage.' I looked at him blankly, feeding him. 'And that would
be my good self and big Baz.'

'And it's appreciated,' I told him.

'I mean if it was left to you, you'd still be sat there gurgling
vodka and –'

'Yes, yes, whatever you say. You and Pine can fight between
yourselves for the credit.'

'So, give with the details.'

'Well, actually' – I lowered my voice and looked round – 'I
kind of fell asleep before anything happened.' I could see his
face light up. 'I woke up on a chair with Ali sleeping in the
other room.' Stan, another true friend, didn't laugh either. At
least not until I told him about the snoring.

'Have you told Pine yet?'

'Not about the snoring.' I frowned and shook my head. 'I'm not so in need of ridicule that I went that far.' He nodded. 'But I was talking to him earlier and he said that he was going to ask Molly –'

'. . . To marry him. I know.' He nodded. 'You know we're not to say anything to her, he's going to surprise her after we get back from Mull.'

I could see the cloud fall round his ears as he looked at Ting and thought about Mull.

'You know I told you I saw Kirsty yesterday.' I spun my cup on its saucer.

'Yeah.'

'Well, she's getting married as well.'

'Married?' He put his hand over mine to stop the grinding that had him grimacing.

'I know.'

'Shit, how are you with that?'

I shrugged and took my hand away from the cup. 'Happy, I guess. I haven't really thought about it, I just gave her a hug and said congratulations.'

'It's all happening at once,' he said, shaking his head. 'Too many things are changing. I want to sleep for a week and wake up last month when our biggest decision was what to listen to or how to get the next shag. Now it just seems that Ting started something that's running out of control and we're getting caught up in it and dragged along. Too many new things, I mean Pine talking about getting married, Kirsty not marrying you –'

'I never asked her, remember?'

'Yes, but you know what I mean, and me being impotent –'

'Stan, you're not fucking impotent, you were drunk.'

'Whatever.' He dismissed my comments with a tired wave. 'I just need to rest for five minutes and I'll be fine, I don't know what's got into me today, I just can't fucking shake this.'

Pine came back with a joint and we went outside to smoke it.

'Right,' said Colin as he walked towards us ten minutes later. 'Let's go.'

As we walked to the truck, he was staring at Ting's bag in Pine's hand.

'Do you think you could put that' – he pointed loosely – 'in the car. It's making me feel uneasy having it in the cab.'

Pine smiled at him in understanding. 'No problem,' he said, 'but we'll need to ride in the car with him, Colin. It is a wake, and, well, it'd be rude not to, wouldn't it?'

Stan and I both nodded in agreement and so reluctantly he set off again with us sat on the back in Stan's car.

We settled back, Stan making an obvious effort to lighten his mood as we pulled back onto the road. I rummaged in the glove box for a cassette. To the opening refrain of 'Rhinestone Cowboy', Stan opened the windows as Pine finished rolling. For the next couple of hours we drank, smoked, and screamed at the top of our voices to every song on Ting's *Kitsch Kountry* double cassette.

Now this was the only way to travel.

past love

We were off the motorway and onto the spectacular drive along the West Coast of Scotland, an assault of wind, colour, and shape. I changed the music to one of Ting's same-song-different-artist collections that he'd done for Stan and breathed in the world as we took turns at telling stories. Ting stories that fell off the tongue in random reference.

Each song acted as a catalyst. A sound bite that tracked a time or an event and squeezed detail from memory stores. Exciting as I found it to recollect and occasionally recoil from our past, I was conscious not to dwell too long on any flash of history. Pine had come late to our small fraternity and I didn't want him to feel any less a part of us because he wasn't with us growing up. His history with Ting may not have had our longevity but it was at least as intense, the two of them being almost twin-like in their personalities and life views. In any case, I needn't have worried, he held his own.

In the way that hostages in captivity develop thought processes unnecessary in their everyday lives, abilities that open doors of perception and allow them to recollect entire film scripts or recite poetry thought forgotten, so Ting's death was stimulating me to find memories that I never knew I had.

We were animated now. Competing with each other and the rushing wind that flew in the windows, we spent our time smiling or shaking our heads as we relived our history.

Ting suspended from school for kissing Andrea Matheson in the style of Elvis. Playing commandos in the woods that became a building site that became a housing estate. The irony of pulling trees down and naming the streets after them was lost on us at such a young age but we adapted our games accordingly. Sneaking round with sharpened dolly pegs thrust into our belts, we became urban guerrillas, stealing pallets for Harry from under the noses of night watchmen as the houses that replaced the trees gave us new stomping grounds in which to live out our fantasies and make some money.

We shook our heads at the words Ting used. Slang, patter that he seemed to grow into as he got older. The further he got from his Scottish heritage the more he compensated by cultivating his identity, thickening his accent, deepening his brogue. A conscious effort that he said paid in spades with the ladies. Then we remembered the nights he sat educating us in the use of his slang, lessons that left us tongue-twisted and aching-faced but that could still be recognised in how we spoke today.

Pine and Ting spending the night crying when we were designing the café because they each, in separate and to this day unfathomed incidents, ended up with chilli powder up their noses. While Pine remembered the night, he was still at a loss to explain it.

We laughed at Ting's need to park his car tidily, always between other cars for uniformity. And his rigid pizza-eating order: second most tasty-looking piece first and tastiest piece second to last in case he was too full to appreciate the final slice.

Two stories in particular I remembered most fondly. They captured the essence that made him who he was. By turns funny and sharp, compelling and considerate. One I was there for and the other was what we agreed was the least likely of tales, our own urban myth that he'd only ever laughed at. Ting and his English teacher. The story was that she started by leaving Ting an apple on his desk at the beginning of each class and then leaving him notes and coded messages when she returned his work after marking it. Always passing him. Playground gossip had him seduced by the end of our final year. While Ting was the most vehement in trying to quash such slanderous accusations, his case was not helped by her subsequent transfer to another school the following term. Or his history of detention.

The other one was when we were working as waiters in a well-heeled restaurant one summer and sneaked to the toilets for a fly smoke away from the prying thighs of the maître d'. Suddenly the door burst open and in crashed one of the diners, the biggest guy either of us had ever seen. We immediately took up position at the urinal. He ran up and stood next to Ting, unzipped and slapped out what looked like a penis, only much much bigger.

'Ahhhhh,' he sighed from his equally well-proportioned boots and turned to Ting with a diamond smile. 'Just made it.'

Ignoring all toilet etiquette, Ting looked down, then at me, then at himself and finally back to the gargantuan. He tilted his head and looked up.

'Do you think you could make me one?'

▭ * ▭

And on and on past the milestones, real and remembered, to Mull.

After a while I slipped into a comfortable silence where I continued to reminisce in the halls of my mind until I reached the present again.

I left Pine and an emotionally wavering Stan talking quietly as I closed my eyes to find the strength that I would need to see beyond the past and prepare myself for this ending that we were about. And where to then?

I was Abbott without Costello, Laurel without Hardy, Roobarb without Custard.

From thoughts of his death and the need to believe that something would come from his ashes, my mind jumped and twisted, stretching then squashing until all my memories, all my futures became one. How I saw that future was down to me. Not conditioning or habit, but choice. There because I was, here until I died. And much as I blamed myself for Ting's death, it was my responsibility to live better because of it.

Could it be that my whole life, my mediocrity, had been nothing more than a refusal to face the future? A protective urge that stopped me picking the daisies. I saw it clearly now, felt it through the cold leather of Ting's bag.

Once, when we were at school, Ting in his place at the head of the gang and me running around the periphery trying to get in, I hated him. He made it look so easy. Being popular, the star striker, digital watch and an enthusiasm for the girls that bordered on perverted, even at that age. Everyone just knew he'd be the first to get pubic hair.

In spite of the fact that he was friendly to everyone, I had it in my head that he didn't like me. He never picked me for his team and always took the ball away from me when he tackled. On its own, the taking the ball away would have been acceptable – everyone who tackled me got the ball – but combined with his obvious refusal to have me on his all-star select, I got the message. I spent weeks secretly praying for his downfall before finally plotting it myself.

After a particularly gruelling Religious Ed class with Father McGonagall, I waited for the cantankerous old lush to finish drinking his 'medicine' and stand with us for prayers. Mine had already begun as I stood up with the rest of the class. Lumbering to his feet, he scraped his chair back and turned, leaving us staring at his back, left hand on heart, right arm extended as though about to start a dance. Facing us again, he thundered in a voice he usually reserved for talking about Protestants: 'Who put chewing gum on my chair?'

Frozen by his frosty breath, we stood transfixed as his whisky-fuelled words flew round the room. The Holy Spirit searching for the unjust.

'Nobody moves until somebody tells me who did it.'

Drawn by his yelling, the headmaster stepped into the room and spoke quietly with him. My legs had started to shake as I realised the enormity of what I had done. Father McGonagall was livid and I knew that, unless I owned up, his considerable wrath would fall on Ting, the class joker. While that had been the whole point initially, I had clearly overstepped the mark.

The hairs on the back of my neck stood up and I turned slightly to my left. Three inches from my eyeball Ting's outstretched finger pointed directly at me.

'Right then.' The head was addressing the class and I turned back to the front. 'Someone tell me who did this.'

The outraged Father was supping noisily from his medicine, oblivious of the head's disapproving frown. I thought I was going to collapse when Ting stepped forward and put his hand up to speak, but I settled on wetting my pants.

'Well, Sweetson, do you know who did this?'

Ting stood and shook his head, even at that time a master of timing and tension.

'I don't, sir. But I think it was the same person that spat in Father McGonagall's medicine.'

Later as we sat in purgatory waiting for the lift to hell, Ting was surprised, shocked even, that I thought he would grass me up. He considered us friends. Of course he didn't want me on his team, he told me.

'Everyone knows you're shit at football.'

'Sweetson!'

Swearing outside the head's office got him into even more trouble.

I was still doing it now. Projecting. Too clever to wait and see how things will turn out, I predict the future with the precision of a misfortune cookie and live within its shell. Too caught up in what I think will go wrong, I miss what doesn't.

▭ * ▭

The last few days must be catching up with us, I thought, as I turned and found Pine and Stan both staring despondently into space. Too much thinking, not enough doing. I sniggered at the lie and watched a kestrel soaring above the valley. I knew I was still bouncing around Ting's death. But I had started to move with it, not let it be a waste. I was finding a spark of life in places I'd long thought dead. Ting was off flying on some new adventure, and when I met him next he would be so full of it that I'd wish him still gone, if only for a second. I had to move on if only to have something to talk about other than his ghostly philandering.

I'd always fought against conforming, or thought I had, refusing to sensibly pension for my future. Why waste money best spent in your prime, when you might not even live to see your dotage? And if you do, how many bars on a fire can you need? Better to live now. But I hadn't. I hadn't done anything. No sign that I ever existed. I thought about the plague of babies suffered by my sister and how foolish I considered her. Live first, parent later, was my cry. But I hadn't, my best child-raising years were meant to be the hell-raising years, and I'd avoided one only to misspend the other. I'd meandered along with no substance to anything. Ephemeral. At some point I may have had it. Before I found my own amazing mediocrity and sat down in triumph. A moment of madness that I'd been trapped in ever since, too afraid to move on.

I all but ran from the safe middle-England nest in a flurry of heaven-sent wings, my sights set on writing my name in the stars, dreams of fame and fortune and life among the grown-ups. My parents migrated south the same winter and never came back, their brood having flown the coop. University and the universe straightened me out; I could fly if I wanted, they told me, but do you really want to? I'd looked around and seen what I could become in the suits and briefcases that surrounded me. Ignoring the promise that going up to London offered, I reached my going down year and never looked back. First interview out of uni and I walked out, two bellicose Masonic barristers shaking their heads at the affront as I left. What did they know? I had years yet, plenty of fun time to be had before working too hard, adventure knocking on my door to see if I was coming out to play. I took a year out, but somehow it had become two years, and then I needed a job to keep me while I looked for a career, and that's what I was doing, still. I developed a lifestyle that fitted so seamlessly that I hardly even listened at the door or wondered if I was out when adventure came calling.

It was surviving dressed up as living.

My wings clipped, I had stopped looking at the heavens, forgetting in my comfort what it was that I had set out to do. Nothing earth-shattering, I had no illusions, but something more, more than this. My life was pretty hollow, or had been. My conversation yesterday with Ali had been another milestone in my understanding. I wouldn't look back any more, it was time for a little self-belief. If tomorrow wanted to tell Father McGonagall it was me, we would stand shoulder to shoulder and spit in his rye together. I felt as though I wasn't nearing the end of this journey now, I was only beginning.

Thoughts of careers and domestic bliss swept me off to the never-never land of the future and I realised that there was an alternative. A choice. And so like the thousands of other souls who want to do things differently, to get a taste of adventure in their lives before the weight of responsibility pulls them under, I decided that when we got back I'd go travelling. Up and off. Just like that.

The sun appeared briefly from behind the clouds and the kestrel flew up and up and up. I smiled at the imagery and whispered, 'I'm going travelling.'

▭ ⋆ ▭

Stan turned to me and arched his brow.

'What?' he asked rather abruptly, pulled from his own musings.

'I'm going travelling after this,' I said again, louder. 'I'm going to pack up and go away for a while, come back and get a career and all that stuff. For me and my cat.'

He twisted round in his chair and faced me, frowning.

'You've always said that you'd go travelling, Pennance, but you never do it. What makes you think you'll actually go this time?'

Stan was right of course, but it seemed rude just to come out and say it like that.

'Because this time I'm not just saying it, I'm doing it.'

'Okay, whatever.' He closed his eyes and leant back.

I went back to the mountains; if he didn't believe me that was fine.

I knew.

'Pennance.' Stan was back, his changing moods swifter even than my own. 'You're always "gonni do" something. Going to book the train, going to learn Spanish, going to get it right. You are the Gonni Man. The Mañana Man. It's always tomorrow with you.' Stan was warming up now. 'You never do anything. Just for once, do something. Don't tell us you're going to do it. Don't do it tomorrow. Just fucking do it!'

I picked up a can from the seat and began shaking it as he continued to rant at me. So what if he was right? This time was going to be different.

'What you doing with that?' he asked as I held it in front of him.

'I'm not telling you.'

When he laughed, I sprayed him with beer to show him that I loved him too, even if he was a prick sometimes.

'Fuck you, faggot,' I shouted above his screeching. 'I'm going and you can kiss my arse goodbye.'

He jumped across the chair just as Pine began showering us with more beer.

'Do you two need some privacy?'

A mass of elbows and teeth, we spent the next ten minutes administering Chinese burns, horse bites, knucklies and choke holds to each other.

Pine was lying on his side on the floor lodged between the front and back seats trying to prise my fingers from his ankle. I was giving him a Chinese burn while kicking at Stan to stop him reaching me. He had Pine trapped between his scissored legs and was typing on his chest with one hand and swiping at me with the other. Pine scuffed my wrist with his shoe and I screamed at him, loosening my grip and allowing him to scurry out of reach as best he could. He twisted and kicked like a ferret, taking Stan by surprise and pushing him onto me. Still rubbing my wrist, I was pushed against the door as Stan got on top of Pine again, before pulling me into a headlock. Uncomfortable as I was, Pine must have been worse. He was pinned on his stomach with his legs kicking at the other door and Stan's knees either side of his head. He was slowly turning his body, trying to get onto his back, while Stan rained knucklies on my head. Just as I began to bend Stan's finger, he froze. I could see him look down in fear as he realised that Pine was lying face up, staring at him, with his teeth closed ever so gently around his scrotum. As carefully as he could, Stan edged himself up, allowing me to sit back and smile as Pine made a deal of sitting up victorious. Our cathartic display over, we opened all the windows and sat cooling off, laughing when Pine remembered to feel the pain from the welt on his calf.

'Fuck sake, that is not even fucking funny,' he said, rubbing his leg.

Stan fluttered his eyelashes. 'Diddums want me to kiss it better?'

'Fuck off, you.' Pine swatted at him with his one good arm. 'Just you get on with kissing his arse.'

'Thank you, Pine,' I said, genuinely pleased that he had faith in my decision.

'You know you want to anyway,' Pine continued. 'Remember what Greg said.'

Pine dodged past Stan's outstretched arm and cowered behind me giggling.

Then we were off again.

◻ * ◻

Pine and Ting had been in St Pete's one night – I was away for a last-ditch dirty weekend with Kirsty – when Stan turned up with Greg, his new boyfriend. I'd met him only a couple of times and couldn't stand him at once. He began every sentence with such redundancies and irreverent openers as 'This is the funniest story . . . It was hilarious . . . You'll love this . . .' and used expressions like 'legendary wankered', 'bonkers' and 'gosh'. And he was Welsh.

He was a friend of Josh's and worked at the casino, and that was where they had been and why they were arguing when they sat down with Pine and Ting. Greg had accused Stan of fancying the dealer at the blackjack table. Even though I wasn't there that night Ting and Pine had told the story so often that I could picture the scene easily.

Stan told Greg to stop talking shite and it had gone downhill from there. By the time they got to the café, Greg was accusing him of chasing anything in trousers. Pine and Ting became engrossed in this lovers' tiff and were trying to remain inconspicuous so as not to interrupt the proceedings. Greg then listed his accusations, details supported by tears, of at least four separate occasions when Stan had 'flirted outrageously' with a fellow called Simon. All of which Stan steadfastly denied and accused Greg of being a melodramatic manipulative cocksucker. Ting had almost choked at the last and Pine had to kick him under the table as he stifled his laugh. Greg had shot them both a look of hatred, risen indignantly and minced off to the bar, leaving them to compose themselves. Stan shook his head and said sorry, but Pine needed more.

'Don't apologise,' he said in his best cloak and dagger. 'Just tell us, do you fancy Simon?'

Stan looked at him and snorted. 'Of course I do, but that's not the point, is it?' He brushed at his fingernails as Greg returned with their drinks.

Things settled down for a while then, until just as Ting was leaving. He told Stan to call me in the morning to confirm a poker night and Greg blew into his glass.

'Stan and Pennance playing poker?' he snorted. 'Who'll be poking who?'

Pine pulled Ting back into the seat as Stan went ballistic and Greg got more paranoid and petty.

'Greg, shut the fuck up and stop being such a prick.'

'Stan, you are a slag, face it.'

'Fuck off.'

'Wanker.'

'Prick.'

'Arse bandit.'

'Shirt-lifter.'

'Dinner masher.'

'Sausage jockey.'

'Uphill gardener.'

'What?'

'Fuck you.'

Pine and Ting looked on in fascination until Greg stormed out under a barrage of slanderous sobriquets. A smirking Stan followed him, leaving them in stunned silence over such a virtuoso performance. Ting and Pine spent the remainder of the night inventing gay profanities. A memorable night, at the end of which Stan had the best sex of that particular relationship and dumped Greg the following morning.

▭ * ▭

Pine suitably chastised, Stan sat in the driver's seat and blew smoke at us.

'You've nothing to fear from me, fat arse.'

Pine pushed me to indicate that that meant me.

'Fairy muff.' I shrugged, conceding the point, not wanting to contest it. I could live with Stan not finding me attractive.

'And you' – he shook his finger at Pine – 'let's not even go to where you've been.'

Pine bravely faced him from behind my shoulder, nodding sagely before punching me in the arm and taking the smoke Stan had passed me.

'Yeah, Pennance, like he'd fancy you.'

'What's wrong with me?' I mocked offence as they looked at each other, eyebrows raised and unsmiling.

'How long have you got?'

'Anyway.' Pine straightened up in his seat, smiling. 'When I first met you I thought you were all gay. That's why I became friends with you.'

Stan tutted and I rounded on Pine.

'Why?'

'Hairdressing.' He shrugged. 'You can't be in with the in crowd if you're straight, and if you're not gay the next best thing is gay friends.'

'Forget that,' I said, thinking back to Saturday night and my wannabe dance partner in the club. 'Why did you think we were gay?'

'Well, I knew he was.' He glanced at Stan, who sat there bemused. 'And do you remember when we first met?'

'I remember it was a party.' But I couldn't remember whose.

'And do you remember what you were doing?'

I sprayed beer as it came back to me.

We'd been sitting on the kitchen steps of a terraced house in Burley where a friend of a friend of Stan's sister was having a party. We didn't notice Pine when he walked into the kitchen as we had our backs to him, but he recognised Stan and shouted hello. Stan, Ting and I turned round in surprise and Pine fled. It wasn't until the following week that we were introduced properly.

He'd interrupted us fellating bananas. We were learning how to put a condom on with our mouths. A skill that I knew would be less useful to me than my Betamax VCR, but a skill nevertheless. Ting's idea. He was aghast that Stan practised safe fucky but not sucky and had hounded him into the practice. Stan, in turn, was teaching us what he'd learnt, progressing from the basic Finger and Thumb Roll that we knew and used as regularly as opportunity allowed, to the master class Tongue and Tight Lip Slip. I didn't gag until we started using flavoured condoms.

'Exactly.' Pine wiped himself down. 'I would have put even money on you both.'

'Eh?'

Stan was smiling away to himself as I looked on, confused.

'Only until we got talking.' Pine held his hand up and continued. 'Then I knew straight away that Ting wasn't.' I'm sure I saw him wink at Stan. 'You took a bit longer.'

'Shows you what you know,' Stan muttered almost under his breath.

'What do you mean?'

'Well, out of the two of them' – he pointed loosely at Ting and me – 'Ting would have been a safer bet.'

'That's what I mean.' Pine nodded.

'No, we're talking about two different things.' Stan shook his head as I sat back in my seat. 'I mean Ting knew for sure that he wasn't gay. This one here' – he nodded at me – 'he can't be sure.'

'Sure as anyone else.' I shrugged.

'Not really.'

'Why?'

'You've never tried it.'

'So –'

I cut myself off as I realised what he'd said. Pine caught it too.

'Are you saying Ting –'

'Yes,' he said almost flippantly.

Pine's questioning look asked if I'd known and I think my slack-jawed stare was answer enough. My mind was racing, screeching round the bends and searching for the thought or picture that would lend credence to Stan's assurance.

'When?'

'Who with?'

Pine and I garbled a volley of questions at him and he waited until we were finished before speaking again.

'Mary Cathcart's party after the trip to Granada Studios the year that we left school.'

'Who with?'

I remembered the party, or rather I remembered not remembering the party. Drunk on cheap cider that we'd been drinking since Manchester, when we got to the party Ting and Stan, almost as far gone as I was, were forced to spend most of the night sitting with me in a spare room to make sure I didn't choke in my coma. Realisation jumped out in front of me as I remembered and I slammed on the brakes at the conclusion.

'With me in the room?' I asked incredulously.

'What?' Pine was even more confused.

'It was him.' I looked at Stan. 'Him and Ting, and I was in the room, I think. Am I right?'

'Inspector Morse, move over.' Stan smiled. 'We have a new champion.'

This was big. This was massive.

Of course it also made perfect sense.

Ting was always pragmatic, even then. He'd decided, Stan told us, that he wanted to know for sure if he was missing anything. Not that he thought he was gay, he just wanted to know for sure what he was missing out on, whether he'd like it or not. Enlightened almost in spite of our education, he was comfortable enough to satisfy the confusion he felt. He just matter-of-factly wanted to know.

Stan unabashedly told us that they kissed and fumbled. Then they talked about it. Ting was satisfied.

'Boys are okay,' he'd said to Stan, smiling. 'But you can't beat the real thing.'

I wasn't sure what to think. Mostly I was hurt that I hadn't known. That's how selfish I can be. It was Pine who was listening properly.

'Jesus,' he said softly. 'How did that make you feel?'

Stan smiled thinly, his lips pressed tight together, white.

'You know how people say that their hearts break? Well, mine shattered. Then and there.' He shook his head slowly. 'Unrequited love. What a cunt.'

'Did he know?'

'Of course he knew.' He laughed gruffly. 'How do you think I knew it was unrequited?'

'Fuck.'

'Tell me about it.'

I was almost jealous of the depth of feeling that Ting and Stan must have had for each other to be able to remain such friends after that.

'How did you cope all these years?'

'What was the alternative?' He shrugged. 'Stop being friends?'

'Well, no. Of course not. But I mean, fuck sake, how hard was that?'

'Hard. Why do you think I've never told you?'

'Neither did Ting.'

'Do I detect a note of jealousy?' He smirked. 'It was me who asked him not to say anything. He wasn't bothered who knew but it was too much for me. I guess it doesn't matter any more. It was a long time ago and he's gone now.'

'Fuck.'

'I'm sorry.'

'Don't worry about it, Pennance.' Stan shook his head, his voice thick with emotion. 'Not even I can blame you for this one.'

'Even so.'

Van Morrison sang in as we faded out. I miss you so much, I can't stand it.

Chapter 16

dream on

Time and distance passed and the music changed. Burt Bachar-ach and the Barenaked Ladies carried me through our silence. Words lost, we fell into ourselves to secure the Ting we would take into the future.

I stared at the twisted beauty of the world as we meandered through the valley, the languid flow of life unaffected by our shared journey, by our mortal hurt. I'd never been disposed to having 'where am I going, why am I here' conversations with myself, I found them too tedious. But now I really wanted to know, I couldn't help myself. What is it all for? What is the fucking point? And above all, where was Ting when I needed him most?

Stan's pain had set me on the dark path to my own and it was Pine, with Jedi-like awareness, who brought me back.

'What about Ali?' he asked quietly.

'What?' I frowned, his words catching me unawares.

'I thought you were going to see what worked out with Ali?'

'So?' I asked, coming back, but still not quite able to catch his thread.

'So what if it works out? Will you still go travelling or are you thinking that she'll go with you or something?'

It was clear from the tone of his voice and his glance at Stan that he didn't. I knew that he was going back to move us on from Stan's confession but I wasn't prepared for the question. I hadn't even considered it. I'd only just decided that I was going and I hadn't thought it through yet, not the actual doing of it. All I had was an agreement in principle. It was enough that I had taken that first step, I hadn't thought about when

I'd go or if I'd go alone. I knew I didn't want to make any firm plans until I saw what happened with Ali, until I found out if we had a future. I was finding open doors all over the place now where before there were only solid walls and, in looking to the future, I was suddenly aware of just how much of it there was or could be. What if Ali was the One and she didn't want to travel with me, would it matter if I changed my mind? What if I didn't go and then found out she wasn't the One after all? How could I know what to do until I'd done it? The best option was not to think about it and to accept my first thought. I'd go travelling because it was what I wanted to do. That didn't mean I had to go straight away though.

'I'm sure she'll come,' I said, half wondering if I could make myself believe it.

'No chance.' Stan was almost vehement, choosing to ignore the sarcasm in my voice.

'Like you'd know,' I snapped, taking umbrage at his tone.

I hadn't even thought about it and here he was taking the fun out of it. Anything could happen, so why not that? I was angry that he was being so sure and so confrontational. His surliness from earlier had re-emerged, refuelled.

'You're not her type,' he stated flatly.

'I was last night.'

'Yeah, right.'

I hate when he's like this. Pine recognised it too and shut himself in a spliff to let it pass. I couldn't. I didn't know if this was a carry-on from his hangover or his fear that he was impotent or his older, remembered loss, but his mood had become anger. He'd been sitting quietly lost as I was and had found something that riled him. Unless challenged, he would fuck with it in his head until he started sniding like this and we would get caught up in his mood.

Taking firm hold of my seat, I asked, 'What's burning your arse?'

He swung round in his chair and told me.

His eyes were red, but not from tears. He gave up the effort of keeping his voice level and by turns shouted and snarled. It would have been comical if he wasn't so serious. He was almost bullet-pointing himself. This journey, the fact that I had fucked up, again, my attitude, Pine's fucking cheery disposition, Colin's rules and most of all, above all, how he felt useless for not having been there for Ting.

The first could be understood easily, but his grief for Ting was something else, even before he'd told us about his feelings. Stan's role as protector in our little circle had been established many times and the impotence he felt was created by his own guilt.

The guilt of not being able to stop the knife as once Ting had shielded him from the barb and blade of the schoolyard bullies. Those homophobic dispensers of comprehensive standing who sought him out for public ridicule. Ting put them to rights with denouncements and sulphuric truths of his own and Stan had been paying him back since he could.

'I feel so fucking pissed off.'

Pine passed him the spliff and wisely refused to be drawn.

'You and me both,' I told him when I was sure he had finished, the hostility draining from me.

I felt it too. The debt of friendship that I'd never be able to pay back. Not in this life. The despair in the quiet moments we try to avoid when we have to be alone. I understood his anger, his guilt. I shared it. I told him about my confession to Ray, about Ting taking my place, everything that I had thought and done, about how pissed off I was.

'That's why I am so pissed off with you.'

I was brought up short, my run-away tongue still flapping although I made no sound. Hormone overdrive. Was he listening to me? Was I saying it wrong? It wasn't my fucking fault. I think I was looking for a more supportive response. I looked at Pine, but he shook his head and made it clear he was not getting involved. I turned my head slightly.

'What?'

'That's what I mean,' Stan said bitterly, confusing me further. 'Fucking Mañana Man, you're so fucking irresponsible. If you were given enough rope you'd fucking lose it. You never do anything you say you will. I mean, fuck sake, does this look like a fucking train?'

'Ting understood.' I looked at Pine. 'He told you to chill out about it.'

'What?'

'Pine?'

'Sorry, Pennance, I made that up to make you feel better.'

Stan was shaking his head. 'Why didn't you just take the fucking things back yourself?'

'What?' I snapped my head round to stare at him. 'You're saying you wish it was me?'

'That's not what he's saying,' Pine answered for him but I ignored him, too caught up with Stan to care.

'Don't fuck with me, Pennance, I'm not in the mood.'

'I'd say you're plenty in the mood, Stan.'

For the first time since we'd met on the monkey bars over twenty years ago, I found myself head to head with Stan. I didn't relish the thought on any number of levels, but he had gotten my dander up good. Talking to Stan was like line dancing – two steps forward, one step back and kick. I couldn't let it go. I wasn't sure that I would be able to find the focus again if I did, and Stan ... well, Stan was being downright unreasonable. At a time when we were getting strength from each other, facing a shared loss and life, when we most needed to be there for each other, we went for it like a couple of banshees.

'WILL YOU TWO SHUT THE FUCK UP!'

I turned towards Pine, surprised that he had shouted. Any irritation I felt at his intrusion was short-lived when I saw the tears on his face. Stan hung his head and I shifted uneasily in my chair. Pine was seldom this vitriolic.

'You're going on like what you're saying actually means something.' He sniffed his tears away. 'You're shouting about blame for something you had fuck all to do with and something you can do fuck all about. Ting's dead. Wake up. It wasn't your fault, either of you, we're not to blame here.' He sagged in his seat, spent, his tears running freely as he looked at nothing outside the window. 'Do you want to know what guilt is, Stan? Do you, Pennance? I can give you guilt.'

I looked up when he stopped speaking, Stan did the same.

'I know I'm only alive because Ting's dead. Don't you see that? Don't you think that fucking haunts me? Do you two retards ever think about anyone else except your fucking selves? Tell me, why wasn't I home the night those jazzfucks threw a petrol bomb through my window? Where was I? Eh? Where was I?'

I didn't know if he was waiting for an answer because I was looking at my feet, too ashamed to look at him.

'I was with you two and Ray because Ting was fucking dead. If he wasn't, I would have been at home. Me and a Molotov Cocktail.' He tapped his head against the window. 'Fucking cheery disposition, my arse.'

Pine fell silent and Stan turned and met my eyes as I lifted my head; the fire was still there but I was fairly sure the well of tears behind it would put it out any time soon. He pushed himself forward and reached for the door handle.

'See,' he hissed as he left, 'now you've gone and upset Pine.'

Before I could protest, he threw the door open and stepped onto the truck. Slamming the door behind him, he stood and let the wind rob his tears of their hold on him. Pine started to giggle and I looked at him as he pinched at the bridge of his nose. Stan slumped himself back into the car and Pine patted him on the shoulder in consolation.

'What?' I asked, sitting up as I realised we were slowing down.

'There was a police car overtaking us when he stepped outside.'

■ * ■

Back in the cab with Colin I was still too pissed off to talk to Stan and followed Pine's lead in falling asleep. It came easier now. I woke when I heard the crunch of stones again as we came off the road at a greasy spoon caravan balanced on the side of a mountain. I pushed Pine awake but he grumbled back to sleep and I jumped out of the truck, stretching and yawning like a pensioner on a coach trip. Stan ignored me as he walked around from the passenger side and followed Colin to the caravan.

By the time I found a bush that stopped the wind spraying hot extract of Stella back at me, Colin and Stan were drinking tea and deep in conversation with the greasy-apron-wearing beard who was frying piles of what looked like roadkill. My turn to return the civilities, I ignored Stan, and ordered tea and four bread rolls with haggis on the recommendation of the chef. One look at me from above his spitting hot plate and he said fried food was what I needed, assuring me of its stomach-lining high fat content, especially tasty with a hangover apparently, and its almost miraculous recovery properties. Short of deep-fried Mars Bars and battered lard, he said, nothing else was guaranteed to make me feel better.

Picnic benches had been concreted into the hill side as though in fear of them falling down the valley. I picked a table and sat gazing in tasteful silence, following the road we'd driven along and thinking that a seat belt would have been useful to stop me tipping off the bench and down the mountain side. It was cold, the bite of wind leaving teeth marks on my soul, and I shivered as the giants blew frost up the valley towards me. The haggis dripped fat, congealing on the table ready to feed the birds that cowered from the elements in hollows along the rough-hewn wall behind me. I could feel their stares as they weighed up food against possible harm. The chef, all hair and tattoos in his stained wife-beating vest, was right about its healing power, and I knew that if I could hold it down I would feel better than I had all day. Awash with tea and fat, I lit a smoke and braced myself against the elements, wind burning tears in my eyes as I took a belt from nature's pick-me-up and watched the trees below march off into the fog.

This was it, I thought. We'd come through the fun part of the journey. The remembrance of laughter past, a falseness that let us forget what we were actually doing, and why. It was appropriate, possibly even necessary that we stop smiling, stop being happy. Stan and Pine seemed to have come to the same conclusion; our fratching and tetchiness which were so out of place were almost palpable here and now. I looked behind me at Stan, tight with Colin, and felt my mood darken with the sky. Honey and cinnamon faded into a bruise that stretched past me on its way to Mull. With the wind came the rain and the thought of heading back to the cab to avoid getting wet. But it was only a smattering so far, not enough to get me running yet.

I sat alone and listened to the wind rushing by, carrying the sounds of life past me and up the valley, each shiver revealing another chink in my emotional armour as memories came at me and the barbed tips of sadness ran through, hot as angry words. I smoked and drank tea, lost in myself and in the valley. Colin shouted above the roar of my silence that we were setting off again and I crushed out my cigarette. Staring as the sparks of fire disappeared, I was thinking about a single shattering instant.

Ting's light stubbed out. A point of totality for him as final as me crushing out my cigarette. The ash caught in the breeze and I was carried with it back to when.

Ten o'clock in the morning. Ting had spent the night at my flat and left me at nine to take the costumes back. Ten o'clock in the morning and I was fighting to catch my breath, a run in the park instead of a run into town. Counting my pulse, feeling like my heart would burst.

Mine didn't, Ting's did. My pulse was one hundred and thirty-six when Ting's stopped. I remember I had been worrying about my recovery rate. Ten o'clock in the morning, one hundred and thirty-six. Some things are not important, even when they are.

An old man asked me for a light and then ambled stiffly to sit nearby with his friend, both weathered and grey, the look of eagles about them. Watching the fog roll in under the rain on the valley floor, I listened to them talk, their voices scraping at the bitterness in the wind. They'd known war. The madness of the world incarnate, the experience of great and unjust loss shared by a generation teethed on hardship, caught in events that would change them forever. How many comrades had they lost? Friends even? They spoke of tea and other such matters of consequence and shook their heads at the caterpillar of caravans advancing up the valley. Leaving them my lighter in a gesture of solidarity, I walked to the car knowing the bag in my hand was my own Omaha Beach or Culloden. The point that marked where my world became less solid, less sensible even if it still went round.

We humans are complex creatures. Opposable thumbs and a capacity to touch the stars. But we still couldn't get the right of it. Life unsullied by death's touch. The knowledge that we have no get-out-free card should give us comfort when faced by it but it doesn't. We fight it and feel lessened by its inevitability, the regret etched in our faces like mountain crag scars if we survive too long. Somebody shoot me when I'm happy, I thought sadly, not meaning it at all.

I felt the wind tug at my jacket and angry spots of rain fall on my face as I stood and looked back down the valley. The two old men were crouched together, huddled against the cold, sitting with their backs to me. I smiled at them, two old soldiers watching over the valley, guarding against the coaches. Irrepressible life.

▭ * ▭

Once, when I was younger, I'd thought that cars were time machines. At an age when everything was a possibility and reality unfolded in the pages of Jules Verne and Robert Louis Stevenson, I'd shut my eyes and be hurtled to the future, securely belted behind the pilot's seat. The journey would pass as we slid through the wormhole, bending time in part-remembered images of possible realities until the engine cut and we were no longer in the past or the promise of the future, but actually there. Catapulted in the blinking of my eye.

As the soothing tempo of the truck threatened me with sleep

I opened the window to try to forestall the inevitable. A tail of wind sought refuge in the cab and punched Pine awake for the time it took me to close it, earning me a stare from Stan that drew the heat from the cold. I turned away and followed another, or maybe even the same kestrel, pacing us along the side of the mountain. Ting would have liked it here. This was where God would come to cut the grass.

'Just get on with it, don't think about it.'

Ting was taking me climbing for the first time and was waiting at the top of the boulder for me to finish the last pitch.

'It's just like the bits you've done, not harder, just different.'

I'd climbed over sixteen feet already and was sweating like a fat guy climbing a boulder. My leg was doing an Elvis and my forearms were in spasm. I listened to him or rather I heard him and made a final push, reaching for a jughold six inches above my right hand. At full stretch my fingers hooked over the top and I shifted my weight to raise my left leg to a lip above my knee. I could feel the nip of my harness as Ting kept the rope tight. My left foot against the boulder, I began to push and pull up using my left arm to reach above and search for a hold. The lip under my left foot snapped and I scraped down the boulder. With all my weight on the jughold, I hung by my right arm, kicking to find purchase below me. Before I could find anything, I lost the strength in my arm and fell off the rock. I swung like a pendulum until Ting lowered me safely to the ground where I trembled like a junkie in rehab.

'Better luck next time, mate.'

But that wasn't true. Next time I fell he wasn't there. It was Ali's turn, but she let me fall for her. Ray picked me up and poured me into a bag and I was clipped to Father McGonagall's collar. A red-eyed dog carrying a scratching Kato in his tail called himself Sir Azz and talked to me about his itchy pussy.

'What do you know about foreign cars anyway?'

I guarded the door at the top of the pyramid and saw the world slope away in layers, each side a different colour, and Helen hoovered Ting and told me she sank the ship.

'Iceberg, Goldberg, what's the difference?'

I slid into the water just as my parachute opened and threatened to smother me. Choking on the ash, I settled down and dried in the lava lamp's glow. I was waiting for the fire to come and take me just as the big finger stabbed me in the eye.

'It could be you.'

Who the fuck is Hugh? I thought as sand filled my head upside down. Exhausted, I closed my good eye and felt everything stay the same.

'Wear hair.'

Sir Azz told me the password, whispering it in my ear and taking a chunk from the lobe in recompense. I pulled the finger from my eye and put it in my pocket beside the emergency sledge and the wig. Pulling a mirror from a sneeze, I saw that I had caught a camera in the glass and ate it without reflection as I slipped on the syrup. And then I fell again, into a pit of teeth fighting to find a wig from the twists of a wet parachute.

'We're here.'

I opened my eyes when I recognised Pine's voice. Heavily, my muscles not yet awake, and not even sure if I was, I looked around and stared at the sea. Lifting my watch to my face, I smiled. Thoughts that became dreams in the closing of an eye had driven me to my future again.

we are family

The first thing I noticed was the smell of fish.

My body woke up to the cold as I tried to stifle a yawn and shivered as I got out of the truck. Straightening up, I looked round at Stan. He was holding his hand out, tight-lipped. Standing in front of him, I wiped my hand dry on my trousers and glanced around. We were parked facing the harbour wall in the belly of a horseshoe bay. A small fleet of fishing boats, real ones with oil and dirt under their nails, snuggled against each other, jostling for position against the wall, away from the swell surging in with the rain. The whole bay was no bigger than a football pitch. To the right of where I stood I could see three or four large grey buildings sitting there as though in protest at the encroaching sea, squatting in their coolie hats, arms folded, just daring the water to rise. Since the only other buildings around were half a mile up the hill behind us, it seemed reasonable to assume that at least one of them would be a pub, the King Canute probably. In front of the buildings there were lobster pots and cages, strewn around as though they'd just been shaken from a giant pocket. Seagulls screeched in delight as they swooped in and around them. It felt like a ghost town and the roll of an empty barrel against the railings on the wall in front served as the tumbleweed. The road led to the buildings and split to become the wall and a slipway to the harbour. The wall stretched across the mouth, leaving room for only one boat at a time to pass. The whole place looked drained of colour, even the hills around us had a touch of grey. Our happy-glo yellow truck was as at home as a cold sore on New Year's Eve.

'Pals?'

I wasn't angry any more. Stan's tantrum was his release and I knew that he was only trying to deal with Ting's death in his own way. That we had arrived here made it all the more necessary not to be angry, to help each other to move on. Free from destructive emotions, I knew that my calmness, my forgiveness, came from understanding that I was ready to go, face the future and become the person I wanted to be. Or if not Elvis, then at least someone who did something for once. Ting's death was becoming revolutionary and I was discovering new truths. That was how I was going to get through it. Stan needed something different and until he found it I knew he would be up and down like a tart's drawers.

'Pals!' I echoed through the rain, reaching out with my hand.

Leaving me hanging, he lifted his outstretched hand and put his thumb to his nose, stuck his tongue out and blew a raspberry.

'When you two have kissed and made up' – Pine walked over, hunched against the driven rain – 'I wouldn't mind getting out of this.' His hair was lying in rat's tails against his face and he was staring boggle-eyed at us as though we were conspiring to drown him. 'Do I look part fish?' He shook his head and the water ran off his hair and down his neck. 'Urrggh . . . can we go please?'

Stan went to speak with Colin about what would happen to his car, while Pine grabbed Ting and we began walking along the path in the other direction from the buildings and seagulls. Mrs Cromerty's guesthouse was round the headland. Stan caught up with us a few minutes later and we walked together with our heads down against the stinging rain and spray as more clouds squeezed into the sky.

'Where's he taking your car?' I shouted above the gale.

'Back to Leeds.'

I carried on walking before I realised that Pine had stopped. He was standing looking at Stan, his arms hanging at his sides, dripping. Ting was dropped at his feet.

'When?'

He didn't shout but I heard him anyway and wondered at his behaviour. Behind him Colin was driving back up the hill, a drip of colour rolling off the page. Stan pointed behind him and Pine slowly turned and dropped his head.

'What's up?' Stan walked over to him. 'Did you leave something on the truck?'

I was looking at Stan and shrugged as Pine began to nod his head.

'Our ride home.'

We stood watching until Colin fell off the edge of our world.

▭ ＊ ▭

Mrs Cromerty looked as old as her house. Once we had worked our way round the bay we'd followed the gravel path to a boathouse, bleached and picked at by the wind. Its door swung open and shut with the regularity of a bass drum complementing the splash and cymbal of the crashing waves. Behind it sat a gleaming whitewashed cottage, bowed in the middle as though sat on. It hadn't as much been built as seemed to have grown from the earth. Its lack of symmetry suggested that if it was man-made then the bread dough they used as bricks didn't have enough yeast. The roof was a mixture of corrugated iron and tiles running to a porch that balanced four feet from the ground.

'Like a bad toupee on your grandmother,' was how Pine described it.

Sally's Mini was parked outside and we quickened our pace as the promise of shelter became reality. We were herded in with the efficiency of a practised cowpoke before we had even told her who we were. I suppose it was reasonable to assume that she'd worked it out but, still, I usually open the door with the chain on. After introductions were made and she'd run us through evacuation procedures, the names of her cats and how to use the immersion heater, and had us sign her fire register, she told us where the girls were, picked up a tray of tea and bid us follow her. She was Mother Munchkin, round like her home, as though she had needed layer upon layer of woollies to keep her warm in the Giles cartoon she had obviously stepped from.

She shuffled along before us, her coat sweeping the worn flags. We passed her private rooms and the kitchen before she led us up the stairs to a small sitting room with an empty fish tank, a radiogram and the girls sat round a fire. She placed the tea tray on a side table – she had shrugged off our offers to carry it – and attacked the fire with a poker before leaving us in a shower of sparks.

Wetter than fish spit, we pushed our way to the fire as we said hello and exchanged journey tales. We didn't explain why Stan felt the need to feel the wind through his hair at sixty miles an hour. Their trip was leisurely by comparison and enviably hassle-, stress- and bribery-free given that they'd only decided to come at the last minute. I was beginning to understand what Stan meant. Molly reached over me and lifted money off the mantelpiece and held her hand out. Stan and Pine each gave her a tenner as she stood beaming.

'What's that for?' I asked, narrowing my eyes.

'We had a sweepstake,' she told me gleefully, 'and guess who won?'

She stepped away from the fire and I eagerly took her place, forgetting to ask what the bet was as Ali smiled, handed me a drink and changed the subject.

'So how are you getting home?'

Pine looked at her and shrugged, we hadn't spoken about it walking here. Once Colin had disappeared, Pine had opened a bottle and we each drank until we got the giggles, the moment too celluloid to be real. We were still sniggering when Mrs Cromerty had opened the door. Eventually we were all looking at Sally. When she realised what our eyes were asking she laughed and that set us off again and in spite of how shitty things had been hours before, or maybe because of that, I knew now that we would be able to give Ting the wake he wanted.

Up until now, everything we had done was for us, the clubbing, even the skullcaps, the weekend, the whole shebang was designed to make us feel better. The different discussions we'd had in forming our wakes, in planning them, morbid as they'd seemed, were to ensure that whoever was left was happy, gaining a moment. Every time we forgot that or couldn't handle it we took something away from what we were doing, carrying out the last wishes of our friend. It had nothing to do with scattering his final mortal remains. He wanted us to remember this, his final event, as he put it, as the best weekend he'd never attend.

'The thing is, boys,' he'd said, 'you don't get to phone up the next morning and ask how the party was. You, Stan, you'll have to trust that you throw a better party when you're dead if you want to be remembered well.' He'd held his hands up as Stan raised his eyebrows. 'That's my point, you already have great parties, but to be able to do it when you're not there' – he clicked his fingers – 'that's got to be the best. That's your moment.'

'So what are you saying?'

'We need to promise now' – he'd held Sindee up like a holy relic and spoken gravely – 'that no matter what, we'll party, not for ourselves but for the one of us that's gone.'

If Ting was right, and I agreed with him at the time, then feeling sad was being selfish and there was no mitigation. Put up or shut up. Shit or get off the pot were his actual words. Now, crouching for heat against the cold reality, our laughter chased the doubts out of the room and I knew what he meant. We weren't supposed to be happy he was dead, we were supposed to be happy for knowing him and knowing he loved us enough to want us not to be sad. Otherwise what was the point in carrying him to Mull? It was the memory not the action that he wanted. Immortality in a smile. For the first time it felt like he would get his wish.

— ∗ —

The girls went to get ready to go to the pub and we were in the sitting room talking to Mrs Cromerty. They had gone to be girlie, primping and brushing their hair before letting the wind work its magic. It's raining, it's blowing, the hairdryer's going, but even suggesting leaving the house without making a vain attempt to achieve a 'do' would have been tantamount to crazy talk in a world where girls 'make up' before swimming or sweating at the gym. We sat round the table while we waited for them.

'What's the local pub like?'

Stan was adding a bit of whisky to Mrs Cromerty's tea as she held up her china cup.

'S'pose it depends on where you live.'

Stan choked on his tea, bubbles of the stuff fell from his nose back into the cup in Escher-like perpetual motion.

'Suppose we lived here.' Pine half laughed, shaking his head at Stan.

'Oh, it's no easy living here, son.' I glanced at Pine as she carried on off the plot. 'The cold, the rain, the reek of dead fish.'

'I'm with you there.' I held my cup in salute.

'I'm sure it's not,' Pine said, pointing out of the window. 'But it must be beautiful when it's not raining and the sun comes out.'

'Ah wouldn't know, son.' She shook her head and pursed her lips. 'Ah've only lived here seventy-three years.'

The pub, she eventually told us, was at the other end of the bay as I had guessed. She didn't, however, have an opinion on its character, having not set foot in it in over forty years. As a Presbyterian, a collection of people even Catholics have been heard to say are 'a bit fucking brainwashed', she preferred the church hall for her recreation in spite of the attendant uphill trek. She laughed when I asked her if the beach was nearby.

'Aye, just follow the sign for the deckchairs. They're right next to the ice-cream and umbrella van. If you still canna find it ask one of the men in yellow coats, they'll be the ones on the boats in the morning shouting "Hi-de-hi".'

I began to think that the lack of backbone to her house was because she had worn it away with her acerbic tongue until it had slumped in defeat. I appreciated her humour all the more for its incongruence. She just didn't look that sharp.

Pine explained why we wanted a beach and not the slipway outside the pub as she suggested and she made the sign of the cross, a reflex comforter I associated with my own grandmother who performed the same ritual every time she swore or someone mentioned the dead. At the end of the path, opposite the boat-house, there was a break in the rocks where a small slope led to the water's edge. Not so much a beach as a gravel pit. We could go there, she told us, otherwise it was a two-mile walk away from the bay.

'That'll do fine.' I looked and got agreement from Pine and Stan. 'Will it be okay if we light a fire?' I asked hesitantly, not wanting to sound too New Age.

'If you can find something that'll burn and isn't mine you can do what you want,' she said, standing up. 'There might be some wood in the boathouse. Will you all be wanting a fry-up in the morning?'

Maybe it's age that lets us dance with the reality of death and then move onto a new partner as the music changes. When you're losing friends at an increasing rate as your fifties become your retirement years and you shuffle noiselessly into your cool-down, death is as much a friend to you as once were the boozer or the club.

'He's gone to the club.'

'Oh, right. You want sugar in that?'

If youth was wasted on the young then resignation was misplaced in the old. The experience needed for acceptance only came after a lifetime of playing every day as your last, banking on the certainty that one day you'd be right. Getting older and tired, the game less adventurous and too much like hard work, the promise of a heaven-sent armchair and coal fire hazed between a dream and a rumour. Where we were trying to make sense of Ting's death, relating it to us and our futures, Mrs Cromerty dismissed such nonsense with the experience of age. I wasn't put out by her casual acceptance of our story, I was absolutely fucking sure her script was being written by Ting, her attitude and logic being supernaturally attuned to our frequency.

'Breakfast is normally between seven and eight.' She paused by the door. 'Since you'll be busy in the morning, I'll make an exception. But no later than nine, I've got chapel at ten.'

She left us a front door key, free rein in her kitchen, and walked off to bed. It was almost six o'clock.

We were opening the second bottle of Jack before the girls joined us and we finished it between us as we waited for their varnish to dry before we could get wet.

Within minutes of leaving the house all their work was blowing in the wind, the rain finding its own path under their hoods and through our clothes. Ting's bag was darkening and getting heavier with every raindrop but I refused to think about the symbolism. The girls linked arms and set a staggering pace through the gloom, attracted by the beacon of the pub sign around the bay. Half a mile as the seagull flies. If only.

Following suit, we walked arm in arm behind them, swinging Ting to keep time and singing into the wind. 'Raindrops Keep Falling On My Head'. We let the words carry us along.

▭ ★ ▭

The inside of the pub was strangely eclectic. In the lounge bar, the room directly off the street, tartan of every weave assaulted the eye. It blurred perspective and gave the room the feel of a padded cell. Deer roamed across purple landscapes with free abandon or stuck their heads through the walls in morbid curiosity. Probably asking themselves how they came to end up in a fishing village. Shaded lamps and an open fire created light that hung between ghostly and warming, throwing shadows of misshapen talismans of heritage and belonging. About as real as Disney but without the budget.

A real enough smile welcomed us in from the rain and Pine ordered a bottle of malt as we shook ourselves out of wet coats and took a table by the fire, taking turns to steam and dry. Stan was looking round in wonder, his eyes wide and his mouth agape.

'It's like a souvenir shop was melted down and sprayed around the room.' He held his tongue while the barmaid brought us a bottle and six glasses and left a jug of ice water on the table. 'I mean, fuck sake.'

Pine poured our drinks and smiled in agreement. Somewhere in the distance, close enough to hear the sound but not the song, someone was singing. Silently toasting Ting, I strained to hear above the crack of the logs and laughed at Stan's amazement.

Of course it was overdone. A Celtic caricature for the tourists in search of William Wallace, or maybe Rabbie Burns. All fire and faith, hairy-arsed and impassioned. They saw everyone coming, and as Gary Larson said best it was, 'Anthropologists! Anthropologists! Quick, hide the VCR.'

This was the Scotland found on shortbread tins and Hollywood blockbusters and what the tourists came to believe. It reminded me of Ye Olde Electrical Shoppe I'd once seen in Stratford.

The only others in the bar were three surfer-generation backpackers, drinking heavy and gaping in wonder below their baseball caps at the treasure displayed above their table. It was no less than the actual war axe of one Robert the Bruce, complete with a calligraphied account of its history. Never mind that the handle had been replaced four times and that the axe head had last been replaced by something from Taiwan, it was what the brochure had promised, a real life-taking slice of history. Also available in scaled reproduction gift sets from the tackle shop next door, according to the enthusiastic assertions of the drawling Americans as they stood up, kilts swirling and toe caps clumping, and stepped out the door. Off to dream of brave hearts of old glory.

A giant with one hand walked in behind them and disappeared behind the bar and through a door at the back. Before the fire had smothered the draught, he was back wearing an apron, like he was in a New York piano bar. He picked up the empty glasses from the kiltless table.

'You got a jukebox here, mate?'

He looked around the empty room before realising that Stan must indeed be speaking to him.

'Naw.'

He shook his head and walked away.

Stan shrugged. 'Probably just as well.'

I watched the barmaid have words with the giant and smiled at her as she crossed over to our table.

'Are you the ones that brought Ray's boy back?'

She spoke shyly, in an awkward way that had me straining to hear. Pine and Molly stopped talking and turned from the fire. Sally and Ali sat with Stan, their glasses motionless in front of their lips.

How bizarre.

She was out of place in her costume. She would have been at home running a saloon. Her voice was soft as though unsure, but I knew that once she was sure, about whatever, she would be what my mother calls blowsy. But there was a gentleness in her eyes, and maybe a little weariness drawn in the lines around them. They hid in their depths her own story – even in this closed-off and dead-end corner of the world lives played out and bore their own sorrow. I knew this to be true without knowing why, the softness of her voice speaking volumes.

'Yes.'

Stan looked at me and I shrugged.

She smiled then as though breaking a spell, passing it on until we all wore one, albeit gingerly, uncertain as to whether it would fit.

'Stevie' – she made a half-gesture to the bar – 'said you were asking about a jukebox.'

'Yes.' Stan nodded. 'Or a CD player or something?'

'No, not in here.' She rolled her eyes round the room. 'But there's a karaoke that we use at weddings in the back room.' Her smile got wider. 'You can use it if you like. It means I can shut this bar and have a go myself. What do you think?'

Stan was already on his way, arm in arm with Molly and Sally, before I got to my feet. Pine and Ali were straight behind them as I grabbed the whisky and coats.

'I'm Moira,' she was saying as I passed through the door behind the bar. 'Ray and I grew up together, it's my mother's guesthouse you're staying in.'

'Ahhh.' I stopped. 'That's how you knew who we were.'

'That and who else would have reason to be here on a night like this?'

'It's not exactly Blackpool, is it?' I raised my eyebrows as I looked round the empty bar and smiled.

'No.' She shook her head and looked round with a shiver. 'But it could be.'

◻ ⋆ ◻

This was where they hid the VCR.

Formica tables around which clustered cracked plastic chairs straight from school dinners. No effort had been made to smooth the ancient wooden floor and the only tartan in sight was on the tap for Tennent's Special. In the corner where they had taken the fluorescent tube out and hot-wired a mirrored globe, a state-of-the-ark tape deck accompanied Stevie. Over the course of the night we listened to him croon a lounge mix of 'Flower of Scotland' every time the stage, the pallet, was empty and his hand was likewise. He only knew the words to that one song.

Moira left us at a table close enough to the bar to be able to talk to us as she worked.

'It's an awful business,' she said to no one in particular. 'Sure, I never met the boy, but all the same. How's Ray taking it?'

'He's getting there,' I told her, not knowing what to say. 'Fairly balanced, considering.'

'Shame right enough.'

I wasn't sure she even heard me. Her eyes had a distant quality, measured in years. 'He's a fine man, always was.'

'A thieving wee bastart's wit he was.'

Other than Stevie, lost in the roar of immortal combat, there were two young men at one table, ourselves at another and a hat rack belting Glencheapest at the bar. It was he who spoke.

'Donald, you mind your tongue,' Moira admonished him. 'Don't speak ill of the deid.'

'He's no deid.'

'It's his flesh and blood they're carrying, noo wheesht. You're upsetting our guests.'

Stan was bristling.

The old man had turned to our table and Pine took hold of Stan's arm as he tried to stand. The two men at the table across from the bar stopped talking and looked up. Stan only had eyes for Donald. He was taking his comment at face value and didn't read the small print. Pine did.

'Stan,' he hissed. 'Don't be fucking with this. Have you seen *The Wicker Man?*'

My thoughts exactly.

Donald did a funny thing then. He laughed. First a tight giggle, but very soon after it changed into a chortle, out of place coming from such a shrunken man. There didn't look to be enough air in his body. But there was, and he was laughing, and before I knew it I was laughing. There I was, laughing at nothing and knowing it was funny. It reached Molly next and then Ali. Sally held out longer but gave up at the same time as Pine. Soon only Stan was left, but, faced with such odds, he put his head down and giggled, not quite sure whether to go the full hog.

'Don't mind me.' Donald got hold of himself under Moira's heavy-laden gaze. 'I liked the boy. Ray, I mean.' He winked and looked at Stan. 'But the wee shite used to steal my pigeon eggs.'

Stan laughed to cover his embarrassment. Squaring up to a pensioner proving to be too much for him, thankfully. Stevie stopped singing and we burst into applause as Moira beckoned him to the bar and he reluctantly put the microphone down, scowling uncertainly at our whooping and stamping.

Their eyes locked in common purpose, Sally and Stan scraped their chairs away and raced to the stage, pulling at each other as they went, the embarrassment of only moments before abandoned in the race for the mike. Cadaverous Donald lifted his glass and slid onto Stan's seat.

'Looks like he'll be away for a while.' He smiled and held his glass out as Ali lifted the whisky. 'I'll have that drink you were about to offer me and you can tell me what happened. Ray was a good enough boy, and his mother, well . . . Does she still like the dancing?'

'Donald, you behave yourself noo.'

Moira took Sally's chair and looked expectantly at me but I pointed at Pine, letting him take the floor. Happy as ever to have an audience, he shook his head slowly and began telling them what had happened. My gaze wandered as he spoke.

Sally and Stan were at an impasse. He held the mike out of her reach but she controlled the deck and the song sheets. Sensing Stevie glancing agitatedly from the bar in longing for the mike, they quickly compromised. Sally held it and Stan got to sing 'I Will Survive' in salute to karaoke lovers everywhere.

Their choice of songs was limited to an album of ballads by Runrig and two compilations with labels reading 'Loud' and 'Smootchie' penned across them. Out of these Pandora's boxes they surprisingly managed to find the classics.

'Stand By Your Man' led them to the 'Green Green Grass of Home', and Sally went 'Crazy' before Stan found 'Angels'. Between them they covered side one of Smootchie and were cueing up Loud, as Pine came to the end of his tale to much tutting and head shaking from Moira and Donald. Somewhere in the telling I watched Ali looking at the stage. She was smiling but it hadn't reached her eyes as Stan sang of 'Angels' and Pine spoke about madness.

'What about the polis?' Donald asked as if it mattered. 'What are they doing?'

'There's nothing to do.' Pine shrugged. 'The guy's back in a hospital somewhere with a clothes peg on his tongue. Case closed, sorry very much indeed.'

'Fucking crackpots.'

His denouncement drew the attention of our neighbours for the second it took them to realise he wasn't addressing them.

I emptied the last of the bottle into Donald's glass and shook my head.

'The man's insane.' Molly's tone was pitiful. 'He didn't even know he'd done something wrong.'

'Not him,' Donald spat. 'Those fuckin' eejits that run the country, that let things like this happen, them, they're the fuckin' mad ones.'

'I'll drink to that.'

We felt and thought the same. Pine sat back in his chair and reached for Molly's hand; he was drifting back into the cold again, and he wanted an anchor. Donald saw the change come over us as we fell silent.

'The worst of it is,' he said in a lighter voice, 'the very same thing could have happened to me a few years back.' He answered Moira's questioning look with a badly disguised wink.

'Seriously?'

Molly looked surprised and Pine sat up straight again, leaning forward, waiting to hear more.

'Oh aye,' he assured them. 'Lucky for me I decided that fancy dress was too much of a palaver so I didn't go to the party and I was okay in the end. It was touch and go for a while though.'

Pine shut his eyes and lowered his head as Donald began to snigger. Moira was with him now and I realised how astute he was; the hot air from his inane comparison brought us round again to where we came in. Laughing. Right on cue, Stan found the Steve Miller Band's 'Joker' and Pine pushed me off to the bar.

◻ * ◻

It seemed to take Stevie an age to serve me. By the time I got back to the table Donald was leaving with the only other locals in the bar and Moira was locking the door behind them. I sat next to Ali. I hadn't had a chance to speak with her since we arrived, not really, but now she was almost on her own as Pine and Molly sat opposite her swinging a chorus line for Stan and Sally.

'You going to get up?' I asked her, nodding to the stage.

'No.' She shook her head, brushing her hair across my shoulder. 'I don't think so. I'm too sober.'

'I've just the thing for that.' I smiled, handing her a glass.

As she took it I snuggled back in my seat and closer to her. Make or break time, I thought.

'About this morning –'

'Shhh.' She held her glass playfully against her lips and pushed at me with her hips. 'You're not going to apologise again, are you?'

Well, of course I was – how else could I find out where it had left me? – but obviously I wasn't now. Carry on regardless, as Paul Heaton would sing.

'No, I was going to say thanks. I had a great time before I fell asleep.'

'There was no before you fell asleep.'

'I meant in the café, in your kitchen.' I shrugged. 'All of it, I suppose. I had a good time.'

Her eyes sparkled as she sipped at her drink. 'Me too.'

'ME NEXT,' Pine shouted and stood up as Stan and Sally ran out of breath and let their last note fade. He grabbed me and pulled me up, thrusting me towards the stage.

Ali was grinning inanely, knowing that I was in the middle of bowling her over. Her eyes puckered as she shouted after me.

'Can you even sing?'

Not particularly well, I thought, as I allowed myself to be led to the stage, but that didn't matter.

Back in the first days of the café, Stan had experimented with karaoke. It didn't last long, but its impression did. From the start I was too concerned about how bad I'd sound. I'd listened in the bath. But Ting and even Stan had told me to forget about that.

'If all you're worried about is making an arse of yourself,' Stan had said, 'then fucking go for it. It washes off.'

I sounded like a wounded hyena chewing its tongue.

'It's not how it sounds,' Ting had assured me. 'It's how it feels.'

If only the rest of the café had agreed.

But I got the bug. We all did.

Not so as we actively sought out the buzz and hiss of the mike, but enough that we couldn't turn our back on it when it found us. Stan sang well of course, as did Pine. Ting and I didn't. He didn't care that he couldn't sing, it felt great. Even without a mike we would spend hours singing, driving here, walking there.

We would sometimes talk only using song lyrics. At that Ting was king, as long as he wasn't singing them. I knew the first lines to hundreds of songs, the rest I had to make up unless I'd absorbed them osmotically from the others.

Music was important to us, not anorak so, but enough. Finding karaoke here tonight could not have been an accident. Particularly in view of the fact that it fulfilled perfectly the criteria necessary for us to enjoy it. It was in an empty pub.

'Of course I can sing,' I tutted back to her before prising the warm mike from Stan's clenched fingers.

He reluctantly let it go and retreated back to the table with a petted lip. I wasn't sure if it was because he wanted to keep singing or if it was because I was about to, but I didn't have time to think about it as Pine cued up a song and we started to sway in time to the rhythm. I followed Pine's lead.

'Lonesome Pine' in the style of Laurel and Hardy.

For the next bottle of whisky I didn't find an opportunity to speak with Ali as we all got lost in the music. Sometimes singing along to the tapes and sometimes making it up as we went along. Ali sang like the angel she was. When I wasn't singing on the stage I tried to approach her to carry on our conversation. She, along with Molly and Sally, immediately covered her ears as I walked to the table, yelling at me not to sing any closer. I took it in good humour and took advantage of their purposeful deafness to leave them a gift that one of their other senses would sniff out before too long. I picked up a bottle and blew back to the stage.

If Ting was right about music touching the soul, about the soundtrack of life, I'd say that big Stevie had a hand in recording it. Just for us and just for now. For hours we all alternately screamed through the mike, crooned into our glasses or danced round the tables as our wake finally woke up.

Pine sang along with Andy Williams and I spun Ali in my arms.

Too good to be true.

And they were right. I couldn't take my eyes off her.

Stan and Sally harmonised in the background as Moira shadow-danced as she cleaned behind the bar and Stevie shuffled and cued up the next track.

We sang and we danced, the songs changing tempo and beat but the mood staying constant as we said our true goodbye in the way we had promised. There was even a bit of Elvis in there.

▭ * ▭

Stan and I were cooling down at the table while the girls held the stage. Sisters were doing it for themselves.

'Where's Pine?'

'Toilet.'

'Okay.' He smiled, looking at the girls. 'When he gets back it's time for the Brothers Gibb.'

A different party a few years ago at Stan's house. Stars In Their Arse, we'd themed it. Ting was going through a Bowie period and Stan talked Pine and me into being the Bee Gees. Camped up, hairdressing salon singers was how Pine insisted we play the night. Another solid party, one we even got to. The night ran like the plot from a seventies soft-focus porn flick: lots of lying around running fingers through hair, schmoozing about styles and style, folk music on an acoustic guitar, glimpses of thigh. When the lights dimmed I got lucky lucky lucky with Kylie Minogue.

Pine appeared and we approached the stage. Barry, Maurice and Robin.

The mike was hot to touch and the girls had to be grudgingly coaxed off the stage. I stepped close so that Ali would have to brush past me to get back to her seat and managed to convince myself that she lingered when she did.

And then we were in character.

Stevie had found us the Bee Gees.

We had the whole clicking thing going on, we had the hips swinging, toes shuffling, heads swaying and shoulders rolling. And we were in time.

'I know your eyes in the morning sun . . .'

Click, swing, shuffle, sway and roll.

'I feel you touch me in the pouring rain . . .'

And then the girls were back up.

By the chorus we were raising the roof.

'How deep is your love . . .'

Take that and party.

Chapter 18

a lifetime tonight

Our lock-in over, we all helped Stevie along with his song before he put the dust covers on his equipment.

I was in shock, almost drooling.

When I'd sat down to take a break from the singing, Ali had squeezed in next to me and held my hand. She'd smiled and it became my trembling hand. We sat like that, watching the others fight over the mike, until Moira told us that it was time to go. She asked them to let Stevie have the last song and then joined us at the table as backing. Once we'd clapped our appreciation, Ali slipped her hand back into mine and I glowed with her warmth. No mistake this time.

Moira said that her mother could sleep through winter so we could make as much noise as we wanted when we got back. She even gave us a bottle of Glenmorangie for the road.

It took a while for us to get going, the extended goodbyes and hugs for Moira and Stevie surprisingly emotional given that we'd barely spent the night with them. But Ray was right about this place, it was coming home, even for us walking away and pushing towards the unknown. They'd made us welcome; more than that, they'd helped to give us the moments that made our journey worthwhile. I would be leaving Ting's ashes tomorrow and taking in their place a feeling of having done something right. Gained as well as lost. Pine and Molly set the pace as we went, with Ali and me hand in hand behind Stan and Sally, who were carrying Ting between them. We all staggered home, along the dock of the bay with Otis and the Sixteen Men of Tain.

— * —

Swinging our arms and dancing as we went, we were sung up and whisky downed as we passed the boathouse. It was still raining and we were soaked but I didn't care. In sight of the house the others ran for the door, squealing and giggling as they did. But I walked, with Ali. I didn't want the moment to end so I was dragging my feet.

'Are you all right?' she asked, her voice husky from singing.

'I'm perfectly unhappy, thank you very much for asking,' I told her with a smile as I lifted and kissed the back of her hand.

'That's an oxymoron.'

'I'm not sure' – my smile got bigger as I looked around and squinted into the distance – 'but I think it's a cow and I know it's definitely a bit harsh to be calling me stupid when I tell you how I feel.'

She rolled her eyes into mine and showed me what a smile could really do in the hands of a professional.

'What about you?'

'Knackered.' She pulled at her wet trousers and they sprang back to her thigh with a squelch. I'd never been jealous of cotton before.

'And I want to get out of these clothes.'

'Oh.'

I couldn't hide my disappointment as I kicked at the stones as we walked to the door. I was hoping she was going to stay up and let me charm her to bed or at least wear her down enough for a kiss and a cuddle. Wasn't that why she took my hand in the pub?

'What about you?'

'I'm fine, honestly.'

'I know that,' she teased. 'But do you want me to get out of these clothes?'

I very nearly came then and there.

'That,' I said, stopping outside the door, 'I would like.'

'Me too.'

She pulled me into a hug against the wall under the eaves and I hoped that she wouldn't be bounced away by the intensity of my thumping heart. The rain fell forgotten as we kissed gently, unhurriedly, through my smile.

I stepped back hesitantly as the sharp sting of how we came to be here resounded with the crashing waves behind me but she drew me back to her warming contours. I groaned at the release she was affording me, perfectly unhappy, crest-of-the-wave stuff. The ups higher and longer than the downs.

She nibbled and whispered in my ear, 'Ready to go to bed and wake up smiling?'

'First- or second-date night?'

'Second.'

'Mmmm.' I pretended to think about it and wiped the smile off my face. 'It might take me a couple of goes but I'm willing to try.'

'Good,' she sparkled. 'Me too.'

She bit me gently, winked and laughed her way into the house, leaving me to float in behind her.

This was the balance that I knew I'd been searching for. The shifts I had to make from one to the other were less gut-wrenching, unforced. I meant it, I was perfectly unhappy. I couldn't be anything else. Ting was dead, Ali was here in my arms. The contrasting emotions left me dizzy, unstable; the pangs of longing left me unhappy, sad but also strangely exhilarated. What had changed, what gave me the strength to think about them, feel them and then smile and joke, was the belief, the crystal-clear and granite-hard fact, that it was okay, perfectly okay to be sad about the past as long as I remembered to look to the future. I knew why I was sad, but more importantly I knew now how to be happy. It was what Ray had told me: don't try, be.

The fire was still burning in the sitting room and the others were sunk in the chairs around its glow, glasses in their hands and songs soft on their lips. Torn between staying with my life-long friends caught in the hypnotic draw of the flames, and taking Ali back to the room for the few hours we had left before morning, I decided that friendship was the most important thing. Trusting my instincts, I emptied the glass Stan passed me and offered Ali my hand. The others stood to kiss and hug good night and I knew I'd been right. Pine and Stan were true friends and we left them smiling as Ali led me to our room.

▭ ✶ ▭

'Do you want to have a shower?'

'Yes, I think so.'

'You don't mind sharing with me, do you?'

'Mind sharing?' I shook my head and answered. 'It's hard to believe that I never thought to suggest it myself.'

I wasn't sure if she meant the room or the shower, but either way it seemed my smile was here to stay.

While we waited for the water to heat for the shower we sat on the bed and had a smoke. I was wedding drunk in the way that you can drink all day and still be sober-ish, dancing and cavorting into the night and sweating the alcohol out. This was the end of days and the beginning of days and it just wouldn't do to be straight. Ali was relaxed, lying back on the patchwork throw-over, flapping her arms as though making snow angels and I sat against the padded headboard wondering why she was here. I knew I'd been a prat when we first met and she'd been drunk when we almost got together last night. It didn't feel like I'd only known her for a few days. Her coming to Mull had surprised me and, happy as I was to be sitting watching her breathing and stretching, my heart quickened at the thought. My emotional outpourings yesterday morning over her kitchen table had done nothing to discourage her, or she was happy to hide the fact that I was hard work. I knew that given time and my new fearless resolution – *carpe diem* and fuck the consequences – I could be a successful low-maintenance boyfriend. The sound of our clicking had been muffled by circumstance and snoring, but I was becoming convinced it had been there, the fitting together of two seemingly random pieces on a double-sided jigsaw.

I'd moved on from thinking of her as Ali the Unattainable and let the knowledge that she was as interested in me as I was in her flood my body, filling me with a sense of worth that had been missing since I split with Kirsty. Sitting on the bed was like waiting to take off on a magic carpet into the unknown, with Ali holding my hand and keeping me from falling to earth. It could be that this was the only travelling I would need to do.

I thought of Stan's assertion that if I went away she would not come with me. Maybe she already had. She came with Sally and was staying with me, her choice. All my prevarication and petty insecurities aside, she had picked me, and my instincts were back on track; she gave me validation. Ting used to say that being single was a transition period where we prepared for the eventuality of romance. Every action played out with the understanding that it's almost the rehearsal for real life, a way of gathering skills and competencies that make the next scene flow smoothly over the rocks that tripped the last time. I tended to agree. It wasn't a conscious thing either. I didn't cry into my pillow at night wishing I was in a relationship. Yet sitting on a bed with a beautiful girl, knowing that she has just travelled three hundred miles to hug you asleep, makes you realise that life may be the same, the same programmes and pictures, but being alone felt as complete as a TV without a remote control. Not looking for a relationship, I had stumbled into one in spite of being at a low ebb, biorhythms all over the place, and behaving like some Neanderthal with a drink problem, and although I was going to hang on to it with the tenacity of a limpet, I was still unclear exactly what Ali was going to get out of it.

Of course I considered myself a catch. If not exactly handsome, I didn't hit every branch on the way off the ugly tree. I could make her laugh more than a mirror, and didn't always look as though I got dressed in the dark, but I knew she could get that from anyone, probably one wrapped in designer labels and charm. I didn't want to examine it too closely though, in case I found the fault.

She flipped onto her stomach with ease and crawled up the bed until she was lying beside me, her head in my lap.

'It's good to find hard men,' she said languidly.

I laughed. 'You mean hard to find good men.' I was beginning to believe my own press and spoke with confidence.

'No.'

Then I knew what she meant and laughed at my own attempt at being clever. We embraced roughly and I pulled at her clothes as though they were on fire.

She pushed me away and stood up. 'I'll just be a minute.' She stepped into the en suite. 'Try not to fall asleep.'

I poured us some wine and walked round the room, turning out the light and taking deep but quiet breaths. The shower could wait. The rain belted against the window and the open curtains let an elemental light wash over and beyond me. In spite of last night's debacle I opted to wait for her in the wicker chair facing the storm. No rocking allowed.

◫ ★ ◫

With her glass lazily drinking from her lips, Ali meandered over and lowered herself in front of me. Kneeling there, she held my star-bright gaze and kissed me. It wasn't the wine that was intoxicating although I felt its warmth as she dribbled it between my teeth. The faint taste of mint threw me until I realised that she must have brushed her teeth while I was setting the mood. I stifled a smile as I imagined her in front of her mirror telling herself: 'Don't blow this, that's Pennance Ward out there!' Somehow I didn't think so but it was a good thought and the timing was even better as Ali, seeing me grin, blew me away with her smile. I stood and lifted her to her feet, her body pushed against me and we began undressing in a rage of desire that wouldn't let us stop kissing until I fumbled at her zipper when I realised she had no underwear on.

Slow down, I thought, this is no place to be fucking around. Ali sensed my hesitation and peeled herself away from me, leaving me with a swollen lip as she kissed and bit herself free.

With Ali sitting at the edge of the bed, I felt self-conscious standing naked in front of her and moved closer, the old demons driving me to my knees before her, out of sight. She leant in and I took a nipple on my tongue as she drew me to her. The hairs on the back of my neck stood on end when I felt her nails run lightly from my shoulders to map the contours of my tightened backside. When she took hold of my erection, she gave me a squeeze that tightened every muscle, then she cried out as I bit down on her nipple in involuntary response. Far from eliciting chastisement, it brought a flush to her throat and a gravelled edge to her voice.

She whispered against my ear, causing me to jerk in her hand. It was a close thing, and I owe a donation to the RSPCA for the volume of images that led me back from the edge.

Holding her face against my neck, she slid off the bed and left a trail of hot breath in my hair as we met and merged. My eyes opened and I made a sound that would only have woken dogs. Nestling on my thighs, she kissed me deeply. I couldn't move. No thrusting possible, or possibly even allowed, as Ali seemed to be content taking control and moving me with pelvic dexterity. I contracted my muscles and pushed gently at the bottom of her spine with the heel of my hand and heard her breath quicken and the redness reappear at her throat. The blotchy contrast to her perfect skin followed the line of her neck, between her breasts, and spread as though searching for my touch.

Too close to continue, I pushed her back onto the bed and lay next to her, dragging a finger along her body watching the swelling of goosebumps and the fractal display as heat became movement. Kissing her neck and shoulders, I let my hand come to rest on the non-roundness of her belly, rocking her slightly. She responded by lifting her hips and pushing at me. Bizarre images of my cat looking for attention leapt to my mind and for a moment I thought I could hear purring. Maybe I did, I wished hopefully. I kissed the length of her body, paying attention to every pore. While the eroticism of this certainly added to her arousal, it was essentially an exercise in erection retention as I was under no illusion as to the effect any direct stimulation would have on me. I was ready and set to go off. From the radiating warmth of her inner thigh, I looked up to find Ali propped on an elbow, in turns smiling and pouting. I kept eye contact until I pushed through her pubic hair and saw her lips part as she closed her eyes and fell back onto the pillow. Her clitoris sought out my tongue. She kicked her leg behind my back and guided me with her hand until she arched and slipped into an orgasm. I didn't stop until she grabbed and crushed me to her chest.

Her clamminess answered the questions about intensity and realism that normally accompany first-time sex, and even from within the protection of my drunken armour I was relieved and not a little pleased. Too hot to remain lying on her, I rolled to the cool side of the bed and relaxed, thinking, somebody shoot me while I'm happy. Meaning it this time. Then it all went by in a blur as, unencumbered by any such thoughts of embarrassment or self-consciousness, Ali pulled the trigger.

I've had good sex before Ali, but can't recall ever feeling as exhausted. I wanted to close my eyes but she dragged me from the bed and kissed me awake under the dripping shower, its pressure less than that of the rain outside. We worked ferociously to get into a lather, sweat running faster than the water. Ali cleansed me of the dust and grime of my journey, and the guilt. It may have been the whisky but, with my eyes closed, I immersed myself in the ritual cleaning, being born again in her purifying touch. The only thing missing was the white linen smock of the high priestess, and that was a bonus. She dried me with a coarse towel and, completing the formal rites, lay on the bed, her arms outstretched in welcome. Starry-eyed, I knelt beside the bed again, an acolyte before Eris, and began to worship.

Curling up together afterwards, we listened to the storm posturing loudly against the glass in the thick moments before sleep arrived and took her. It tried to come for me too, but I was making it wait, as sometimes it had me do, until I had etched the rise and fall of her slumbering form in the mindscape labelled 'Oh My Fucking Lord'.

Chapter 19

tom sorrow's night

Sleep wouldn't come when I thought I was ready and I slid out from the bed, careful not to wake Ali, but making sure I got another look at her perfect nakedness.

I was restless, my mind firing off in random thoughts.

This night was special. This weekend. Ting had given me a platform and I was centre stage, the play finally taking shape, finding direction. I looked out the window at the dark brooding clouds and caught, just for a second, the glint and shine of a star.

Gazing up, I knew that the stars were always there even if sometimes I couldn't see them. It was just a matter of believing. I knew that this was important stuff I was messing with and I seemed to be on the edge of understanding it. My guilt, my fear and my sadness were all veils that clouded my soul and hid the bright lights of the future. Was that it? Was the storm passing? Before I could grasp it, it disappeared. Ting would know.

With that thought I quietly dressed and slipped from the room. Stan or Pine might still be up and I hoped that Ting would be with them.

They turned and smiled as I stepped into the sitting room. 'Couldn't sleep?'

'Ali chuck you out for snoring?'

I looked archly at Stan as he hastily inspected his navel.

Pine gave me a wink as I took a seat next to him and Molly. Sally had gone to bed not long after Ali and me. Ting's bag was sat on a chair next to the antiquated radiogram as would be his wont. They were talking about Tom Night.

When I'd gone to bed they'd decided they were hungry and had found a couple of pizzas in the freezer. Stan coaxed life into the record player and dusted off an album he'd found behind the fish tank, Tommy Emmanuel, an antipodean fingerpicking maestro. Just the sort of thing that would make a great find for Tom Night.

We'd each had different nights. I'd had John and Paul, Pine had Steve, Ray and Elvis, Stan had William and Bruce, and Ting always chose Tom.

Conceptually it was simple enough, but putting it into practice was more than a little complicated at times depending on how bum-nipped we got about detail. Acceptable, Borderline and Not Even With a Shoehorn were the categories, and each of us had a veto that neither Pine nor I had used, but which Stan and Ting used almost automatically. Our theme nights encouraged us to search out more and more obscure entries, each night being devoted to all things Ray or Bruce or Tom or whoever.

On finding the Tommy Emmanuel record they had slipped into the memory of our last Tom Night with Ting, remembering in detail the detail. Ting had a formula for his night and a list of what was appropriate.

The acceptable were the likes of Mr Waits and Mr Jones. We could watch Mr Cooper, *Dr Who* – the Baker years, *Tom and Jerry* and anything with Terry-Thomas in it given that the h was silent. If we used the PlayStation we could only play Lara or Tommi Makinen's Rally. The detail was exquisite, Ting had been tireless in his search for Tomness. Only food was fairly straightforward, anything with ketchup, but we restricted ourselves to certain alcohol until the sun came up. Old Tom and Thomas Hardy Ale – reputably one of the strongest beers in the world and a favourite of Ting's any night of the week, Tomatin single malt and Tom and Jerry cocktails.

Those nights were our mothers' sewing bees or our fathers' club nights, our equivalent of pyjama parties and makeover nights for the boys. Our nights of Tomesterone, blanketed from the world, in the isolation booth that came from being in 'The

Club'. The theme gave reason to the need. Sitting at home listening to dodgy sounds, playing computer games and getting wasted is considered tickety-boo if you're nineteen, live at home and wear concert T-shirts and ponytails. Approaching thirty, it's a bit sad. But with a theme like Tom Night, or poker or comedy night, it becomes not only acceptable, but something worthy of comment and value through its exclusivity and exoticism. In short, a club.

Normally, it would only be the four of us. Only once before had we invited non full-time dick carriers to a night, and the change in dynamics had been disastrous.

We'd had a Ray Night at Pine's, and Zoe, his then muse, Kirsty and Sally had joined us. Things started well enough, even if most of their contributions except Mssrs Charles and Winstone were vetoed. We drank, we ate, we talked shit. Stan asked Ting, 'Breathing underwater or flying?' while we watched Ray Liotta help bury a wise guy. Ting showed no hesitation in wanting to fly, of course; nor did Stan and I, with only Pine going subaqua. He turned his attention to the girls. 'And you ladies?' That's when the wheel fell off.

'If I choose one would it mean . . . ?'

'Could I fly underwater holding my . . . ?'

'Do you mean flying in a plane or . . . ?'

Arrrgggh. Just play the fucking game. That's what the vibe told me the other X-chrome-deficients in the room were thinking behind their frowns. And I agreed. Black or white, hard or soft, answer or procrastinate, do we fire our electrons in totally different ways? Same information, different summation.

'It's just a fucking game, don't analyse it, feel the answer before your brain tells you.'

Ting was only trying to be helpful, but Sally was having none of it. Zoe and Kirsty made room for her on the couch, and all three sat and took the huff together, saying it was a stupid question.

Well, maybe it was, but it was what we did; we spent time answering stupid questions. Maybe we couldn't fly, but did that mean that we shouldn't think to heaven and wonder what if? More probably, it's that the answers can be foolish, or stupid even, but in spite of the opinion of those who missed their true vocation with the fall of the Third Reich and so became priests, no question can truly be stupid, unless it's 'do you want to go to hell?' And asking questions of the fluff that fills the cracks in our state-agendised force feducation was pretty much how we filled the commercial breaks in our lives. But apparently we did it differently. Temperaments and aptitudes differentiating those who were with us and those who . . . well, those who had less testosterone. We, boys, were good at asking the questions that we subconsciously knew we needed answers to. That's our thing. Girls are good at different things, like taking stuff back to shops and noticing changes in hairgrip fashion. We major in different arenas. Questions that appear inconsequential – even if they aren't – sticks, throwing stones and other such indulgences that make our hair hurt if we don't care about them. We don't do *Eastenders* – unless pant-driven – soft furnishings or the new improved Clinique range, and we don't take the huff when girls do.

'When was the last time you dragged a stick along a fence?' Ting had used his most placating voice.

'I'm not patronising you,' was his best defence as he tried to slide around the death stares of three decidedly Teflon-friendly girls. And that was his point. How could they enjoy our nights of escapism when they refused to appreciate a good stick or climb to our level of awareness and sophistication in addressing life's less visited importance? He had the good sense to leave out his previously prepared and thus highly fucking patronising monologue on the disrespect their bringing Ray Burr's *Ironside* showed to the gravity of the night.

Pine in the role of host had tried to defuse the situation with strategic use of chocolate from a Sting Ray collector's set that he'd ordered specially, a nuance well lost on the girls who spent the rest of the night somewhere else.

As I joined them reminiscing, Molly punctured our bloated sense of esotericism and stick-led superiority by digging a bottle of Tomintoul from her bag. Ting's favourite. She was going to give it to us in the morning to toast Ting away, but guessed at the importance of this night's farewell. Our ramblings had become an impromptu Tom Night into which she slipped with the stickiness of pheromonal lubrication. Which is to say with ardour and ease. We didn't have the videos or the games, but we had our imagination and it held us entranced.

▭ * ▭

An hour later only Molly and I still functioned.

I was unsurprised at her ability to go the distance, having witnessed first-hand, albeit under her own protection, her model dysfunctional family party. The first time I met her father, he was perched on the top of a jukebox explaining the principle of thermal uplift with the help of a newspaper and gum combination, Harry and Jack. Harry was holding a paraffin heater under one arm and swigging from the Jack. Outside of myself and Molly no one was listening.

The masses within the Lower Side Liberty Club's snug bar were happy enough that the unplugging and placing of the Wurlitzer at the top of the stairs meant they could hear more of the growls from the bare-knuckle fighters in the makeshift ring. The smack of flesh and blood. Quite literally. The two men descaling each other were doing so for the entertainment of the octogenarian matriarch whose birthday we were celebrating. Their and Molly's grandmother. Her mother was refereeing.

At a time when the majority of her family were either comatose through alcohol or pugilism, Molly was still cognisant enough to be able to point out the flaws in her father's logic at launch, in the air, and as he hit every step. In that same time I managed to say 'Fuck'. Harry had shaken his head and wandered off to watch what his brother had married into, leaving Molly and me to hold the heater up again.

Stan lay curled in front of the fire, competing with one of Mrs Cromerty's cats for its warmth. Pine was lying on the couch sleeping like a stroke victim.

'Too ugly.' Molly pushed at him until he turned away from us. 'That's better.'

I had to agree. As with most things, Molly was right. She handed me the last piece of cold pizza.

'So.' She shuffled herself comfortable. 'I finally get you to myself.'

I could only nod and chew.

'You and Ali an item now then?'

Another nod and a cheesy smile.

'So, what's up?'

Molly knew me, I mean really knew me, and for that I was glad. We'd lived together in a student house for two years and had a thing that lasted one full weekend. In our first year, we were giddy just from being away from home and out in our new real world, full of righteousness and dungarees. We were model students in our apathy to the system. Fuck lectures; we learnt in the bar and got drunk on our loan-given right to make a difference. Not one of us suspected we were being manipulated by overdraft-hungry bankers and publicans with an agenda of their own. Back then we were hyped on campus shenanigans. One night we'd had the de rigueur D and M after a union disco, even though I didn't know what it meant. I just knew that if I wanted to get anywhere with her it was required. Possibly as a consequence of us both being off our face, we hit it off. The next two days were spent alternatively having student sex: shallow and frenzied, and student conversation: deep and meaningful. By Monday we had become close enough for her to tell me that we would never have sex again, ever, and that I had just become her new best friend. I said 'oh' and that was the start of it.

After halls of residence, we shared houses in Brickend Road and a seven-bedroom affair in Queensway that nearly cost us our finals due to its proximity to the pub. Friends ever since, it was only when she started going out with Pine that we stopped snogging at New Year. After graduating, when I came back home, she moved to Bristol, but we were still in regular contact thanks to her company mobile phone and Beemer. Promotion, family and boredom brought her to Leeds, and after three weeks of getting to know everyone, she asked Pine out and has been in love ever since. At this moment she had her feet pushed under the table and was nestling her back into his bum.

'Why aren't you in bed snoring the sleep of the exhausted?'

'I couldn't sleep.' I shrugged.

'So, what's up?'

'Well, I'm a wee bit pissed off about that whole Ting getting killed thing . . .' I pushed my chin out and shook my head. 'Apart from that . . .' I was already one step ahead of her and ducked to avoid the lighter that hurtled past my head and narrowly missed Stan's ear, striking him firmly on the nose. He swatted at it, but didn't wake.

Molly brooked no nonsense when she felt she was on course for a d and m, our understated carry-on from longer-hair days. And she was a thrower. With little provocation and less warning, she would propel any object to hand if she thought I was being clever. Or trying to be.

'You know what I mean,' I said, still flinching.

She did know, but that's not what she was talking about. And she knew I knew it.

Ergo: gas-fired missile.

'Come on.'

I shrugged and ate my pizza, thinking about everything that had happened in the last few days and how I could explain what I was thinking.

Ting of course, Ali, even Donna. Travelling and my future. The time-honoured pursuit of 'what happens next' that kept Russell Grant in pullovers.

Pine farted and Molly punched him but remained where she was. True love, I thought.

'I don't really know,' I told her. 'I'm trying to make sense of what's happened. Trying to move on from here.'

And then the thoughts came to life with my breath.

'I feel as though I've been given a second chance, an opportunity to start over.'

'You mean a kick up the arse?'

That's exactly what I meant.

'Remember when Kirsty and I split up and I got over it by getting a hobby?'

'Seven,' she reminded me.

'Whatever. Well, this time living is going to be my hobby. No more tomorrow man.'

I knew I meant it as I told her. About Ali and how she made me feel, about Kirsty getting married and how it confused me because I didn't feel anything about it. I spoke about Ting and how he was pushing me from beyond the grave to do something different before it was too late. To move my life on.

Words that surprised me, describing a new world of opportunity and adventure. Just like the old days. Molly frowned at me when I said that. But it would be. Not really the old days, but their hyperbolic memory updated and brought to life by the power of new dreams.

'And the new dreams are?' she asked.

That's when she stumped me. I wasn't sure. Travelling? Ali?

'Well, I don't know that yet, but I know they're coming.'

I sat up and rubbed the pins and needles from my feet. Molly was watching me and nodding.

Ahab, Mrs Cromerty's cat, woke and stepped over Stan, stretched himself out and jumped onto my lap. I wasn't used to a cat that was so soft. If Kato jumped on my lap I tended to sit frozen until she became distracted or her tail stopped flicking and I could make my escape. We'd agreed that if her tail was moving it wasn't a good time to touch her. Ahab unnerved me by being friendly.

'I've been trying to explain that to you for years, and you're just getting it now. Go figure.'

'Well, thanks for letting me work it out myself, Mum.'

'Like you could do that.' She raised her eyebrows. 'I told you when you and Kirsty split up that she was still in love with you, but you wouldn't see that either.'

'Couldn't.'

'Wouldn't. I told you to . . .'

'Okay, I get it, I'm crap and you're great.'

She leant in closer to me and cupped her ear.

'I said I'm crap and you're great.'

'Excuse me?'

'The greatest.'

'Thank you.' She practically sang it as she reached for the last of the Tomintoul. 'So when does this new Pennance step up to the plate?'

I emptied my glass and looked at her, recognition lighting her eyes a fraction before reaching her smile. We said it together and laughed.

'Tomorrow!'

feeling groovy

The curtains were closed and the lights were off as we sat in the tempered glow thrown by the log fire. Shadows and flames lending ambience to our silences. We were both still starving, and with our unofficial Tom Night officially over with the sun up, I pushed Ahab from my knee and we swayed to the kitchen to kill the munchies.

'Right.' Molly rubbed her hands, all *Ready Steady Cook*, and attacked the fridge.

Not surprisingly she homed in on the bacon straight away, and in no time at all the fat was spitting its surrender.

'How long will this take?'

'I'm guessing ten, maybe fifteen minutes?'

'Too long.'

So we microwaved chips: nine minutes. Too long. We made toast: four minutes. Too long. We settled on a bowl of corn-flakes in the meantime, and both agreed we had them bad. Molly grated cheese and then spread both mayonnaise and brown sauce on the toast banjo.

Back at the table we sat quietly, eating in detail. Every bite a taste sensation, and then a sharp shot of Jack to fire the sauce.

'You should have married Kirsty.'

And there was the connection that demonstrated deep friendship. It was Kirsty that I'd been thinking of when Molly spoke. She knew me very well. Of course, she would have been on target if she'd gone for Ali, Donna, or any of the girls from *Friends*. I felt no remorse in thinking about other girls when Ali was only a few feet away sleeping off our amour. It was, I knew, only natural. Nothing shameful. The species programming that kept us aware of the possibilities. I wanted things to work with her, I had a good feeling that they would and was sure she would let me keep my fantasies. She must have had her own.

'What about Ali? Don't you think I should marry her?'

'We're not talking about now. We're talking about then. You should have married Kirsty when you had the chance.'

'I didn't want to marry Kirsty.'

Over the years I'd become accustomed to Molly and her tangential thinking. Conversations rarely followed a prescribed route and she paid scant attention to the nuances of general discussion, like the use of reference, for example.

'Yes, you did.'

She was also prone to the non sequitur.

'Don't talk daft.' I waved her off. 'I'm not sure I ever loved her.'

''Course you did.'

I screwed up my face and stuck my finger in my mouth, sucking the fawn goo from my fingers. She was lying on the floor next to Stan now, blowing smoke rings to the ceiling.

'You're just saying that because she's marrying someone else. You're protecting yourself.'

'No, I'm saying it because it's true.'

She propped herself up on her elbow. 'Something smells fishy here.'

'No, I'm serious. I think that's why I was so ready to be happy for her.'

'I don't mean Kirsty.' She sat up and looked around. 'Something really smells fishy.'

Molly was staring at me.

'What?'

'Can you not smell anything?'

With a flashback to Saturday, I tucked my feet under me and closed my eyes.

'Fish?'

'Fish.'

'The whole place has been reeking of it since we arrived. Where have you been? Don't throw that.'

Too late.

'Over here.'

She was stood in front of and away from the radiogram and I could see her wrinkle her nose in discomfort as she gestured in the general direction of Ting's bag.

'It's somewhere round here.'

I snaked my way along the floor to her, pulling myself onto the arm of Ting's chair.

'God, it is stronger over here.'

Then Molly gasped and pulled me out of the way as Ahab exploded from Ting's bag, a furball in tinfoil hissing past my ear.

I turned in time to see him streak past the door and, jumping over Stan, I gave chase.

'It still smells.'

Molly was staring at Ting's bag and I stopped as I reached the door. I hesitated and let that particularly unsavoury image take hold. Taking a John McClane moment to compose myself, I turned back to her. Something in the bag was smelling like three-day-dead house guests and it was down to me to face it. Molly stood aside as I reached a hand to the bag and took hold of one of the straps and began lifting it towards me.

'JESUSFUCKINCHRIST.'

I jumped back and turned to a giggling Molly.

'Don't do that.' I tried not to laugh as relief washed over me with a chill. 'Do you want to do this?'

'Don't be such a baby.' She took a step back and clasped her hands behind her back.

'Well, then.'

With one eye on Molly, I lifted the bag until it fell open enough to see inside.

'Looks like a big jar of coffee and a tuna sandwich.'

'Take them out.'

'You take them out.'

'Oh, for fuck sake, give me it here.'

'Don't take that tone with me,' I whined. 'You know I hate tuna.'

I cleared space and Molly placed the oversized jar and two half-eaten tuna and sweetcorn sandwiches on white bread beside each other on the table. We looked at each other, we looked at the table, we shook our heads and began skinning up at the same time, neither of us having spoken. Minutes passed while we stared, both of us agog.

'Do you want to go first?'

I looked at her and shrugged. 'I have absolutely no idea. The cat obviously smelt the tuna, but why was it there in the first place? I don't have a scooby.'

'Me neither, but no wonder it's stinking. Look at the bread, it must have been in there for days.' She shook her head in question. 'Munchies?'

'Again?'

'No. Did someone put them there in case you got the munchies?'

In what some alcoholics call a moment of clarity, and half-way down my smoke, I figured it out.

'Ting.'

'Ting? You think Ting made you a sandwich for the train?'

'No. They were there in case Ting got the munchies.'

I told her about his gran making sandwiches when Ray told her Ting was going away. Then I went in search of the cat. Kato, I had no doubt, could have ingested the tinfoil wrapping easily but I wasn't so sure about the rotund Ahab's robustness and my conscience didn't want to test his constitution. With the assistance of a stout stick, I chased him from the kitchen, forcing him to surrender his catch, and walked back to find Molly staring into the coffee jar.

I stood frozen in the doorway.

'You've opened it.'

'Haven't you?'

I threw a glance at Stan as I walked over to the table and knelt opposite her, not yet prepared to look. I'd thought about it before, but had shied away. Absurd as I knew it was, I thought that if I looked and saw him it would somehow become more real. He would be dead. Carrying a bag and calling it your friend is almost acceptable social behaviour – rucksacks made from unstuffed toys, all with personalities and names, it's barely eccentric. But to actually do it – to take your friend out in a bag – that requires something more. And for me it was denial. I had to mask the truth behind the unrealness of it. Right up until the last moment I was expecting Ting to sneak up behind me and ask me what kind of fool thing I was doing partying with his bag. Didn't I get the note?

'No. We didn't even look in the bag.'

Molly gazed behind my eyes and her voice softened as she asked if I wanted her to close the jar. I shook my head. I thought of what Stan had said about knowing Ting was there, only not. He was right about that but not in the way he thought. What was the point in closing the jar? There was nothing in it that mattered.

'It's not Ting.'

'What?'

'That, down there, it's not Ting.'

'What do you mean?' she asked softly. 'Who is it?'

'It's nobody. That's who. It's just a bunch of ash.'

Molly has a way about her of cutting to the chase. She gets behind the words and pushes them aside, finding the thought that gave rise to them and working from there.

'You sure?'

'Only one way to find out.'

I followed her gaze and let out a breath as I looked down. A twinge. No more than a brush of cold wind. The storm outside didn't even bother to lend its thunder to the occasion. I was expecting a hand squeezing my heart, a kickboxing match in my stomach. I got a shock. It was ash. Coarse ash.

Not soul dust.

I flickered a tight smile at Molly before reaching into the jar.

'Pennance?'

It scratched at my nails as I dug my fingers down. I felt its texture and its coldness not sending chills down my back and realised that I was fine. This was sleeping with the light off for the first time, knowing that from that moment on it didn't

matter. Another tick in the box and move on to the next challenge; light on, light off, it was old news. I knew I was stone
drunk, but I knew I was going to be okay. Any fear I had about
putting my hand into the lion's mouth had disappeared; it was
a pussy cat and I'd tamed it.

Ting wasn't in a jar, he didn't need one where he was, it
couldn't hold him. It was us who needed it. We who carried
it, close to our hearts, treating it with deference and imbuing
it with mystic qualities, we were the ones that it was for. It
gave us a focus, a receptacle for our emotional outpourings,
somewhere to point the finger and say, 'That's why I'm sad.'
My fear for this jar of earth yesterday seemed laughable now.
If I'd found a turd in my toilet and knew it was Ting's, I
wouldn't frame it or pickle it, I'd flush it into the sea without
a second thought (except maybe to think how gross it was that
he'd left it there, the dirty bastard). Just as we would be doing
tomorrow with this dry, finger-scratching nothing in the jar.
The bits he had finished with.

'I'm sure now.' I looked up. 'He's not here.'

'I know.'

She said it with such conviction that I was embarrassed for
myself.

'Weez cool.'

'Good. Now can we get rid of that tuna before it burns
through the table?'

It was just about then that the lion snapped its jaws. Shaking
my hand out of the jar, I started to stand and rewrap the
sandwiches. Ahab leapt from behind Molly and took a swipe
at the rustling tinfoil. He caught me by surprise and I jumped
back, dropping the tuna and spilling the jar on top of it.

I landed on Stan.

By the time I'd reacted, Molly had the jar upright and was
scooping handfuls back in, all the time with one eye on Stan's
restless form. The cat sneezed in the corner and shamelessly
stared at me as I described his death and scooped. Stan was
getting to his feet as I zipped the bag closed, firmly, and slid it
under the table.

'What hit me?' he asked, rubbing his back.

'The cat jumped on you.'

'I'll kill that fucking thing.'

'Be my guest,' I said flatly. When he turned towards the door, Ahab made like a posse and disappeared in a cloud of dust. Molly passed Stan a smoke and he sat on the edge of the table, nodding his yes at my offer of Jack.

'What's that smell?'

'Tuna.'

'Is there any left?'

'Trust me.' I handed him a shot. 'You wouldn't want it, it's off.'

'Smells fine.'

'And you run a café?' Molly asked, wide-eyed.

He shrugged and walked to the kitchen. 'Anybody want water?'

Molly and I sat in silence until he came back and lay down in front of the fire and fell asleep again. I picked up the Jack and took an almighty hit straight from the bottle.

'Oh Christ.' Molly was covering her mouth and shaking her head. 'We are so going to burn for that.'

'It's only ash,' I said bravely, biting my lip.

'True.'

'But we'll still go to hell.'

'Absofuckinlutely.'

We took the giggles bad then and Molly had to go and splash water on her face before we could talk again. Then she straightened herself up and once more demonstrated her ability to know the right thing to do. She moved on.

It really was only ash.

▭ ＊ ▭

'You should have married Kirsty.'

Progress made, she knew not to dwell on a subject.

'Didn't we just do this?'

'We didn't finish.'

'You sure?'

Of course, she did have her blind spots.

She arched her eyebrows in challenge and I conceded the point almost before she picked up the remote control.

'You always marry Kirsty.'

'Not any more I don't, she is officially out of the game, there's a new player in town.'

'Ah!' She held her hand up. 'But you admit you did?'

'Only if she was up.' I gave her the point. 'And only if Elisabeth Shue wasn't. You know that.'

I reached behind me and tugged the curtain open, releasing an army of dust. Molly made like a vampire, so I fought it shut again, the dust retreating after the sun.

'Far too fucking bright. Fool boy,' she said, screening her eyes. 'Not like some I could mention.'

I gave her the finger and told her to fuck off, only I didn't say it out loud. No need to prove her right.

'If you've got your finger up when I turn round, I'm going to break it off.'

'You're not my fucking mother, and you don't get to wash my mouth out for swearing either.' I stuck my tongue out and she caught it with the remote.

Pine had been stirring on the couch since my brief encounter with the sun, and finally managed to swing his legs over the side and growl his way to the toilet. When he came back, Molly was lying on the couch smiling at him. He tutted past her and lay next to Stan, covering them both with the duvet he'd taken from his room.

'Ain't he sweet?' A kiss floated from Molly's lips and Pine reached up, caught it and pulled it down to his chest, his fist held closed as though it might escape.

'What you on?' he asked lazily as he got comfortable and closed his eyes, heading back to the back of his mind.

'I said he should have married Kirsty.'

'No,' he mumbled. 'Marry Elisabeth Shue, shag Kirsty, and throw Molly off the couch.'

'Pine, shut up and go to sleep. Elisabeth Shue wasn't up.'

She tutted at him but he was already gone or wisely chose to pretend.

'Right.' She looked at me with an evil grin. 'Here's your three. Lana Turner, Marilyn, and Catherine Zeta Jones.'

'Marilyn the transvestite pop sensation from the golden age of Sta-Prest and legwarmers?'

'The other one.'

'Tough call.'

I lay across my chair and got comfortable – this was going to be a long one.

━ ✳ ━

Depending on your perspective, it was either very late or really early by the time I crawled back into bed with Ali. Molly had fallen asleep on the couch and I'd covered her with a blanket. I'd sat for a while in the quiet, holding Ting and looking for sleep, but when the fire burnt down to its ember bed I decided that I wanted Ali's warmth. I kissed her softly on the lips as I moved in beside her. She moaned gently and entwined herself round me as she turned in her sleep.

I closed my eyes and thought about earlier. Did we have sex or were we making love? Could we do it again please just to be sure? Unhurried and tenderly.

I could hear the sharp cries of the fishermen break through the glass of the window as we lay together, her sleeping, me listening. Unwilling now to sleep for fear of losing the moment, I was equally wary of waking up. I was looking forward to the morning with the fear and trepidation of what we had to do.

Ting to be cast asunder, life to go on.

The more I thought about it the clearer it became. It wasn't fear of the future that was holding me here, I was caught in the now. The guilt and the fear were consigned to the past and a smile tugged at my lips. Ali turned her head towards me, awake, a question in her eyes.

'Penny for them?'

'I'm not thinking about anything,' I said, shaking my head

and letting her see my smile. 'Well, nothing startling anyway.'
I pulled her to me and she nestled against my shoulder. 'I'm
thinking I like how this feels.'

'Me too,' she purred and shut her eyes.

'You think we'll be okay in the morning?'

'It is morning and you've just said it yourself, we are good.'

'You know what I mean.'

'We're fine, we'll be fine.' She curled her finger and absently
tugged at my hair. 'As long as you believe that and you want
that, we'll be fine, you'll be fine.' She accentuated every word
with a tug and I had to kiss her to shut her up.

'I believe it.' I kissed her with every word.

'Keep talking.' She smiled and we became one again.

Chapter 21

is this kansas?

I was lying in a field of poppies that ran to a pine forest barely visible in the hazy rise of the morning air. I could feel the cushion of grass as I curled against the cold. The music of a waterfall rose behind me, splashing the day awake with the freshness of an infant. Angel song flowed around the basin created by the mountains, echoing the breath on my lips. Jagged fingers of cold attacked my toes and I instinctively kicked the duvet over my feet.

Letting my memory awaken before my body, I took a hit from remembered passion and swelled in the morning glory that always follows. The body's safety check before facing life. Making sure that we can rise to the challenge of another day with the hunter-gatherers. As dreaming and reality took a step apart, in the moment before you really wake up and hear the alarm for what it is and not for the fire bell that it was born from, I watched the forest mutate into a spider plant and the waterfall reduce to mere showerly proportions. At a time when the last thing my sleep-infested mind wanted to do was to wake up, I opened one eye as a compromise to my bladder's insistence that I shake a leg. I froze as reference met context and led my bleary gaze to Ali standing behind the misted glass of the shower singing Janis Joplin.

The vision in frosted glass confirmed what I had begun to suspect. I had spent the night wrestling with a fallen angel. Purity and perfection wrapped in the gossamer wings of sexuality. Eris returned. And now here I was enchanted again.

Unwilling to encourage fate, I watched her while I prodded at my hangover with a stick.

Across the bedroom, a distance measured in the life of stars, Ali emerged from the shower surrounded by a crowd of steam that danced around her and clung like imps imploring her favour. I closed my eyes, not willing to lessen her mysticism or my rapture as she dried. I could hear her work the towel as she lightly hummed another Joplin number.

Then silence. I strained to hear but she was *Mary Celeste*. Then I heard her. I opened my eyes, the way you have to push your head all the way back so that you can look out the bottom. She was having a pee. She must have assumed I was still asleep, or was happy to ignore the fact that I was pretending. Feeling the guilt of the voyeur, I made the effort to go back to sleep so as to negate the lie, but like purposefully growing or forcing yourself to like jazz, it was futile.

My senses heightened in response to my eyes being closed and I listened to her walk round the room. Janis became Dino and I smiled before I remembered to be asleep.

'Get up and have a shower. It's too late to sleep.'

I used a little theatre to wake up and smile groggily as she threw her towel on the bed and walked naked to her bag. The warm dampness of the towel gave rise to thoughts of kidnap and harems and a life of sheer unadulterated longing.

'I know you're awake, you were watching me in the shower.'

Caught like a schoolboy thumbing the Grattan's catalogue, I protested my innocence for all of the two seconds it took her to challenge my assertion of sleep by pulling the duvet off the bed.

Pulling a sloppy T-shirt over her head, she ordered me up.

'Go on,' she insisted as she plugged in the kettle that was on the dresser. 'I'll make us some coffee.'

□ * □

The shower surprised me and knocked any thoughts of returning to bed from my body with the subtlety of a sand-blaster exposing a forgotten wall. Gone was last night's trick-ling excuse and in its place a suddenly high-pressure power shower, every girl's friend, that I was forced to hold well away from me as it fired sizzling needles that tried to pierce my flesh. I became accustomed to the pain, found my voice and began following Ali's rendition of Dino's 'Somewhere There's a Someone'. When I finally looked to the audience for appreciation, I turned to find Ali brushing her teeth and watching me through the porthole she'd made in the mirror. Whilst I'm not particularly shy, especially in light of last night's performance, I do have unresolved confidence issues with my body image and I could feel the tightening in my gut as I reflexly breathed in and blushed under her gaze.

'Stop that,' she admonished me with a spit. 'It makes you look stupid.'

'Stop what,' I asked, turning to profile and lathering a cover for my embarrassment.

Ali turned and leant against the sink. 'I'll just wait here until you breathe out again if you'd like.'

'I am breathing out.'

With that she plonked herself on the toilet, pulling a brush through her hair. Unaware of my training under Guru Kirsty, she thought to wait me out but was forced to concede when the kettle boiled and she went chasing after its whistle. Taking my cue, I stepped out into a towel, brushed my teeth with a finger and crossed back to the bedroom. The curtains were closed and we sat on the bed in semi-darkness, me against the wall, Ali cross-legged in front of me. She laughed as I buttoned my shirt.

Dismissive as Ali was about my complex, a wave of forget-about-it, I was too well programmed. Looking at her, I knew why.

My sex life had been, up to this point, a predictable path of least resistance. While I would happily stand proud to demonstrate and explain my attraction to each and every one, if not their attraction to me, which I rarely understood, the difference with Ali – and I was only now realising it – was that she was hard.

I knew soft. Pliant flesh that moulded to suit, shook with

pleasure and quivered in anticipation. Ali was hard. She had a flat stomach when she lay flat, as I did, but when she stood up, or lay on her side or sat cross-legged, she didn't go Buddha. Holding her was strange in a way that I wasn't sure I understood. She was sexy, hell, sexy isn't enough of a word. From her perfect feet to her manicured nails, everything in between cried healthy, toned and hard. Apart from her breasts – they were sublime.

I couldn't voice my insecurity, I couldn't explain, not to the perfection in front of me. She could afford to be dismissive, we had no commonality on that front, my front. In the past I'd shared the embarrassment of sober awareness with girls I knew less of and thought of not at all. We would be united in our careful avoidance of actually seeing each other naked and sober without darkness to cloak us, but we'd both know it and so it was almost fun. Ali was one of those unaccountable aberrations who actually did look better without her clothes on. Here, now, I could open up about my insecurities, my fears and hopes and such, but not *the* insecurity. I couldn't get that naked yet.

'Why are you getting dressed under a towel?' she asked, lighting two cigarettes and handing me one. 'In case it's slipped your mind, I've seen you naked. A bit late for modesty, don't you think?'

What could I say? She blew smoke, and gave me a moment's grace before saving me from having to answer.

'Don't I get another look? Don't you like me this morning?' This was said while she twisted her hair round her finger and made use of her dimples.

'Stop taking the piss,' I said, following her lead and employing a petted lip. 'I was drunk and you took advantage of me.' I supped at my coffee and furrowed my brow. 'As a matter of fact I'm beginning to suspect that you drugged me. I never get naked on a first date. Too much to lose.'

'Second date.'

'Whatever.'

'Bollocks,' she said. 'You need to get naked, otherwise how will you know if you want another?'

'You're the second-date girl. You tell me.'

'Women's prerogative.'

'Well, there are other things, you know. Sense of humour, conversation.'

I stumbled then as she stubbed her cigarette out and pulled at her shirt. 'Oh yeah? Tell you what, you talk and make jokes if you like.' The shirt climbed, seemingly of its own volition, to her chest. 'Or' – and the dimples came back – 'we could get naked again.' Her breasts fell out from below the shirt. Only they didn't fall. 'You can even breathe in the whole time if you like.' Before I could think of anything suitably funny to say, she put my coffee to one side and placed her hand on my shorts. 'I'll take this as a yes then.'

◻ ＊ ◻

Last night the sex was drunken and still a bit hazy; it would take quite a while before it all came back, if indeed it did. But this was different. We had energy. And Ali, as she told me in a whisper against my thigh, was a morning person.

We lay together breathing hard, Ali on top of me, lying on her back and me inside her. She was using her hands to bring us both to another orgasm. Before we left the bedroom we were both in need of another shower and I was in serious need of talking at my friends about it. Still flushed, we had sex in the shower. Good clean fun.

Afterwards I sat on the bed waiting for her to make up before we went to find out if the others were up. Ting was by my side. This was a good morning to be alive. A guilt-laden cloud flitted across my horizon but was blasted away by rays of pure gold every time I looked up and caught Ali's eye. More up than down. I tried to concentrate on that but lost it when Ali disappeared into the bathroom. I spiralled. Drawn inexorably by my need to feel bad, I plunged into a vortex of despair. How long I was gone I don't know. I returned, sweating coldly, to Ali standing over me, confusion on her face.

'It's okay to have fun you know.' She kissed my cheek and

continued putting her hair up. 'You can be sad for Ting, but you need to keep going. Otherwise you might as well be dead yourself.'

I looked up, unsure whether to be offended at this unsolicited advice or surprised at her insight.

'Am I so transparent?'

She kissed me again. 'Call it honest. Your face doesn't hide what your heart is feeling. It's refreshing, you're one of the lucky ones.'

'No good at poker though.'

'Oh, I don't know.' She smiled. 'You had a couple of good hands earlier.'

And then I was bewitched again.

Chapter 22

bravehearts broken

We met in the sitting room for breakfast. It was a quiet time, our heads thicker than the dripping toast that came with Mrs Cromerty's tray. When I'd seen the amount of food she'd cooked I'd looked out the window to see if a coach party had arrived. There may indeed have been a coach in the drive, there could have been anything out there, hidden by the unremitting blanket of rain that had probably continued unabated since Noah packed up.

Fortified and square-jawed, we rallied to the cause. Ting was ready to go.

We ran from the house to the shelter of the boathouse, screaming our defiance at the storm. A six-headed tangle of uncoordinated limbs flapping at the rain and sliding through slushing mud and stinging gravel. Ginger beer and brownies in the bag and Stan barking at us to run faster and faster. We pushed through the unhinged door, grinning in breathless exhilaration. I opened the bottle of whisky that we'd put in Ting's bag and passed it round while Pine kicked about for firewood.

'How are we going to get a fire started in this?' Sally asked as we gathered up bits of old boats and chairs that covered the floor. 'We'll need more than a Zippo.'

'A torch.'

Ali tore the cover off a three-legged chair, wrapped it round the end of a broken oar and had Sally pour vodka over it from a flask she had in her pocket. Magnificent and resourceful.

'Don't any of you watch *Xena*?' she sniggered. 'Right, load up and I'll lead the way.'

We stepped from the boathouse in single file and our exuberance fled faster than we walked. Rain be damned. Ali led our slow procession, carrying her torch ahead of her, as we followed with our offerings. I smiled at the sight of us, hunched against the rain, determined to enact some pagan ceremony. Thoughts for Ting fused with last night's cleansing. Emerging from the temporary sanctuary of the boathouse, we had set out on a new path, less inclined to frivolity or haste. Our arms burdened, as temple slaves we followed the priestess from the sacristy, each step heavier than the last. I thought I was experiencing some quasi-religious existentialist piss-take. If Ali had started doing the conga as we snaked through the bushes that led to the pebbled beach, I would have been shoogling my arse and skipping along with her, making it into part of the rite. It was as though her solemnity was keeping me in check. We approached this end with the inherited knowledge that we should be grieving and, despite our assurances to Ting and him wanting otherwise, we were still at it.

'Dun, dun, dun dundun.'

Pine was walking behind me and I heard him hum a deep-throated chant.

'Dun, dun, dun dundun.'

My ears pricked up as his voice rose above the noise of our shuffling progress and I lifted my face up to the clouds' maw. I wore a full open-mouthed grin as humility struck me with every raindrop. My head started bopping in time as I walked. I should have known Pine would be with me. Thoughts of Ting filled me as I closed my eyes to find the sound and let my feet look out for themselves. I sniggered as I found what I was using my ears to look for.

'DUN, DUN, DUN DUNDUN.'

Stan's voice sang out with Pine's. Ali stopped and turned at the sound and I waved her on with my fingers.

'DUN, DUN, DUN DUNDUN.'

I sucked in until my ribs pushed at the planks in my arms fit to burst a lung and bellowed as they continued.

'DEHREY, DEH DEH DEHREY.'

By the time we had piled our caches on the sucking pebbles of the beach, the girls, in perfect counterpoint, had taken up the call and we sounded like the magnificent seven we were.

□ ★ □

At last the flames took hold. Sharp pink tongues lapped at the bubbling wood, drinking the vodka and spitting flames. Pine hugged Ting to his chest while Stan and I threw the last crate on the fire. We stood watching as the rain fell on our faces, salt stinging as the world cried with us.

Desolation looked me in the eye. A black ending of sky and water hazed by Ting's beacon, biding its time before reaching for that temporal light and swallowing the ashes. Standing awkwardly on the pebbles and brink, unwilling to make the final cast, I looked at the others, sharing a sigh with them, and forced the first last step.

'Let's do it,' I croaked.

Nobody spoke. The moment here and their voices failed them; only sharp nods and the shuffling stones announced their hearing. The wind however roared its agreement, fanning the flames for a final push.

We huddled round Pine as though talking tactics, the ball held between us. Stan extended his hand and Pine opened the bag. Relieved to be passing the burden, Pine's hand sought Molly's. The fire crackled behind me, egging us on, counselling against time-wasting. Like us, cowering and flinching against the encroaching tide, it knew it was time to go. Suddenly the wind died. Or it may have. I heard the rub of stones becoming as dust under my feet, the slap of rain against Gore-Tex, the numb wet bark of a scared dog, a sea of blood breaking against my skull, the slow turning of a lid, screaming in the silence as the world called for its own.

Stan poured into cupped hands.

Drawn to the deeper darkness within, I leant forward with everyone else, our heads together, and peered at the ashes. In this imperfect chamber our bodies creaked, the wind returned with renewed force and swirled hair and more, while we let it steal Ting from our hands.

With open arms.

In the fanned light from the fire the last of Ting took wing and flew away, disappearing into the heavy sky to start again.

When all that remained were six closed fists we picked our glasses up from where they sat at our feet and walked to the water's edge. Standing just beyond the touch of icy eternity, I raised my glass in salute and cast my last hold on Ting into the abyss.

'In the next life,' I whispered.

Either side of me the others did the same, sending him off with their own silent goodbyes.

I raised and emptied my glass against the loneliness.

Coughing malt and more, I squeezed my eyes shut and waited. Stan was spluttering and Pine was crying – I could feel his sobs in the wind. I took a deep breath and felt my throat burn, a grazing and rasping as I swallowed back the pain. When I opened my eyes I saw that I wasn't the only one, Stan was choking and smarting as Molly slapped his back. Ali stood quietly, her face unreadable as she stared into the grey. Lost with the flame that had finally surrendered its light, she didn't even notice Sally slip her arm around her shoulders. Pine was crying.

It was only ash, I kept telling myself. Images of Ting sneaked through my brain unbidden. And this was a gesture. Ting down and holding his shin, a numpty from the big school towering over him as the ref booked him. This weekend, this weak end, was nothing but a symbol, an act of faith. Our teacher knelt beside him, the bucket and sponge from the art class in his hand. It was only ash. It wasn't important. Ting was an essence, a sense, something intangible that couldn't be defined by matter. The ash didn't matter. I understood that. The magic sponge, dipped in self-belief, wiped away the pain. It stopped the tears, maybe not forever, but long enough to see the game through.

Molly turned with Stan and held her hand out for Pine. He

took it with a tight smile as he looked at me, sniffed and wiped
at his face.

'Got some Ting in my eye.'

The wind pulled at his words and I laughed before I could
stop myself. I held my hand out and Stan took it, smiling and
choking, as he looked at Pine through glazed eyes. We stood
and half-heartedly brushed the sea and more from our clothes,
making the mental adjustments needed to move on. Stan was
still coughing as Pine held out his arms and we fell into a bear
hug, six deep. Inappropriately perhaps for such an intimate
moment, Stan hacked deep in his throat and spat at our feet.
Amid cries of disgust, he shook his head and ran his tongue
around his mouth, gulping like a guppy.

'Why the fuck can I taste sweetcorn?'

Molly nudged me so hard I thought she'd cracked a rib as
I laughed and tried not to choke as he continued to hack deep
in his throat.

Back on track.

The seriousness of the moment shoehorned into the box
marked 'not to be opened until very fucking drunk', we stepped
back and watched the sea take claim.

When the tide had done its work with the remains of the
fire, we turned away for the final time and walked back to the
house. Shoulders back, head high. Heart enriched, enlightened
and heavy. Back on the bike after the fall.

We walked behind the girls, arm in arm as we reached Mrs
Cromerty's.

Stan decided that we had to be ready to leave in half an
hour. 'We should get back to the café.'

I didn't argue. We weren't finished yet.

Ting wanted us back in St Pete's, he wanted to be sure we
didn't dwell. Get back, get pissed and get on.

▭ ✱ ▭

When I got to my room Ali wasn't there. We'd packed up
before we went for breakfast so I had nothing to do except

change into dry clothes and sit at the open window, staring at the rain and trying to look at nothing.

After a while she came in. I smiled as she came over and put her arms round me from behind.

'Hi,' she said.

'Hi.'

'You okay?'

'Yeah. You?'

'No.'

Well, neither was I really, but I thought we were being polite. Stiff upper lip and all that. I turned and returned her embrace as she wiped at her eyes.

We stood like that for a moment before she sighed and moved past me to lean on the windowsill like I had been doing. I loved her vulnerability. In a good way.

I took up position next to her and breathed her in.

I realised with a certainty I couldn't explain that something had changed.

'Those clouds are lighter, it looks like it might stop raining.'

It didn't and she sounded tired, as I was, and well she should be, but it was more than that.

'I feel as if a weight's been lifted,' she sighed, 'or it will be soon.'

I followed her eyes as she searched the heavens.

'I think I'm in love, Pennance.'

That I wasn't expecting.

I thought she was talking about on the beach, about Ting, but she wasn't, she was talking about me. I was glad she wasn't looking at me when she spoke.

Frantically I tried to find my voice but it had skulked off when my heart stopped. I reached over and took her hand, squeezing it in encouragement, urging her to go on, to say something else, buy me some time to let it sink in and find out how it felt. She loved me.

Looking at the boats in the harbour, I felt that it was they who were anchored securely on terra firma and that it was I who fought for balance. It was a bit sudden but then again these were stressful times, drawing every ounce of emotion from every second and exposing us to the raw feelings we are left with when grief and joy bind us. It's all about timing.

She was in love with me and a new future presented itself, a whole possibility of anything at all was introduced with those words and I felt nothing but heart-gripping excitement to hear them. Surprisingly, wonderfully so.

'There I've said it, no going back now.' She stood straight and pushed her hair back and I had to catch my breath as her dimples reached for my heart. 'Pennance, I'm sorry, but I realise it now. I know my timing is awful, but I don't know what else to say.'

Nothing. If you're smitten, you're smitten.

Oh, my God, she's smitten.

'Listening to Pine last night talking to Donald and Moira' – she leant back on the windowsill – 'Ting this morning . . . it made me realise that if you see a chance you've got to take it in case you don't get another. If something's meant to be' – she sighed and took a deep breath – 'good or fucked, it's meant to be.'

Of course I agreed. But why was she sorry?

'Do you understand?'

'I think so,' I said uncertainly. 'You're apologising for falling in love with me?'

She shook her head and her hair fell over her face again. Ignoring it, she pushed up against me, looking at me from the corner of her eye.

'No, stupid.' She bit her lip. 'I think I'm in love with Sally.'

I laughed and hugged her.

On the strength of Ali choosing to share a room with me, I had assumed, with surprising inconsistency, that we would in fact become an item. In the looks and touches we shared at an emotionally charged time, when my heart was vulnerable to her, I sensed a closeness. But I didn't expect this. That Ali would fall for me was too great a leap.

I turned and held her, wrapping myself around her to protect her from the cold, from the chill of exposing herself to me and trusting her instincts. I hadn't expected her to fall in love with me. A dream maybe, in idle moments when fancy connives to force a smile, but not real actual love. And that's what was in her voice, that's what she hid behind her joking, that's what was in her tear-drenched eyes, she'd fallen in love. Before I knew it I told her I loved her too.

And I meant it.

'Pennance.' She pushed me away and folded her arms. 'You don't love me.'

'I think I do.'

'Oh, God.'

I shrugged and moved to hold her but she stepped back.

'What?'

'I don't love you.'

'But you just said –'

She stepped forward and held my outstretched hands as I began backing away, confused now.

'I'm serious.' She grinned somewhat sadly. 'I think I'm in love with Sally.'

'But you're not gay.'

She was back to biting her lip.

'That's the problem,' she said softly. 'I kind of am.'

'How much kind of?'

'Apart from you?'

I nodded, numbly.

'Kind of all of me.'

'You're kidding, right?'

'If only.'

So that was that.

I was wrong. I wasn't expecting her to fall for me, then she did, only she didn't, and suddenly I was dating a lesbian. Ting would just die when I told him. My heart lurched four foot to the side and back as I remembered and it took a minute before I got a hold of it. By now, Ting probably already knew.

'What about Sally?'

'Her too.'

'You sure?'

'More sure than I am.'

'And have you two . . . you know . . . ?'

Welcome back to school.

'Not for years.'

'What about Molly?' I asked, thinking about Pine.

'No, Molly's straight.'

'I mean does she know about you and Sally being gay?'

'Bisexual.'

I made a note to ask Pine if she'd told him. I looked over at the boats and thought about priorities. Here was my girlfriend, technically speaking, confessing to being in love with my friend's, terminally speaking, ex-girlfriend. Exactly where I was in the picture hadn't occurred to me, nor had my declaration of love and its subsequent rebuff made an impression on my ego. Above the need to save face or avoid embarrassment, beyond my right to be indignant and feel spurned, I concentrated on visualising lesbians. All very twelve years old and flicking through *Razzle* at the back of the class; I was doing it before I knew not to. But that had to stop. My mind was racing as I finished the movie in my head – Molly had a cameo.

I guessed Stan would be right, I'd be travelling alone. But still, looking at it from a different perspective, one that knew the stars were always there even if out of sight, I smiled and stored another moment. This was sweet torment, the bastard-faced reality of the bum's rush covered in smooth sexual fantasy. As clarity arrived I had a curious thought.

'Did Ting know about Sally?'

Ali was happy enough to be answering my questions, she knew that I needed time to comprehend what she'd just told me, she was uncommonly perceptive, and regretfully I knew that that was one of the qualities that I found attractive in her. To stop such harmful thoughts confusing me I had to remember she was a lesbian. It helped me think straight.

'About her connection to the Romanovs?'

'Romanovs? No, about her . . . yes, right, very funny.' I shook my head in mock exasperation while she grinned innocently. Moment rendering. 'Did he?'

'Yes.'

'Fucking hell, he never said a word.'

She arched her eyebrows. 'He wouldn't, you should know that.'

Of course he wouldn't, I realised with wide-eyed certainty, thinking back to Stan's confession. We shared confidences; we never broke them.

'Does Sally know about you?'

'I told you that we used to go out together.'

'Yes, but I didn't know you meant together together at the time. Does she know that you're in love with her?'

I found it passing strange that I was even having this conversation. Less than ten minutes ago Ali was facing playing a big part in my life, travelling aside. I thought that if this was the opportunity to go on, to move on, then I could do a lot worse than tying my flag to her pole. As I slid back to earth, my pennant fluttering off in the wind, I was skirting round the question of what happened now, knowing that the finality of that answer was matched only by its inevitability.

'That was what this weekend, well, this week was meant to be about. We'd arranged it before . . .' She looked at me and I nodded. 'A kind of spend-some-time-together-see-where-it-goes thing. If it worked out we were thinking about starting to see each other again.'

'So what happened?'

'Sally was upset about Ting, she needed this wake to help her get through losing him.' She took a deep breath. 'Losing his friendship was something she never thought she'd have to deal with.'

Yeah, yeah, I thought, enough about Sally.

'We were supposed to spend the weekend together and so she asked me to come along. I guess I had my own things to work out. That's when I met you. The rest you know.'

'Right now I feel as if I know nothing.'

'I'm just as confused as you are, Pennance. Do you think I want to be having this conversation? Or be in this situation? I'm confused, I'm scared and right now I really need a hug.'

I was nodding again. Inanely.

Okay, enough about you. 'What about us?'

She sat back against the window and held me in her arms. Her face carried an openness that let me know she was still speaking from her heart. Honest with no need for duplicity or mollycoddled condolence.

'I don't know. I hadn't thought it through. I just needed to tell you. It seemed the right thing to do. I know the timing's shit. Why are you laughing?'

It was more of a snigger and I was thinking how good I was at reading people. Women, Kirsty, Ali. Maybe it was me after all, living in a looped tape of my own reality, edited to suit, ready to believe only what I saw and heard though my own distorted speakers. Stan had obviously seen it.

'Never mind.' I smiled. 'It just seems all the women in my life are full of surprises at the moment.'

'You mean Kirsty getting married?'

'Who told you?' I asked her, embarrassed that she not only knew what I meant, but who I meant. But it would have been Pine, of course. 'Never mind, I already know.'

'He said you were talking about going travelling.'

'I am now, that's for fucking sure.'

We laughed together, the danger zone passed and I felt a sharp stab of regret for what might never have been anyway.

▭ ＊ ▭

Pressure off, us became me and her stood leaning into the rain, our futures mostly unwritten but with the outline shading done.

'So will I get a postcard?'

'Of course.' I smiled.

'You know, Pennance' – she took my hand and held it to her as she wiped away her unannounced tears – 'it's just possible that you're a lot sweeter than you think you are.'

'What?'

'You heard.'

'You take that right back,' I said sternly. 'I've got a repu-
tation to keep.'

'Don't worry,' she sniffed. 'Your secret's safe with me.'

I squeezed her hand and we stood quietly, lost in our own
thoughts until Stan knocked on the door.

'This is it,' I said as we picked up our bags. 'Once we walk
out that door it's too late.' She looked at me confused as I
smiled. 'Are you sure you're gay?'

'Bisexual.'

'Last night didn't change your mind?' I glanced at the bed.
'Or this morning?'

She shook her head sadly and I decided to ask her about us
again.

'So,' I said, reaching for the door. 'Was I your first?'

'You wish.' She pushed me through. 'But if it's any consolation you'll be the last.'

Now how was I meant to take that?

'Oh well.' I kissed her as we got to the stairs; the others
were waiting at the bottom. 'At least I can tell everyone that I
gave a lesbian multiple orgasms.'

'No, you didn't,' she insisted, quietly walking down ahead
of me.

'Yes, I can.'

Chapter 23

lost luggage

I sat cramped and moaning in the back of Sally's car as she raced the river home. I wished I hadn't eaten so much as I tried to sleep my way to Glasgow. I'd decided to visit my sister before going home. The thought of travelling to Leeds in the back of a Mini had convinced me. I thought it was probably a good idea anyway, since I had decided that I was definitely going away. I'd catch the Leeds train at Glasgow and stop off in Newcastle and see Grace for an hour or so before getting home and going about changing my whole life. I called and arranged to meet her.

Ali and I had stood at the bottom of the stairs before we left, hugging out of sight of the others. Our lips together in a final farewell to us.

'No regrets?' she'd asked as I opened the door to face the future.

'None.'

I smiled and we walked away from our past. I knew it wasn't strictly the truth – of course I had regrets but they were fewer than if nothing had happened and now I had the memory, not of what if but of what was.

At the door we said goodbye to Moira and her mother, fresh back from chapel.

'Did you find what you were looking for?' Moira had asked quietly, glancing from me to the others.

Ali bit her lip and her eyes shifted from me to Sally, and Pine took Molly's hand. Stan nodded slowly, understanding what was only now coming to me. I hadn't known that I was looking for anything. The wake had started as a joke and become our quest. Not one fraught with danger, but as arduous as the search for any Holy Grail. I got it now though and, looking at my friends, I knew it was different for each of us, a goodbye to the past and the hope of a new and better future. Ting's death was the point when I began to understand it all. Everything was squeezed into the last few days, compressed to fit into my reality since Ting left. Donna; Kirsty; Ali; Stan and I fighting; Pine deciding to get married; these were all events or episodes that normally I would have written off as unrelated, isolated experiences that ran independently from one to the other. But here, all at once, I recognised them as signposts that could guide and direct. All I had to do was give myself permission to follow my own road. That, as much as having the wake for Ting, was what this was about. Not grieving, although that played a part, but recognising life and, in its way, death for what they were: a sea of opportunity where only the unaware couldn't keep their heads above the water. Ali had helped keep me afloat.

'I think so,' I said uncertainly, sure what I knew but unclear if that was what she was asking. She might have been talking about the karaoke and a warm pub, but then, perhaps, they were both the same thing anyway if looked at correctly. My voice became firmer. 'The meaning of life,' I said, surprised that I didn't immediately cringe. 'But I didn't find it. I think it's always been floating around waiting.'

Pine giggled and Molly nudged him quiet as she led him away; maybe I was being a cliché but that didn't make it any less true. Moira nodded her head slowly.

'That'll be about the right of it.'

Moira waved us off as we elbowed and nudged our way comfortable. As comfortable as six people could get in a car the size of my shoe.

□ ＊ □

I was woken by the sound of nothing, the absence of noise. We were at a rest stop and Sally had gone for a coffee with Stan and Ali.

Working on the same principle of leaving a twisted ankle in a boot, not risking it swelling and not fitting back in, I'd decided to sit tight until we got to Glasgow. Molly and Pine were of a similar mind. Unfortunately only Sally was insured to drive the car. Ali had taken the first stint in the passenger seat and Stan was up for it next. I was smoking out of the window, leaning on the back of the driver's seat when Molly poked me in the ribs.

'So what's going on with Ali and you?'

'Nothing.' I shrugged, acting casually. 'It was a fling.'

Pine made a confused grunting sound, his usually vocal cords having been strained last night.

'So that's it? Just like that?'

I used the only impersonation that I can carry off with any degree of success. 'Just like that,' all Tommy Cooper. I flinched and tentatively opened one eye, confused that I hadn't been poked, flicked, punched, pinched or struck, but Molly had sat back and was smiling.

'What are you talking about?' Pine croaked. 'Why are you talking about a fling? I thought Ali could be the One, that's what you said. What happened to that?'

'She wasn't.'

'And you know just like that?'

'It's like Stan said.' I was pleased I was still smiling when I came out with it, the words making the thoughts my reality. 'I'm not her type.'

He shook his head. 'But I don't . . .'

Molly held her hand up and looked at me.

'Be my guest,' I told her magnanimously.

She knew all about Pine's chequered past and had accepted his history as easily as he had hers, she also knew that he professed his prodigious track record had left him with a legacy: an ability to judge, categorise and label the straight from the bent, or in his words 'the ones he could pull and the lesbians'.

'Ali's gay.' She puffed up and told him as though it was more obvious than a perm. 'I thought you knew.'

His eyes narrowed as he waited for her to laugh, then he shifted his gaze to me.

'Bisexual,' I corrected her.

'Fucking hell. You're serious.'

I sniggered with him until a grin took over my face. 'Can you fucking believe it?'

He shook his head and fucking helled until Molly tutted.

'I can't believe you never knew.'

'Fuck sake, Molly,' I said in his defence, 'I didn't know myself until she told me this morning.'

'You're as bad as him. The two of you must walk around with your eyes shut.' She glanced quickly between us. 'Or at least looking at the wrong things.' We both blushed as she moved on. 'You're sure it's just a fling?' She narrowed her eyes. 'We were talking yesterday and she said she thought she was falling in love.' She held her hand up quickly. 'I'm not trying to frighten you, I don't think she's a bunny boiler or anything, but love at first sight and all that shite.'

'It's not shite!' Pine said seriously, knowingly.

'That's what I'm saying,' she soothed him. 'Maybe you should look at it differently, Pennance.'

'Are you even bothered?' Pine moved back into Jedi mode. 'Don't forget what you said yesterday on the way up. She's not really your type, bisexual or not.' He shivered. 'And just think of the baggage she'd have.'

'I'm fine with it.' I grinned tightly, knowing that it was the truth. 'I mean how could I not be?'

He smiled in agreement as Molly asked what I'd said yesterday and I told her about Ali's hardness, possibly making more of it in my mind than it was in my hand but knowing that Pine had called it well, his years of experience working truer than Molly credited.

'Don't get me wrong.' I shook my head at her dubious expression. 'She has an amazing body.'

'Figure,' she said distractedly as she stopped Pine nodding with a look.

'But I like to have to guess if I'm holding a boob or a tummy, you know what I mean?'

She reached up and kissed me. 'Oh, that's such a lovely way

of putting it.' I had momentarily disarmed her, but it didn't last long. She turned to Pine again. 'I hope you're taking notes here.'

Now that wasn't fair. Pine held his tongue while Molly made a point of crediting me with his words, and it seemed only fair that I should even the score.

'She's in love right enough though.' I nodded and gave the impression I was thinking it through, then I looked at her quizzically. 'But with Sally.'

We had a re-run of before, only now Molly played Pine's part. He was looking at me and I nodded, then winked and turned back to Molly.

'I thought you knew.'

Pine warned us that they were coming back to the car and she unrolled the magazine and left me be.

'Anyway,' she said with a smile, 'I still think you should go for it.'

'She's in love with Sally.'

'Ah! But you've got bigger boobs.'

Pine had to separate us when Stan opened the door.

The rest of the journey was a nightmare. Stan and Sally sat up front singing along to the Lighthouse Family and I was the only one awake in the back. I wanted to sleep but I couldn't relax, we were so cramped that I had to put all my weight through one foot so as not to crush Ali as she curled over and under me like a cat. My time was spent trying to catch a glimpse of Sally's boobs and wondering if that could swing it for me. Then I remembered the nipples and concentrated on planning my route round the world.

Chapter 24

training for life

They dropped me off outside Central Station and I tore through the traffic out of the rain. I'd phoned from Mrs Cromerty's as we said goodbye and knew that I had about fifteen minutes to get a ticket and catch the train. I looked warily about me as I approached the counter, idly wondering if my photofit had been faxed through from Leeds by a vindictive or bored clerk. Shaking such nonsense from my head, I stood in line at the counter and watched the beggar work the queue beside me.

She wasn't having much luck as she appeared to be invisible to those she petitioned. Her scabrous dog was another matter as they skipped and twisted to avoid its wet padding. My eyes were drawn to the girl in front of me. She gathered her hair in her hands and ran the rain from it as she tilted her head to the side. She turned and smiled an apology to me as it splashed at my feet and I realised she was a Honey. Thoughts of Ali ran from me as I smiled back and waited for her to say something. She missed her chance.

'Any spare change?'

I never understood how it could be spare but reached into my pocket anyway. The beggar looked to be no more than a streak of snot and was shivering harder than her mutt. I knew I had more to spare than her.

'Aw, cheers, big man, yir a diamond.'

She hacked a cough and walked off, pulling at the rope as her dog shook itself dry. When I'd brushed my legs of raining mongrel the girl in front was leaving the counter and once again smiling at me, but I lost her when the clerk buzzed me forward.

I almost felt good walking to the platform, more content

than I thought I would. It was a strange feeling, forged by Ting, tempered by Ali.

Tested by a smile.

◻ ★ ◻

I worked my way through the carriage and spotted her sitting at a table looking out the window at the station rapidly disappearing behind us. The carriage had only about seven people in it and as I drew closer I saw that there was a man sitting opposite her reading a paper and drinking coffee. She looked up as I came alongside the table.

'Anyone sitting here?'

I pointed to the seat next to the man. He looked up at me and then at the twenty or so empty seats immediately around him. He didn't sound very friendly as he grunted and shook his head. I waited until he'd lifted his briefcase and sat down next to him, enjoying his discomfort as I invaded his personal space.

I knew exactly how he felt. I'd have been the same myself if the circumstances were reversed. I couldn't actually remember when I'd last enjoyed a train journey from wherever to anywhere when I wasn't drunk, drugged, or snoring for that very reason.

Typically, particularly from King's Cross late at night, unless you happen to be the drunk, the dopehead, or the snorer, you spend the whole journey thinking of all the things you would do if 'they' came near you. Quintessentially British, we normally feign sleep or death when any itinerant reprobate even looks in our direction, quietly emitting anti-personnel disgust vibes in the two-foot area immediately surrounding us.

My preference for remaining sane throughout those despicable journeys was to indulge in role play and I had a particular fondness for the hero fantasy. Me in a church, in a particularly slow and long queue, in the supermarket, on a bus, and even more likely on a train. Enter nutter – this could be anyone on the train that I took an instant and irrational dislike to – and on goes the daydream where I save everyone from said nutter using only a plastic cup and some string and spend the remaining time basking in the pinky haze of non-British bullishness whilst avoiding the sexual advances of every red-blooded girl within testosterone-sniffing vicinity.

Sounds like the script from a B-movie or a night in the life of Steven Seagal, and it's about as close to real life as that particular fantasy ever gets. A bit like the other one that includes twins called Svelte and Lilly and a large snake called Walter.

The point was the need for some kind of mental stimulation to get through the journey without going mad myself. Not just a little peeved, but actual mad.

Trains and sobriety don't mix well unless you're the driver and even then it's necessary to be locked up away from harm's way in a cell at the front or, more worryingly, at the back of the train. Even when you book a seat, some freak of nature rips off the reservation ticket, takes up residence and proceeds to get all indignant when you meekly point out that they're in your fucking chair. Of course it's important to remember that last week when you were the drunk it was you who got stroppy, telling Mr Anal Ticket Holder to get a life and another seat because you weren't moving, while still chewing on the reservation ticket that you had liberated from the back of the seat. I hated travelling by train and I wasn't proud of my behaviour now either. I was worse than the drunks of my memory because I was sober and having the same effect.

My neighbour huffed and puffed himself comfortable, throwing me looks of ice and making his offence at my choice of seat clear.

In less than a minute he scowled, stood up and moved to a different seat, muttering under his breath about manners and consideration. Some people are just really unfriendly, I thought, and smiled as I handed him his briefcase.

I slid into the window seat opposite her and made a show of settling in. She pointedly ignored me. Maybe I'd been too obvious. Thinking about it, I knew there was no maybe about it. But I was determined to make a play.

No risk.

Outside chance.

The sun broke through the clouds and I put my sunglasses on. All the better to see her with. I leant back as if looking out the window and watched her, not sure yet what to say to her. It was probably too early anyway. Chill out for a bit, don't choke, but don't wait too long either, I reminded myself. Remember Caroline Moon?

A New Year's party where I spent two hours working up to talking to her only to lose her to Ting. He'd arrived later, scoped the room and headed immediately for her. After being in the room ten minutes, he'd ended up taking her home and leaving me wondering why I was such a fuck-up.

Don't wait too long. As if listening to my thoughts, she shuffled across the seat into the aisle and walked off without a backward glance.

Bastard.

I did get to watch her go, I thought, consoling myself, and her bag was still here so she was coming back. Toilet probably. With her gone, I looked out of the window and saw the miles roll away in front of me. Lost in thought, I didn't notice her come back until she sat down, placing a coffee in front of her. I turned and smiled at her as she glanced at me. I looked back at the window and watched her reflection lean over and rummage in her bag.

Now is the time, let her get comfortable and then . . . She put on headphones and picked up a magazine, settled back and took a drink from her coffee.

Bastard.

Another missed opportunity.

So much for Ting and his power of positive flirting.

◻ ＊ ◻

After a time she laid her magazine down and reached into her bag again. I'd been watching her closely. The way she absently pushed at her hair, the shape of her lips as she drank, her chest rising and falling, her chest rising and falling. When she rummaged in her bag, I could see the muscles in her shoulder and arms, the blonde hairs whispering shadows that spoke of strength. The strength of a swimmer or an aerobics instructor. I laughed at the stereotype and she looked up, at the same time placing a card and pen on the table in front of her. Embarrassed, I glanced down and saw that it was a cartoon.

She opened the card and started writing. The cartoon was one I recognised. A group of deer standing in a forest, one of them had a bull's-eye drawn on its chest. 'Bummer of a birthmark,' it read underneath. Now things were looking up. Admittedly I still hadn't managed to talk to her yet, but when I did I was fairly confident that we'd get on. She liked the Far Side and that in my book was a prerequisite.

When she'd finished writing the envelope – to someone called Hannah something or other – I said a big thanks to the universal mother. No SWALK and no kisses. Unless my experience with Ali was the beginning of a trend, and surely to fuck nobody's got that kind of luck, then it was still worth a go.

Soon as she takes those earphones off I'm in there, I thought. Biding my time and needing distraction, I took my book out and began reading. I'd found it by chance at the bottom of my bag last night. She looked over when I started reading, obviously checking the cover to make a judgement on my taste. This added further strength to my backbone. I thought she looked puzzled for a moment but I must have imagined it as she went back to her magazine, ignoring me again.

I wasn't really concentrating on reading but was watching her flick through her pages, too fast to be reading, I thought, and wondered if maybe she was sharking too. Looking bored, she put the magazine down and finished her coffee. I saw her glance over again and quickly looked back at my book, worrying that I'd been busted. When I checked again, she had taken a book from her bag and was reading it. The Walkman sat on the magazine. My heart was pounding now. In my peripheral vision I'd seen the cover of her book. No detail but a collection of colour and images.

She was reading the same book as me.

This has got to be the time to go for it. Surely. This has got to be a gift. I thought of Ting and the Cosmic Coincidence Centre he believed was real and not the white elephant of conspiracy theory lore that I'd always told him it was. I had a change of heart then and pictured him at the control desk, turning outsized plastic dials and clicking buttons to arrange things to help me wake up and get with the programme.

She was further through the book than I was, judging by the thickness on each side of the spine. I read a couple more pages and then laughed out loud before turning and immediately catching her eye.

Make or break time, Pennance, I said to myself as the laughter dried in my throat and I went for it with the confidence of a shopping trolley learning to swim. She'd glanced up when I'd laughed and was still watching me; she didn't look away. In the frozen moment between thought and action, I realised what I was doing. I was making a play.

And I was sober.

I hadn't done this straight for longer than I could remember. Where was my beer bottle? My cannabis confidence? I was about to attempt to dazzle a Honey and I was straight. The implication of this suddenly spun in front of me, setting off a flock of big-winged birds in my stomach.

Faint heart never fucked a pig, I blustered inappropriately.

Starting again, I tried for a chortle and came in somewhere between a guffaw and a choke followed by a snort. Then a whine.

'Stuff like that never happens to me.'

She looked at me over her sunglasses. 'Sorry?'

Smiling as though embarrassed, I put the book down and looked into her eyes. Chocolate brown.

'Sorry. I didn't mean to say that out loud.'

Deeper and deeper I dived into the bucket of smarm that had replaced my pool of wit and charm. I nodded at the table. 'It's that book, it's so clichéd.'

She raised her eyebrows and I hoped it was because I'd

questioned her chosen reading matter, not that that gave me any comfort, the very thing I was hoping to build a conversation round. Ting's first day at the controls and I'd labelled the connection facile, but not before opening with a thinly veiled, innuendo-laden line. Nudge nudge, wink wink.

Undeterred by my own compounding stupidity, I proceeded with the subtlety of a hobnailed boot meeting a swinging testicle at speed and went for bust.

'I mean, come on, that whole meeting strangers and having casual glancing sex.' I raised my eyebrows, hers were still up. 'A bit far-fetched, don't you think?'

So that was that. I'd taken the plunge. All that could happen now was that she would leave me to drown. Or she could call for the guard.

For a moment she looked at me as though I was a leper offering her a sook on my lollipop. Then the corners of her mouth curled, just slightly, her nostrils flared, giving her glasses a rise that covered her eyes again. Deadpan, she replied, 'Happens to me all the time,' and went back to her book.

I just stared. A twelve-year-old with his first glimpse of the forbidden fruit of a cherry nipple, my mouth agape and my eyes wider than a South London gangster. She glanced up with a look that suggested I should lift my jaw off the table. Gobstruck, I turned as though I'd suddenly seen something of interest outside. Something more interesting than what was happening here, now? I don't think so. The fields and pylons dragged my eyes as they fell out the window in a blur. Now would be a good time to say something, anything, but I froze, confused. Yes, she had spoken to me without using the words wanker, off and fuck, but she'd returned to her page, signalling the end of the conversation. Or did it? That's why I was confused. Was I supposed to probe her now? Poke away at her? Question her as to why that should be the case? Give her a synopsis of Ting's hypothesis that the natural laws of the universal conspiracy that guard against dreams coming true didn't apply to her and get her views? Or was I supposed to sit catching flies?

I hid behind my sunglasses and watched her mark her page in the book with her ticket and place it on the table alongside mine. I watched from behind the protective lenses of my glasses as she lifted a packet of crisps – salt and vinegar, my favourite – and placed them delicately one at a time on her tongue, licking her fingers and lips each time. Naturally, I was able to make that action erotic and stored its memory for later use. She sat with her head against the window oblivious of the havoc her T-shirt was wreaking in my mind as the strap fell down her rounded arm revealing the top of her bra.

Realising that I was regressing again, I was honest enough with myself to know that I'd already given up on the play. Christ, 'that never happens to me', I couldn't believe that I'd said that. She would now be worrying about how to move away without me stalking her, or wondering whether to call for help. Excuse me, could you possibly remove this sad loser from my personal space? No wonder it never happens to me. I knew me and I was cringing. I hadn't stumbled as I was talking, I'd fallen flat on my face with my adolescent chat-up line and now had no recourse but to sit and be seen and not heard, just like my mother had told me little boys should be. From a smorgasbord of cheesy lines I'd opted for the most eyewateringly twee and embarrassing. I might as well have asked her to suck my dick and be done with it.

Still pretending to look out the window, I saw her turn towards me and hold the crisps out. Was she offering me one? Or was I being tested on the saddo scale to prove that she knew I was watching her while I was trying to make it obvious that I wasn't? If I accepted a crisp I'd confirm her Peeping Tom suspicions and if I didn't I would miss the opportunity that I thought I'd already lost through my stupidity. Either way I was in an untenable position of my own making. Just like always. Snafu. As I sat drowning in a sea of indecision, she threw me a line.

'Want a crisp?'

I made a theatre of turning from the window, the smile on my face genuine with pleasure and relief. Maybe I hadn't been busted after all, maybe my opening gambit, while inappropriate and unusual, had got her thinking. Here's a guy, she'd reason, who doesn't use lines, isn't embarrassed to say what he's thinking, and is only trying to be friendly to a stranger on the train.

'Thanks.'

Still wearing my sunglasses, I took advantage of her stretching to offer me the crisps to look alternately between her eyes and her cleavage before she leant back and thoughtlessly lifted the strap back to her shoulder, robbing me of any further opportunity. Class 101 flirting.

'I was only joking before,' she said when she was fully adjusted. 'You know, about it always happening to me.'

Mouth full of half-masticated potato, I could only nod and smile, hoping that I didn't remind her of one of those nodding dogs on the parcel shelves of Volvos and Clios that bounce their heads at traffic lights.

'It's a good book though,' she continued. 'Even if a bit far-fetched. Makes me want to travel, not to have sex in toilets on trains' – she gave me a level gaze – 'but actually go and do something. Maybe not for a year, but certainly somewhere other than Greece or Spain for two weeks, something more adventurous, I suppose.'

With that statement she was pulling me out of the mire and I felt my waterlogged brain searching for a way to capitalise.

'I know what you mean,' I answered after holding my hand up and making a show of hurriedly swallowing. 'I'm actually going travelling myself.'

'Where are you going?'

'I've got one of those round-the-world tickets; you know, Asia, Australia, America, that sort of thing.' I was listening to myself and wondering why I was lying.

'Man, that sounds great.' She sat back in her seat and stretched her legs under the table, kicking my feet. 'Sorry.'

'It's okay.' I smiled and gave her more room. 'I've got another one.'

She looked behind me and I thought I'd lost her, but she

reached for her bag and turned to me as I heard the refreshments trolley wheel up from behind.

'Do you want a coffee?' she asked.

Turning as the trolley stopped, I put my hand in my pocket.

'Let me get them,' I offered, but she already had his attention and shook her head as she ordered.

I thanked her as she stirred her drink and slid my money towards her.

'You can get the next one,' she said and pushed it back to me.

Inside, I was churning with promise. The Next One. She gazed out of the window at the passing fields, and her eyes had a distant look about them, as though seeing beyond the grass and the trees.

'I've always wanted to do that.' She looked back at me. 'Go travelling, I mean. I just never got around to it.'

'I know what you mean.' I tried to appear nonchalant, sipping suggestively at my coffee and burning my mouth. 'I've been saying I'd go for years but there's always been something else happening or it was too much trouble.'

She laughed and nodded her head, causing her hair to fall over her face. 'I'm always going to do it next year.'

'Me too.'

I smiled tightly and took a drink to stop myself laughing at the irony as I watched her run her fingers through her hair, throwing it down her back. She absently pulled her T-shirt strap from her arm where it had slid again and brought the front an inch or two higher on the chest in one of those unconscious movements that girls do when they remember they have tits. We sat in comfortable silence then, sipping our coffee and pretending to look out the window. Her face was unreadable as, I imagined, she thought about all the far-flung places she wanted to visit.

This was going great as far as I could make out. Not only was she talking to me but she'd bought me a coffee with the promise of further caffeine on the way. My only concern now, having made contact, was the undeniable fact that I had lied to her with no good reason and any further conversation, or, dare I dream, further meeting, would be sullied.

Excusing myself, I went to the toilet and stood looking in the mirror.

Moral Dilemma.

Faced with the prospect of spending time with a Honey, should I come clean or continue with the lie?

Come clean: guilt

Continue with lie: guilt.

Standing with my hands on the sink and looking at my face in the mirror, I sneered at myself and waited for my reflection to dazzle me with an insightful answer to my dilemma. Unfortunately for me this was no movie and, looking round, I saw no one waiting to help the hero, no supporting cast and definitely no talking mirror.

Guilty on two counts.

I didn't want her to think I was someone I wasn't. The guy who was going travelling, the guy who doesn't flex and tense every time he sits with a Honey.

The new me was hard work. Comfortable, fat and honest, with just a pinch of twenty-first-century humility. End-of-an-era stuff really. I made my decision. The ticket I would come clean about, the other I would keep up. For old times' sake I'd use a pretence. A play. I'd lead her to believe that I really was comfortable with what I looked like. I sagged in the mirror and thought of Ali this morning. If she thought I was attractive like this then why not the Honey? Game on.

I had to go back to my seat. I'd been gone five minutes and I didn't want her to think I was so uncouth as to take a shit on a train. Toilets should be reserved for number ones and sex, at least that's what the book said.

I took a deep breath, checked my trousers for stains and walked back. Squeezing back into my seat, I watched her take off her headphones and put them in her bag.

'I'd given up on you.' She smiled. 'I thought you'd met someone back there.'

'Me?' I laughed in reply. She knew where I'd gone.

'You know toilets on trains' – I think she looked embarrassed – 'no one spends any time in them unless they're' – she held up her hands and motioned with them – 'you know.' Her eyes were laughing and now I felt embarrassed.

'Unfortunately no.' I tried to sound cool. 'I told you, nothing like that ever happens to me.'

She smiled again and before she could say anything else I took a stand. Plucking the pubic hair of common sense, I came clean.

'Actually, I was weighing up the pros and cons of admitting to you that I kind of lied a little bit earlier when I said I was going travelling.'

There, done it, that wasn't so hard. I waited for a response but her only reaction was to take her smile out of my reach.

Shit.

Keep talking.

Keep talking.

'It wasn't a lie as such,' I wheedled, 'more an exaggeration.'

She folded her arms and I got images of being on Ricky Lake or Jerry Springer, fighting to be understood when I'd been billed as Pennance the Serial Liar.

'Go on,' she instructed me coldly.

'I am going travelling.' I could feel the sweat patches form. 'Well, what I mean is I'd like to go and I've been thinking about it seriously for a few days now and this time I'm going to go.' I looked at the table, squaring the books. 'I haven't got a ticket yet but I know where I want to go and I've got the money and the opportunity. I just need to get the ticket.' I knew it was true as I said it and the more I thought about it the better I liked the idea.

I was going travelling. Honest.

'And that's it? That's your lie?'

'That's it,' I assured her as she looked quizzically at me.

'And do you often feel the need to lie to complete strangers on a train?'

'Well, not normally.' I rolled my finger on the table, playing at being six. 'It just kind of came out before I'd thought about it really.'

'So why the need to fess up?'

That's the cruncher, I thought, why did I? It wasn't a major lie, it probably wasn't even a lie at all as I'd planned to get a ticket. It was just that it didn't sit comfortably with me. I wasn't sure why, but no, of course I was.

'I felt guilty.'

How could I explain that it wasn't her I was sorry about lying to. It was myself. I didn't need any more guilt in my life, and I didn't have room for it. I was trying to be a new Pennance, a reduced-guilt version.

This morning Ali had told me that my guilt about Ting wouldn't last forever. Shit can't last forever, it's got to go to make room for new shit, she said. Everything moves on. So I was trying, determined to do it today.

She looked at me through narrow eyes, the touches of a smile playing round her mouth, and I shrugged back at her.

'I'm only playing with you,' she confessed. 'You've not said anything to feel bad about, everybody exaggerates.' She looked around conspiratorially. 'Matter of fact, I've just got a new job and, between you and me, I lied, well, stretched the truth, if you will, on my application.' She relaxed her arms and the smile spread to her eyes. 'And as for the interview . . .'

We laughed together then.

'That was cruel,' I teased her through petted lips.

'Sorry,' she continued, trying to keep a straight face, 'but you made it so easy and, anyway, I'm sick of people lying to me so I was interested to see what you had to say.'

'Thanks very much.' I hoped I sounded injured but think she saw through me as she just tilted her head and smiled like a goddess.

'Shall we start again?'

Chapter 25

outplayed?

I offered her my hand.

'Hello, my name's Pennance, Pennance Ward,' I said formally, clicking my heels together under the table and bowing my head.

She shook my hand and held it.

'Hello, Pennance Ward, the name's Bond, Jane Bond.'

I almost attempted a joke but figured that she'd appreciate it more if I let the obvious go. I must have been reading it well because she gave my hand an extra squeeze in the ensuing silence as though to say well done.

'My pleasure.' I grinned and let a little Connery slip out in spite of myself.

'Good one.' She nodded, eyes wide, and let my hand go. 'No one's come up with that one before.' I took my hand back as though scolded, thinking that I'd fucked up again, but she grinned and shook her head. 'Don't take everything so seriously.'

Relax.

This was going better than I could have imagined and there I was giving psychotic signals at every opportunity.

How not to make a play.

She settled back and asked why I'd been in Glasgow and we moved on to a conversation that allowed me to explain my behaviour. She listened to the story of the weekend and the trip to Mull. Every sentence came easier than the next and suddenly I realised I'd been talking about stuff that I didn't even speak to my friends about, again. First with Ali and now here, I was finding it disconcerting the ease with which I was talking about things that had always been left unspoken.

Feelings.

I wondered fleetingly if there was a connection between my relaxed muscles play and my liberal display of emotional openness. Conscious that I didn't want to scare her off with my intensity, I stopped talking and looked at her, embarrassed.

'I'm not always this fucked up, you know,' I said by way of explanation and not for the first time in the last few days, but she was already nodding at me.

'I'm sure you're not,' she answered. 'I think I'd be pretty fucked up myself.' She seemed to be searching for something to say. 'I think your friend's dad is right.'

'Ray?'

'Yeah, Ray. I think he's right. You shouldn't feel guilty, certainly not about your friend's death.' She hesitated, but I didn't feel like breaking the silence. 'I know it's not my place to say' – she looked up – 'but you need to get on. Go travelling, do something, but don't just sit there biting your lip, mulling it over.' She put her head down and blushed slightly. 'No pun intended.'

'None taken.' She smiled through her lashes at me as I pushed myself up straight and laid my hands on the table. 'Anyway, enough about me, this is too heavy a conversation for a train.' There was only so much soul searching I could do when I was on a time limit and I was determined to change the mood. 'What about you? Do you always sit and talk to strange men on the train?' I looked confused, accusing. 'What? Are you a counsellor for the Samaritans, or one of those weirdos that . . .' I stopped and stared at her like the penny just dropped. 'Ah, I get it, you are a researcher for Oprah. You're looking for saddos to put on your show, aren't you?'

'Damn, you've sussed me.' Her hands were up and she looked at me shyly. 'I don't suppose there's any chance that you live in a trailer or that you used to be a woman or anything?'

'Well . . .' I glanced back over my shoulder and then beckoned her forward, whispering, 'I've always wanted to and I'm happy to lie about it if there's any money involved.'

'What, say you were a woman?'

'No, live in a trailer.'

She leant back and laughed. 'You couldn't handle it, Pennance, too much guilt.'

'Being a woman?'

'No, lying for money.'

'True,' I laughed, 'but the being a woman part, that must be fairly easy.' I waited to see if she'd bite.

'Get over yourself,' she said with deliberation.

Right on cue.

'Okay, fair comment,' I agreed, watching her, trying to see if she was taking me seriously.

'You men have got it so easy.'

Bang, every grumble every woman has ever had.

'. . . And that's before you even start thinking about having kids, gravity, osteoporosis, dickheads and thrush.'

'Whoa, I'm kidding, I'm kidding.'

Now I was worried that she was taking me seriously. Fucking great, Pennance, could you piss her off any more?

'Well, don't,' she said, sounding offended. 'If you say stuff like that I'll never be able to convince Oprah that you were a woman.'

She was watching me totally straight-faced and it took a couple of seconds before it dawned on me that I'd just been had. I snorted in acknowledgement and she lost her composure as she gave in to the giggles.

'You're just jealous because I've got a willy,' I huffed, trying to get the upper hand again. 'Pennance envy, it's called.'

'Oh please.' She rolled her eyes so hard I heard them click. 'I can get as many of those as I like.'

'Ha ha.' I resorted to taking the huff again. 'Kick a man when he's down.'

She laughed maliciously. 'That's the best time.'

'True.' I nodded furiously, trying to find something funny to say to get back on an even footing. 'But you've got to admit, apart from all that stuff, women did get all the good bits.' She looked confused. 'You know.' I shrugged and pointed with my chin. 'A PlayStation for a body, multiple orgasms, a bus pass five years before us, what do we get? We get to pee standing up.'

'Get real,' she laughed. 'Haven't you seen *The Full Monty*?'

'Yeah.' I played my trump card. 'But we can get pressure, we can have height and distance competitions, even write our names.'

'Woo.' She held her hands to her face in mock amazement. 'I wish I was a man.'

I stopped smiling and looked directly at her, all or nothing on my next line.

'I'm glad you're not.'

And there it was. And it was cheesy.

Silence.

She held my gaze as her hands slid off her face.

Too needy, Pennance.

Looks like you've blown it.

She pulled at her T-shirt self-consciously again and I willed the train to go faster. Go faster and faster and faster, go fast enough to go back in time and I'll start again and this time I won't be such a dick. And I'll flex and tense.

'I'm not, you know.'

This not unsurprisingly woke me from my self-flagellation.

'Sorry?'

'I'm not a researcher for Oprah.'

Thank you, thank you, thank you.

She knew that my last outburst had left me feeling foolish and yet here she was, getting me out of it.

'Really?' I smiled at her in acknowledgement. 'Why don't you tell me who you really are then? I feel as though I'm sat here naked before you. It's your turn to expose yourself, metaphorically speaking of course.'

'Of course.'

▭ ★ ▭

'Okay, you get to ask me three questions and then it's my turn again. Sound fair?' she said.

'Three questions?' I sat up straight as though in an interview but with more smiling.

'Yes.'

'And you've got to answer them?' I rubbed at my chin and pursed my lips as I spoke.

'Yes.'

'About anything?' I grinned.

'Yes.' She mirrored me. 'My turn now.'

She found out that I'd once buried a VCR in the garden, that Miles Davis made me want to pee and that I'd prefer never to read a book than never to hear music, before it was my turn to ask the questions again. She was as open as I'd been.

Jane Bond, twenty-seven, moving to a new job and a new life away from a boyfriend who'd cheated on her and a mother who wanted grandchildren.

'So you're off into the great unknown to start again?'

'Something like that.' She shrugged. 'I just had to do something. I guess I realised that life shouldn't be something that just happens to me and that I was the one who would have to make the difference. It was my responsibility.' She smiled. 'So here I am. Moving on and terrified.'

'That explains the smell then.' I grinned and made her laugh, lightening up. She kept talking and I asked questions in the right places and shook my head when it was appreciated, but all the time she was talking, my mind was racing. I was listening to her and couldn't stop thinking that I liked her. I liked how she looked, how she thought, how she moved. I liked how she made me feel. And all this after an hour. After Ali.

'It's not like I'm running away,' she insisted. 'I just needed something new, that's why I took this job.' I nodded in agreement, encouraging her to continue. 'That's why I'm talking to you,' she said plaintively. 'Normally I'd ignore any sad bastard who used such lame lines. I mean, come on.' Her eyebrows climbed into her hair. ' "That never happens to me." '

I could only look sheepishly at her while inside I felt waves of embarrassment wash over me until even my ears were blushing. Of course, she knew I'd been making a play, how could she not, it's not as though I was good at it.

'You're so obviously not good at this that I was embarrassed for you.'

'Huh.' I sulked. 'I told you I've been having a bad time lately.' I searched for an excuse but couldn't find one that didn't have me marked out as a loser or pathetic. Once again I was left with honesty and was becoming worried about the regularity with which it was proving to be my only option now that I had used it once. 'Cut me some slack here. I'm sorry I'm not a professional Don Juan but I'm not normally that bad.'

'Are you sure?'

'Yes,' I tutted, unconvincingly. 'I'm sure.'

She looked as though she was weighing up whether to believe me or not.

'Okay, I'll give you the benefit of the doubt.'

'Oh, thank you very much!'

'Hey, look, I'm still not convinced that you're not only sitting there because I soaked your shoe; for all I know you saw me buy my ticket and decided to stalk me. You cut me some slack.'

If she hadn't been laughing as she spoke, I'd have been moving seats; so persuasive was her logic, I almost doubted myself.

'Don't worry.' I grinned. 'It was definitely the Carlisle train I wanted.'

'This train doesn't go to –' She stopped and stared. 'Touché.'

◼ * ◼

With the freedom of strangers we talked about ourselves, sharing confidences and fears for our futures, equally unknown. It didn't seem odd to me that we had moved beyond the small talk of passing interest and opened up to each other free of the masks that friendship thrust upon us. This was how it should be.

These were the moments before familiarity bred conservatism.

'Have you ever been in love?' she asked quietly, comfortable and removed enough to be casually intimate.

'No, I don't think so,' I answered her easily, as relaxed as she. 'I thought I was, but now I'm not so sure.'

She smiled. 'If you have to think about it you haven't.'

'I love people. I mean, there are people I love and a couple that I thought I was in love with.' I considered Kirsty and, more surprisingly, Ali before I continued. 'But looking back, I don't think I was.' I shrugged. 'How do you know if it's love?'

'You'd know it,' she said certainly. 'You think differently when you've been in love. You see things differently.'

Her voice softened and she spoke hesitantly, as though she was simultaneously thinking and talking about something for the first time; she was opening up to me and I felt too enthralled to stop her. And what she was saying struck a chord with me.

'You can't unlearn what you know from being in love,' she lamented, 'and that's why you see things differently.'

She was confusing me now.

'Surely that's a good thing?' I asked, thinking that all learning was good learning.

'Sometimes,' she agreed, 'but sometimes it's a pain in the arse.'

'Like when?'

She shrugged and shuffled in her seat. 'Like when I'm single and I know what it's like to be in a relationship. To not have the things you've had before and to want them – new ones, better ones.'

'Don't you enjoy being single?' I asked in a neutral tone even though I was conscious of the question implied by asking.

'That's just it.' She smiled. 'Sometimes I do and other times I don't.'

'But most people are like that,' I countered.

'I know,' she said defensively, 'but I'm only just coming to terms with it. It doesn't matter that everybody else is the same, this is me going through it and having to work it out for myself.'

We passed through a tunnel then and sat in silence in the

momentary gloom. I could feel the rough material of the seat ride against my arm as I shuffled my weight to ease the numbness in the cheeks of my bum. I could feel the noise of the wheels more pronounced as if the sudden echoes of the tunnel intensified both sound and feeling in equal measure.

My outstretched leg rested lightly against hers and I tingled when she didn't pull away. With a suddenness that attacked my eyes, we shot from the darkness. She scowled at the sun and put her sunglasses on and continued speaking as though the tunnel was a pause for breath.

'The thing I've got difficulty with is that I enjoyed being in a relationship,' she admitted. 'If I'd never been there, I'd never have had anything to compare being single to and I wouldn't be caught in this mess.'

'I've been in a relationship,' I told her, 'and now I'm single, but I don't think it really matters that much. You just get on with it.'

'Yes, but you're obviously not the brightest spark in the box when it comes to these sorts of things, I can see that and I've just met you. If you'd been in love you might well think differently about it,' she insisted and I chose not to hear her character assassination.

'What about it's better to have loved and lost . . .'

'Do you believe that?'

I shrugged and smiled. 'I will if you will.'

'Can't argue with that.'

'So you want a boyfriend,' I said, teasing her, 'so that you can be a happy bunny again?'

She smiled deliciously and leant her head on the window.

'No, all men are bastards.'

'In that case' – I stood and sidled out of the seat – 'I'll go get us a coffee as a gesture of reconciliation on behalf of my illegitimate brothers everywhere.'

'Don't forget chocolate.'

■ * ■

I watched the rain blur into the sea as we hugged the coast and rattled along before turning inland and approaching Newcastle. I was dozing off when the train began to slow and Jane nudged me and reminded me that I was getting off.

She was going straight through to Leeds and I was feeling guilty for thinking that I would stay on the train with her and let Grace down again. Someone had called her on her mobile and she was still talking when the train stopped.

'Go on.' She pushed me, still holding the phone to her ear. 'Go say goodbye to your sister and get yourself off round the planet, it'll do you the world of good.'

That answered that question.

I had almost asked her for her number before she said that and I'd thought it was reasonable to expect that she would have given it to me considering that we'd just spent the whole journey in each other's head. My instincts had proved to be as reliable as ever as I mouthed goodbye and walked from the train, unwilling to look back in case she saw the disappointment in my face.

I'd done too good a job in being the new Pennance, too full of enthusiasm for starting again and wanting to get away. She'd taken me at face value and had faith in my conviction in what I told her I wanted to do, and waved me off as though I was stepping from the train and onto a plane today. I wasn't, but I would be. I knew that for the fact it was. How could I not now?

I'd walked away from one possibility because of my insistence that I needed to follow another to validate my life. I'd convinced myself that travelling wasn't a dream any more, it was my reality and, stepping from the train, I knew that that was why I didn't ask for her number. That and her almost curt dismissal as we'd lumbered to a stop. So I would go and say goodbye to Grace, I would get on and get out, and I wouldn't look back at what might have been. For sure that way indeed lay madness. At least on my travels I would be misreading the signals for the right reasons, language barriers instead of congenital stupidity.

'Here.'

I turned as I felt a hand tap my shoulder as I approached the gate.

'You left this on the train.'

I looked first at her as she smiled and turned back towards the train, and then at the napkin she had thrust into my hand. Before I could say anything she had stepped past the queue behind me and jumped back on the train as the guard closed the doors and it pulled out of the station. I shook my head and grinned. Using all my teeth.

Jane Bond.

06775023674.

I really was about as bright as a blackout on a dark night.

lost without grace

I ran from the station to a café across the road and shook off my coat. Even on the twenty-metre dash from the station I got soaked. The rain hadn't let up all morning and the café was preparing for its early-afternoon rush from the ciabatta and cappuccino crew. The daily run of lunch on the hoof as the suits assured themselves of their need to be seen to be busy. Look at me, I'm too busy to have lunch. A sandwich at my desk is about all I can manage.

I stood at the back of the queue smelling wet dog from the overcoat in front of me and smiled as it reminded me of Jane.

'A latte, an espresso, double-grain Italian peppered ham on rye, a decaf cappuccino without chocolate and three sugars, Brie and lettuce in a cob, tuna melt with mayo and Lea & Perrins and could you bag it to go?' It was only the accents that helped me to remember that this was Newcastle not New York.

'Can I have a cup of tea and a sausage roll please.'

At twelve pence for a sachet of sauce, I declined the offer and walked between the steaming briefcases and took a stool by the window, my tea and sausage roll looking out of place on the counter of European super-bread sandwiches.

Waiting for Grace, I tuned out from the inane chattering of the secretaries on my left moaning about their boss and the bum-fluffed solicitors on my right boasting to the mobile phone. Same old same old.

I spent my time watching the rain and the scurrying of the suits, trying to preserve their twenty-quid hairdos. It kept me amused as, umbrellas up, newspapers over heads, collars up, they half ran to avoid the taxi splashes that found them anyway. As that grew boring I couldn't avoid it any longer. Trying not to grin, I took the napkin Jane had given me and smoothed it out flat on the counter in front of me.

Jane Bond.

06775023674.

As I smiled through the fantasy of when I'd call her, it was a moment before I caught sight of Grace getting out of a cab across at the station. I hadn't seen her since she'd told me she was pregnant again, and looking at her, blooming, I was glad that I'd made the effort to see her now, even if it was only for an hour or so. While she waited for the traffic to slow, I went to the counter and ordered two more teas. She was wet and probably cold, Grace was always cold and I knew that I would get masses of brownie points for the tea. I headed back to the window just as she came through the door and unbuttoned her coat. She looked up and rewarded me with a smile when she saw the steaming mugs in my hands. She folded her coat over her arm and waddled over to me, reached up and gave me a kiss.

'Hey, big brother, it's good to see you. I hope one of them is for me.'

She took the proffered mug out of my hand and looked for a place to sit.

'I'm over there by the window.' I nodded and looked over to where my coat and bag sat.

'Shit.'

The waitress was clearing away the secretarial debris from next to where my stuff was and running a cloth along the counter. She picked up my empty plate and mug and put them on her tray. Stumbling towards her in my haste, I kicked my way through the tables and spilt tea on my hand and sleeve.

'Pennance?'

Grace followed in my wake, picking up the briefcase and coats and smiling at the suits in apology, as I ignored them and pushed on to the window, sucking on the back of my scalded hand.

'I haven't finished yet,' I started over the music. 'Don't touch that' – too late – 'napkin.' In her efficiency, she used it to dry the counter and popped it in one of the cups on her tray just to make extra sure that I was totally fucked.

She looked at me through blank eyes as I rummaged on her tray and lifted the brown soggy mass that ten seconds ago was a paper key to the house of happy.

'I don't fucking believe this.'

'I'm sorry, I thought you were finished.' She backed up, glancing from me to Grace. 'Sorry,' she mumbled again and disappeared off to the kitchen.

'What's up?' Grace was looking over my shoulder as I tried to straighten the sodden napkin out on the counter.

J e Pcn

0o7

The ink had run and the napkin was a brown and blue smudge; my new beginning looked like a patch of bruised skin from Hannibal Lecter's fridge.

Outside a car backfired and the bang was the noise my bubble made when it popped. Welcome back to your reality, Pennance, it shouted. I looked at Grace and pointed at the napkin as she sidled onto a stool beside me.

'I met a girl on the train and she gave me her phone number.' I quickly told her about the journey. 'I thought that maybe this time it would work out. Christ, she got off the train and gave me it.'

I knew I sounded pathetic – it was only a phone number – but things looked like they might have gone well; we had the same interests and outlook on life, she made me laugh and, more importantly, laughed at my jokes. It didn't get much better than that. I'd bottled it and scurried off without so much as a by-your-leave and she'd run out after me in spite of it, and if that wasn't a sign then it was the biggest foul-up since Moses took ten tablets, got stoned and saw a burning bush. I looked back to the kitchen and scowled as the waitress peeked through the window at me.

'Stupid bitch.'

Following my gaze, Grace tutted. 'Well, shit happens, Pennance, you can't blame the poor girl for doing her job.'

'I know that, but I've got to blame somebody. It's hardly my fault, is it? Man, I don't fucking believe this, the things people do when you don't have a gun.'

Grace smiled and let me ramble for a few minutes. There was no rescuing the phone number, no reason to keep the napkin, but I squeezed the tea out of it and put it in my pocket anyway, a reminder of what might have been and tangible proof for Pine and Stan that I had made a successful play if nothing else.

My hands were stained with ink but I didn't notice as I rubbed my forehead in resignation. Oh well, welcome to another day. Grace laughed at me and I glared at her in annoyance. Can't she see I'm having a crisis here? She licked her thumb and before I could stop her she started rubbing at my forehead like mothers have done for years with their children.

'Urggh, stop that.' I wiped her saliva off with my sleeve. It was blue. I rubbed at my forehead until she assured me it was gone.

'Grace, I'm sorry I'm in a mood, it's just the last few days have taken a toll on me and I thought Ting was watching out for me when Jane gave me her number. Trust me, if you knew how my luck was running you'd understand; it's been one hell of a week.'

With a jolt I realised that I hadn't even told her about Ting yet. Boy, did I feel good now.

◼ * ◼

Grace stood and put her coat back on and pulled me up from my seat.

'C'mon, we'll go whilst the rain's stopped and you can tell me all about it.'

I finished my tea and she held the door open for me. Outside we linked arms and headed down the road.

'Where we going?'

'Shopping.'

'I don't want to –'

'I'll shop, you talk,' she said, leading me down the street. 'So come on, tell me what you've been up to, you haven't been here in months and then you just turn up.' She looked at me closely. 'Are you all right? I mean really you do look a bit fucked.'

'Well, it's like I told you on the phone this morning, I was in Mull and thought it would be a good idea to call in and see you on my way home, so here I am.'

'Yes, so you said on the phone, but what were you doing in Mull?'

'I was at a wake.'

'In Mull?'

'The funeral was in Leeds, we took his ashes to Mull.'

'Whose funeral was it?'

It started to rain again so we jumped into a shop.

'You remember Ting?'

'Of course I –'

She tightened her grip on my hand and a couple of tears squeezed out of my eye.

'Oh no, don't tell me that.'

'Last week.' I nodded and wiped at my nose. 'We took him home to Mull.'

'Jesus Christ, Pennance, I'm sorry.'

She gave me a hug and shook her head in disbelief as I told her what happened. Tears ran freely as I spoke to her and she glared at the other shoppers if they gawked too long at my discomfort.

Grace had moved away years before and was happily married with two kids and her Geordie husband Phil. She knew Ting from when we were kids, although it was probably over ten years since she had last seen him.

We didn't keep in contact that much although when we did see each other, we always had a good time and the intervening weeks and months dropped away in moments. I told her about Ting's death and the stag wake at Mull as we dodged the rain and I found a different café.

Then I told her about Ali and finally Jane again.

'So true to form and with total disregard for any sign she was giving me, I said goodbye and got off the train. As I was giving my ticket at the gate, she pushed up to me and thrust this napkin in my hand with her phone number on it. The train was leaving so she ran back on before I could say anything.' I was shaking my head. 'You know the rest.'

She shook her head in turn. 'Pennance, it's not the end of the world.'

She'd been upset about Ting and sympathetic when I'd told her about Ali, now she was being matter of fact. A mother putting the plaster on a scraped knee.

'So what, if you can't phone her? So what if you don't see her again, it's enough that someone wanted you to phone them.' She looked at me closely. 'Don't you see? If she gave you her number then somebody else can give you a number. You just have to put it down to experience and move on. Shit happens and we deal with it.'

'Thanks, Grace, that's just the help I need right now.'

Her tough love approach to my latest catastrophe was beginning to piss me off.

'What else are you going to do?'

I'd taken the hump with her but she brushed off my mood and carried on regardless. She was filling me in on what had been happening with her but, whilst I was paying lip service to what she was saying, I was too caught up in feeling sorry for myself to really listen.

I would have called Jane tonight if I still had her number. I knew that that was risking appearing too keen, but she was the one who gave me her number so I thought it could have been okay.

'Hi, Jane, it's Pennance. You want to go for a beer tomorrow?'

'Hi, Jane, it's Pennance. How would you like to come travelling with me? . . . You would!'

'Hi, Jane, it's Pennance . . . Pennance . . . From the train . . . Erm, you gave me it, remember?'

'Hi, Jane, it's Pennance . . . That's right . . . Yeah, I'd love to!'

Not now though.

Bastard.

She'd be getting off the train now, walking through the station and out of my reach forever. Walking out of the station . . .

'Grace, have you got your mobile on you?'

'What?' She looked at me, brought up short in her monologue that I wasn't hearing.

'I need to use your phone.'

'Why?'

'I'm going to phone the station and get them to Tannoy for Jane.'

I knew she was weighing up whether or not to tell me that she thought I was being a bit sad. Making a decision, she fumbled in her bag and brought out her mobile phone.

'You sure you want to do this?'

'What do you mean?'

'You don't think it's a bit . . .'

'Sad?'

'Fucking scary is what I mean. How long did you talk to her for?'

'It's not the length.' Pissed off and wired as I was, I couldn't help but smile as she held up the phone. 'It's the quality.'

'Yeah, dream on. Here, go for it.'

So I did.

'Hello, yes, you can.' I'd been put through to three different people and was explaining again what I wanted to another confused bovine. 'What I'm looking for is someone to put a call out for a friend of mine who should be getting off the Glasgow train right now . . . Yes, I know that but by the time it takes to get from the platform to the gates she should still be there . . . Please!'

I glanced at Grace who was looking out of the window trying not to smile.

'. . . It is an emergency.'

Grace turned and frowned.

'Okay, thanks.'

I put my hand over the mouthpiece. 'I'm on hold. And it is an emergency so stop looking at me like that.'

She just shook her head. Saddo.

'Hello, yes, hello, I've already explained what I want to . . . Oh, okay, thanks.'

I beamed at Grace.

'I don't fucking believe it, they're going to do it.' I made a fist and whispered yes.

'That's right, if you can ask Jane to go to a phone and . . .'

And what? Phone Pennance? She didn't have my number.

'. . . And . . . would you be able to put her through to me if she got to a phone at the ticket desk or something?' I mean, great plan, Pennance. 'Okay, I've got it, can I leave you a number so that when she answers the Tannoy you can give her it? Excellent, thanks, the number is . . . wait a minute, I just have to get the number.'

Grace was looking at me strangely.

'No way are you giving my number out over the Tannoy in a train station,' she said, folding her arms awkwardly.

'I'm not, just give me the number and I'll leave it with this girl on the phone. She'll pass it to Jane when she answers the message.'

'No.'

'Are you kidding? Come on, Grace . . . please.'

'Leave your own number.'

'But I won't be there, will I?'

'Do you think that makes any difference, you've got a machine and you're getting a train in twenty minutes. Use your head.' She said it in a tone that ended the discussion. 'And hurry up with my phone.'

Bastard.

'Hello, I'm back, sorry about that. Okay, can you ask Jane to leave Pennance Ward her phone number on . . . What? . . . Yes, I met her on the train . . .' Grace was rolling her eyes at me and mouthing 'no' but it was too late and I hit the heel of

my hand against my head with enough force to rattle my teeth.
'. . . But it is an emergency.'

I could feel the hairs on the back of my neck drip as the
sweat ran down my back and I started to panic.

'Look, I'm being honest with you, I've only just met her on
the train, she gave me her phone number and I've lost it . . .
this is the only way I can think of to get in touch with her . . .
please . . . please . . . please.'

The people at the tables round us were staring now but I
didn't care.

'Oh come on, help me out . . . please . . . please.

'Thanks for fucking nothing, you jobsworth bastard . . .
What? . . . No, that's not my real name so I don't care who
you rep—'

I held the phone out and snarled at it as I turned to Grace.
'Can you believe she put the fu—'

She grabbed the phone from me as I sat and used the table
in lieu of the brick wall that I needed.

'And you can stop staring,' I twisted and spat at the table
of smug couples sat beside us.

Grace punched my leg and hissed, 'Pennance, calm down.
It's not their fault.' She smiled an apology at them. 'Chill out
for fuck's sake,' she said through gritted teeth.

I was too angry though. My last-ditch brilliant idea to get
to Jane. Fuck, it was just like a film; it could have been romantic
if it had worked, a story to tell our grandkids about how we
tracked each other down after a chance encounter and lived
happily ever after together.

A waiter came over and looked at Grace; he jerked his thumb
at me pounding my head against the table. 'I'm sorry, I'm going
to have to ask you to leave.'

'Oh, come on.' She glanced at me and shook her head,
accentuating her stomach. 'He'll be fine, won't you, Pennance?
He's just kind of flipped a wee bit.'

She looked up at him and half whispered. 'He's just been
to a funeral and he's a bit strung out, that's all. Cut him some
slack, he'll be fine, honest.'

She kicked my ankle as he made a show of thinking about it. 'You'll be fine, won't you?'

I stopped banging my head when she kicked me and sat back in the seat trying to blow spit bubbles. Grace was seven months pregnant, the waiter possibly even thought that we were together and there was me losing my rag because I couldn't contact a girl I'd just met on a train. She was right, I was completely fucking bananas. I'd gone possibility crazy.

Aware of all my opportunities and fiercely determined to get the most from them when they appeared, I was going off the scale when they didn't live up to the promises that I made for them. A couple of days with Ali and I was ready to tell her I loved her and a few hours on a train later I was lamenting the newest lost love of my life never to be. All I could hear was Mr Pitiful.

'Sorry, mate.' I looked at him and grinned tightly. 'I'm fine now. They just pissed me off.' I forced a smile at the other table. 'Sorry about the swearing.' I started twitching. 'Please, just let me finish my coffee before the voices come back.'

He didn't look convinced but a quick glance at Grace seemed to reassure him.

▭ * ▭

Grace was refusing to look at me. She stared out the window as the traffic raced through the rain in first gear. I sat squirming. I couldn't shake off the feeling of wanting to strangle that cow on the phone, I imagined that it was the same one who had my collar felt in the train station.

Grace wasn't talking to me. Her display with the waiter was designed to keep us in from the rain and nothing to do with having forgiven my behaviour. I felt about two inches tall. The waiter was watching me as he worked the floor. I ordered two more coffees and he gave me a look of warning as he brought them to the table.

'Grace, I'm really sorry.' She spooned sugar into her coffee and I made to stand. 'I can only say it so many times.'

She shrugged.

I couldn't blame her really. I had acted like a dick.

'Look, if you'd rather, I'll just go now and wait in the station. I don't want to be like this, upsetting you. I'm sorry, I was a dick.'

She sipped at her coffee and I didn't know what to do now. I'd said sorry and I'd offered to go. Did that mean she was calling my bluff?

'Okay.' I stood up and made a show of straightening myself ready to go.

'Pennance, sit down and stop acting like a drama queen.'

I sat down, concealing my smile.

'You are an enormous fuckwit, do you know that?' She shook her head. 'What am I going to do with you?'

I looked up from contemplating my cigarette packet. My ego bruising, I gave her my best puppy dog eyes until she laughed.

'And don't even think about smoking in here,' she said disgustedly as I drew a cigarette from the pack. 'If you really want to go, just light that up and I'll throw you out myself.'

'I wasn't going to smoke in here.'

'Well, you've got a cigarette in your hand, haven't you?'

'I've got boxer shorts on as well.'

And then everything was okay again as we remembered that we did actually like each other and I made allowances for her being a control freak and she coped better with my emotional mercury switch. We began garbling as time threatened to catch us up and this time I paid attention to her, pushing my problems out and learning what my own family was up to.

Grace was the linchpin in our family. Where we had each gone our separate ways, our separate lives, she was the catalyst for family gatherings.

'Dad says you haven't spoken to him or Mum for months.'

She had moved directly into lecture mode, forgetting totally that ten minutes ago she wasn't even talking to me. No wonder she didn't want me to go, she never ever missed an opportunity to play families.

'You are going home for Christmas this year, aren't you? You promised last year and didn't, so you better be sure this time.'

'I'll let them know.'

'Just make sure you phone them and if you're not going to visit then have a good excuse this time and not something as ludicrous as last time.' She shook her head. 'Growing your fucking nails, I can't believe they let you get away with that.'

'What if I'm not here?'

'Don't be getting morbid on me, Pennance.'

'I don't mean that, I mean what if I'm away travelling?'

'If you're making an excuse at least use something more believable.'

'I'm serious, Grace, that's why I came here. When I get home I'm buying the ticket and going. I mean it this time.'

'Oh, I know you're serious, it's not as though you're thinking about anything else. It's all you've been able to talk about since you arrived.' She threw her eyes this way and that. 'Travelling this, travelling that.'

I stuck my tongue out and decided to drop it. I knew that no one would believe me until I had the tan and the inflection in my voice to prove otherwise.

'Well, you can believe it this time. I'll send you a postcard, T-shirts for the kids.'

'Yeah, whatever.'

'You'll have to send me a photo when the baby's born, I don't know where I'll be though. Have you got a name sorted out yet?'

'Don't change the subject,' she scolded me, not quite finished with her lecture. 'It's about time you started thinking about others and stopped being so selfish.'

'I'm not selfish,' I said, not really believing it myself.

'Then why don't you ever phone Mum and Dad? Or me and the kids?' She went for the jugular. 'Do you even know when Steph and Joe's birthdays are?'

'Of course I do, the end of July and the middle of February.'

She looked at me as though waiting for a more precise answer.

'I'm sorry.' I realised what she was waiting for. 'I guess I missed Steph's birthday again. I meant to send a card but when I remembered it was too late.'

'And you didn't phone because . . . ?'

She could see me trying to find the right answer but didn't make it any easier on me. She sat back waiting.

'It's not that I'm selfish, it's just that . . .' I didn't really have an excuse.

'Forget it, it's not me who's bothered, but you better have a good reason when Steph gets a hold of you, she's well miffed. Matter of fact, maybe you should leave the country for a while.'

Brilliant, I thought, more woman trouble and this one's only six years old. Like mother, like daughter.

I hadn't seen Steph or Joe since last Christmas. I knew I should have made more of an effort to see them, get to know them. On the few occasions that I did visit I loved spending time with them. They were a tonic, everything else took second place as I was usually too intent on making sure that nothing happened to them to think about anything else. Because one time I took them out.

We went to an adventure playground, more for me than them, and to the fair, candyfloss and sugar dummies. It was the first time that I'd been out on my own with them and I remembered walking around with the buggy, playing dad, smiling at the other parents and not correcting them in their assumptions about me.

We'd chased a ball round the park and fed the ducks, running for the sake of running and not walking on any cracks. I could get used to this, I'd thought at the time. Steph and Joe were full of gurgling laughter and spontaneous beauty. I understood then what it was to be broody. On the way back home it started raining and Joe had sat on Steph's lap in the buggy, sheltering from the rain as I ran down the path. I was leaning forward and talking to them as we went and my heart nearly stopped when Steph's foot caught the strap at the front of the buggy and they both catapulted out and scraped to a halt on the gravel with me pushing the upturned buggy over them and jumping to avoid stomping on them.

I'd panicked as Joe screamed, his hands scraped raw as he broke his fall. The scream cut off as Steph slid over him, her momentum increased by the buggy following her. Blood was streaming from Joe's chin as I picked him up and held him tight to my shoulder in alarm. Steph was rolling on the path kicking the broken buggy to one side when I knelt by her, trying to see how hurt she was. Her knee was bleeding and her lip was burst but I didn't notice either of them until later. I passed out when I saw the way her arm had bent. I came round to Joe slapping me and a tear-streaked Steph screaming for me to wake up. They probably didn't even remember that it happened but I would never forget it. I remembered that date easier than their birthdays. It was the day I found out I wasn't cut out for parenting. Everyone was very understanding about it and how Phil resisted the urge to flatten me was always a mystery to me. But that was the last time I'd accepted the responsibility of babysitting regardless of Grace and Phil's assurances that it could have happened to anyone. Like Ting's death, I couldn't believe that it wasn't my fault.

'So you do believe I'm going away then?'

She looked at me quietly, weighing up her answer.

'Of course I believe you.' She knew what I wanted to hear. 'It could be just what you need.'

'You don't think it's a bad idea?'

I'd expected her to try and counsel me away from the rashness that she would think my going was and was pleased that I got her blessing.

'I think it's crazier than toffee, but that's just me. If it's what you want, then you go for it.'

'Thanks, Grace. That means a lot to me.'

'No charge, bro.' She smiled and looked at her watch. 'Now tell me quickly, was this Ali really a lezzie?'

Chapter 27

re connect

I'd left Grace at the station with a promise of phone calls or at least a postcard or two and drifted off to sleep as the train pulled out with Cornershop singing me down 'The Road Back Home Again'. I dozed throughout the journey, my mind feverish with anticipation. Perhaps, portentously, the rain hadn't followed me. We pulled in to Leeds station and I jumped in a taxi. All the tea and coffee from before was forcing my mind to concentrate on not peeing myself as I was bounced all the way home. I dumped my bag in the hall and rushed into the toilet with my pants round my thighs.

'Do you mind?'

Instinctively I covered myself, pinching my foreskin while my brain tried to shut the tap off. I stood too far away from the toilet to reach but was too far gone to contain it. With Helen in the bath to my right I swivelled my head towards her and my body in the opposite direction emptying my balloon into the sink before once more covering myself, the flow having been cut off.

'Sorry.' I blushed. Nurse or no nurse, there are some things no one needs to share. 'I didn't know you were here.'

'Well, now that you do could you find something else to look at?'

She was shaving her leg when I came in and now sat hugging her knees, returning my stare. Apart from the fact that she was sitting in my bath, which was reason enough to stare, I was preoccupied by the sliver of nipple visible against her thigh and was rapt by its thereness.

I'd begun thinking of Helen as a sister almost since I'd moved into the flat, I was one of her girlfriends and we avoided any complications to our neighbourly platonic relationship by mutual accord. I'd never seen her in the bath before though. Naturally the blood rushed from my head and I began to grow in a different way. I saw Helen's nipple, and Jane's face. Confused, I crab-walked out of the toilet and made us a coffee.

'Do you want this water?' she shouted through the door.

'Urgghh. You were shaving your legs. That's disgusting, bloody well wash it out and run me another.'

She sat with me on the couch and brushed her hair while my bath ran. Her dressing gown was pulled tight and she wore mule slippers which Kato was taking an unseemly interest in. It was strangely comforting to come home to someone, even if it was unexpected. There was a normality to it that brought perspective to my week so far.

'My boiler's up the Swanee again,' she tutted from behind a wall of hair before flicking it behind her ears. 'How are you?' She looked up. 'Did you get on all right?'

'It was okay,' I laughed and corrected myself. 'Actually it was more than okay, different, but better than okay. Bizarre too, I'll tell you about it over a beer.'

'Can't tonight. I've got a date, maybe next week.'

'Ah.' I nodded in understanding. 'That's explains why you're using my razor.'

'Could be.'

She smiled coyly and told me about her weekend. She raced through to the part where she paid for her meal at a drive-in and drove off without it, stopped at some traffic lights where a car pulled up next to her and a smoothie handed her her veggie burger and fries. He asked her out and so she was shaving her legs.

'You know what I've been like, Pennance,' she said seriously. 'This could be the One. Helluva first impression, don't you think? I mean how long have I been waiting for a boyfriend that showed some gumption, some what do you call it, va va voom?'

You and me both, I thought, feeling the touch of Jane's hand on my shoulder.

'Helen.' I stopped her as she stepped to the door to go home and begin making up. 'Will you feed Kato again for a while?'

'Sure, where you off?'

'I'm going travelling.'

'For how long?'

'Six, seven months.'

'No problem,' she said, picking up her clothes and opening the door. 'I'll see you in the morning and we'll have breakfast and you can tell me all about it, okay?'

I gave her a hug as she left. 'Good luck tonight.'

She turned on her heel as I was closing the door.

'Luck, my arse. What do you think a cleavage is for?'

◻ * ◻

I was lying in wait. Soon I'd have to resurface. Through my goggles I was watching the rim of the bath, waiting for Kato. I knew that when she jumped up and looked in the bath all she would see would be the bubbles. I'd wait for the confusion to register in her eyes and then I'd spring the trap. The new Pennance.

Fearing that she was ignorant of my designs and running out of breath, I was about to surface when she jumped on the rim and looked quizzically at the water.

She hit the roof and shot out of the bathroom as I erupted from the deep with a scream. Throwing my goggles off, I coughed and spluttered the water from my lungs before splashing round in victory.

I sat like that as the water drained from the bath.

The last of my doubts disappeared with it down the plughole. When it was empty and I was sure the last of them had gone, I stood and faced the mirror and smiled reassuringly at my reflection. I successfully fought the temptation to tell myself I was a beautiful person on the grounds that it was too

American but did allow myself to wink as I stepped from the bath and dried off to Abba.

I was in a strange mood. Excited by the prospect of booking my ticket and everything that came with it, I kept catching myself thinking about my friends' faces when I threw the confirmation letter on the table and announced I was going. Ting, Stan and Pine dropping dead at my feet in surprise.

I'd choked in the bath when I first did it. I'd been thinking of Ting as still being alive. The memory made me smile now. Any guilt I had about even momentarily forgetting he was gone poured out with the bath water. I wasn't supposed to tremble every time I thought about him and I knew that while ever I was thinking that he was still part of my life he would be. He was an inseparable part of my future and because of that he would always be alive in my memory. Every time I looked back on the future I would know that what I did after this point was influenced by him as much as if he was still here. If Pine thought he was alive today because Ting was dead then it was equally true that I would live a fuller life for the same reason. Maybe I would have gotten round to it later but certainly no sooner. Ting's death had given me the proverbial toe up the backside.

Determined, I let Abba play out and found Paul Weller.

'The Changing Man' on repeat.

I booted up my computer.

━ * ━

I dressed purposefully and stepped out of the flat. I wanted to see Ray and let him know that everything went well in Mull before I went to the café. Mrs B was in her garden and waved me over as I walked by.

'So you off to the dancing again?'

'It's a bit early, Mrs B.' I smiled. 'Maybe later.'

'Tea dances, Pennance, can't beat them. If you're free one afternoon I'll take you and show you what I mean. You'd be amazed at the energy we coffin dodgers have got when we know we can have a nap straight afterwards.'

Even as she was talking to me she couldn't help plucking at the weeds growing at the foot of the wall and putting them in her pocket.

'You sure you could tear yourself away from your garden long enough?'

'It grows by itself anyway.' She looked at me with a gleam in her eye. 'All I do is talk to it and I'm sure it wouldn't miss me rabbiting for a couple of hours, especially when it sees how good I look with you on my arm and dancing shoes on my feet.'

'Please.' I put my hands on my cheeks. 'You're making me blush.'

'So what do you say?' she laughed. 'Have we got a date?'

'We have indeed.' I grinned at the thought. 'But only if you return the favour and come raving with me.'

'No problem. What's that?'

Helen had told her where I'd been and she had taken it upon herself to cheer me up. I hoped that she hadn't been sitting out waiting to do just that as it wasn't the warmest of days and not only was my new dance partner prone to gout but she was of an age where hypothermia was only a sneeze away. I held her rubbish bag while she pruned and reacquainted me with her roses.

'There's only one thing that doesn't grow, Pennance,' she said as she finished and stood back to admire her handiwork, 'and that's grief.'

I smiled and watched her walk to her door, humbled again. If her dancing was as good as her gardening and as sharp as her mind then I was in for a fun afternoon. I waved and set off to Ray's as she closed the door behind her.

⌑ * ⌑

I caught him as he was leaving the house. He looked well, better than before at least. He was going to see his mother. That was the only parallel we had with last week as we walked down his path and along the street. It's not that we were upbeat, that would have been crass, but the air of guilt that had choked me then was gone now. Even if only for the time being, although I was working on its permanency. Harry and Jojo had dropped Ray off this morning and he had a lightness in his step that spoke of things faced and dealt with, if not forgiven and forgotten, and I knew that we'd both been on a journey.

'You were right about Mull,' I said as we walked. 'A magical place, right enough.'

'I told you you'd love it.'

'You could have told me about the rain,' I huffed, 'or the fish even. Yes, definitely about the fucking fish.'

'Why do you think I left in the first place!'

He lost himself in a smile when I told him about our night, reliving his own memories of Donald and Moira.

'She was the reason I set the school record for the egg and spoon race.' He grinned as he told me. 'When the whistle blew at the start of the race I was watching her on the swings behind the finishing line. As we started running, everyone else concentrating on their eggs, I was distracted by a flash of light as the sun glinted off the chains on the swing and Moira jumped off.' He shook his head. 'All I saw was the threat of a bra below her T-shirt and I was gone.'

'How fast did you go?' I imagined him haring along. 'What was your time?'

'Nine minutes and forty-three seconds.'

I stopped walking and waited for him to turn round.

'How long was the race?'

'About twenty metres,' he laughed. 'I was eleven at the time and she was two classes in front of me. I never even spoke to her but she gave me the shakes that day, I'll tell you that for nothing. They'd run the next three races before I crossed the finishing line and I had to sup my soup through a straw for the rest of the day.'

He walked off, shaking his head, and I followed, doing the same.

It was easier to talk about Ting when we were laughing. It didn't so much hide the fact that it hurt as chase the pain away.

Remembering him with a smile instead of a tear didn't lessen his memory, it encouraged it.

I told him about our journey and pretended to be aggrieved at his lack of faith in me as he handed me a tenner to give to Molly when I explained about the train. He knew which beach we'd stood on and guessed that he'd probably sat on at least one of the chairs we'd burnt. The boathouse had been his own No. 7 and old Donald's too. It turned out that Ray had indeed stolen Donald's pigeon eggs.

Then I told him I was going travelling.

'About fucking time, son,' he said heartily. 'I thought you'd never get round to it.'

'Well, I'm round to it now.' I grinned. 'It's for definite.'

We stopped outside his mum's house.

'Well, I'm glad to hear it.' He winked. 'Again.'

Before I could protest he laughed and seized my hand. 'Only kidding, Pennance.' He looked over his shoulder. 'We'd better finish this another time, I need to get in and see my mum. I can feel her twitching at the curtains behind me. Unless you want to come in? She's making sandwiches if you're hungry?'

'No, Ray. Thanks, but I better get to the café.' I didn't think I could face another one of her sandwiches yet. 'It's the last night of the wake. Get drunk and get on.'

'Of course.' He nodded. 'Don't let me keep you, I'm late myself.'

I arranged to meet him for a pint and gave him the piece of paper I took out of my pocket.

'This is for you,' I said, hiding my grin.

'What's this?' He unfolded it and frowned. 'I gave you this. It's the phone number for the guesthouse.'

'I know,' I said casually. 'Moira asked me to give it to you this morning.'

'Well, I'll be . . .'

He shook his head and slipped the note into his pocket and I saw Ting sparkle in his eye.

'Maybe I'll be taking a drive up the road after all.' He gave my arm a slap as I turned to go. 'Looks like we're going to be okay, Pennance,' he said, grinning, all eleven and dropping his egg again. 'You have a good night and try not to lose me any more of my money if you can help it, eh?'

'No chance.'

Chapter 28

until tomorrow i'll just keep moving on

I sat and counted my money.

I made a show of losing my place and starting again twice before they chased me to the bar to buy a round with my unexpected windfall. Served them right after the affront of their 'how would Pennance get to Mull' wager.

I'd left Ray and come straight to the café, the confirmation letter that I'd printed off burning a hole in my jacket.

For less than it cost to buy a good suit, one that an executive with no chin could afford, I was going round the world. Calling in to eight or nine countries along the way. It was tailor-made to fit and I would be looking good.

I could have waited until the travel agent's opened in the morning, but that was so old me. Why wait until tomorrow when I had a computer today? All very twenty-first century, I bought my tickets over the internet.

www.dontwaituntilyour.age

It was exciting, booking the tickets, even paying – fighting the panic about how I was going to afford it was a different kind of excitement.

Not only had I memorised my flight schedules but I almost had the planes and flight numbers down pat by the time I got to St Pete's.

Stan and Pine were at the booth when I got there and casually dropped the confirmation letter on the table as I sat down. Molly's coat was thrown over the back of the booth and I guessed she must have been in the toilet. I knew Sally and Ali wouldn't be here but I still felt a pang of regret when I didn't see them.

I was disappointed when they ignored the envelope while

we caught up and they asked about Grace and the kids. I told them how pissed off she was about them not going with me in an attempt to change the subject, hoping they'd maybe pay attention to the letter, all but shrieking with whistles and bells on the table in front of them. Even when Molly came back from the toilet and I waved it in front of them they remained undeterred and almost studiously ignored it. Resigned, I began to tell them about Jane and the napkin but I couldn't concentrate, I couldn't take my eyes off the envelope.

Every time I'd stopped talking they'd asked about something else. Pine had skinned up and Stan had even moved it aside when reaching for the lighter.

I couldn't understand why it appeared to be invisible.

I picked it up myself in disgust and thrust it into Stan's hand.

He read it and handed it to Pine. Both their faces were expressionless as Molly glanced at it and reached into her pocket. I was still waiting for a response, the smile faltering on my face at such underwhelming enthusiasm when Molly unfolded two tenners and handed them to me with a sigh. Stan shook his head and I took the £20 note he handed me along with another from Pine before any of them spoke.

'Bastard,' they said together.

Then the smiles and the toasts began, to friends gone and friends going.

Since their sweep didn't have a contingency for my actually having bought the tickets, actually doing something I said I would, they had no option but to give me the money. They didn't want to and that's why they stalled and sent me to the bar to gloat when they grudgingly handed it over.

'I can't believe you're going.' Pine shook his head, not for the first time. 'I was going to buy Molly a ring with my winnings.'

'You could have put it towards the cost of the box it comes in at least,' Molly said drily.

Pine flinched; there was no joke behind her smiling face.

'We're getting married,' Molly told me matter-of-factly as though it was something she did every day.

'Well, I'm flattered, Molly, and I do care about you.' I raised my shoulders in a shrug, by now drunk enough to be careless. 'But what about Pine?'

She shook her head. 'He won't mind. It was almost his own idea,' she said affectionately, surprising me by not reaching for a projectile.

'Thanks, Pine, but I think you should be the one that marries her.'

It was Stan who hit me first.

Going travelling was going to save me a lot of bruises, maybe I'd meet people who'd think I was as clever as I did.

Pine didn't get the chance to shop for a ring, with or without me. When they got home from Mull she decided for him.

'I'm pregnant.'

'You're pregnant?'

'Why does everyone keep saying that?' She looked meaningfully at Stan and Pine. 'Yes. Now are you going to sit there catching flies or am I going to get a hug?'

◻ * ◻

The night turned out to be what it was supposed to be. It was strange without Ting but we got on with it as though he was simply away again, due to come back through the door at any time and dazzle us with his latest scheme or conquest.

Stan hugged me senseless until I told him that Ali hadn't left me heartbroken and then left me speechless when he told me that he was going on a date with Colin the patrolman. I almost asked him to get my hundred quid back as an introduction fee, but decided against it for health reasons.

Ting would know that we were getting it right.

Get back and get on.

We were smiling on with our lives.

I was monopolising Pine. I knew I was boring him with the tales of derring-do that I planned to get up to while he was up to his ears in nappies and poo when I realised that he wasn't paying attention to me. I turned in my seat and stretched over the booth to see what had so enthralled him.

'Pennance?' Pine called after me.

I was already halfway to the bar before he realised that I was gone. Stan was standing at the door and I raced over, tripping up on a bag that stuck out from below a table. I fell headlong and landed in a heap at his feet.

'Hi.' I smiled and lounged on the floor as though that had been my intent from the start. 'Fancy meeting you here.'

Stan frowned as he looked at me then kicked me gently and told me to get up, but I ignored him.

I only had eyes for Jane.

She grinned and shook her head as Stan glanced at her and rolled his eyes.

'Hi, Pennance, how you doing down there?'

I jumped up, in too much pain to flex or tense and led her to the bar. Stan followed and I could see Pine watching as Molly emerged from the stairs and walked past with a questioning look on her face.

'Are you here on your own?'

'Yes.' She pointed to the tray that Stan was carrying. 'Your friend here helped my aunt out with a cake on Friday for a christening and she asked me to drop it off.' She turned to Stan. 'Are you sure you don't want some money for it?'

'He's fine,' I told her, reeling from the connection. 'He wouldn't dream of taking your money.'

Stan looked confused but shook his head in agreement.

'Why don't I get you a drink?'

She sat on a barstool and I nodded to Stan and he mumbled off to open a bottle of wine. My heart was climbing out of my mouth as I watched her take her jacket off and settle. Before bringing our glasses, Stan put the soundtrack to *Casablanca* on and I smiled over at him.

In all the cafés in all the world.

'I can't believe I've bumped into you,' she said, fidgeting with her hair. 'When I gave you my number and you never said anything I assumed you weren't interested and I'd never see you again.' I tried to keep my face straight and my eyes away from her rapidly rising and falling chest. 'I thought that you would think I was crazy or too needy or something and that you'd throw it away, thinking you were well shot of me.' She flicked her hair back and smiled. 'Don't think it was a normal thing for me to do, I just thought . . . well' – she shrugged – 'I don't know anyone in Leeds and you seemed like a nice guy.'

The words were running from her mouth and I was struggling to catch up with what she was saying above the pounding in my veins.

She sounded like me.

'I know that you're jaunting off round the world but I'd hoped that we could spend some time together first, you know, maybe show me around, that kind of thing.' She blushed. 'When you didn't ask for my number I thought I'd misread the signs, made a mistake. But I thought what the fuck, nothing ventured and all that. I mean when you told me that you were going travelling I was pleased for you.'

I cringed as I remembered but took heart that I could now show her the letter and prove that I was a man of my word.

'But when you admitted that you didn't have the tickets I was pleased for me.'

She cringed.

'I know it's selfish but the idea of coming here and knowing no one, having no one to talk to or go out with, the idea of spending all my time alone with me was depressing me and I was ready to give up before I'd even started. Then you arrived and I just thought . . .'

She lifted her eyes from the counter and looked at me through her lashes. '. . . You can help me out any time you're ready here, Pennance.'

My smile erupted and she started to giggle.

'Bastard.' She glanced at the door. 'Do you want me to go now or should I keep rambling and see if I can't embarrass myself a bit more?'

'You're doing fine,' I told her, 'but can we go back to the bit where you said I was a nice guy again please.' She punched me as Stan brought us our drink.

'So were you going to phone me?'

'Of course I was going to –'

Stan began humming the Batman theme: gonni gonni gonni gonni, gonni gonni gonni gonni, and she smiled as I shot him a withering look.

'I can't believe I just asked that.' She put her head in her hands. 'Now I do sound needy.'

'No, not at all,' I said reassuringly. 'Believe me, I would have phoned.'

She peeked at me through her fingers and I felt the hand of fate squeeze gently round my heart, forcing it back into my mouth.

'What, when you got back from Outer Mongolia?'

'I'm not going to Mongolia,' I laughed. 'Wait here and I'll show you. I'll be right back.'

Stan stepped out from behind the bar and walked back to the booth behind me. I reached into the drawer for the confirmation letter as Pine and Molly stared and pulled me onto the bench.

'So who's the Honey, Pennance?'

Molly let that go as she was just as intent on hearing the answer.

When I took the envelope out of the drawer I lifted out the napkin Jane had given me too and placed it on the table in front of me.

I pointed to the napkin and they understood.

And then I did.

I looked from the letter in my hand to the napkin on the table.

The napkin, blurred and illegible, and the letter clear as day. The future printed.

Adventure knocking on my door.

I saw the letter with its definitives and I knew.

The not knowing. The excitement.

The buzz of the unknown.

Irresponsible?

Irrepressible.

I smoothed the napkin out on the table and took their money out of my wallet and handed it back to them. They looked on in confusion at the money in their hands, at the napkin, and then at the envelope in my hand.

'What are you –?' Stan began.

I held the confirmation letter in two hands and slowly tore it down the middle, casually throwing it on the table. It was a class act of symbolic theatre.

'That's Jane,' I told them with a nod to the bar.

'Why have you just done that?' Stan picked up the torn envelope.

'I told you, that's Jane.'

I'd come back to the table to get the letter to show Jane where I was going.

Show her how focused I was on making the change that I'd talked about when I told her how Ting's death had got to me.

It was at that point that I realised that I might as well be in Outer Mongolia if I was going to go anywhere.

When I took the flight schedule from the drawer I couldn't remember where I'd arranged to set off from, never mind where I was going, and when I'd looked at the napkin all I could see was Jane's eyes sparkling through her fingers. I knew then that I'd been going in the wrong direction anyway. Everything I was going to find was sat twenty feet away, tingling the hairs on the back of my neck with her smile.

'So what about this?' Stan held up the torn printout.

'Put that back in the drawer before I bring her over to meet you,' I said as I stood up, 'and don't mention it yet or I'll tell her what you said about her aunt.'

Pine had his arm round Molly and they sat agog as I explained how she came to end up at St Pete's. I kept Ting's role at the Cosmic Coincidence Centre to myself.

'Tell me that's not a wake-up call.'

Stan shook his head and frowned. 'So does this mean that you're not going to go away then?'

'Of course I'm still going,' I tutted as I turned to go.

'When?'

Jane was waiting at the bar and I could see her chewing on the end of her hair as I moved towards her.

I knew I didn't need to say anything because Molly and Pine were already shaking their heads and Stan had started to giggle at his own stupidity. But I'd learnt now that when an opportunity in life presents itself so obviously it's only a fool who ignores it.

I smirked over my shoulder as I went.

'When do you think?'